# GREEK KEY

# GREEK KEY

### K.B. Spangler

**A Girl and Her Fed Books**

*Greek Key* is a work of fiction. Names, characters, and events are the creations of the author. Settings are either fictional or have been adapted from locations in and around Washington, D.C. and Greece for purposes of storytelling. Any resemblance to actual persons, living or dead, is entirely coincidental.

All characters, places, and events are set in the universe of A Girl and Her Fed, found online at www.agirlandherfed.com

Printed by CreateSpace, an Amazon.com Company.
Available from Amazon.com and other retail outlets.

*For everyone who wanted a Speedy novel.*

*You're all delightfully nuts.*

# CHAPTER 1

I'm still in the phonebook. Quaint, right? It's a holdover from when I was a kid, I think. I used to get such a kick out of flipping open the phonebook and seeing my mom's name. Some of the blush wore off when she married my stepdad and our names changed, but what can you do? You're all of four years old, and suddenly there's a dude behind a desk telling you that your last name isn't yours anymore.

I decided to make that new name mine. I held that name through my stepdad's funeral, and made sure the name outlasted those others who came and went in my mom's life. That name's still mine, even though I got married myself last October.

And there it is in the phonebook: *Blackwell, Hope.*

I love it. When I start my medical residency, one of the first things I'll do is call up the White Pages and tell them to add a little *MD* suffix to my name.

The problem is, when your name and number and address are in the phonebook, it makes it phenomenally easy for those many assholes who hate your husband to break into your house at three in the morning.

Yes, I'm aware—*painfully* aware, thank you—that we live in the Information Age, but our family's data isn't easily found online. I'll get to the whys of that in a minute. Because all of this is my polite way of explaining why I'm starting this story from underneath a couple of police officers.

I might have been swearing.

There were ambulances parked out front, too, which explains why my husband hit our front door so hard it flew off of its hinges.

That wasn't really his fault. Sparky's built like a linebacker and moves twice as fast. Get a little adrenaline pumping, and things tend to break around him.

He took in the room while he was moving. Five men, broken and bloody, each of them with an EMT shining a penlight in various places. Me, lying prone on the floor, two police officers standing not *quite* on top of me to make sure I stayed there...

Bad scene.

Both cops' guns came out when the door flew across the room. Those guns didn't go down when their owners recognized my husband. Instead, the hands holding those guns began to shake, their fingers on the grips of their guns began to turn white...

Worse scene.

"Guys," I said. "Don't make me get up."

The guns went down.

Sparky doesn't smile much in public, but if you're looking for it, you can see the corners of his eyes twitch.

"Everything good here?" he asked me.

I shrugged. Bit of a mistake, as the officer with his boot resting on my back flinched, and I gained another fifty pounds of twitchy cop. "'s fine," I grunted. "Some members of your fanclub showed up with baseball bats."

And tire irons, and crowbars, and even a sledgehammer. I hadn't been nice to the one who had brought the sledgehammer. Sledgehammers mean business.

"They came in through the back, Agent Mulcahy," said the officer who wasn't crushing my shoulders into mush. I liked him. "They cut through a plastic tarp in the construction area."

"Smart," my husband said. "Our alarm system doesn't cover that zone yet." He knelt beside one of our wanna-be assailants. The man's head lolled sideways before he fell forward into the EMT's lap.

"He had a sledgehammer," I offered.

"Ah," Sparky replied. He looked at the officers. "Now, why are you standing on my wife?"

God bless the man for trying.

The cop with the heavy boots sputtered something about

how when they had showed up, I had been armed (I hadn't), and how they had shouted for me to get down on the floor (I had), and how things had gotten sloppy from there.

The real story had more threats, the majority of them not made by me. Boots-Cop did *not* like my husband, and his emotions had gone bonkers when he saw me.

Being famous is one of those things that sounds great until it actually happens to you.

Sparky listened and nodded in the appropriate places before asking if I was under arrest. The officers traded a glance heavy with paperwork and bad publicity, and I breathed easier as the boot came off of my back.

I stood and dusted myself off as best I could. I had stopped sleeping in the buff years ago (Reason? See: the current state of our living room), but I had gone to bed in nothing but one of Sparky's tees and my granny panties, and modesty hadn't been my first thought when I woke to the sounds of glass breaking and strange voices downstairs. Still, his shirts were long enough on me to count as a sundress, so I pretended I was wearing a classic somethin'-somethin' from a French designer instead of a threadbare shirt with the logo for the New England Patriots.

I don't think it worked: it was kinda cold.

Whatever. They were in *my* house.

I cracked my knuckles to work out the kinks, and the officers moved a good few feet away from me and Sparky. This put them closer to the bad guys, and both cops and bad guys were okay with this. It didn't bother me—I'm weird, Sparky's weirder, but to the average cop, home invaders are a stupid kind of normal.

"Are you pressing charges?" Boots-Cop asked me.

"Yes," said Sparky, at the same time I said, "Nope."

My husband's eyebrow went up, so I added, "It's not like they'll be coming back."

"Split the difference?" he asked. "Yes to trespassing, no to assault?"

I walked over to Sledgehammer, who was being kept at the edge of consciousness by his EMT. He was a heavy dude, in black biker leather over worn jeans. He saw me coming, and woke up enough to start squirming towards the kitchen.

I knelt beside him as he wiggled across the floor, his handcuffs leaving fresh scratches in the cherry wood. I would have rapped him on the head a time or two for that but, hey, I'm a paramedic myself, and I've got the whole medical school thing going. Last thing I needed to do was aid and abet his concussion. "Hey," I asked. "Am I ever gonna see you again?"

"No!" Sledgehammer curled into a ball. His EMT glared at me as he tried to drag Sledgehammer back to an upright position. Sledgehammer was having none of it, and batted at the EMT with weak chained hands.

"How 'bout this? You spread the word to leave us the fuck alone, and I'll let you tell your buddies in community service that I didn't kick your ass to Friday and back."

Sledgehammer nodded so hard I heard his teeth click.

"Right, then." I jerked a thumb at his EMT, who hauled Sledgehammer to his feet and towards the waiting ambulance. It took a few minutes for the EMTs and Boots-Cop to clear the rest of them out, with Boots-Cop doing the ride-along to the hospital. The officer who stayed behind had a decent attitude once he got some distance from his scared rabbit of a partner. We gave him some juice (Yes, he asked for juice. Some people like juice, and we had juice.), he took my statement, and then he left.

Leaving us to stare at the chaos where our living room used to be.

"Sweetie…" Sparky sighed.

"Don't start."

"I was going to apologize," he said. "This never happened to you before I showed up."

"Yeah, well…" I hopped up on my toes and gave him a quick kiss. "It did, and even if it hadn't, you're worth it."

He tipped the loveseat upright while I went on a cushion hunt, and then we collapsed in a gentle heap. Three in the morning is a hard place to find yourself after a long, long day.

"How was the…thing?" I asked.

"The welcome reception for the new Director of the EPA," he said, as he brushed my hair away from my neck. "Decent food. Terrible conversation."

"That doesn't sound like OACET business."

OACET is shorthand for the Office of Adaptive and Complementary Enhancement Technologies. Sparky's responsible for it, and the four hun—

Right, sorry. Let's try this again.

Let me tell you about what happens when you unravel a major government conspiracy: if you live through it, your life doesn't snap back to its usual shape. No, you have positively wrecked any chance of normalcy. Unless you're sitting on a trove of blackmail documents that will keep you and your loved ones alive, you'd better learn how to adapt to your new status quo.

Sparky and me? We had that trove, but we decided it was our nuclear option, to use only when our backs were against the wall and that wall was made of acid-drooling lions. Instead, we went public. We took everything that had happened to Sparky and the other members of OACET, and we threw it all on the ground. Look, America! There's your politicians' dirty laundry, bloodstains and all.

This made a lot of very powerful politicians extremely pissed at us.

If you think this is the reason for Officer Boots-Cop's twitchy trigger finger, just wait. It gets better. Or worse, depending on how you like your English.

See, back when they were fresh-faced kids in their early twenties, Sparky and a bunch of other up-and-comers in the federal government were asked to participate in a top secret intelligence program. They were told that September 11th had proven that those many hundreds of different agencies, military organizations, departments, divisions, and whatnots which formed the federal government had to learn to work together. Improved communication among different government entities was the goal, they said.

But their sneaky idea was to network the people.

So, five hundred people—sorry, I should have said *kids,* as the oldest of these five hundred said people had just celebrated her twenty-fifth birthday—had their heads strapped into a three-pin skull cradle and went under the laser-guided craniotome. It wasn't pleasant. Sparky's scars are hidden by his hair, but man, they're brutal. They took the top of his skull clean off. Sure, they replaced it with alloys that can withstand the impact of a speeding car, but it's squicky to think that somewhere out there, a surgical orderly could be using my husband's parietal bone as an ashtray.

After that, they stuck an organic computer chip deep inside Sparky's brain, and sensors on his optic and auditory nerves. And then, once he and the other OACET Agents had healed up, they cut them loose and pretended they didn't exist.

Think about that for a moment. You wake up from brain surgery, and all of your equipment—both your factory originals and the aftermarket add-ons—seems to work as promised. Sure, you'd like it if the buggy Artificial Intelligence unit could be turned off, and you're not really sure how to keep the other Agents out of your head, but at least you didn't die, right?

Then you learn the same politicians who greenlit your conversion to cyborg status decided this top-secret experiment wasn't working out as planned. Too bad for the volunteers: they're stuck dealing with an AI that won't shut up, not to mention they're permanently linked into the neuroses of four hundred and ninety-nine others going through the exact same crap. This bugginess kept getting worse and worse, and the Agents couldn't escape it. It wasn't as though they could take the implants out: those chips were grafted to the cerebral cortex, and as collections of cells go, that particular one is fairly important.

It all collapsed into an endless screaming mindfuck for the cyborgs.

And? Since it was a government program, and elections and

publicity were involved, everyone who might be able to help decided it was safer to stay as far away from that buggy cyborg program as they could.

So that's exactly what they did.

Back when I first met Sparky, he was drugged out of his gourd and doing scut work. He'd been like that for five whole years. Five years of living like a goddamned zombie, shuffling through the motions, unable to let himself think or feel. He turned out to be a really stellar guy under the antidepressants and the sleeping pills, and once he got himself back together, we decided to learn what we could about that chip in his head.

Turns out the implant does a lot more than allow Agents to talk to each other over distances. The implant is the ultimate encryption breaker—if you've got one, you can access and control *any* networked machine.

Take a breath and let that sink in.

Now, if you just looked around and took inventory of how many networked machines you own, or can access, or have heard of from a friend of a friend who works in That Place, and then immediately thought, "Well, that's pretty fucking terrifying," you are one bright cookie.

*That's* what we took public.

We became overnight celebrities. There was the cyborg thing, of course, and government conspiracies are always sexy, but Sparky and me? We make a *fabulous* couple. He's riding that tall, blond superspy vibe, and I've won more gold medals in judo than anyone else alive. Add that to the story of how we fell in love while fighting to set him and his buddies free?

Photogenic magic.[1]

Except?

For every person who thinks you and your husband are heroes who did the right thing, there's one who thinks you didn't. I don't think I need to tell you which of those two is louder.

---

1 Anna Kendrick played me in the movie. She did right by me, I guess, but I still think she needed to put on more muscle. I was really worried about her during some of those action scenes.

Folks, fame ain't worth the price tag. Trust me: a pack of moderately-armed morons breaking into our house is barely worth a mention these days.

It's better than it used to be, though. Sparky and the other surviving OACET Agents have been out for almost a year, and everybody is gradually getting used to the idea of near-omniscient cyborgs in their midst. Sparky was on the political A-list. Yeah, I don't quite know how that happened either, but everybody in Washington wants a piece of him. And tonight was the first time in over a month that I've needed to wreck the living room.

Our poor, much-abused living room...*oy*.

I looked over in time to see our front door, which had been stuck in the drywall by its knob alone, come free and clatter to the ground.

March in D.C. is still too chilly to leave a gaping hole where a door used to be, so I shrugged out of Sparky's arms, and went to get the tarps and duct tape. When I returned, the loveseat was empty.

"In here," came a woman's voice from the kitchen.

I dropped the tarps by the door hole, and headed for the kitchen. Rachel Peng had her hands wrapped around a fresh cup of coffee. I can usually keep myself from picking up emotions, but with every step I took towards her, the more exhausted I felt.

Rachel's head came up, hard. She's an empath, too, but her abilities come from her implant and are more developed than mine. She can tell you exactly what you're feeling at any given moment, and has no problem asking questions that can peel your psyche open so she can pick through the bits. It's *extra-freaky*.

I pretended not to see how she was watching me like a starving predator, and went to pour myself a cup of coffee. Exhaustion was normal; it was three in the morning, and anybody with good sense and a good schedule would be tired. Rachel's head went back down.

Perfect. She doesn't know about me, and I'd like to keep it that way.

"Hey Rachel," I said as I went for the cream and sugar. "What's going on?"

"Hope," she said by way of greeting, and nodded towards Sparky. "I noticed Mulcahy was still up, so I asked if it was okay to drop by."

Rachel doesn't drive, but before I could open my mouth, she said, "Santino drove. He's taking a nap in the car." And *then*, when she saw that her throwaway comment had put me off, she added, "Sorry. Didn't mean to read you like that. It's been a long day."

See what I mean by extra-freaky? This is the reason I'm the second-worst psychic in the world. My emotions should belong to me and me alone, and I'm not about to snatch anybody else's straight out of their soul.

I dropped into the chair beside Sparky and threw my feet over his knees. "Everything okay?" I asked her.

Rachel shot a furtive glance at Sparky, and they did that too-silent thing that happened when they were talking through the cyborgs' mental link.

I used it as a chance to give Rachel the once-over. She's been out of the Army for close to seven years, but she's usually as crisp and tidy as if she were still in uniform. Tonight, she had the look of a woman who was miles from her bed.

She sighed as she turned back to me. "Sorry," Rachel said again. "National security. Secrets. You know how it goes. Had to check with the boss first."

"The boss says it's okay to tell his wife," Sparky said.

Great. This had all the hallmarks of OACET drama, and now I was miles from my own bed, too.

# CHAPTER 2

"We're investigating a robbery," Rachel said to me.

No surprise there. Rachel Peng is OACET's liaison to the Washington D.C. Metropolitan Police Department. She and her team are specialists who get called in when the crime is due north of normal. They're usually tapped to handle assassinations, bombings, criminal masterminds, and etcetera.

Come to think of it, robbery is pocket change for her.

"A man was found murdered in the basement of the White House," she continued. "It looks like his death was used to cover up a theft."

Bingo.

I yanked my legs off of Sparky's so I could sit up. He didn't flinch: not at me, and not at what Rachel had said. I was the only person in the room who hadn't known about the corpse. "What?! Why isn't this on the news?"

Rachel shrugged. "Because he was found murdered in the White House. I'm under a gag order, myself. Ah...Hope?"

I pantomimed zipping my lips.

"Thanks," she said. "Since the crimes took place in Washington, the Secret Service is working with the MPD to solve the homicide. They're also handling the robbery."

"Wait," I said, my fingernails tapping against the ceramic coffee mug. "Play that back. I thought you said—"

"I did." Rachel cut me off. "There's the official story," she said, and held her hand at eye level. "And then there's us." Her hand dropped below the tabletop, out of view.

I nodded.

"We're reporting to the Secret Service, as well as our supervisor at the MPD," she said. "So it's not like we're doing this off the books. We just get a little extra flexibility."

"What happens if this blows up in the press? Is it gonna come back on OACET?" This is a new mode of thinking for me, by the way. Not too long ago, I thought I'd grow up to be a reporter. Then my world turned into spycraft and code names, and I've had to train myself to look at it through reputation-colored glasses. Trust me, life's just easier when you're not trying to stare through the shit you've created for yourself.

"No," Rachel said. "We're covered. If this comes back on anyone, it'll be on the Secret Service. They were the ones who asked us to help; they want to show they're making every effort to put things right."

"What's the problem?" Sparky asked. His voice was getting some rough edges from lack of sleep. "I thought the case was over. Your team caught the suspect."

News to me. They weren't being rude. Rephrase: they didn't mean to be rude. Their native language isn't spoken aloud. Those of us who can't headtalk have to pick up fragments of spoken conversation and fit them together as we go along. It is annoying as fuck, and Sparky and I have had more than a few fights about it.

Rachel winced as my mood dipped towards *grrr! Cyborgs.* She ran both hands through her short black hair. "Sorry," she said to me. "The short-short version is the crimes have been solved. We're done. It's over. But the loose ends…"

She sighed. "There's something bigger happening, and I can't quite see what it is."

"Did you find the object?" Sparky asked. "I'm assuming there was a reason it was stolen."

"Yeah, we're working that angle," Rachel said, her hand moving towards the inner pocket of her suit coat. "It's hard to explain… Here." She took out a small black box made from carbon fiber, sleek and shiny and durable as hell.

Rachel glanced up at me. "This was entrusted to me for tonight only," she said, answering a question I hadn't gotten around to asking. "I nearly had to sign away my soul before the Secret Service would release it to me."

"What is it?" The box was the right size for a medium-sized piece of jewelry. A bracelet, maybe. My brain had jumped to gold and diamonds, maybe an antique brooch studded in gems. It'd have to be precious if it was worth storming the White House.

Rachel popped the lid and moved aside a protective sheath. An old corroded piece of metal about the size of my palm lay on the batting.

I gasped. I couldn't help it.

Have you ever seen something—a place, maybe, or an old tree—and just *known*? Known there was something more to it than just the object itself? That there's a layer of history to it that just…makes it more than itself?

This pitted chunk of brown-black metal on my kitchen table was screaming history at me.

I wanted to run and hide.

Instead, I reached out and gently ran two fingers along its surface. The screaming bubbled away until the object was nothing more than a piece of crumbling bronze and a new memory.

"Hope?"

I pulled myself away from the box and its contents. They were looking at me, Sparky and Rachel both.

"Hope?" Rachel repeated. "What's wrong?"

"Where did you—Um, where did the White House get this?" Oh, answering questions with questions. So useful.

"Gift of State from the Greeks over a century ago," she said. "Do you recognize it?"

"Should I?"

A tiny angry line appeared between her eyes; she knew I was dodging. "Not unless you study ancient computers."

I laughed. "That's not a computer. Whatever that is, it's thousands of years old."

"It *is* a computer. It's…" Rachel pushed back from the table. "It's complicated. Let me get Santino. He's better at explaining these things."

Sparky and I watched her leave until she was out of earshot, and then he leaned in close. "What happened?" he asked.

I dragged the box towards me so I could study the metal. There were tiny flecks of golds and greens under the corrosion. "Every so-called psychometric I've met has been a stone-cold fraud," I whispered. "But if there are psychics who can tell what happened to an object in its past, they'd *kill* to get their hands on this."

"What is it? Can you read it?"

"No." I shook my head. "I know it's important. I just don't know why."

There were footsteps on the flagstones where our front door used to be, and then Rachel returned with her partner in tow. Raul Santino, a tall guy with dark hair, was wearing a suit as rumpled as Rachel's and was rubbing his face with both hands to wake himself up.

We exchanged the usual hellos, and Santino funneled coffee into himself until he was good to talk. He'd been to our house a bunch of times, and the thrill of chatting it up with Rachel's famous boss was long gone. Santino was more fun to be around now that the hero worship had vanished. The man's a total sassy-pants.

"Right," Santino said, reaching across the table to grab the polished black box. I had a quick flash of irrational anger as he took the strange piece of metal away from me. Rachel's head came up again before I locked myself down. "Can I have a tablet? Mine's in the car."

Sparky grabbed one from a nearby charging station on the counter. There's always a tablet handy when you're dealing with cyborgs: it's a translation device to help them talk about what they see in their heads. But, as Santino's fingers pounded away, it was clear he wanted to show, not be shown.

He spun the tablet towards me. A Wikipedia page was on the display, the only visible graphics looking suspiciously like the chunk of corroded metal on the table.

"The Antikythera Mechanism," Santino said. "The oldest

known computer. Discovered in 1900, but built nearly two millennia before."

"Wait, what?" I was sure I misheard him as I mathed my way backwards through the centuries. "Like hell there were computers back then. Might as well claim Jesus Christ used to email progress reports to Dad every few weeks."

Rachel took a noisy sip of coffee as she tried not to laugh, but Santino just sighed. "Different kind of computer," he said. "The Mechanism was driven by gears, like an analog clock. Whoever invented it used it as a celestial calendar, among other things."

Sparky gave a small grunt. His eyes were unfocused: he was reading websites as fast as he could. "A lunar calendar... looks like it had a zodiac component, too... It was a very crude device," he said. "Should it really be considered a computer?"

"Yes," Santino muttered. "The Mechanism computed. Ergo, computer."

Rachel took a breath that was just a little too quick. From her, that was the equivalent of gasping and falling into a dead faint. Santino glanced at her, then back to Sparky as he realized he had snapped at her commanding officer. "I'm sorry," Santino said. "I've spent the better part of the day explaining this, so I'm a little burned out. Computers aren't defined by consumption of electricity, or how many processors they use. They're defined by function. The Mechanism performed complex equations. As far as we know, it was the first of its kind.

"And..." Santino paused. "The Mechanism was so complex, it wouldn't be duplicated for another fifteen hundred years."

*Shit.*

Sparky and I locked eyes.

Rachel's head came up a third time, and she bounced between me and Sparky as she tried to figure out why our moods had shifted. "What?" she asked him.

Sparky pretended to misunderstand her. "Rachel's right. I don't get it," he said to Santino. "What do you mean by fifteen hundred years?"

"Just that," Santino said. "The Mechanism wasn't just the first computer of its kind. It was so unique that it's considered an out-of-place artifact. You might think it's a crude piece of metal, but the Mechanism was technology that was so advanced, whole civilizations had to rise and fall before its like was seen again."

I knew it. Just *knew* it. But what I said was: "Damn. Dude who built it musta been a real genius."

"Yeah." Santino got up to refill his coffee. "Not like we'll ever know who that was. Not for sure. There's no historical record of the Mechanism. Cicero has a brief mention of a complex device built by Archimedes, and some archaeologists swear that the calculations of the Mechanism include the date of an eclipse in Archimedes' era, but other scholars believe that Posidonius built it after Archimedes' death—"

"Santino?" Rachel cut in. "Nerd it down a notch."

Her partner glared at her as he dumped sugar into his cup. "*Any*how," he said, "the backstory's irrelevant. Point is, all of the known fragments of the Mechanism are considered national treasures of Greece. They're kept in the National Archaeological Museum of Athens. If this is part of the Mechanism—"

"It is," Rachel and I said together.

She rounded on me. "Okay, what's going on here?" she snapped. "I can see the writing stamped on the metal—I know it's an ancient artifact!—but how in the hell do *you*—"

"Agent Peng," Sparky said, soft steel within his tone. "Take a walk."

Rachel sat motionless, her dark eyes fixed on him. I felt her anger roll back under her control. "Yes, sir," she said to Sparky. "May I use your restroom?"

He nodded, and Rachel disappeared.

(I hated seeing that. Rachel doesn't realize it, but she'll go along with almost anything Sparky says. Even when she thinks it's indefensibly stupid. She's got this default setting in her subconscious which is flipped to **Obey!** around him. I think some of it is due to her Army days, and the rest of it is because of the collective. She treats him like a cross between an officer and an older brother. Not the fun kind of older brother, either.

Sparky is that one brother who works in a prestigious law firm, and shows up on birthdays and holidays to make you feel bad about yourself by example. Rachel should know better than to jump when he says frog, but I don't think she'll ever realize she does it.)

Santino, still standing by the coffeemaker, fidgeted. "It's late," he said. "We should probably leave."

"Please," Sparky said, and gestured towards Santino's chair. "Sit. I should explain."

Sparky doesn't like to lie, and I don't like to laugh out loud when he's doing damage control, so I went in search of Rachel.

We've got a bunch of bathrooms, and it took me some time to learn she hadn't headed towards any of them. I found her sitting on a pile of landscaping boulders in the half-finished greenhouse, a dark shape under the plastic canopy and a fuzzy-filmed moon. I came up beside her, and plopped down on a nearby rock.

My patience gland is seriously underdeveloped. I waited nearly thirty whole seconds before I said, "It's not like we want to keep things from you."

"I know," Rachel said.

I hoped she'd follow that line up with something a little more descriptive, but she's a cop and an empath. She knew all she needed to do was give me enough silent air and I'd fill it. "We can't talk about what happened before we rescued you guys," I told her. "There are some secrets we promised we'd keep."

"Half-truth," she said.

"What?"

"That was a half-truth," she repeated. She flipped a chunk of plaster into the dry trough that would soon turn into a fake streambed. "I can tell when people are lying to me, and you were getting close.

"But," she sighed, "it was more truth than lie. Thank you."

"You're welcome. I'd tell you more if I could."

I saw her teeth flash white in the dark: she was smiling. "That was completely true."

"Yeah." I tossed a second piece of plaster after hers. It bounced and skittered over the concrete, kicking up dust as it went. "I hate this spy shit, by the way. I never wanted to live my life around secrets."

Rachel chuckled. "True."

There was a gust of wind, and the flap of plastic that the group of moderately-armed yahoos had used as a door snapped open. I shivered: the stones were cold, and I was still in my nightshirt. Rachel didn't feel it, because cyborg. Their metabolisms are like portable nuclear reactors. I, on the other hand, was freezing my thinly-clad butt off on slabs of geologically-displaced granite.

"Come on," Rachel said, as she jumped down from the rocks. "Let's get back before the boys come to find us. You're freezing."

"I *hate* it when you do that," I muttered, but I hopped down beside her.

"I know that, too," she said. "And I'm going to keep poking that button until I figure out what it's connected to."

"Have fun trying," I said. My life is hard enough to figure out when you're living it. "So. Back on point—what's bugging you about this weird Greek clock?"

"It's…" She threw up her hands. "Something about this case is nagging at me."

"The bad guys?" Ugh. *Bad guys.* Is my spy jargon lacking or what? "Someone had to know that fragment was in the White House's basement. Was it the Greek government? Santino said the clock's a national treasure."

"No." Rachel shook her head. "Nobody at the White House knew what the fragment was until today. The White House did a digital inventory of their gifts of state about five years back, but they didn't realize the fragment was a part of the Mechanism. If they did, we'd have offered to give it back to the Greeks out of goodwill—better that than having to manage a scandal if they learned we were keeping it from them. The Greeks know this, too. If they ever learned we had a piece of their famous clock, they'd just ask. There's precedent for sitting Presidents giving gifts of state back when asked. It'd be good press for everybody."

We passed into the house proper, and I tried not to dance around as my feet hit the floors. In-floor radiant heating is usually a godsend, but if your feet have adjusted to a cold night in early spring, you might as well have jumped straight onto a summer beach at high noon.

"Private buyer?" I guessed.

"Yeah." Rachel glanced down at my feet before adding, "What we think happened was that a photo of the fragment was spotted by an information broker, and a private buyer commissioned the break-in."

"How could the buyer know it was from that old clock? Seems a pretty big risk to take based on a photo."

"The locations and dates of discovery line up. Also, another Agent did some digital modeling, and the archived photo of the fragment fits into the pieces of the clock on display at the Museum. It didn't take him more than a couple of minutes, so if the buyer has access to a good digital artist, he or she had access to the same information."

I tossed the facts around, and they kept falling into the same pattern. "Enough reasons to steal it, I suppose. If you desperately wanted a piece of an old clock, that is."

"Exactly. And that's what's nagging at me," she said, as we reached the kitchen. "Why *would* anyone want that fragment?"

Sparky and Santino had their heads together over the tablet. All was forgiven, apparently. Sparky took a moment to search my face before giving me the slightest smile—*Thanks for the save, Sweetie*—while Santino said, "Hey, *I* might commit murder for a piece of the Mechanism. Lots of people would."

"Sure," Rachel said.

"We've been arguing about this all day," Santino said. "I know it's worth theft and murder. Rachel politely disagrees."

Rachel politely disagreed again, this time using words that made me blush. *Me.*

"Well, you don't murder people over rusty shoehorns," I devil's-advocated. "But getting your hands on part of the world's oldest computer might be worth a deep shivvin'. Seems a better reason to kill someone than wanting their Toyota."

Still.

I didn't need to be part of the collective to know that Rachel and I were sharing an *uh-huh, right* moment.

Santino sighed, deep and long. "Okay," he said, poking the table next to the fragment in its box. "Do I have to remind you guys that people do really, *really* shitty things to get their hands on advanced technology?"

Sparky's and Rachel's eyes went cold, and maybe a little dangerous.

"Didn't think so," Santino said. "What's known about the Mechanism is incomplete. There are pieces missing. If this fragment is part of the clock, there's enough writing on it to help fill in those blanks.

"The Mechanism was unique to its era," he continued. "It might—*might!*—still contain information that we don't have today. Celestial events that were written into the calendar, for example. Maybe even mathematical formulae we've never seen in practice. This fragment could answer a lot of questions."

"All right," Sparky said. He was already in risk management mode. Santino must have convinced him when Rachel and I were out of the room. "What can we do to help?"

"Get the word out," Santino said. "OACET has connections. We need to learn if any private collectors have requested detailed information of the Mechanism over the last five years."

"I'll put someone on it," Sparky said, holding out his hand. "Thanks for bringing this to our attention."

Sparky is a master at throwing people out. He and Santino shook hands, and he even gave Rachel a brief no-hard-feelings hug.

Rachel winked at me on her way out.

Rachel and Santino took a moment to tape up the plastic tarp over the hole where our front door used to be. They did a much better job of it than I would have—being married to the Cyborg King does have its perks. Or maybe they did it just because they needed to see themselves succeed at something, and securing a piece of plastic in place was about as good as it was going to get for them today.

*It's sort of heartbreaking how everybody's just trying to do the best they can.*

Sparky waited until they were in Santino's car before he sighed and dropped his head into his hands. "What did you and Rachel talk about?"

"I guess she's decided to treat it like a game," I said. "She's got Army DNA, Sparky. You've told her she doesn't need to know, so she won't force the issue. But if she can figure it out on her own from the clues we leave lying around..."

"Great," he muttered. "Just great. She already sees too much as it is."

"Yup," I said, as I reclaimed my coffee cup. "We're generally screwed. She's trustworthy, though. Maybe we should just tell her and get it over with."

He shook his head, his dark blond hair sliding back and forth between his fingers. "Not with this," he said. "It's too big. Not unless we don't have a choice."

"Right." It came out a little on the sarcastic side, and Sparky pulled his head out of his hands.

"What?" he asked.

"It's starting to blend together again," I told him. "OACET and...and *everything*. That old clock is proof."

"Yeah. We might not know where Rachel's case is going," he muttered. "But I have a good idea where it started."

"I'm way ahead of you," I replied. "Do you have an early day tomorrow?"

"Always," he groaned, scrubbing his forehead with his fingertips again.

"Okay," I said as I stood, and gave him a quick kiss on the crown of his head. "Go get some sleep. I'll make the call."

# CHAPTER 3

Let's start with time travel.

(I know, I know, most people tell stories from beginning to end. I can't do that. I need to start with the fundamentals, because when time travel is involved, you can*not* pick a single beginning without going screaming bonkers.)

Time's elemental. The idea we have any control over time itself is insane. We might as well try to control the ocean. We build docks and clocks, sure, but those are just us thumping our chests at the infinite.

We like the *idea* of time travel because time is possibilities decanted. If we could move through time, we tell ourselves, we could change the past, control the present, manipulate the future...

Nope.

The idea of time travel is great. Actual time travel, however, is bullshit, and when I say that time travel is bullshit, you should listen. I'm something of an authority on this subject. I can't travel through time myself, but I know a bunch of people who can. And do.

Well, not so often anymore (although when you're talking about time travel, words like "often" and "anymore" get a little clunky). Not after (clunk-clunk) Sparky and I had a long sit-down with them and made them tell us the rules.

There are only three rules for time travel, and they're fairly simple.

First, there's no such thing as paradox. Time doesn't allow itself to be treated like a toy. There is no possible way you can change events. You aren't that powerful. *Nothing* within the scope of human influence is that powerful. When you play with time, you play by its rules. Ask your grandmother for a picture of how she looked back in high school before you debate this point with me.

Second, you can only go forward. The past is fixed. Since going back in time would change history due to observer effect, it simply cannot happen.

Third, you can go forward and return to the present at the same moment you left it. You can spend as much time in the future as you want, but you shouldn't count on that particular future coming to pass. Everything is possible, and everything is in a constant state of change. You have a one hundred percent chance of traveling to what could happen, and an almost zero percent chance of landing in the future that *will be.*

So, why bother to time travel at all?

The trick, my time-traveling friends told us, is to follow probabilities. If you track something that exists right this moment forward in time, you'll see the possible futures for that specific object. The longer you follow it forward, the more possibilities you'll encounter. Stretch the trip into months or years or decades or centuries, and there'll be too many possible futures to find the one which will come to pass.

But if you keep your trips short—say, an hour or two at most—then you're much more likely to see realistic probabilities. Think of it as bristles on a broom. The closer you are to the shaft, the tighter the bristles are bound. Move away from that tight center line, and the bristles may travel in the same general direction, but there's a lot more space between them. By staying close to your point of origin, and by following one specific object, you're limiting deviations.

There's also an important corollary.

Pay attention.

Ready?

If that object is significant—*seriously* significant!—within history, then it's more likely that following it forward won't have the same degree of uncertainty. Things like volcanoes. Massive dinosaur-ending asteroids…

The Gutenberg Bible.

If you follow these significant objects forward through time, you'll be able to trace their paths in history. They'll still be multiple futures, there's no escaping that, but you're likely to see outcomes that will come to pass as a direct result of that object. Significant objects are bound into the human experience; they've defined it, and once they pop up, you'll never see one without the other.

Imagine you're a time traveler, and you follow the Gutenberg Bible forward. You'd see massive societal shifts. Literacy, communications, information... All of this evolves from something as stupidly simple as movable type.

Now, imagine it's six hundred years later and you want to see what's going to happen to all of these new cyborgs walking around. Our buddies followed Sparky's implant forward. They did this a lot, by the way, both before and after we went public. They wanted to know what types of new technology might evolve from this first generation. What they found...*ugh*.

They found the impact of the implant everywhere. *Ev-er-y-where*. They were ubiquitous as cell phones and computers. As was the peripheral equipment. You know, embedded hard drives which could be coded to a specific person and whatever.

And the changes to society...?

As I said...*ugh*.

Sparky and I decided we needed to call quits on getting our information from time travel. Not that the technique doesn't work! It does. It absolutely does. Trust me on this. I made a fortune on day-trading this way, before Sparky and I decided that having access to infinite futures was far more dangerous than having no access at all. But time travel is *not* a sure thing: no matter how close to the present you stay, no matter how carefully and cautiously you follow that one object forward, you're still going to trip over different possibilities. I've taken a lot of tumbles in the market on stocks that seemed like sure things. Once Sparky and I started playing on a level where lives were at stake, we asked our time-traveling buddies to stop. We didn't want to hear about the *mights* and *coulds* and *maybes* when the only certainty was that the other OACET Agents were counting on us to keep them alive.

Our buddies didn't like it when we told them to stop. Power's fun, and knowing pieces of the future is about as powerful as you can get. We couldn't just ask them to not tell us what they saw, either. No, they needed to *stop*. Our buddies give us a shit-ton of good advice and we want to hear what they have to say, but if they're still poking around the future, this advice would be tainted by what they've seen.

Well, maybe.

This whole scenario is tripping dangerously close to paradox, so maybe it wouldn't have mattered at all…or maybe it would've changed the outcome completely.

Let me walk you through the problem. *If* Sparky and I made decisions based on advice that was informed by what our friends had observed, *then* we would be making decisions which would affirm the future as they had seen it. It's like hearing that your dining room will be such a nice color of blue once you paint it, and then deciding to buy cerulean paint. Ipso facto paradox. Since time doesn't tolerate paradox, we're pretty sure there are two outcomes: one, this decision would be one we would have arrived at on our own, without help, or two, the decision is completely the reverse of what we would have decided. We don't know which of these is accurate—or if they're both accurate at different points in time—but in either case, it's a good enough reason to not bother with advice from the future.

See what I mean? Bullshit, all of it, and distracting bullshit at that. It's hard to live in the moment when you're dealing with endless possibilities and second-guessing your own thoughts. Not to mention that if you invest your energy in a possible future that doesn't come to pass, it's a hard knock to your confidence. Sparky and me, we weighed the pros and cons. Then we weighed them again. And again. And at the end of a lot of talking and arguing and actual fist-swinging fighting, we decided time travel was the equivalent of snake oil: total bullshit, except when you have a squeaky snake.

Time travel is nonsense for so many reasons, and the lack of opportunity to apply common sense is a big one. Instead of relying on the dubious outcomes of time travel, we just made sure our snakes don't squeak. We told all of our time-traveling buddies to knock it off. We said that if they wanted to play in our reality, then they should *stay* in our reality, and no more gallivanting off to hypothetical quasi-potential futures or whatever.

They...

Well.

They weren't happy about it. Giving these guys an ultimatum is like shoving your hand into a garbage disposal and hoping they aren't in the mood to flick the switch. But they agreed to stop. We had to spell it out for them using tiny words and motherfuckin' flowcharts, but they did agree.

(Between you and me, I'm sure they still slip through time, but at least it's mostly on beer runs. Future booze is *a-maz-ing!* Alcohol is one of those universal constants. The way our friends tell it, humanity's historical record is defined by the set evolution of alcoholic beverages. And yes, this is sort of paradox-y, because no matter what the future holds, I know it'll involve distilleries and a barley-centric civilization, but it gives me a headache when I think about it.)

Now.

Ancient out-of-place mechanisms, time travel...

I hope you see where I'm going with this. A couple millennia ago, someone decided that gears were pretty nifty and wanted to see what would become of them. And they either got really lucky with picking the right future, or gears are like the Gutenberg Bible.

I'm pretty sure it's the latter.

As I mentioned, I'm the world's second-worst psychic. I know the world's worst psychic, and he's awful on principle. If he ever decides to develop his abilities, I'd immediately be bumped down to the bottom of the psychic roster.

I do have one specialty, though. I'm *great* with the dead.

This is mostly accidental. For the longest time, I didn't think I was actually talking to ghosts. I sort of...

Look, shit happens. Back in college, some asshole slipped me extra-strength LSD instead of a roofie.

Then, suddenly? A dormant part of my brain flipped on, and I could see ghosts.

Not just ghosts, but the ghosts of really famous dead Americans.

It worked out okay, I guess, except my best friend and surrogate dad has been dead for more than two hundred years.

Or, another way to think of it is that I can summon the ghost of Benjamin Franklin whenever I damn well please.

I hope my rambling about time travel makes more sense now. You and me, we can't hop into multiple potential futures whenever we please. A ghost, though? The image of a person made from powerful purposeful energy?

Not such a big deal for them.

# CHAPTER 4

The floor was icy under my bare feet as I walked towards the construction zone. The home invasion dudes with their assorted hardware had cut a giant hole in the plastic separating the main house from the site of the future greenhouse, and the cold had settled in. I taped it closed as best I could; I was a lot sloppier about it than Rachel and Santino had been with the hole in the front door, but I was mostly killing time.

I thought about Ben while I ripped tiny slabs of tape from the roll with my teeth. He usually comes when I call, but I try to avoid that unless it's an emergency. Ben has a life (haha) of his own, and it's rude to yank him away from it. But if I'm alone, and if he's occupying a large space in my thoughts, he'll usually pop in on his own.

He says we're linked. An interesting word, *linked*. It's what Sparky and the other Agents call their networked connections. Sparky says that if another Agent is thinking about him, he can feel it. It's got to be sustained thinking, though. He says that back when they were new, he used to feel it when another Agent thought about his name, or his eye color, or some other trivial detail that came up a zillion times a minute. These days, they've gotten better at keeping each other out, and now they have to concentrate to make contact.

I'm not quite sure what it means to be linked to Ben. He almost never talks about what happens in the Afterlife. Most of the ghostly factoids I've learned about death and dying have been assembled over my years with him, a puzzle made up of pieces from a million conversations. I do know that while the link between Sparky and the Agents goes both ways, it's not like that with me and Ben. He might be able to feel me, or hear me when I call, but I have no clue what's going on with him unless he tells me.

I'm pretty sure he can't read my mind, though. Even the best psychics in the world can't pick up much more than emotion, and for all that Benjamin Franklin was in life, he was never psychic.

All of this was running through my head when Ben popped into our dimension. The sky didn't split open or anything nearly as dramatic. There was a quick puff of wind, and he was just *there*.

"Dearest," he said.

If you need to know what he looks like, do a Google search and check out a portrait or two. He hasn't changed much. Hasn't changed at all, really. Same receding hairline, same tiny wire-rimmed glasses perched on his nose. Same clothes, too, except for the sneakers. He discovered Chucks in the 1940s, and never went back to hard leather shoes.

Oh, and like all ghosts, he's bright blue.

"Hey, Ben." I dropped the spool of tape and moved in for a hug. It doesn't matter if he's mostly made of light and the occasional stray molecule; when I get a hug from him, it's always warm and solid. When I broke away, he took a look at my face, and *knew*.

"Not a social call, then," he said quietly. "What has happened?"

"C'mon," I said, waving for him to follow me as I headed for the nearest heating vent. "Us fleshy folk are freezing."

The air around me grew thick and comfortable, as if a wool blanket had been wrapped around me. I grinned up at him. "I'd forgotten about that trick."

"We are a long way from your college drinking days."

"Everyone used to wonder why I never froze to death during bar crawls," I said, remembering how he used to shape the air around me, a bubble of protection from the elements. Nobody was ever the wiser. Ben was one of the most powerful ghosts around, but he was almost always invisible to everyone except psychics. It made him a handy guardian angel, especially if you were the type of college kid who was prone to acting without thinking...

Ahem.

We snuggled together against a stack of lumber, me curled within the crook of his arm. Ben waved a hand, and two cups of coffee appeared. Mine was light and sweet, and the mug fit my hand like it had been made for me.

(By the way, if you're wondering what it's like to have a best friend who's a ghost, let me assure you that it's flippin' *fantastic!*)

"What's troubling you?" he asked after a few minutes of catchup chatter.

"The Antikythera Mechanism," I said. "Out-of-place artifacts in general, I guess."

"Ah, yes," he said, nodding. "God save the living from dead men with a sense of humor."

"I thought that was you."

He laughed. "That shipwreck was long before even my time, Dearest. But yes, my people have been known to seed the imagination."

"Is that what ghosts call changing history?"

Ben tensed.

It was oh-so-slight, and I wouldn't have noticed if I hadn't been watching for it. "Gotcha," I said, poking him in the holographic equivalent of his ribcage. "Spill. And none of this 'Keep the world of the living and the dead separate' bullshit, okay? You can*not* bring me coffee and still trot out that line whenever you want to dodge a question."

Ben sighed. "Be gentle," he said with a small smile. "Remember, the dead are curious, too. We wish to learn, to grow, as much as we did when we lived. It is why some of us have chosen to stay upon the earth, even after our days on it have come to a close."

"Sure," I replied. "So. A dead dude built a magic skyclock. Makes all the sense in the world."

He pulled his arm away, and curled in on himself to rest his chin on his knees. I'd say he hunched over, but that's not a

Benism. Not unless I'd managed to find one of those rare topics that tore him up inside. We've all got those, and when we're with those whom we love, we do our best to avoid them unless it's absolutely necessary to pick at the scabs. Me and Ben, we're no different; by now, I knew mostly everything that hurt him.

This was new.

I waited.

"The past cannot be changed," he said.

I nodded. "Because paradox."

"Because paradox, indeed. There is, however, nothing to prevent the dead from duplicating what they have seen in the future in their own time."

"The magic skyclock was built by a ghost? I assumed it was yanked out of the future, whole, and then dumped in ancient Greece."

He laughed, a sad chuckle. "What have I brought you from the future, Dearest?"

I had the answer ready. "Information and alcohol. And this." I held up my right hand, with its ugly resin ring on my middle finger. It was a cross between a pager and a GPS, and it was keyed directly to Sparky's implant. Anytime I needed him, I could press a hidden button, and he—and nobody else—would get the signal.

"Don't you think that's odd? You've often asked me why I haven't brought you your own personal antigravity device. Barring that, a jetpack."

"I assumed you didn't want to scrape me off of the ceiling."

"That, too," he admitted. "But the technology to build that ring already exists within this time. The physical footprints for global positioning systems and pagers, both? That ring could have been made by someone with the knowledge and ability. I violated nothing by bringing that ring back to you.

"Now, an antigravity device? The traces of that technology might exist in ideas and experiments. There are some steps taken towards such a device within today's laboratories, but these steps have left no significant imprints. One day, they might, and on that day it may be possible to bring you that device."

"Ah. Paradox."

"Yes. If there is no foundation in the timeline, an item should never be moved from the future."

I couldn't shake the feeling that Ben was fretting. "*Should never*, or *can't be*?" I asked.

He gave me a sad smile. "Very astute of you, Dearest. If I were to bring an item from the future back to the present, it would be unmoored in time."

I tossed this idea around in my head, looking for a way to apply paradox to it. It took me a moment.

"Oh shit," I said, very, very quietly.

Ben nodded. "Oh shit, indeed."

You remember what I was saying about what might happen if information from the future informs our decisions? How what we decide would either be what we'd have done anyhow, or how the option might simply reverse itself?

I had just realized there was a third option.

"I can bring alcohol back to you, as alcohol may as well be a natural law in that it seems to violate nothing. I made a decision to bring back your ring, as the technology that informs it is already fixed within this time. I will not risk bringing back much else, as…"

"…it might cease to exist."

"Perhaps," he said. "And if that is indeed the case, it might erase parts of the timeline with it."

"There's no way to know for sure, is there? How would we know if we just stopped…existing?" I asked. I glanced down to see my hands still wrapped around my coffee cup, the same cup that Ben had—"Hey!" I said, as I dropped the mug on the floor and kicked it away from me. "Where'dja get this coffee?"

Ben laughed. "A diner in Brooklyn. Don't worry," he said, pushing the mug back towards me. It had been refilled with that same perfect blend. "I have found that teleportation may violate the rules of physics, but not those of time. The physical realm is much more forgiving than the temporal one."

"Uh…"

"I always leave a tip, and I make the effort to return the cup. It is a darling place. I have no desire to help nudge it into bankruptcy."

Good enough for me. I took up the mug, and let the heat sink into my hands. "If we violated time and it erased itself…" I started. The coffee still had streams of white from the cream. As I watched, these melted away. "We'd never know it happened."

"I have a theory," Ben said. "I don't believe that timelines cease to exist, but I do think objects of paradox can become lost."

"That's a relief. It'd be better than just…disappearing."

"Perhaps," Ben said.

That same sense of sadness kept coming off of him in waves. It was getting hard to pretend he wasn't feeling miserable, but the thing about Ben Franklin? He needs to think he's five moves ahead of you, or he starts feeling even *worse*.

"You think this is why we've only found that one clock?" I asked. "The others got lost?"

"If there were others," he replied. "Lesser devices similar to the Mechanism were described by numerous scholars, but this one has always been recognized as exceptional."

"So…" I began. My poor brain hamster was turning its wheel as fast as it could. "If those lesser devices didn't have the same footprint as the Mechanism, and if the Mechanism was built by a ghost who wanted to develop ideas he or she saw in the future… The Mechanism could inspire others, who might expand on its advanced technology instead of working on technology native to their own timeline. Boom! Paradox. Unless it somehow…*didn't*."

"Yes. As such, the Mechanism vanished off of the face of the earth, never to be seen until—"

I sat up straight and finished his sentence for him. "—until technology evolved to catch up with it."

"Yes," he said. "Intriguing, is it not, that we have yet to find an out-of-place artifact that we cannot easily explain? By the time we discover them, our science has surpassed their merits."

"I figured that's because our technology was better than theirs."

He gave me that same sad smile again. "Such ego, Dearest. The joy of discovery is admitting there will always be something we cannot understand."

Ben stared down at his mug. I felt the cold starting to creep back in as his concentration slipped and my metaphysical energy blanket fell apart.

"Ben?" I asked. "What's bothering you?"

It took him a minute to answer, and when he did, it wasn't an answer at all.

"Dearest? I think I must ask you to go to Greece."

# CHAPTER 5

There was too much sun when I woke up.

*The curtains are open*, my brain informed the rest of me. *You closed them when you went to bed, and Sparky wouldn't have opened them, not when you went to sleep at dawn...*

My body didn't want to be awake, and it told my brain to shut up and deal with it. The cunning application of pillow to eyeballs would solve this problem. The pillow didn't even have to be moved. No, I could just turn over, and—

My brain had me up and rolling into a *zenpo kaiten* before I could drop back into sleep. I was halfway across the bedroom before the crowbar crashed into the exact spot on the pillow where my head had been.

Let me tell you about sugar.

My high school history teacher used to say that sugar was the catalyst for the Industrial Revolution. I checked his dates and he was off by a few decades, but sugar plus coffee did hit Great Britain right around the time that steam engines finally hit their stride. Imagine that for a second: the British and stimulants, together at last!

Shit got *done*.

Now, let me tell you about koalas.

Cute? Yes. Cuddly? Definitely. Stupider than rocks? *Fuck* yes. They have some of the least-developed brains in the mammalian kingdom. Their brains are so tiny that they're basically bobbing around in the koala's skull. When a koala does manage to process a thought, it's almost always focused on one of three basic drives: they eat, sleep, and procreate, and they do this with the literal single-mindedness of a brain capable of holding just one thought at a time.

They're fairly durable, though. If you were a mad scientist

who wanted to write on a blank slate and see if you could enhance intelligence, you couldn't pick a better test subject than a koala.

Except, around your third koala, you'd realize that the animal's metabolism is causing problems. The critters only eat eucalyptus, and when they're not eating or fucking, they're asleep. So you start to tinker with the koala genome so they can live on a variety of plants, and don't need to sleep twenty-two hours a day.

At Koala No. 4, you decide to see if you can also get them to metabolize grains. Fresh vegetation can be hard to find, but every supermarket has a cereal aisle.

By Koala No. 17, you've gotten the process nailed down. Brains, guts, everything works. You start to test the limits on what can be done to improve a koala's smarts. Under the right conditions, can a koala become as intelligent as a monkey? A great ape? A *human*?

These experiments go great. So great, you run into communication problems. It's harder to test the intelligence of an animal that can't vocalize. You decide to tinker with their vocal cords.

Finally, you get to Koala No. 26. This one's a total dud. Every single modification went right—better than on any previous test subject, really!—but the animal is a lump of stupid squeaking fur. You decide to euthanize and start from scratch.

Except Koala No. 26 beats you to it. The little bugger has been playing dumb all along. You're proud of him, probably, in the instant before he shoots you between the eyes with your own gun.

Young Koala No. 26 spent a rough couple of days running scared in suburban Missouri before he was captured. And then escaped. And captured, and escaped, and captured, and escaped, and captured...and finally, a certain government agency got news of this "speedy devil" that could break out of any cage. They whisked him away to one of those subterranean buildings that form the stuff of nightmares, and performed unspeakable tests until they learned he had about 200 IQ points more than the average Harvard graduate.

Koala No. 26 sat in a cage and broke codes for years. Sparky rescued him. This...

Um.

Yeah.

This probably wasn't the best decision Sparky's ever made.

It's not like he could release this koala into the wild, or even put him in a zoo. So? Sparky decided this koala was his responsibility. For a while, he made sure the koala had his own apartment. These days, he lives with us.

I love the little fucker, I do, but let's face facts: if the entire Industrial Revolution was the outcome of moderately caffeinated cultural sugar high, a superintelligent animal with three all-encompassing drives and regular access to Cap'n Crunch becomes its own force of nature.

And he is an *asshole*.

Case in point: said asshole got his paws on a crowbar.

"Speedy!" Shouting was a mistake. Lack of sleep made my own voice bounce off the backs of my eyeballs. I tried again. "Speedy? The crowbar?"

"Found it in the kitchen," he said. He's got a smooth, dark voice, somewhere between a tenor and a baritone. It's slightly disturbing. A talking koala should sound like a big squeaky chipmunk, not a radio talk show host. "Thought you might want it back."

"I'm sure." I crossed the room and grabbed the crowbar before he could smash anything. "Thanks."

"Don't mention it." He hopped off of the headboard and settled into the hollow of the sheets.

Look, it's not like he actually wanted to bean me with the crowbar. If he had, he wouldn't have bothered to warn me by opening the curtains, or by waiting until I woke up enough to know to move out of the way. What he wanted was to cuddle with me in a warm bed. He just has an extremely violent way of asking permission.

I shoved him aside and got back under the sheets. Somehow, purely by accident, I ended up with the soft crease at the backs of his ears under my fingernails. I sighed and started scratching.

"What happened last night?" he asked.

"Where were you?"

"Out."

"Do I get anything more than 'out'?"

He tilted his head so I'd hit the itchy spots. "Nope."

"Fine, then. No gossip for you."

"Oh?" He peered up at me. Whatever he saw there set him to grinning. "Oh-*ho!* Someone was visited by three spirits last night."

"One spirit. The Ghost of Paradox Present."

The koala batted my hand away and climbed on my stomach. "I was running an errand. Now, what's up?"

"An errand? That's all I get?"

Speedy's eyes traveled to my hand and back, and he gave me a wide smile. It wasn't a nice smile. Smiling isn't a natural gesture for a koala, and they have a lot of teeth.

"Don't even think about it," I warned him. "A bunch of guys broke in last night, and I'm running on zero sleep."

"Cops show up?"

I nodded. "We had a...logical misunderstanding. They saw all of the bodies on the ground, and me standing over them."

He snorted. It was a sound somewhere between a grunt and a happy kazoo. "You'd think they'd have heard of you by now."

"They had, but protocol is protocol," I said, shrugging. The motion tipped Speedy sideways, and his claws bit into my ribcage. (Pro tip: if you're ever given the choice between being on the business side of a koala's teeth or its claws, go with the teeth. Those fuckers don't sprint up the sides of trees because Ben Franklin's ghost brought them invisible jetpacks.) I waved the crowbar at him until he climbed off.

This time, he snuggled against my arm. He was tired. We usually went a few more rounds before he settled down. "You tell me yours, and I'll tell you mine."

"Fine."

"Got a commission from the Smithsonian. They wanted a second opinion on a few Babylonian texts."

"You speak Babylonian?"

"Nobody speaks Babylonian except for scholars, and they butcher the pronunciation so badly that you can't call it speech," he said, rolling his eyes towards the ceiling. "I *read* all of the Semitic languages, Akkadian included."

Right. Speedy is a genius, remember? Specifically, a genius with languages. If he doesn't already know a particular language (unlikely), give him a book and a week. Lately, he's been dabbling in dead languages for the local museums. He doesn't do it for the money; he says breaking the spirits of overeducated thumb-monkeys is a delight.

Of course, said overeducated thumb-monkeys don't exactly enjoy having their work discredited by a thirty-five-pound marsupial. So the museums bring him in at night, when there's fewer people around to witness the swearing and the sobbing.

"'bout you?" he murmured into my armpit.

"Ben is sending me to Greece to track down the origins of the Antikythera Mechanism, since he thinks it might have something to do with ancient ghosts."

Speedy sat up so quickly that there were little *rip-POPS!* as his claws poked through the sheets. "That rat *bastard!*" he hissed.

Okay, one last thing about koalas' thought processes? They aren't creative thinkers. Speedy can logic his way to the moon and back if he's got the pieces of a spaceship laid out in front of him, but he'd never even dream of putting pumpkin, spice, and latte together in the same cup.

He had seen something I missed.

Whatever. Solving puzzles is what he did. And I could either beg and plead for him to tell me, which he wouldn't, or I could annoy the shit out of him by ignoring him.

I rolled over and hit the button on the curtain remote (everything is remote-controlled in a cyborg's house, a fact that

I remember only when I'm conscious), and pretended not to notice that Speedy's ears had flattened against his head.

He hunkered down beside me, grumbling.

I started scratching his ears again. They gradually unplastered themselves as he relaxed.

"Hey, Speedy?" I whispered. "Want to come with me to Greece?"

# CHAPTER 6

The world's worst psychic was waiting for us at the airport.

Mike Reilly is as Scots-Irish as they come. He's medium-height and stocky, with the obligatory green eyes, red hair, and freckles. Slap a kilt and a sporran on him, and he'd blend right in with those dudes who toss whole telephone poles for fun.

He was arguing philosophy with a baggage clerk.

Which is in character, really. Mike will argue philosophy with anything willing to talk to him. (This is why his partner's parrots all scream *"How do you know?"* when the phone rings.) The baggage clerk seemed quite happy arguing back, so I chose a different line.

"This is Speedy, the talking koala," I said to my own clerk as I passed him Speedy's papers. "He doesn't travel in a carry-on, and he's had all of his shots. He's cleared to visit Greece, and they're expecting him at the airport and our hotels."

It's a rule of my life that I manage all of Speedy's affairs before I manage my own. First, it's not as though I could pretend he was a Cocker Spaniel and sneak him aboard a plane in a carry-on, and it's hard to miss a koala sitting on a woman's shoulders. I think that's remarked upon even in Australia, let alone Dulles International Airport.

Second, it's best to deal with Speedy as quickly as possible. If you don't, Bad Things Happen.

The clerk peered down at us from behind his desk, and started out with the usual question: "Is this a joke?"

"Yes," Speedy replied.

I'm really lucky Speedy loves to show off. All he has to do to totally screw me with airport security is play dumb.

The clerk dropped everything to fawn over him, which gave me time to wander over to Mike's line and let him know we had arrived. He was walking the clerk through Aristotle's *Nicomachean Ethics,* and they were knee-deep in the definitions of virtue and happiness.

"Don't," I whispered.

Mike's fuzzy red eyebrows moved up a couple of inches. The man pretended pure innocence. "Don't what?"

"Don't talk him into quitting."

The clerk glared at Mike.

"He does this all the time," I said to the clerk.

"She's kidding," Mike assured him. "Once, our waitress walked out in the middle of our lunch. Just once! But I'll never hear the end of it."

"Has he asked you if you've assessed the ultimate value of your life in relation to your personal and societal obligations yet?"

The clerk blinked at me a few times. "Hey!" he said, as his brain put the details together. "You're—"

"Hi," I said, giving him a little wave. "Hope Blackwell, yeah. And my husband isn't with us." Honestly, I don't even need to participate in conversations any more. The same questions just come and come and come.

The clerk didn't believe me, but as he looked around to see if he could catch a glimpse of Sparky, he noticed Speedy sitting a few counters away. "Oh, it's Speedy!"

Yes, folks, I wasn't kidding—the koala is famous, too. Try being me and taking your not-so-nuclear family out for pizza. Just try it, I dare you. Clear your schedule first.

It took us another hour to get through checkout and security. Speedy and I signed a bunch of autographs. Someone got in my face and started screaming that I had just caused the last good politician to resign from office: when she realized I wasn't going to respond, she spat on me. Mike spent the entire time laughing. All in all, a typical day.

Once upon a time, before I married a cyborg, I would have hauled Miss Spitter around the airport by her tongue. These days, I carry moist towelettes and make sure I dab off the spittle before it crusts over. Somewhere between the spitting and the dabbing, I use those magic words: "Yes, I will press charges, thank you." I've learned the hard way that if a dude breaks into my house and I kick his ass, I am much less likely to get slapped with a countersuit than if a random stranger spits on me and I, quote, *overreact,* unquote.

If I dab it off with a wistful smile on my face, I end up looking the hero on the evening news.

People are weird.

The flight went fine. Speedy took it as an opportunity to catch up on his sleep, which left me and Mike to hash out the details of the trip. And eat. Mike and I never turn down a meal, and while airline food has earned its reputation, the business-class dinners were still edible.

Mike had insisted on bringing a paper map. This, he had spread over my seat, our empty dinner plates, and most of a snoring koala. He was making careful marks with a blue pencil, sketching out the roads between villages.

"Was Ambassador Goodwin able to arrange the meeting with the…um…" Mike didn't know what to call our contact in Athens. Neither of us knew the shorthand for a professional tomb robber.

"Archaeologist," I said. It seemed as safe a job description as any. "And yes, he asked one of the museums to contact a freelancer they know, a guy named Atlas Petrakis. Goodwin thinks we're operating on OACET's behalf to track down other pieces of the Antikythera Mechanism."

Speedy and I had come up with this story before we had even considered leaving Washington. It was a better reason for us to move around a strange country than sightseeing. I was on good speaking terms with Jack Goodwin, the American ambassador to Greece, so I had emailed him and gushed in giant wordy paragraphs about how finding the first fragment of the Mechanism had won OACET a ton of positive press, and how I wanted to come to Greece to see if I could locate any others that had gone missing.

Oh, and I'd be bringing some friends. Greece is *so* lovely at this time of year...

It was the kind of bullshit excuse you'd get from a spoiled rich girl who wanted to rationalize a vacation, but Goodwin was a politician. He had sent a polite reply saying that it was a fabulous idea, and promised to do what he could to help. A few email exchanges later, and he claimed to have found me the male version of Lara Croft.

I wasn't too happy about working with a stranger, but whatever. As much as I would have loved to touch down in Athens and merrily wander about a strange country, several facts needed to be taken into consideration.

Fact: I'm famous. Like, ridiculously famous. Not to mention how I'm usually running around with this talking koala. The only one of us who could pass for an average tourist on this trip was Mike. Traveling incognito was out.

Fact: During the ten-day period when Mike and I were preparing to travel to Greece, Rachel had solved her murder mystery. The story had blown up in the media, and had resulted in the resignation of a prominent politician from office (see: Miss Spitter). The whole world was now obsessed with the Antikythera Mechanism, so we couldn't ask questions about it without getting inspected and dissected.

Fact: Senator Richard Hanlon—sorry, *former* Senator Richard Hanlon—had wanted the fragment of the Antikythera Mechanism. He had wanted it so badly that he had hired a thief to break into the White House to steal it.

Fact: If Hanlon was involved, shit had gotten real. Mike and I weren't just dealing with a millennia-old mystery: we were dealing with crazy-making evil geniuses and their schemes...

Without looking up from his map, Mike reached over and took the plastic knife out of my mouth.

I tasted blood, and my tongue found where I had accidentally cut my lip on the edge of the knife. "Thanks," I said, as I pried a piece of plastic from between my teeth.

He nodded, and passed me a napkin.

(Business class had linen napkins and plastic silverware? What a strange world this is.)

"What's on your mind?" he asked. His big fingers trailed across the map, charting a path from Athens to where the Mechanism had been found.

"Hanlon."

"Ah."

"I'm thinking that we might want to check and see if Hanlon's been to Greece lately."

"Mmm," Mike said. He made a tick mark on the map. "Your husband knows every move Hanlon's made over the past ten years. He would have mentioned."

"Maybe Hanlon sent a proxy," I said. "Or maybe he's already got connections in Greece. Seems like breaking into the White House is a last resort. If I were Hanlon, I would have checked to see if I could find any fragments of the Mechanism in Greece before I went that far."

Mike nodded. "True."

"Is this a trap? This doesn't feel like a trap."

"I don't think so," Mike said, and then grinned at me. "But wouldn't it be fun if it were?"

I cackled so loudly that the other passengers poked their heads up to see what had happened. I waved them off, then said to Mike: "You are a *shit* pacifist."

"I practice nonviolence," he corrected me. "Not pacifism."

"Shouldn't you stop hanging out with me, then?" I asked, half-seriously. We'd had this discussion before, but I was always worried that one day Mike would finally stop rationalizing his way through our friendship. "Seems like when you associate with someone who puts you in a position where you have to commit violence on a regular basis..."

"How can one be sure of their beliefs unless they're tested?" he replied.

I chuckled, much more softly this time. "You just enjoy beating people up."

"I enjoy practicing the evolving applications of an art I've dedicated my life to learning," he said.

I rolled my eyes at him, and Mike patted my knee. "It's okay," he assured me. "It'd be one thing if you went looking for conflict, but you don't—it happens naturally."

"And now we're back to the issue of whether or not we're walking into a trap," I said.

"I vote no," Mike said. "Even if Hanlon knew we were going to Greece, there's no reason for him to come after us."

"Hanlon knows every move Sparky makes, too," I said. "They hate each other. That's reason enough for Hanlon to try and bag me, especially if he's in a whole other country and can claim he had nothing to do with my accidental demise."

"Hanlon wouldn't try that," Mike said. "That'd turn his cold war with OACET into open murder. Your husband would destroy him."

I grinned.

Mike stretched, already tired of being caged in an airbound metal tube. The map across his lap crinkled with the movement. "Do you think we'll bump into any of the regulars?"

"Definitely," I said. "I don't know what they'll be like in Greece, though."

Wherever I went, I could count on being followed by a bunch of goons who OACET's various enemies hired to keep tabs on me. Usually they just watched and took pictures, but sometimes they tried to beat me up. Speedy, Mike, and I had *tons* of fun fucking with them—it was like running our own personal paparazzi obstacle course.

"We face what comes, when it comes. But I still don't think this is a trap. I think we've got other things to worry about," Mike said, and fluttered a corner of the map at me.

"Yup," I said, and the two of us settled down to plan our route.

We weren't starting in Antikythera. The Mechanism had been built elsewhere. We didn't know where, exactly. Nobody knows where! Sparky had put OACET's research team on it, and they had come up with a pile of facts tied together by guesswork. It's about eighty pages long, and so dry that it might as well have laid down to die in the Sahara ten years ago. Mike and I read the entire thing cover to cover, and we kept copies on our phones in case we needed a refresher.

Speedy had it memorized.

We were starting in Athens, because when you go to Greece, you start in Athens. From there, Rhodes definitely, and maybe some other spots along the way. There were a couple of names that kept popping up in relation to the Mechanism, and the big ones were Archimedes and Posidonius. These two dudes were phenomenal mathematicians and astronomers, and were separated by about a hundred years, with Posidonius refining much of Archimedes' earlier work. And they had both built complex mechanical orreries which were centered on the movements of the Sun.

Now, I'm not suggesting that Posidonius wasn't a genius in his own right, but when you're looking for evidence of ghosts, you start by checking into legacies. It'd be so much easier if ghosts just clanked around your attic and went *Boo!*—but no, they like to hang around and poke at the living. Genius or not, Posidonius was our best lead, and he'd set up shop in Rhodes, so...

"There's a problem," Mike said, poking the map with his pencil. It left a little blue pucker on Rhodes, which fluttered up and down as Speedy snored. "Posidonius spent years living in Roman territory. It's likely he made it all the way to northern Africa."

"Yeah," I said. "It's a lot of ground to cover." I didn't see it as a problem, but I love to travel. Speedy, on the other hand, is a territorial homebody. I figured I had about a week before his instincts kicked in and I had a furious Queensland koala to manage.

"Not that," he said. "New work by Archimedes keeps turning up. I wonder..." His voice trailed off.

I nodded. I had the same thought.

Have you heard about the Archimedes Palimpsest? In the

13<sup>th</sup> century, a bunch of monks got their hands on some used parchment, cleaned it up, and wrote a bunch of prayers on it. Seven hundred years later, a British dude realized the original writing on the parchment was mathematical theorems. There was the usual academic headbangery, followed by the discovery that some of those theorems were developed by Archimedes, they had been written down over a thousand years after his death, and they had never been recorded in print anywhere else.

Do a little light reading on Archimedes, and you'll find coincidences like the Palimpsest all over the place. It's almost like Archimedes didn't stop making or inventing or discovering shit after he died.

Listen, I know human history is rife with coincidence, and lost artifacts are turning up all of the time, and blah blah blah. If you dick around with powerful ghosts long enough, this sort of thing is a red flag.

Maybe Archimedes' ghost was still kicking around.

# CHAPTER 7

I'd never been to Greece before.

We landed at night, which muffled the edges of the city. I've done a lot of traveling, and when you're tired and hungry and jet-lagged, every airport looks like the same. I dragged Mike and Speedy across Athens, got us checked into our hotel, and hit the sheets for something like ten hours until the boys decided they were ready to explore and the best way to wake me up was to sit on me.

I forgave them as soon as I made it to the window.

I had booked us a room in a hotel on the edge of the old city, a fact I had forgotten until I saw this amazing landscape of white and gold laid out beneath us. The sun was high enough to bounce light off of limestone and marble, and the entire place glowed like an ancient gem.

I might have squeaked.

We were close enough to the Parthenon to pick out the details. It looked as if a giant had smashed a club against its roof, leaving columns and craters. The rocks running across the hill were this glorious tumble of rubble. All I wanted to do was explore.

We were off and running.

I think I've mentioned how I'm new to the spy game, but one of the first things I learned is that bad guys get bored. If Speedy, Mike, and I were being followed, we could do worse than play tourists for a little while. The bad guys—if there were any— wouldn't quit following us, but they'd take out their phones and start Candy Crushing or whatever the cool hitmen are playing these days.

Bored bad guys are sloppy bad guys. After six hours of us acting like jerky tourists, we'd be able to recognize them.

We usually just waved and blew kisses. Sometimes, if they're really extra-terrible at their jobs, we pay someone to bring them coffee or beer.

(Speedy and I *love* to buy drinks for our bad guys. It scares the *shit* out of them.)

The walk up the hill to the acropolis was steeper than it appeared from the hotel room. Mike and I took it as an opportunity to run sprints. I won; he was wearing a heavy backpack and an additional thirty-five pounds of male Queensland koala. By the time we got to the Parthenon at the top, we were both winded. We figured it'd buy us some time to talk freely: any bad guys who had followed us on foot had probably *died*.

Mike deposited Speedy on a nearby chunk of fallen marble, and the three of us took in the view.

Spectacular.

"Did Archimedes ever visit Athens?" I asked as I passed a canteen of water to Mike.

"Nobody knows," Speedy whispered. He was stalking a lizard across the rocks. "Probably, but there's no record of it. We know he made it down to Egypt—*ach!*" He mistimed his pounce, and missed the lizard by a mile. It scurried behind a clump of tawny grass. This, he ate.

"Greece and Rome were at war when he was alive," he continued around a mouthful of grass. "Archimedes lived in Syracuse. There was bad blood between Syracuse and Athens, and Greece was hell to move around in, but any scholar who made it all the way to Alexandria must have also hit up Athens."

"So what can we expect to find here?" Mike asked, thumbing through Archimedes' dossier on his phone.

"For Archimedes? Jack fuck-all shit. But Posidonius studied in Athens when he was a student."

I leaned back on my rock. Athens morning sunlight, folks? Absolutely *divine*. "Have we just outright accepted that Archimedes was haunting Posidonius?"

"Yes," Speedy said.

"Maybe." Mike was always open to alternatives. "But if Posidonius did bump into Archimedes, where did it happen? Their geographies didn't overlap."

"We should find a Greek ghost and ask," Speedy suggested.

"Working on it," I muttered.

There was another reason—a darned good reason—we had started in Athens.

We were looking for ghosts.

The Afterlife is...

Okay. Imagine a bag of marbles.

Now, imagine a bag of marbles a *billion* times the size of that one. And dump all of those marbles on the metaphysical floor.

Now, imagine you have to move from this nice Cat's Eye here to that lovely Aggie *aaaaaaall* the way over there, but only, like, one out of fifty of those marbles are connected, and you have no clue how to locate these connections.

That's the Afterlife.

Please remember that ghosts don't tell us shit about shit. Everything I know about the Afterlife is conditionally vague. Since I'm, you know, still alive, my impression of the Afterlife is that it's not so much Heaven as it is your own personal version of Better Metaphysical Homes and Gardens. You and your buddies who have chosen to remain in the Afterlife, rather than dissipating into the aether or getting reincarnated as bunnies or whatever, get to play with your own section of space-time. It's yours. It's your own slice of paradise to manipulate as you see fit. You want to live in a cave? Bam! There's your cave. You want to live in Kim Kardashian's mansion? Bam! There's your mansion.

(I'm not sure if a facsimile of Kim Kardashian comes with it, by the way. I've never asked, because *ugh*.)

But this little slice of paradise? It's *private*. Unless you're the type of person who's okay with strangers barging into your home, your borders are impenetrable.

From what I've gathered, this creates something of a challenge in making new friends. Your old friends can find your home just fine, and maybe you all go hang out in spaces that certain ghosts have created for get-togethers or whatnot, but you can't just wander into someone else's backyard and ask to use their Kardashian cave-pool.

The Afterlife is a very exclusive invitation-only after-party. I had already asked Ben to find a dead dude, who knew another dead dude, who knew a Greek dead dude, who knew either Archimedes or Posidonius. I didn't expect anything to come of it.

So, you know. Go to the source.

I let my mind wander. I felt a bit like Speedy's lizard: mostly enjoying myself in the sun, but keeping an eye out to make sure something bigger wasn't about to eat me.

Ghosts feel like...

I don't know what they feel like.

I know when they're around. They *push* on my brain. They don't do it intentionally—I think the energy they throw off hits my psychic buttons.

Today, my buttons remained unpushed. The Parthenon was unhaunted.

(At least, for me. I have my theories about why psychics can perceive some ghosts and not others. I'll get into those theories later.)

I sat up and stretched.

"Anything?" Mike asked.

"Nope," I said. "If there's anybody lurking about, they're staying off of my radar."

"It was a long shot anyway," he said.

What Mike didn't say was that it was probably for the best. I don't speak Greek, let alone ancient Greek. If we had bumped into an old ghost, Speedy would have had to serve as the translator.

How do you say 'righteously pissed-off poltergeist lynch mob' in ancient Greek?

"We should go to a battlefield," Speedy said. "You always get lucky at battlefields."

"Um…" I had the mental image of getting skewered on a dead Spartan's spectral spear. "Put a pin in that idea. I want to keep trying here."

We played tourists for the rest of the afternoon. It was incredibly pleasant. The Parthenon has a snack stand.[2]

The Acropolis at Athens is a wickedly arid place. Most of it is dusty and dry, but we ended up at the southern end of the ruins, in a space that was more green than brown. We were the only people in sight. The walk was rough for the average tourist, but there were plenty of signs to show we hadn't magically discovered this place. Candy wrappers, used condoms, the occasional shoe, that sort of thing. Made sense: there was a cluster of apartment buildings down the hill, just barely visible through the tree line.

"Where are we?" I asked. There was a set of columns sticking up from the ground. After spending the better part of a day in the old city, the magic of turning the corner and tripping over (literally) those surviving scraps of buildings was beginning to wear off.

"The Asklepion spring house," Speedy replied. He was back up on Mike's shoulders, inspecting the ruins from a height. He had run afoul of a scorpion on one of his lizard chases and was done with the ground for a while.

"I thought that was on Kos," Mike said.

"Asklepieia were healing temples," Speedy sighed. "Like hospitals. The Greeks built more than one of those fuckers."

He inspected the rocks around us. Most of them were giant slabs of cut stone left over from when the archaeologists had tried to stick the temple back together. Behind those was the mountain, with chunks of crude caves here and there. "Try again," he told me, as he stared into one of those caves.

"Speedy?"

"Healing was another form of science. The library's gone, and so's most of the art, but there's still water here. Try again."

"I don't see a spring," I started to say, but caught myself when I saw all the trees. Underground water is still water. "Right."

2 Speedy says the Parthenon has always had some version of a snack stand. Go figure.

I found a big flat stone, checked it for scorpions, and sat. The sun was behind the mountain, and it was getting chilly. "This entire week is going to be about me freezing my butt off on cold rocks," I muttered quietly to myself.

Speedy has the *unbelievable* hearing you'd expect from an animal whose ears take up a majority of its headspace. "Don't care. Find ghosts."

"Hush," Mike told him. He was keeping watch back the way we came. "We finally picked up a tail."

Speedy glanced over Mike's shoulder, and grinned at the two men far down the trail.

I shut my mind off as best as I could, and waited for something to push my buttons. *Bird song. Bugs. What sound does a scorpion make? Do scorpions make noise, anyway? They're not like wolves...maybe they are. There was that thing on the Discovery Channel about wolf packs and how they don't howl when hunting. They just pick their moment and strike. Sometimes they howl. Howling's like...I guess it's a cheerleader thing...*

I had made the mental jump to wolves in cheerleader skirts (*Rrrrah! Rrrrah! Go team go!*) when I felt that unmistakable twitchy-itchy sensation I get when a ghost is nearby.

"Guys? We're on."

Mike shooed Speedy off of his shoulders, and slipped off his backpack. He had carefully wrapped the liquor bottles in sweatshirts, and they didn't even clink as he pulled two of them from the bag.

Let me tell you about ghosts and liquor.

Wait, no. I don't really need to bother with this one. It's self-explanatory. Loooong story short? Only the most powerful ghosts can travel through time. They're the ones with ready access to future booze. The rest of us, both living and dead, have to take our alcohol as we find it.

I've yet to meet a ghost who'll turn down a free drink.

Mike and I had picked up an assortment of Greek alcohol at the duty free shop. We'd gotten a sharp look from the clerks when they realized we were buying all of this stuff while traveling into the country, not out of it, but fuck 'em. Ghosts are territorial buggers. A bribe is more likely to work if it's familiar, so wine and ouzo it was.

"Should we do this now?" Mike asked, looking down the trail.

"Yeah," I said. Mike and I can tell fellow psychics at a glance: we've got this weird blue aura. It goes away after you make physical contact, shaking hands or whatever, but it's great if you want to find strange psychics in a crowd.

Not that we ever did find other psychics, but I'll get into that later.

(Listen, I'm sorry my life is complicated, okay? I'd explain everything to you at once if I could, but for the moment we should focus on how Mike and I wanted to get ancient Greek ghosts liquored up.)

Mike broke out the ouzo. I took the first drink.

I'd never had ouzo before. It was…uh…

It's an acquired taste.

Mike waited patiently until I stopped choking: Speedy laughed his ass off.

"Well, that got their attention," I said once I could talk.

"Two psychics and me?" Speedy said. "They knew we were here from the moment we hit the hill."

He had a point. Ghosts are attracted to psychics, and there's nobody, alive or dead, who doesn't want to know the deal with the talking koala.

"Salud," Mike said, toasting the invisible air around us.

"Wrong. *Stin iyia mas*," Speedy corrected him.

"*Stin iyia mas*," Mike and I parroted.

The ouzo was better the second time.

Then we put the bottle on the table, and waited.

Let me tell you about ghosts and memories.

A very few ghosts, like Ben, are super-powerful. They're *remembered*. Everybody knows their name. Those memories are a source of energy, and these superghosts can use it to travel through time and whatnot.

But not everybody who dies was a legend. Most human beings are average schmucks just trying to survive. Four generations—at most!—and we're just a blurry name on the back of a yellow photograph. The vast majority of ghosts don't have enough energy to manifest.

There are motherfuckin' ghosts *everywhere*, guys.

(Don't freak out. Ghosts are like bacteria. Your body might be covered in invisible crawling things, but they don't affect you unless you get a papercut or something. Same with ghosts. They aren't invisible stalkers—they've got their own shit to do.[3])

We were trying to attract a powerful ghost. We figured if we got lucky, we'd get a philosopher or a scientist, somebody whose name was written down in an ancient text and remembered by resentful college students cramming for midterms.

If such a ghost showed up, it didn't mean we'd be able to see them. Even for the best psychics, talking to the dead is a crapshoot. It's simple physics. Strong ghost plus strong psychic? Conversation. Weak ghost plus shitty psychics? Zilch. Zero. Zip.

I'm really good with the dead, so if we got a strong ghost's attention, I'd probably be able to talk to him.

If I could see him.

Which I couldn't.

Not unless he picked up the bottle of ouzo to tell me *exactly* where he was, so I could focus on him.

Bribes are a time-honored method of communication between psychics and weaker ghosts. Some cultures refer to them as offerings, as in, "Hey, I offer you this bribe in exchange for favors." It works mainly as a gesture of goodwill. As I said, ghosts have their own shit to do. A bottle of good ouzo proves we respect his time and want the conversation to be worthwhile for him.

(People, really! The absolute worst *worst* **worst** thing you can do when dealing with ghosts is think of them as the living's little

---

3 Okay, so there aren't nearly as many ghosts as there are different types of bacterium. Sorry. I just like that analogy. They're still everywhere, though. Ghosts *and* bacteria. Now go wash your damned hands.

blue minions! They're human beings, and they deserve respect. Also, they're invisible human beings who can walk through walls—do *not* piss them off. If you're lucky, the least they'll do to you is hide the toilet paper.)

The bottle didn't move.

We waited until the sun went down. Mike had brought a deck of cards, and we played poker. It was next to impossible to win, as we always dealt out four hands instead of three, and that fourth hand stayed flat on the stone.

No, I don't know if long-dead Greek ghosts know how to play poker, but it never hurts to be polite.

Every fifteen minutes, I'd do that thing where I let my mind wander. Yup. There were still ghosts nearby. They just weren't making themselves known.

"Fuck it," I finally said. It was getting late, we were hungry, and the ruins looked savage after dark. Plus, the local kids would start turning up for their nightly hump-n-bump sessions. "We're not getting anywhere."

"Maybe we're not wanted," Mike said, gazing around at the broken marble stones.

"Or maybe they tried, and they're not strong enough to lift the cards or the bottle. Or maybe it's the culture problem and they can't manifest to Americans. Or maybe…" I waved my hands uselessly and gave up. There were too many unknowns when dealing with ghosts.

We dumped everything into the backpack, checked to make sure our goon buddies were still lurking around (they were hiding behind some bushes, but the glow of their phones gave them away), and left the half-empty bottle of ouzo on top of the rock. Either the ghosts would spirit it away (hah), or the local kids would have a spectacular night.

We started down the nearest path. It wasn't a hard walk, but it was dark, and Mike and I had to watch our footing. So we didn't bother to look back the way we came until Speedy tapped Mike on the head and said, "Guys? The bottle."

Mike and I turned around.

The bottle was gone.

# CHAPTER 8

The dudes on our tail waited until we'd eaten dinner before they pretended to mug us.

I thought it was really nice of them.

We went out for authentic Greek food, which was ridiculously good. Or maybe Mike and I were still a little drunk on the ouzo. Whatever. Even Speedy enjoyed it, and he's pickier than a toddler who just learned how to scream *NO!*

We were walking back to our hotel when one of them popped out of an alley, and the two dudes following us tried to ambush us from behind while we were distracted. I had the one with the handgun against the wall before he knew what had happened; from behind me came the sounds of manic koala laughter and shoulders leaving their sockets.

And crying. Lots of crying.

"How we doin'?" I called to Mike and/or Speedy.

"Done," Mike grunted.

I took a moment to check on them. Two large men in T-shirts and jeans were on the ground, sobbing uncontrollably, with Mike standing over them like an avenging Irish angel.

Speedy was sitting on one of the men. The fur around his mouth was bloody.

I felt an arm twitch in my hands as the man whose face was currently half flesh, half brick prepared to squirm away from me. I upped that fraction to two-thirds brick, and he relented.

"So what is this?" I asked him. "Attempted kidnapping? I'm guessing attempted kidnapping."

There was a string of mumbled Greek from him.

"Speedy?" I asked.

"'Filthy bitch. Queen of the maggot-infested cooches, I don't have to tell you anything.'"

"Speedy, we're on the clock."

The koala sighed. "Just that last sentence."

I added some more brick to the face-plus-wall equation. The man's eyes widened and he screamed.

(Look, there's a reason certain wrist locks are illegal in judo. Just because I don't normally use them doesn't mean I don't know them.)

Then I threw him.

Speedy and Mike knew it was coming. Speedy ducked; Mike added a hammer kick. The man went from flying to flattened in a millisecond, stomped straight into the pavement by Mike's Size 13 shoe.

The sound of sirens had begun. I glanced around and saw we had an audience. You don't hold a fistfight on a busy city street without attracting attention.

"Speedy? Do what you can. You've got thirty seconds."

I walked towards the crowd, shouting and waving like an absolute moron. The cell phones and their cameras turned from the koala to me, and I began asking, loudly, if anyone had seen the whole thing because we'd need witnesses and *ohmyGod* what is *wrong* with this city we were just on our way back from dinner and yes, I am Hope Blackwell, I'm here on vacation and *Officer!* Thank goodness you're finally here! These men *attacked* us!

The police stations in Athens aren't that pretty. The country is in the middle of a vicious economic crisis. The main parts of the city were spruced up for the 2004 Summer Olympics, and that was the last time anybody could afford to throw paint on them. The station still had toilet facilities, so while Mike and his infinite patience described what had happened in the alley to three officers who barely spoke English, I spirited Speedy off to the women's bathroom to rinse off the blood.

I plopped him on a little ledge beside the sink, and held a hand beneath his mouth. "Spit."

He grumbled something in Greek.

"Don't make me go in there."

He opened his jaws, and two goodly-sized pieces of human fingers fell out. They had been chewed to hell, but they both still had their nails intact. This seemed…weirdly ironic.

I threw these into the toilet, and flushed a bunch of times to make sure the fingers would never be seen again. "Jesus, Speedy, you're the dictionary definition of an herbivore. You literally can*not* digest meat."

"I enjoy the flavor."

There weren't any paper towels, so I made do with toilet paper. Blood is hard to get out of fur, by the way. It's sticky, and the harder you work to get it off, the more saturated the surrounding areas become. I futzed around and made things worse until Speedy got so fed up that he shoved his face under the running water and started to clean himself up.

Tee hee.

"What did he tell you?" I asked.

The koala's words were slightly bubbly as he scrubbed his muzzle. "Hired goons. Third-party intermediary. Probably no way to trace the initial request unless we drop everything and concentrate on tracking the source."

"Was it supposed to be a kidnapping?" It wouldn't surprise me. As the Cyborg King's wife, someone tries to kidnap me every third week.[4]

"No," he said. He held out a clawed paw for a clean wad of toilet paper, and began to dry himself off. "Smash and scare. Orders were to injure Mike, and tell us to get out of town."

"Poor hired goons."

"Yup."

Nobody has a proper appreciation for hired goons. They're regular working dudes who weren't hugged enough as kids, or didn't get the chance to go to college, or don't have the smarts or motivation to make it in a steady job. I'd feel for them, except the vast majority of people they beat up don't have the ability to

---

4  I'm getting grumpy about it, by the way. Filling out police reports is really time-consuming, and there's always someone to lecture me on how I should make an effort to not get kidnapped. It's gotten so bad that when a stranger throws off a kidnappy vibe, I run at them while shouting, "Hey, does this rag smell like chloroform to you?"

smack them back.

We left the bathroom and rejoined Mike. He was deep in conversation with the U.S. Ambassador to Greece about Sisyphus, Tantalus, and the illusions of happiness and suffering.

Listen, what Mike does for fun is his own business. If you choose to let him drag you into it, that's yours. But I was getting tired, and poor Ambassador Goodwin was floundering, and I figured breaking up that particular discussion would benefit everybody.

"Jack!" I waved, and dropped Speedy on a nearby table.

"Hope!" The ambassador jumped up and gave me a grateful hug. He's a grandfatherly man, decent and pudgy. We've sat beside each other a couple of times at various political functions back home in Washington, and those can be a real bonding experience if you and the other guy both enjoy telling dick jokes. "I'm sorry this is your introduction to Greece. Please, tell me what I can do."

"Aw, it's no big deal," I said. "Happens all the time. To me," I added quickly, as Goodwin struggled to find a nice way to say *What?* and *No, it doesn't,* and *Perhaps you would like a tour of the inside of a locked jail cell until I can find you a responsible adult to take you home?*

"Which is why she asked me to come along," Mike said with a big Irish grin.

"You've met Mike Reilly?" I asked the ambassador. "Did he mention he's an *Hachidan* in aikido?"

"Eighth-degree black belt," Mike offered. "I teach master classes for American *aikidōka.*"

I just stood there and smiled while Goodwin reassessed the middle-aged frat boy standing in front of him. Maybe their philosophy discussion snapped into context, I don't know, but Goodwin apparently decided I was in good hands.

(Yes, this was teeth-grindingly frustrating. Mike may be a master in aikido, but I'm nearly his equal at judo. I don't mind that he's technically a better fighter than I am—we both started practicing our respective arts when we were five, so he's got a twelve-year head start on his training. But *nooooo*, I need an *escort* because vagina and…snarlgrowl.)

After the paperwork was done (there's always paperwork, and Speedy had to translate part of the forms), we took Goodwin to a local bar as a thank-you gesture for smoothing everything over. They put us on the patio, fire burning all around us in various containers, and the Parthenon shining on the hill behind us.

Halfway through the third round, I realized I had no idea why Goodwin was there.

"So," I said, as I played with the brazier set in the middle of the table, "how did you know we were at the police station?"

Goodwin had the grace to look embarrassed. "Well…"

"Easy," Speedy said. "He knew you were coming to town, and he told the police to call him when they brought you in."

"*If*," Goodwin quickly said. "*If* they brought you in."

The cardboard bar coaster I was teasing through the fire burst into flame, and we had an interesting few moments when we all suddenly discovered the coaster had been soaking in a high-proof alcohol instead of water. And then we learned that the nearby planter hadn't gotten any water recently. And then the manager showed up. By the time I had paid for damages, Goodwin was laughing.

"Okay," the ambassador said, as Speedy settled across his shoulders like a living mink stole. "Now I don't feel nearly as guilty about warning the police."

"Things come up," I sighed.

A few more hours of drinking, and Mike and Speedy called it for the night. They left for our hotel while I stayed behind to talk shop with Goodwin.

"What's the mood like back home?" he asked.

"You saw the news?"

"Yes," he said. "Is it true? What Hanlon did to your husband and the other Agents?"

"It's all true," I said. "Except you've probably read the filtered stuff that Hanlon put out as damage control. Wanna hear the real story?"

He did.

I'll spare you the hour-long *Oh no, nobody could be that cruel!* back-and-forth between Goodwin and myself, and give you the short version.

Remember when I said that the chip in my husband's brain was the outcome of a government conspiracy?

Well, the dude behind that conspiracy was Hanlon.

About ten years ago, his company had developed the technology for the implant. Instead of using it to make himself rich(er), Hanlon had turned around and given the data to the U.S. government. Said they could use it to help undercover field operatives talk over long distances.

Nice guy, right?

Wrong.

See, Hanlon wanted the cyborgs' abilities, but he didn't want to risk putting a chip in his own brain, and he didn't want to go through the bother and expense of making cyborgs himself. By donating his tech to the government, he got the U.S. taxpayers to fund his scheme. But Hanlon also needed the Program to fail, hence the buggy AI that reduced my husband and the rest of OACET to emotionless husks.

Oh, and while this was going on? Hanlon was running for political office, so he'd be in the right place at the right time to suggest that this failed Program should be defunded. *Don't worry*, he'd say. *Since this is partially my fault, I'll offer all of these poor people excellent jobs in my company...*

If you're a sadistic evil genius with enough patience, it's the ideal way to build your own cyborg army.

I couldn't even *think* about Hanlon without wanting to kick down a wall—

"Hope?" I felt Goodwin's hand touch mine, and noticed that I was squeezing my whiskey glass so hard that my fingers had gone white. I shoved the glass away from me before I shattered it and tore myself to hell.

Some psychics can heal themselves. I'm not one of them,

and I scar way too easily to be careless with sharp edges.

"So, how are things here?" I asked. "All we hear about Greece is austerity, austerity, austerity...financial chaos."

"That's pretty much right on the nose," he replied. "No one knows what to do, and none of the major players are communicating with each other. The banks have known that the country was bankrupt for years, but they kept telling the people and the government that they're solvent. The government has known they're bankrupt, too, but they thought they had the European Union to fall back on...

"The people are the ones who are suffering," Goodwin said, his eyes tight. "Jobs are collapsing, and there's no centralized reconstruction strategy. But there are plenty of opportunists out there who are trying to use the chaos as a way to further their agendas. There're several nationalist movements that are—"

His head snapped up. "Be careful, Hope. Americans are easy targets—you, probably more than most."

"I know," I said. "But this country is still safe for tourists, right?"

"Are you kidding?! You were attacked not three hours ago—"

I waved off his concern. "No no, that's just me. I mean, is Greece still safe for the average tourist?"

"In Athens and the more populated areas? Definitely. Out in the country...?"

He didn't want to finish that thought aloud. Ah, politics.

"Good to know," I said, as I topped off our glasses from a handy tumbler. "I'll try to stay in the cities."

Goodwin insisted on seeing me safely back to the hotel lobby; I insisted on waiting with him until his car service arrived. I tucked him into the shopworn Fiat, and promised him I'd call him before leaving Athens.

I was...concerned.

Not about getting kidnapped and ransomed—although I still needed to look up the Greek for "chloroform"[5]—but about moving through the country. I'd never expected to travel

---

5 It's χλωροφόρμιο, which I found to be rather intimidating until Speedy said it's pronounced *chlorofórmio*, so there's that.

unnoticed, but I had expected to be able to *travel*.

Ghosts and goons and a country on the brink of collapse. Whee.

# CHAPTER 9

The next day, I was supposed to meet our archaeologist over dinner. Before that, we went shopping for knives.

Mike and I strongly agree on the topic of edged weapons: we don't like them. In a combat situation, they can be taken from you and used against you. Hands, feet, and other body parts? Much more reliable, and if the dude you're up against is willing to take your body apart to keep you from knocking him around, you've already got bigger problems than a knife can manage.

But knives aren't just for stabbin'. When you're wandering around a foreign country, you want a knife. A good knife isn't a weapon. It's a tool when you're hungry and all that's nearby are fish and bunnies. More importantly, it's a nice piece of universal barter when a local townie has something you need and doesn't trust cash from a foreign yahoo.

Plus, if everything goes well and you get to keep your new knife, you can mail it home to yourself and add it to your ever-growing collection. It makes a really nice souvenir.

Mike had a friend of a friend who knew a guy. This guy owned a shop, an import-export boutique not too far from the Athens Central Market. Mostly knives, we were told, with some utility tools, and thanks for supporting the local economy because *boy* does it need it!

We stopped at the Market on the way, because you can't be near the Market and not drop in to gawk at it. The Market's one of those old-time enclosed halls that seems to go on for miles, and is made up of different pieces of architecture all banged together. Sometimes there are skylights and huge arched windows; other times, you turn a corner and find yourself in a cool, dark alley full of raw meat.

Have you ever seen a basket of live snails? I hadn't. For a couple of Euros, the vendor let me stick my hand in the basket, and all of these snails the size of golf balls started crawling up my arm. It was adorable and *amazingly* ticklish.

(And slimy. I really should have thought about the slime. That goop took two showers and three bars of soap to scrub off.)

And there was food on top of food on top of *food!*

My favorite part of traveling overseas is the food. I love American cuisine, I do, but it's pretty limited, with the same basic meats and vegetables spun into those so-called ethnic meals. Give me something without chicken and tomato any day. Give me something made from tree fruits I can't even pronounce. Give me a taste of this world we *live* in!

We grabbed lunch. It might have been a sandwich, I don't know, but loaves of bread were involved and they had rich, creamy centers.

Mine had meat. I'm not sure what kind. Mike and Speedy are vegetarians, so I couldn't ask them. I think it was lamb. I know it was really good.

(If Speedy and I had been alone, I would have described my meal in detail and watched him squirm in jealousy, but Mike gets a little green when I talk about eating flesh. He's already cut out all root vegetables from his diet, saying that murder is murder regardless of the type of mind involved. The day that science figures out how to let a human photosynthesize will be the happiest day of Mike's life, and even then he'll sunbathe in a parking lot to make sure he isn't depriving the grass of their fair share.)

After lunch, we wandered around the market. It was mostly farm stands, but there were enough trinkets to keep us interested. Plus, Speedy tended to attract a crowd no matter where we were, so he performed a few poems from his perch atop Mike's shoulder. There was the usual bout of laughter, followed by mothers gasping and slamming their hands over their kids' ears.

Have you ever seen small children hauled away by their ears? It's pretty horrible. In their mothers' defense, getting a child out of harm's way is instinctive, but *oh* will those kids be sore tomorrow!

Two hours, another quasi-sandwich, and three streets later, we ended up at the knife store.

It was pretty seedy. It reminded me of shopping in India, where none of the stores have counters. Americans need counters when we go shopping. We're conditioned to counters. We love our many-layered glass display cases, and the crazy amount of variety therein, probably because it means we can feel *so* damned righteous when the owner doesn't have exactly what we want.

Here, it was a few tables in the middle of the room, with short knives laid out on pieces of old cloth. Along the walls were longer knives tucked within the wooden beams, with the occasional sword propped up on the sills.

There was a man in the store, flipping through a magazine with his feet propped up on one of the tables. He glanced up, did a double take, and yelled something at us in Greek.

Speedy shouted something back, also in Greek.

The man's temper rose, then blinked out in a string of halting words as he realized who (what) had spoken to him.[6] He turned and walked into a back room, and I heard the loud pop of a cork, followed by liquid glugging into a glass.

Mike placed Speedy on the floor, and us two humans began to browse the knives.

I wasn't expecting anything fantastic. American imports were on a table off to the side, all familiar makes and models. Nothing exciting, and identical to items we could have easily picked up at home. The European knives were about the same, although there were a couple of custom items from makers that I'd never heard of before.

---

6 I have no idea what they said, but let me translate that for you anyhow:
   "No animals in the store!"
   "Fuck you and the dog who cooks your dinner."
   "Don't talk about my wife...like...koala...what...thing..."

My eyes fell on a Finnish Puukko knife with an inlaid wood handle and a matching leather sheath. I picked it up and flipped it around a little. It was pretty much perfect for me. The right size, the right weight... I couldn't wear it in a city (obviously), but it'd be small enough to tuck under my shirttails when we got out in the country.

"How's it feel?" Mike asked.

I held it out to him, handle first. "Great balance," I said. "Mind if I call dibs?"

He took it, held it for a few heartbeats, and then handed it back to me. "It's yours," he replied.

"Too small for your hand?"

He grinned at me. "Sure."

"Friend of David?"

We turned to see the shopkeeper stumble out of the back room. He was flushed, and he glared at Speedy with a wavering gaze; at least one goodly-sized glass of booze had helped steady his nerves, but Speedy had climbed up the exposed wood beams and was now leering down at him from the ceiling.

"Yes," Mike said, nodding. "David sent us."

"David..." he began, but didn't know the English, and the rest of the sentence stumbled into Greek.

"'David' is a code name. The person who sent us here has a sick sense of humor, and didn't tell him who was coming," Speedy translated.

The shopkeeper gulped. "Yes," he said, still staring at Speedy. "Humor."

"Okay," I said, holding up the Puukko knife. "I'll take this, and as many utility tools as you'll sell me."

Speedy translated, and the shopkeeper went from *Nervous* to *Nervous but Hey, Money's Money.*

"Yes," the shopkeeper said to me, and then a question in Greek to Speedy.

"Utility tools," Speedy replied.

"Yes, utility tools," he said. "Leatherman? Gerber? Swiss Army?"

I nodded, grinning at the universal language of brands.

He pulled out a dozen of these, and these went into a canvas sack along with my new Puukko knife.

Speedy, Mike, and the shopkeeper began haggling over the price of the tools. Speedy is a *huge* cheapskate—Mike needed to make sure he didn't rip the shopkeeper off.

(Keep in mind that this was unnecessary labor for Mike on multiple levels, as I was the one footing the bill for this adventure. Everything's a game to Speedy. The only reason I trust his translations is that you can only torture ants for so long before you get bored, and he got bored with false translations years ago. Plus, he knows that if he really pisses me off, I would totally leave him sitting on a rock in the middle of a field full of scorpions.)

That's when I found the sword.

There was a pile of blue velvet on one of the tables, the smallest flash of metal sticking out from under a fold. I tossed the folds of the cloth open, and...

It wasn't for sale. I knew that just by looking at it. It was a raw blade waiting for a handle and hilt. I guess it was a long knife, technically, but it had a little curve to it that reminded me more of a sword than a knife. There wasn't a speck of ornamentation on the blade, but it was made from real Wootz steel and it didn't need anything to—

Sorry. I should have said Damascus steel. You've probably heard of *that*. But even if you've never heard of either Wootz or Damascus steel, you'd know it if you saw it. Those knives with all of the crazy patterns in the metal? That's Damascus.

It's got a hell of a history, Damascus steel does. It's incredibly sharp and can take a beating, and during the Crusades it was probably the source of those stories where the knights are cleaved clean in twain. There's even a rumor that each new sword needed to be quenched in the blood of a red-headed boy before it could be put to use.

It doesn't exist anymore—the art of making it, I mean. Damascus steel started out in the Middle East in the third century, bounced around the continent until some thousand-plus years later, and then, *poof!* Gone, vanished into history due to new trade routes and globalization and all of that fun stuff. Maybe there was a dire shortage of red-headed boys.

There are reproductions, obviously, made by artisans who've managed to come close to duplicating the original process. These modern versions are arguably better quality, but...

I knew I was looking at the real deal.

Then the shopkeeper noticed what I was doing, and started to shout at me.

Speedy shimmied along the ceiling beams, upside down, like a super-fluffy crawling bat. "Don't!" he translated gleefully. "That's for a customer! Please, miss, don't!"

I nodded to show that I understood, and backed away from the knife a step or two. "Mike, you've got to see this."

Mike reached me before the shopkeeper, and we both stood and marveled at the blade.

The shopkeeper, realizing we weren't about to pick it up and start swinging it wildly, calmed down.

"Where did you get this?" I asked him.

Koala chatter.

It took the shopkeeper a moment to reply. When he did, Speedy laughed. "He's lying," he said. "He claims he took it as a trade from a customer who didn't know its value."

"How do you know he's lying?" I asked.

Speedy shot me a look. "The guy's running stolen antiquities out of the back room," he said. "You think a dinky knife store can stay alive in this economy?"

"Why'd he leave this out here on the table?" I asked.

"It's trash. You should see what he's got in the back," Speedy said. From his vantage point on the ceiling, he could see over the clutter to what lay beyond. "Dude needs to invest in a decent door."

"Hey Mike?" I asked, as the light dawned in my rock-hard skull. "This friend of a friend of yours? Did you ask him to put us in touch with somebody in the black market?"

Mike didn't say a word, but he was very loud about it.

I sighed. Personally, I didn't give two shits if we had stumbled into something illegal. I would have raised holy hell if the dude was selling animal parts, but antiquities? Dead is dead, and I *know* dead. Anyone associated with that Damascus sword had long since found better weapons.

However...

I really didn't want to start any rumors that the Cyborg King's wife was involved in a smuggling operation.

The shopkeeper glanced between us and Speedy, and asked the koala a question.

"He wants to know where you're from," Speedy said.

Before I could answer, Mike said, "Lake Minnetonka."

I slapped my hand across my eyes. You had to know Mike— he didn't lie. So his friend of a friend must have given him a password one step higher than 'David', and now, just like magic, we had become accomplices to trafficking in stolen artifacts.

"Mike..." I groaned.

"This is a complex and challenging world," Mike said, looking skyward. "Who are we to judge how our brothers and sisters stay alive? Especially when we are searching for what has been lost ourselves."

He put some stress on part of that—*we are searching for what has been lost*—and I finally caught up.

Textbooks and museums only hold part of the story. It's sad, but human civilization gets turned upside-down on a regular basis. Lots of stuff has gone missing, or gotten stolen, or wasn't considered important enough to preserve. Archimedes and the Antikythera Mechanism both have large followings within the academic community, and most of what is known about them has been uploaded and dissected and debated and funneled into online journals.

Maybe there was information that existed...somewhere else.

Which made sense, if you thought about it. After all, we were here in Greece because of a piece of the Mechanism that had slipped through the cracks. There could be more of them on the black market, or already in the hands of private collectors. And somebody who was active in those circles might have a better idea of where we should start hunting for Archimedes.

"We're already working with a…an archaeologist," I said.

"Who works directly with museums. I think we need someone off the books."

*Dang.* "You could have told me," I muttered.

"No," he said. "Not if you need to testify under oath that you had no idea what the real purpose of this store was when we first arrived, and that you left after you learned the truth."

"Um…"

"*After* being somewhat relative," he admitted. And, before I could ask, he added, "I already paid for our gear. You're clean."

That tweaked a nerve. The Puukko knife had been expensive. I'd make it up to him.

During our brief ethical interlude, Speedy and the shopkeeper had been engaged in a battle royale over…something. When Mike and I stopped chatting, the shopkeeper threw up his hands in frustration. He locked the front door, and then waved us toward the back of the store.

"What's up with him?" I whispered to Speedy.

The koala let his forepaws come free of the ceiling beam and he dangled in midair, held up by nothing but those wicked tree-gouging claws on his back legs. "He thinks he's dealing with two stupid Americans who want a piece of the Antikythera Mechanism."

"Well, *yeah.*"

Speedy rolled his eyes as he stretched himself towards me. I held out my hands, and he oozed off of the ceiling in a snakelike coil, crawling down my arms to settle in his customary place on my shoulders.

"He's a middleman." His fur buzzed against my ears as he whispered. "He's gonna try to pass off cheap dross as treasures. Don't buy anything—don't even look interested. Just hold out until he puts you in touch with people higher up in the food chain."

"Sparky's gonna shit kittens over this," I muttered.

"No, he won't," he said. "The person he sends to you will have been employed by private auction houses and museums. You can play dumb—the best dealers in the illegal art trade have legitimate connections."

Isn't *that* depressing?

We followed the shopkeeper into the room behind the store, and I stood with my arms crossed as he showed us a veritable buffet of trinkets from lost civilizations. I kept shaking my head as he showed us each item—*nope, nope, nope, not looking for old pots, nope*—until he gave up.

He and Speedy had another argument. I tried to ignore the koala shouting across my left ear as best I could—a real trick, I assure you. I caught the name of our hotel, and nothing else.

Then, Speedy popped me on the side of my head. I took this as a sign to shoot the storekeeper one last stern Look, and then the three of us left.

"Nicely done," Speedy said to me. "He'll send his contact over to our hotel tomorrow. And he thinks you're a complete bitch!"

Well. High praise from Asshole Caesar.

# CHAPTER 10

Apparently, I'd be dining in a fairy kingdom. The restaurant had rooftop seating which overlooked the city. A marble fountain large enough to bathe in was the major source of light: it was surrounded by lanterns, and a soft warm glow swam up from spotlights set below the waterline. Trees grew from huge planters between the tables, carving out niches of space and privacy.

I was accidentally-on-purpose fifteen minutes early, and was wearing something tiny, expensive, and red. Blood red, really, that one dark shade you get when the injury is on the bad side of serious. The sound of my heels smacked down the rest of the ambient noise as the *maître d'* showed me to my table, and I smiled and waved when people called my name.

If I *had* to meet a stranger a couple thousand miles outside of my home territory, I was damned sure I'd make myself some witnesses.

I took a few selfies with the waitstaff, and chatted up a very nice American couple on their honeymoon. Then, halfway through the new bride's story about a dress fitting gone awry, her mouth dropped open and the rest of her face fell slack.

I turned to look at what had caused her mental hard drive to crash. She was staring at the man who had just walked into the restaurant and…

*Wow.*

Let me remind you that I'm usually surrounded by good-looking men. My husband is finger-licking delicious, and most of the guys in OACET are at least on par with him. There may be one—*cough*Josh Glassman*cough*—who is sex appeal incarnate.

What I'm saying is, I've had to build up an immunity to

Grade-A prime beefcake just to get through the day.

But this guy?

*Wow.*

He had thick, dark hair and smoky Mediterranean skin, and was in a suit that was barely a button away from being a full tuxedo. He wore the jacket open, and it spilled in clean lines over a broad chest and a pristine white shirt.

A small boutonniere on his lapel held a rose that matched my blood-red dress.

"Ah," I heard myself say. "This must be my dinner date."

I'm not sure what happened to the honeymooners, since I spent the next thirty seconds watching an authentic Greek god walk towards me. He had that smooth, rolling stride of a man who enjoyed long jogs on the beach, and listening to live music at sunset. His turnoffs included—

Sorry. As I said, *wow.*

He was standing over the table for a good few heartbeats before I remembered I should, you know, talk or something.

I arched an eyebrow instead. It seemed safer.

"Atlas Petrakis," he said with a grin. There was a little bit of devil in it.

"Of course you are," I replied. "Please, sit down."

He reached for my hand. Like a dummy, I thought he was going to shake it. Instead, he kissed it, a perfectly gentlemanly gesture with the bare minimum of lips and spit.

And it still sent a shivering tingle down to my southern inlet.

Some men know what they're doing. Atlas Petrakis *knew* what he was *doing.*

He released my hand—again, not too fast, not too slow, but *juuuust* right—and I gestured towards the other chair. "Please," I said. "Sit down."

Atlas seated himself, carefully tucking his leather satchel between his feet. I noticed he looped the strap around his knee, and realized he had brought samples.

Oh boy.

See, I wasn't quite sure whether I, a wealthy American

tourist, could visit a foreign country and walk off with a part of its history. I *definitely* wasn't sure if Atlas Petrakis was a legitimate archaeologist. What's the etiquette when an edible hunk of a man offers you (possibly) stolen antiquities? Slap him and walk away? Wait for the third date to buy them? I had completely skipped over this chapter in *The Ladies' Guide to Felonies.*

"So, Mr. Petrakis—"

"Atlas, please. Ms. Blackwell..."

He waited to see if I'd give him permission to use my first name, but he wasn't about to get lucky tonight. "So, Atlas, what is it you do? Goodwin said you're the best in your business, but he was vague about what that business actually is."

"Easiest to think of me as a professional treasure hunter," he said. "Would you object if I ordered us some wine?"

I would not object, and Atlas called the waiter over and asked for something in Greek. The waiter returned with a bottle of a local vintage, *Xinomavro*, which I thought was somewhat spicy.

It sure went down easy, though.

"What does a professional treasure hunter do?" I asked, swirling the wine to make its long legs crawl down the side of the glass. The torchlight sparkled within the wine's deep reds. "Tomb raiding, dodging giant boulders, and such?"

Atlas chuckled. "I've played those games. No, I have never raided a tomb. Collectors hire me when they want an item, and I locate it for them. I'm an art broker for antiquities."

There we go. *Art broker* sounded much less sexy than *professional treasure hunter*, but I could wrap my mind around it. When Ben and I first started making money in the stock market, I had gone through a brief period where I acquired paintings as quickly as I could. I sold most of them the following year, when I finally accepted that Abstract Expressionism was lost on me. My rapid churn rate on Rothkos and Kandinskys had been a fast introduction to how the art world catered to the wealthy: if you hired the right broker, you could point and shoot him at what you wanted, and he'd spring out to grab the item like a meaty grappling hook.

"Do you have a client list?" I asked, and he flipped open his satchel to retrieve it.

"Some clients request their privacy be protected," he said, handing me the list. "They have asked to be kept anonymous."

Yup. On of a list of a hundred names, the first twenty were *Anon,* followed by a description of the item that Atlas had acquired for them. All of the items sounded exotic. Like, birds with crazy claw-hands in their wings exotic.

"What's a nábrók?" I asked.

Atlas feigned a shudder. "You're better off not knowing."

"Hah," I said, and poured myself a little more wine. "Now I have to know."

He told me. I regretted asking.[7]

"Where did you find one of those?" I asked, and then amended the question to include the rest of the list. "Where did you find all of these?"

He smiled. "I am quite skilled," he said, and I swear his eyes *twinkled* at me.

"Pretend this is a job interview," I said.

It came out a little harsh, and he sat up and smoothed himself down. "Ah…yes. Many private collectors are willing to part with some items in exchange for others. I facilitate the trade between interested parties."

"Where do the items come from?" I asked. "You know… originally."

"You're concerned about what is legal and what is not?"

I nodded. "Very concerned."

"Collecting relics of lost civilizations is not a new phenomenon," Atlas said, as he ran a finger over his blood-

---

7 Okay. Say you're a man, and you have a really good male friend. You and your friend strike a bargain that the first one of you to die will be skinned from the waist down. This skin has to be removed in a single flawless piece. Then, go steal a coin from a grieving widow, and put it in the scrotum of your new skin pants. Add some ancient Icelandic mumbo-jumbo rituals, and the scrotum will fill with money. Also? You can never get out of these pants or the magic will stop working, unless you convince another really good friend to wear them for you while you go and set fire to your own body while muttering, "Unclean, unclean…" So. Infinite moneymaking best friend corpse pants. That's a nábrók.

red rose. "Much of what I find has been bought and sold many times, long before cultural property was formally recognized. Such items have been in private possession for many years, and are often treated as exempt from current standards. If these items go to a museum, they are removed from private circulation.

"Except..." Atlas gestured over his shoulder, calling my attention to the city spread out beneath our rooftop patio. "Greece? It has many museums. Not all of them will survive our depression. It is sad, but the smaller museums, they are selling off parts of their collections to survive. Many of them have approached me and have asked me to find them buyers for items that will not be missed."

It *was* sad, the idea that museums needed to trade their treasures to keep their doors open. I followed his gaze towards the city, where the outlines of the acropolis were soft against the twilight sky.

I felt his hand on mine. It was warm—like, a sitting-by-the-heat-vent-on-a-January-morning warm. "We are an old people," he said. "This is not our first challenge. It shall not be our last."

And he gave me that twinkling *smile* again.

I decided to fire another warning shot.

"Love your flower," I said.

"Thank you," Atlas replied. "I see we have similar tastes, yes? Your dress, you see? A complement?"

I didn't reply.

"We Greeks believe in Fate," he said. "Perhaps, Fate tells us we shall work well together."

"Sure," I said. "Or you arrived early and waited outside, saw me come in, and then ran down to the florist on the corner to find a boutonniere that matches my outfit. Great trick, by the way. Suggests there's already a bond between us."

He flashed his devil's grin. "Caught," he admitted. "Did you learn that from your friends, the spies?"

"No. It's something con artists do."

The grin disappeared.

"Ms. Blackwell, I didn't mean to—"

"Of course not," I said. "But don't try to jerk me around. Now, do you want to start over?"

He busied himself with his napkin, unable to meet my eyes. "I would like that, yes."

The waiter arrived and we went through the traditional Dance of the Breadsticks. They were delicious, warm and buttery, and I devoured my share.

By the time I had gotten a nice soggy layer of appetizers in my stomach, I felt secure enough to shift from small talk to the real stuff.

"You've heard about the discovery of the new piece of the Antikythera Mechanism?"

"Of course," he said.

"Finding it has been good for OACET's reputation," I said. "If there were another lost fragment out there, OACET would like to be involved in its location and recovery. We would turn it over to a museum, of course. I'm here because they can't leave the country, and they need someone they trust as their representative to put the feelers out."

There. Nice and solid. Probably aligned neatly with what little information he had gotten from Ambassador Goodwin. Who says I can't lie worth a damn?

Atlas Petrakis gave me a very cautious nod. Suspicion, so well hidden I almost hadn't noticed it, left him. "Yes," he said. "I see how that would bring you to me.

"But, Ms. Blackwell," he said, as he reclined in his chair. His shirt shifted slightly, the space between the buttons stretching to show that smooth chest...oh *wow*. "Finding a single fragment of the Mechanism was a miracle. If there are more of them at large, they are most likely at the bottom of the sea."

"Or in a private collection," I pressed. "There might be something out there that's been...lost."

"Many things have been lost," he agreed.

"As you've said, it's your job to recover such items for

interested parties."

He nodded again. "But it's never so simple. Understand, please, that this new discovery is likely to bring out the frauds. Every collector with an unidentified fragment in their possession will think they've had a piece of the Mechanism all along."

I shrugged. "So what? I'm rich, and I bet you work on commission."

Atlas blinked.

"I'm not very subtle," I added helpfully.

"I have noticed," he replied.

"If I decide to hire you, you'll be paid for each possible lead, false or not. I want anything connected to the Mechanism, not just actual pieces of it. Documents, scraps of paper, family anecdotes… It'll all be good for OACET's reputation.

"For the record," I added, "anything you obtain for me must be done legally. OACET is dissected in the media on a daily basis, so I'm going to personally check each lead."

I paused. This was the tricky bit.

"If," I continued, "you do find a solid lead, I'll want to know the source. I'll be checking how that source acquired the fragment. Especially *where* they found it. It doesn't matter if it was discovered five or five hundred years ago—I'll still want to check the data myself."

"It's my job to establish provenance—"

I cut him off. "And mine to make sure anything I bring back to my husband won't bite him in the ass. With that said," I continued, "you'll still be paid for these solid leads, even if the provenance falls apart when I check it out. It's not your fault if a seller lies to you."

He shook his head, bemused. Apparently, this is not how such deals were usually done in the gray areas of the antiquities trade. I wondered how much he'd jack up his price for leads that he knew would dead-end on me.

I also wondered how long it would take him to realize that I was hoping he'd find these dead ends.

"It's my spring break, so I'm here for one week," I said. "Two, if your best leads can't be resolved quickly. Again, you'll get a bonus if they—"

"No." Atlas cut in. "Ms. Blackwell, what you want, it cannot happen. The art world moves slowly. It takes time to find what you are looking for, more time to arrange meetings, and still more time to check provenance."

"Then I hope you're caught up on your sleep," I said.

He stared at me for a very long moment. I thought he might walk out. I really wouldn't have blamed him if he had. Instead, he nodded, as if agreeing to terms.

"Now," I said, as I reached for the bottle to refill my wine. "Before I decide to put you on the payroll, show me what you've brought."

Atlas reached for his satchel.

He was definitely a pro. He hailed the waiter and asked for a clean dishtowel, which he laid on the table; on top of that, he placed a piece of clean white linen which he removed from a large plastic Ziploc baggie. He tucked the plastic baggie between the dishtowel and the linen, making a sanitation sandwich to keep any grease from floating upwards through the layers of cloth.

Then, he started placing small boxes on the linen.

"If these aren't enough to prove my skills," he said, "I have more at my office. Larger pieces, very lovely. But more expensive, of course."

Damn. I realized, almost too late, that he expected me to buy at least one of these samples as proof that I was committed to the hunt. I hoped he took personal checks.

"All of this is legal?" I asked.

Atlas twitched. "Ms. Blackwell—"

"'cuz I'll walk out of here right now if you can't prove that you're the rightful seller."

"Of course," he said, resigned, and reached back into the satchel for the documentation.

He spread this out on the table, tucking each piece of paper underneath its corresponding box. I didn't recognize any of it—all Greek to me, haha—but I took a couple of photos and sent them to Speedy.

The koala answered in record time. Mike must have been typing for him; Speedy's claws are too bulky to bang text out on a cell phone. *"Either authentic or good forgeries. It'll hold up."*

*"K,"* I replied.

"My friend says these look authentic," I said. "I'm sorry if I implied a lack of trust."

"You have made it quite clear how you stand on the matter of legality," he said. "I'll respect that."

He waited, probably for me to say that I'd start respecting his own professionalism.

Nope.

Listen, any dude who smarms his way through the appetizers is probably going to keep pushing me until he gets it through his head that I push back. Sooner or later, Atlas Petrakis would grok me, and then we'd be friendly friend-friends. Until then? Game on.

Atlas stifled a sigh. "Greece is protective of its treasures. If the original owners didn't give me permission to sell these items, they wouldn't be allowed to leave the country."

I nodded, and he began opening the boxes.

He went from largest to smallest, showing me ancient items. Here, a miniature marble frieze. There, a necklace. A strip of leather cut and twisted into the figure of a bull...

Then he got to the smallest box, and that same heart-halting moment that had slammed into me back in my kitchen grabbed me again.

I pretended to inspect the necklace as I ignored what was shouting at me from inside a ring box.

Petrakis lifted its lid. Inside, three pieces of glass—no, three beads, but flattened so they looked more like shards of glass than beads—lay on the satin cushion.

One was a vivid bottle green. The other two, pale blue. They tugged at me in the same way the fragment of the Mechanism had, and I knew these little beads had *history.*

"Aw!" I said in the same voice I'd use if a friend was showing me an especially average cat, and not as if I was strangling myself to keep from grabbing the beads and running. "Cute."

Then I went back to inspecting the necklace.

The waiter arrived and reminded us that our meals were soon to come out of the kitchen, and Atlas packed up his goods with the same careful precision he had used to set them on the linen cloth.

I'm serious about food. I didn't let us talk business during the meal. Fish and meatballs and *spanakopita,* which I had had a zillion times but had never really experienced before, and something that Atlas insisted were fried zucchini flowers stuffed with rice.

And pita bread? The kind that's made on a baking stone and slathered in farm-fresh butter? *Divine.*

Dessert was a custard, which sounds boring until you try it. Lemon, sugar, a thin crust on the bottom? Simple can still be perfect.

Through it all, Atlas told stories about Greece. Ancient Greece, mainly, stories he had come across in his travels. Stories of gods and heroes, of enormous troves of gold and riches still waiting to be found among the islands...

Mostly, he spoke of kings.

Hundreds of kings, with dynasties lasting for millennia, and I was suddenly glad that America only has a few centuries of history behind it. Seriously, I have my hands full dealing with a bunch of Founding Fathers. Thank God and any other deity listening that I was born to a relatively new culture. I don't know how I'd handle three thousand years' worth of ghosts bobbing around my personal periphery all the damned time.

When our waiter had whisked the custard plates away, Atlas finally started on the queens. Hippolyta, ruler of the Amazons. Penelope, who drove men to ruin through waiting. Hecuba, the grieving mother.

And Helen of Troy.

I rolled my eyes when he got to her. I couldn't help it: I'd never been a fan of Helen of Troy. Yay, she was pretty. Everybody cheer for pretty.

"Ah," Atlas laughed. "You're familiar with the American version of Helen. What a shame—did you know Helen was a warrior?"

"Helen, the face who launched a thousand ships? That Helen?"

He nodded. "The mythology puts her as a child of Zeus, but no matter who her father was, she was born a princess of Sparta. All Spartan children were raised in a culture of war. Some of the stories say that she was trained in the martial arts from childhood, and was equal to her brothers in battle."

My memories of seventh-grade world history are a joke. "Her brothers...?"

"Castor and Polydeuces. Legendary fighters. Savage, cunning, and possessed with the strength of the gods. They were among the best of Sparta's legendary warriors."

They sounded familiar. "Gemini? The Twins?"

"Yes!" A bright smile lit his face. This one, as opposed to his devil's grin, seemed sincere. "The constellation of Gemini. Polydeuces was Zeus' son, and when Castor was to die, he petitioned the gods to let his twin share his divine nature. They were transformed into stars, to never be separated, not by death or by distance."

"Helen was a twin, too, wasn't she?"

Atlas laughed aloud. "Yes!" he said again. "Twin to Clytemnestra, who became the wife of Agamemnon."

"Agamemnon... He played a small part in the Trojan War?"

That smile faltered a bit. Apparently I needed to brush up on my Greek myths. Or...poetry. Or history. Something.

"A large part," Atlas said. "He was the brother of Menelaus, the king who married Helen. When Paris kidnapped Helen and began the war, Agamemnon brought his armies to fight by Menelaus' side."

I sniffed. "Helen couldn't have been that hot a warrior. Not if she let herself be taken captive by the Trojans."

"Maybe she didn't," Atlas said. "We know about her from stories in which she was no one's hero. Hard to say what kind of person she was, when she was alive. It's a sad truth of history: men are remembered for their deeds; women, for their beauty."

"If she lived at all," I said.

"I'm sure she did," Atlas said. He returned to his satchel, and removed the smallest box. He was not as careful with it this time, merely flipping his saucer over so its clean underside kept the box out of the crumbs we had left on the table. He opened the box to show the three little beads and said, "The man who sold me this? He claimed they belonged to Helen."

I poked the velvet box with my pinkie. The three beads rolled around their satin bed, and the sound of them brushing against each other chimed like small bells. The sound was barely loud enough to hear, but it bypassed my ears completely. That chiming resonated within my brain, kicking and punching in its eagerness to tell me *things*.

"Sure," I said. "Can you prove it? That these were once Helen's?"

He hesitated. It was quick and hard to notice, but I was already there. "Of course not," I answered for him.

"If I could," he replied, "these wouldn't be for sale. They would be priceless, artifacts owned by one of the most memorable women who had ever lived."

"Uh-huh." I jabbed the box again, and reminded myself that if I grabbed the box and leapt over the edge of the balcony, it would go badly for me. The fall to the ground, for starters. Then, the police, and the arrest, and having to explain to Ben and Sparky that the beads were screaming at me...

"They have been dated to when Helen most likely lived," Atlas said, as he tried to push the smallest items he had brought with him into my checkbook. "Some historians say that such beads were given as prizes in battle. Perhaps Helen herself won these in a tournament."

"A few chunks of glass? Some prize."

"They would have looked different when new," he said. "Such beads were often covered in gold sheaths to bring out the details in the relief."

I craned my neck down towards the beads, and saw that two of the beads might have had faces stamped in them. "So what you're saying is that these are damaged?"

This time, his sigh was audible.

I grinned at him. "Good job," I said. "Spinning a story about a warrior woman because you know your audience. Let me see the necklace again, and we'll pretend Helen of Troy owned *that* instead."

He paused, and then told me why that wasn't possible. The necklace was made during a different period, used distinct craftsmanship, didn't align with what was known of Helen's life or location…blah blah and blah.

So Atlas Petrakis passed that test, too.

I walked out of there with a pretty necklace, and a gorgeous man on my payroll.

And the beads, of course.

# CHAPTER 11

It was the most vivid dream I'd ever had.

I was running naked through the woods, a dagger ready at my side. My legs weren't mine—the skin was darker, white scars covering it in stripes. My feet were calloused from rougher surfaces than a dojo mat. I heard a laugh from somewhere ahead, and knew it was my sister.

The stag broke cover.

It ran south, towards the stream. There was a thicket that way, with dark, hard thorns that would be kinder to a deer's hide than mine. I whistled, and received an answering chirp as my sister raced to get ahead of the stag.

She had a gladder spirit than me, my sister did, and she danced along the low branches, just above the thorns. When she dropped from the trees, the stag stopped and shied from her.

I followed the path the stag had made through the brambles, and was ready when it turned to flee. I moved in, close and quick, beneath the sweep of its horns, and had run my dagger through its foreleg before it could leap away.

My sister giggled like a wild woman, and threw her own dagger aside as she picked up a sharp stone.

It was like that, then.

I threw my own dagger to join hers on the damp earth, and together we closed on the stag.

The beast bellowed, lashing out with its antlers, its hind legs… We moved in and out, cheering each other on as the stag exhausted itself. My sister scored with her rock against a leg, and the stag fell, twice lamed.

We went for its throat, both of us laughing.

We knew well the taste of blood, my sister and I, and it was always better when it wasn't our own.

The stag was heavy, and we were not yet ten. We had to take its head and leave the body.

We stopped by the stream where we had left our clothes, and washed before we dressed ourselves. Then, the stag's head carried carefully between us, we returned to camp.

Father was waiting.

We knelt and gifted the king with the head of the stag, and worried. It was such a small stag, such a *young* stag, and it hadn't yet learned enough of the ways of hunters to give us a good chase...

Father nodded.

Our people don't reward half measures. Had we failed, we would have been sent out again. Or, worse, suffered the shame of not being allowed to try a second time.

He sent servants to recover the meat, and that night we dined on our stag.

My sister and I shared its heart between us.

After, he presented me with a gold necklace. A double strand of beads, the sinew knotted tight around each to keep them from falling off the line when it was cut.

I had drawn first blood. It was my prize to keep. I drew my dagger and sliced the joined strands of beads into two, and knotted one half around my twin's neck. When it was fastened tight, she did the same for me.

Father smiled.

I woke in a grumpy rush, choking on the imaginary taste of deer blood. Beside me, Speedy slept on, undisturbed by my sudden coughing fit.

"What," I sputtered, "The. Fuck. Was. *That?!*"

# CHAPTER 12

Let me tell you the worst thing about being the world's second worst psychic.

Shit happens to everybody. It's part of the human experience. We process this shit as best we can: sometimes it cleans up nicely and we can wad up the toilet paper and flush it away, and sometimes it smears itself all over our psyches. In my weird life, shit happens on a fairly regular basis, and most of this shit is outside the scope of the typical human experience.

My best friend is Benjamin Franklin's *ghost*, for fuck's sake! My perspective on what is normal is somewhat skewed.

So when I have a dream in which I'm Helen of Goddamned Troy—prepubescent Helen of Troy, no less, and hunting a deer while buck (sorry) naked—I can't dismiss it as *just* a dream.

I also can't call up any of my psychic buddies for advice, since I don't have any. Just Mike, and he knows less about this weird stuff than I do.

I didn't have a lot of options, so I did what any sensible person would do when they woke up from something that was half a nightmare: I rolled over and went back to sleep.

The morning came in another bright blaze of golden glory across the ruins of the Parthenon. Mike and I got dressed, deposited Speedy at a nearby café under the watchful eye of a heavily-bribed barista, and went for a jog around the city.

Athens turned out to be larger than we thought. We called it quits after a couple of hours, and took a shortcut through the Plaka to get back to our hotel. The Plaka is this great little neighborhood near the acropolis, kinda touristy but with an old-world charm. We grabbed some slush drinks from a cart, and wandered through the streets. Cars aren't allowed in the Plaka, but small vehicles are, and I nearly got trampled by a donkey.

Then I told Mike about my dream.

I didn't leave anything out. The sounds, the sensations... Most of all, I focused on what I had seen. I have a Hollywood education in ancient Greece, and nothing from my dream matched my mental images of pale stone and flowing robes and curtains. Hell, nearly every adult woman there had had at least one boob showing, and that definitely didn't fit into anything I had ever bumped into while channel surfing.

Mike's noisy when he's thinking quietly.

"What do you think? Did I buy Helen's ghost along with those glass beads?"

He shrugged.

"That's it?" I asked. I popped the lid on my drink and started gnawing on the ice. "No sage advice? Woulda sworn you'd pull out some obscure Buddhist saying and tell me that the dream is significant."

"All things are significant."

"But...?"

He shrugged. "Not all things have meaning. At least, not in relation to our own small scopes of self."

"That's more like it. What about this dream?"

Mike turned and lobbed his empty cup into a trash can, *swoosh*, nice and clean. As the can was across the street and had a fancy iron cover over all but a teeny cup-sized hole, half of the people walking the Plaka turned towards us. Some of them started to point.

I waved. "Damn it, Mike," I muttered as the cameras came out.

We took off running.

We stopped before we reached the café where we had dumped Speedy. "Here's what I think," he said, as we walked the last couple of streets to cool ourselves down. "The dream was probably just a dream, and until we learn otherwise, I suggest we don't worry about it."

I nodded. That's about where I had ended up myself.

Except…

"Ever heard of psychometry?" I asked.

"Oh lord," Mike said, rolling his eyes. "Which superpower is that again? The one where you touch an object and know its past?"

I chuckled. "Yup."

"That's bullshit," he said. "Psychics can't affect objects, or vice versa. We deal with biological matter, whatever form it takes."

"I thought so, too," I said. "But those beads, Mike…"

He shrugged but didn't say anything. When I had brought the beads back to the hotel the night before, Mike couldn't look away from them. When I had asked what he thought of them, he had said they were loud.

I knew what he meant—they were *still* loud. I had expected that the pressure that kept chiming against the inside of my skull would ease over time. Nope. Before we had left for our run, we had agreed that they were still as loud as they had been the previous night. Maybe louder.

"I'm thinking psychometry might be an advantage," I said. "If it is a real talent, it'd definitely be useful on this trip. Even if we can't pick memories off of an item, it could help us separate real pieces of the Mechanism from false leads."

"I'll call my mother," he said, his voice as tight as it ever got. "Maybe she knows something."

I laid my hand on his arm. It felt as if I were touching iron.

Inner peace only gets you so far. After that comes family.

We strolled up to the café. I was expecting a crowd out the door: Speedy tends to enjoy putting on a show. Instead, the koala was sitting on a table, deep in conversation with Atlas Petrakis.

"Wow," Mike said as he caught sight of the antiquities broker.

"I know, right?"

"You said he was delicious, but…*wow*."

"And he's got a sexy accent," I said. "And he's hella smart, and he likes to wear really thin linen, and—"

My mouth stopped working as Atlas looked up from a

spreadsheet and spotted me and Mike. He gave us that million-watt smile as he waved us over.

"Wow!"

"You mentioned," I told Mike, as I propelled him towards the table.

We dragged over some loose chairs on the way, and I flagged down the waiter for some water. Lots of water. Athens is a little arid.

Atlas stood. I needed a few moments to realize that he wanted to help me into my chair.

I laughed and let him. I was such a wreck that I could have wrung a gallon of sweat out of my shirt, and the gesture struck me as hilarious. He tucked me neatly into the table, as properly as if Mike and I had come in dressed all fancy-like.

"Hey, Speedy," I said, as Mike and Atlas got acquainted.

The koala's ears were flattened back. That's...never good. At least they were at three-quarters mast. Half-mast or lower, and you might as well look around for a nice lead-lined fallout shelter.

He grunted at me. It was a typical koala greeting: whatever was bothering him must not have crossed over into his supergenius side.

(That's a big problem with these altered types, if you ask me. Not just Speedy, but OACET, too. Sticking new smarts on top of old instincts sometimes means that the stupid-simple stuff has a hard time getting through.)

"Whatcha working on?" I asked.

Speedy looked up from the spreadsheets. "Tall, dark, and hormonal over there keeps detailed client lists. These are people or organizations who've approached him with items to sell."

I glanced at the spreadsheets. There were organized by item and location, but the far left columns were blank. The clients' names and contact information had been deleted; at least, on the version of the spreadsheets that Atlas had given to Speedy.

"Anything recovered from the bottom of the ocean?"

"Lots," he replied. One of the claws on his right forepaw was tapping against the paper.

Speedy doesn't twitch. Nervous activity is for animals—and humans—in captivity, and Speedy has plenty of outlets for any anxiety that might build up. I followed the tapping claw down to a small column that looked to be nothing but a line of dates.

Speedy watched me track his claws, and nodded. Something was on his mind besides whatever had flattened his ears. Something significant.

Ah. The spreadsheets weren't just lists of queries. They also indicated if these particular clients had bought or sold items from Atlas in the past.

And the same client had bought multiple items around the same time, nearly six months ago.

I took the spreadsheets from Speedy and started flipping through the pages. Yup. Someone had walked this same road before we got here.

"Senator Richard Hanlon," I said loudly.

Atlas Petrakis' head whipped towards me so quickly that I didn't need to ask the question.

I asked it anyhow, mainly for Mike's benefit. "You performed this exact same search for Hanlon last year?"

"I won't answer that," he said. "I respect my clients' privacy."

I kicked the chair back and stood, fuming. "Figure out if we can still work with him," I told Mike and Speedy. "I don't trust my own judgment right now."

I was three blocks away from the café before I realized I was scaring people. Whatever was written on my face must have been absolutely violent. I had the entire street to myself, as pedestrians and cars alike moved to get out of my path.

Hanlon.

I'm not a bad person. Really. But if you put a gun to my head and told me to choose the one person on earth who should die a prolonged, painful death, I'd pick Hanlon.

Eh, let's be honest. You wouldn't need the gun.

Hanlon.

The same guy who was responsible for putting my husband

and the other members of OACET through five years of living hell.

The same guy who had hired a thief to break into the White House and steal a piece of the Antikythera Mechanism.

The same guy who had apparently been collecting pieces of the Mechanism using strategies that mirrored those we were using to track down Archimedes—

"Shit!" I swore, and ducked into an alley to call my husband.

Being married to a cyborg has its perks. I can't remember the last time I had to set a digital clock, for one thing.

For another, our version of phone sex is pretty great.

Remember my ugly resin ring, the one Benjamin Franklin brought back from the future?[8] I activated it. A zillion (ish) miles away, Sparky felt it. He appeared in front of me in a flash of bright green, and smiled down at me.

"Hey, Sweetie," he said.

He wasn't really there. Well, his brain—consciousness, whatever—was, but his body was back home in Washington. Still, he looked as if he were standing in front of me, all fully fleshed and dressed in different shades of green, and when he reached for my hand, I almost expected to feel the warmth of his skin.

I didn't; his hand passed through mine in a halo of neon light. My body vibrated ever so slightly where they blended together.

(I really don't care if that delicious tingle is all psychological or whatnot, thank you. It's real to the two of us, and that's all that matters.)

Sparky pulled his hand from mine as he took in the setting. It was rather...

Ugh.

We were standing in an alley in a city undergoing a massive economic depression. We could count a dozen rats without even trying.

Phone sex would wait.

"What's happened?" he asked.

---

8 *sigh* I know, right?

"Oh, you'll love this," I said. We snuggled up behind a dumpster, out of the way of prying eyes, and I briefed him on Atlas Petrakis. "So," I finished, "I've got my doubts that a guy who worked for Hanlon would magically show up and want to work for me."

He nodded. "Too much of a coincidence. Where is Petrakis now?"

"Mike and Speedy are with him in a café. Mike will stop him if he tries to pull a runner."

"What are you going to do?"

I kicked a stray soda can at a rat who was getting awfully curious about my feet. The soda can sailed over the rat and clattered noisily into a pile of broken glass, and the rest of the pack scattered.

Sparky watched the rats as they ran for cover. "Thought so."

"Yup. I have zero problems covering the same ground Hanlon did. Hell, he saved us some work," I realized. "Atlas wouldn't have been able to come up with that list so quickly if he hadn't already done the same search for Hanlon. If Hanlon's already bought additional pieces of the Mechanism, good for him. I just need to know where those pieces were discovered."

"Think Petrakis will sell you the information?"

"If he's not a plant? Yes," I replied. "If Hanlon's set him on us, he'll balk on the sale and invent a reason to come with us while we travel."

"Even if he knows you're on to him?"

I muttered something and tried not to blush. I was already regretting my outburst at the café. I should have done what Speedy had done—play dumb and string Atlas along. Instead, I had jumped and roared.

Spy stuff? Not my strong suit.

Sparky grinned. "Don't worry about it," he said. "Is Petrakis dangerous?"

I laughed. "No," I said. "Manipulative? Definitely. But he's about as dangerous as a sexy kitten."

"Sexy?" My husband's eyebrows moved up a twitch, and

then up a whole inch as he found Atlas Petrakis' photograph in a database. "Wow."

"Right?"

He groaned aloud. There was a world of emotion in it, ranging from regret all the way to jealousy that another man was roaming around a foreign country with his wife. I would have hugged him but, you know. No body. Instead, I reached out and touched the space where his shoulder appeared to be.

We steal our moments when we can, Sparky and me, so we stayed like that until I needed to head back to the café. He disappeared in another flash of green, with a promise to check back with me later that evening.

I turned down the street and wandered back towards the café. I was walking slowly, pacing my way west in the early afternoon sunlight. Apparently, that's all the opportunity that someone needed to try and pick my pocket.

I was having *none of that nonsense.*

The thief was good; she didn't do that careless bump-and-shove that most pickpockets do. Instead, she waited until a car blew its horn as it passed me, and then used the moment in which I was distracted to drop her hand into the pocket of my shorts.

I slammed my hand down on top of hers and pinned her hand inside my pants (shut up), and then whipped my upper body forward. The would-be thief went tipping forward, her top half shooting straight over my shoulders.

Except for that one hand. I wasn't about to give up control of that hand.

Hey, I was nice to her; I could have snapped her arm like a twig. Instead, I made sure to throw her in the same direction her shoulder rotated. I used our momentum to slam the two of us against the nearest building, using her torso as my personal air bag.

"Apologize," I said, "and I'll let you go."

I couldn't see her face, what with it dangling somewhere near my butt and all, but she squeaked out my name.

"I know who I am."

"David sent me!" she said in English.

I'm not all that quick. I banged her against the wall again (shut up, shut up) before I remembered the passphrase that Mike had used in the knife shop.

I had just beaten up our black market contact.

Well.

I carried her into an alley as rat-infested as the last one, and tipped her gently onto her feet.

The woman was…um…

Let's go with "plain".

She appeared to be a local Greek woman a few years older than I was, and hadn't had the advantage of modern orthodontic work. Or dermatology. Or tweezers. The part of my brain that hadn't come along on my spring break from medical school diagnosed her with a moderate case of hirsutism.

She was also wearing one of the neatest jackets I had ever seen. It looked like a military make, just not any military that I was familiar with—greens and khakis were splashed across her arms and chest, the perfect hues to blend in with the landscape around the Parthenon.

It was long, too, and darker at its bottom than the top. She could squat down in the middle of a Greek field, pull the jacket's hood over her head, and disappear into thin air.

Atlas Petrakis might be polished perfection, but this woman was *real*.

"Why'd you try to mug me?" I asked slowly.

"Heard you were good," she said.

"And?"

She flipped her hand around so I could see her palm. I would have sworn it was empty, but no, there was my wallet.

"I'm better," she said, grinning as she handed it back to me. "Call me Darling."

I didn't reply as I made a show of counting out my credit cards.

"I don't steal from my clients," she said, and did that empty-palm trick again. My Visa card appeared, and she held it out to me.

"You're hired," I said, and she dropped the Visa card into my hand. Followed by a second credit card…she had also snagged my Amex? *Oy*.

"Just like that?"

"Anyone who can rifle though my wallet while I'm smashing them upside down against a wall can get the job done."

"Yes… Tell me," Darling said as she made a show of rubbing her head. Her English was excellent, her accent and cadence similar to Atlas'. "How often will the beatings happen?"

"As often as you try to put one over on me."

"Good," she said, holding out her hand for me to shake. "I will not be doing that again."

We talked shop as we walked the rest of the way to the café. Terms, wages, contracts (Darling laughed at that one), and legality. *Especially* legality.

"I don't know how you usually operate," I said to her. "When I'm paying you, law and order are your key words."

Darling nodded. "I can do such things," she said. "I have the proper paperwork."

With that, I pushed open the door of the café.

Mike always kept a keen eye on his surroundings, so he spotted us the moment Darling and I walked in. It took Speedy and Atlas a few moments more, but when Atlas caught sight of Darling, he lunged to his feet, his chair banging against the stone floor as it toppled backwards. The gorgeous man began shouting angrily in Greek, and to go by Speedy's impressed expression, he was nailing the profanities pretty hard.

None of that held a candle to what Darling had done the moment she had seen Atlas, which was lunge at him with an honest-to-God drawn *gun!*

As she leapt, she shouted: *"You!"*

# CHAPTER 13

When it comes to guns, Mike doesn't fuck around.

He was too far from Darling to control her gun. Instead? He kicked a chair straight up into the air, and then gave it a tap to launch it at her like a wicker missile.

This knocked Darling sideways and put her close enough for me to flip things around, and by *things,* I mean *Darling*. I snagged her free hand and flung her against the ground, wham bam boom.

By the time she was down, Mike was already standing on her gun hand.

"Don't hurt her," I told him. "She's…uh. She's David. You know?" I said glancing around the room. Fortunately, the café wasn't crowded. Unfortunately, this was because most people had had the sense to start running for the door the moment the gun came out. The barista has disappeared, but I saw the coil of an old telephone cord jiggle as it ran from the wall to where she was hiding beneath the counter. "David?"

"Ah," Mike said, and eased most of the weight of his foot from her wrist.

"She is also my cousin," Atlas said darkly. "Who promised she would stop poaching my clients."

"These are not *your* clients!" Darling replied. Her gun had disappeared; Mike's jogging shorts hung a little low on his right-hand side. "They hired me!"

Atlas turned towards me, disbelief clear on his face. I nodded. "I'm pretty sure she's never worked for Hanlon," I said. "Gives her a nice head start on you in my opinion."

"He was just another client!" Atlas insisted. "Hanlon hired most of the art brokers in the country to search for the Mechanism. I was no different."

"Could be true," Speedy said. "No reason for Hanlon to hire just one dude."

And that was the moment when Darling realized the famous talking koala wasn't a hoax or a gimmick or some other kind of ridiculous shenanigans.

It basically shut her down right there.

Put yourself in her place. Close your eyes and pretend Mr. Ed could actually talk. Everyone's told you that he's a real live talking horse. You've even seen him on television. Then, you're walking in the park one day and you bump into this horse who wants to have a conversation with you.

It. Doesn't. Happen.

Not in any semblance of real life you've experienced, that is.

I've seen this happen a billion times. Dumb people tend to find their balance within moments, needing nothing more than an *Oh, right, I heard about this thing.*

Smart people need to shut down and reboot.

Darling was one of the smart ones. She shoved Mike off of her hand and sat up, staring at the koala the entire time.

"You talk?" she whispered. "You are not a fake?"

"Go fuck yourself," Speedy said, and jumped down from the table to find the nearest toilet.[9]

"He is not a fake," Atlas said, a little too smugly. He settled back in his chair and rested his hands across his papers. "He has been helping me plan the next stage in our search."

"Says the man who might be fired," I said.

"May I suggest we resolve this before the police arrive?" Mike asked, as he helped Darling to stand and then made her sit across the table from her cousin. "If you can't, leave now, and we'll be in touch.

"Maybe," he added, as he removed Darling's gun from his pocket and broke it apart to peek inside. He shot me a Look: the woman had attacked her cousin with a loaded gun.

Not good. We should be glad she didn't outright murder him the moment she saw him.

The Petrakis cousins glared at each other, poking around the

9 Or potted plant. Speedy's not picky.

boundaries of civility. I guess one of them blinked wrong or something, because just like that? It was *on*.

The stray thought that they were two strangers running a con on us evaporated when they set against each other in the kind of verbal battle that can only occur between family members. I didn't understand the language, but I didn't need to: there was enough waving and shouting to follow along. Both of them were in it to win it, and it was only a matter of time before one or both of them started throwing punches.

"Enough!"

I slammed my hands down on the marble tabletop, hard. From the direction of the barista's counter came a little yipping noise, followed by more whispered Greek into the phone. "Guys?" I said. "This is getting too dramaculous for me. Go. Talk. Figure out who stays or who goes. At this point, I really don't care, and I'll happily stay an extra day or two in Athens to find your replacements if it means I don't have to deal with your bullshit. Got it?"

They did.

The two of them went outside to have a really splendid whispered fight on the sidewalk. It was all waving hands and pointing, mostly towards us. The Petrakis cousins held their argument in Greek, of course. Speedy hopped back up on the table once he saw that Darling was gone, and us bipedal Americans pretended to be bored as he did a line-by-line translation.

I'll give you the highlight reel: neither of them wanted to work for us. Atlas was doing so for the prestige of putting OACET and Hope Blackwell on his résumé. Darling needed the money. Atlas wasn't about to give ground, and said that since he was here first, she could go [truly astonishing expletive, probably embellished via koala].

Then Darling dropped the bomb...her mom wasn't doing well. Cancer.

That shut Atlas down.

It also shut Speedy down, as he lost interest when Atlas'

face fell and the drama washed away. That was fine—Mike and I didn't need the rest of their fight translated. Atlas reached towards his cousin, who shook off his hands and stood there with the stoic expression of a woman who never, ever lets herself cry. Then, they pushed themselves into politeness, with the kind of awkward pauses that only exist in those conversations you *have* to have.

Listen, I sympathized with the Petrakis cousins, really. Some of my family members are human sewage, and don't even get me started on Mike's family. But I was not in Greece to make friends or play therapist.

It'd be nice if I could save the world without feeling guilty about it.

"How long before the police arrive?" I asked Speedy.

He nodded in the direction of the barista's counter. "They aren't coming. No physical assault occurred, so they aren't spending the resources on it."

"You're kidding. It's a good part of town, and someone had a gun."

The koala did that rolling-shoulder motion that passed for his shrug. "They're tapped out," he said. "Emergencies only. This doesn't count since everybody is still standing."

"Grim," I said, as the cousins reentered the store.

"Reality," he said, and nodded towards the cousins. "Money trumps all else. Watch."

Mike sighed, and went to go put the barista at ease. He took a chair with him, just in case.

Atlas reclaimed his seat at the table, and pulled the spreadsheets towards him.

"I am sorry," he said to me. "I should have realized working for Hanlon would have been a conflict of interest for you. I hope I have made it clear that I respect my clients' privacy; I did not mean to mislead you in any way."

I don't think I grunted or swore, but Speedy still chuckled.

"Our personal problems? They will not be an issue for you," Darling said. Her words were clipped and hard. I got the impression that if I let down my mental shields, I'd be swimming in some rather unpleasant emotions.

"Great," I replied. "We leave tomorrow for…uh…"

"Kos," Speedy said.

I nodded and pretended to know where—or what—Kos was. It was a name that hadn't come up in our briefings or anything… Wait, no, Mike had mentioned Kos when we were exploring the Asklepion. It was a city, maybe, or an island? Possibly both.

"What's at Kos?" I asked.

"Surviving documents from the Library at Alexandria," Speedy said. "Archimedes studied at Alexandria, and there's some anecdotal evidence that Posidonius did, too, since he used the stars at Alexandria in his equations."

"Kos is also a location I did not check for Hanlon," Atlas said. "There may be new information there, hidden in what remains of the Great Library."

"As good a place as any," I said.

Then it was logistics. And more drinks; we tipped the poor barista so heavily she was actually sorry to see us leave. Since I was paying the bill, I was the last one out the door. Darling hung back; I thought she was being polite until she grabbed my arm. It was such a sudden gesture that I had covered her hand with my own before I remembered that I shouldn't hurl her across the room.

She didn't notice, preoccupied with watching Atlas through the window.

"My cousin is an evil man," Darling said. "Beneath that face, he is ugly. Listen to me—I *know*."

# CHAPTER 14

I was back in the dream again, and the long-legged boy before me thought he was a man.

He was standing on a high rock, the sun at his back. There was no doubt in my mind that he had positioned himself as such to appear as impressive as he could.

I walked on.

He had tricked me, and I cursed myself for it. I loved the old shrines more than those in the cities, and, as was my custom, had traveled many miles to make sacrifice to Artemis. As I neared the shrine, I heard the screaming of a rabbit in a snare, and wandered from the road to retrieve it for my Goddess.

Now, I was surrounded by soldiers who did not look to my father.

I almost smiled; he felt he had needed an army to catch me.

He scampered down from his perch, his footing more luck than skill, and pushed past me to bar my way. "They say you're the child of a god," he said.

"They say my mother lay with a swan, who also happened to be a god," I said. "Both of those are stories for fools."

The forest around me rustled, as the soldiers he had brought with him moved ever closer.

I dropped the rabbit as my hand moved to the dagger at my waist.

"Helen, no."

The voice came from the brush behind me. It was that of Pirithous, king of Larissa. Friend to Sparta, or so he had claimed.

"What a lovely thing you have found for me," said the long-legged boy, as he looked upon me with hot eyes.

"Do not touch her," Pirithous said. "She'll gut you like a fish."

"I will," I promised the boy.

"I am a king," the boy said to Pirithous. "She'll show me respect."

"You are a child in the body of a king," I told him.

"And you," he said, as he reached for my hand, "are a queen in the body of a child."

I hit him.

I had yet to come into my own strength. Still, I knocked out a tooth, and smiled as the blood came rushing down his chin.

He would have returned my blow, but Pirithous stopped him. "Theseus! No! It would be war."

The boy glared at his companion. "When I take her, it *will* be war."

The King of Larissa gazed at me, as if realizing only now what was being asked of him. "Perhaps—"

"Look at her, old friend," said the boy. "Not nearly a woman, and still perfect."

Pirithous moved to put his body between me and this old and ugly boy. There appeared to be lines some kings would not cross.

"Your word," Pirithous said. "Your word that you will not touch her until she comes of age."

"Of course," the boy said, as his eyes traveled up and down my form.

The man before me placed his hands on the shoulders of the boy. The two of them shared a size and had lived the same length of years, and still I could not help but think that one had wisdom that the other would never find.

"Your *word*, Theseus."

The boy's eyes moved from me, and I saw there was indeed some age within them. Some men were rendered powerless by women: the king of Athens appeared to be one of these.

His friend shook him, gently, and I heard spears move within the brush.

Theseus sighed. "My word, old friend. I'll send the girl to my mother's house until she is fifteen."

My heart, already choking in fear, seized at the thought of

years in prison.

Followed by a lifetime with this horrible boy.

"I will make my offering before you try to take me," I said.

I did not wait for them to answer. I took up the rabbit that had put me in their trap, and walked the last league to the shrine. There, I prayed to my Goddess, protector of hunters and virgins, and reminded her that as such I was twice in need of her assistance.

Once done, I burned the rabbit.

I removed my necklace and cut it in half, and laid this and my dagger upon the altar.

"Sister," I whispered. "Hear me. Come and find these things, and know I did not vanish in the hunt.

"Brothers, come and find me, and burn Athens to the ground."

I tied the other half of my necklace around my wrist to remind me of all I was about to lose, and then I turned to face the soldiers.

# CHAPTER 15

The train ran low along the coast as we made our way to the port that was the second leg of our journey to Kos.

I had my forehead pressed against the window. A light rain was falling, and beads of water streamed past on their way to the ground. A sleeping koala was using my thigh as a substitute for a tree branch, his warm, soft weight pressed tight against mine.

I was exhausted, but I didn't trust myself to nap—I was ready to be rid of Helen.

I no longer thought those dreams were anything but her memories. My attention span is a notorious galaxy-devouring black hole. I rarely have a full-sensory dream experience, and when I do, I'm incapable of having one with a sustained plotline. Especially a plotline with sociocultural horrors that my waking brain would nope out on before I could accidentally follow them to their logical ends.

Ever been on a wooden ship? Ever been on a wooden ship from two thousand years ago? First of all, there's a lot of slave labor, and while Helen might have been okay with that, I wasn't. It's a living misery.

Second? I...

—oh *God!*—

Okay. Deep breath.

There's only so much a prepubescent girl can do to keep a boatload of men off of her. Helen might have been a hurricane crossed with a wildcat, but *holy shitballs!* If that nice King hadn't guarded Helen at swordpoint the entire trip back to Athens, last night's dream would have been a literal fucking nightmare.

I was drinking way too much today, and I didn't mind at all. There was a knock on the door to our private car, and

Mike returned with another couple of bottles. I grabbed one gratefully, and had downed most of it before I realized it was only soda pop.

"Damn it, Mike," I snapped. "You said you'd find more beer."

"I did," he said. "Then I left it where I found it."

I detached myself from the koala and stood. Speedy, grumbling in his sleep, waved his forepaws in the air where my leg had been before he settled down. "Where's the club car?"

"Four cars towards the rear," he said. "Or, you could talk to me."

"We've already talked," I said, and went in search of alcohol.

I regretted taking my frustration out on Mike the moment I shut the door on him, but...

In those dreams, I was a powerless observer. Absolutely powerless. I couldn't even wake myself up. And since I was riding along from her point of view, if something unspeakable happened to Helen, it'd also happen to me.

Yes, was a selfish thought. Yes, I felt miserable for that poor little girl, all alone and stolen from the family and the land she loved.

Hell-to-the-fuck *no!* I didn't want to be gang-raped, vicariously or otherwise.

Mike thought I should simply meditate my way out of it, the epitome of *clear your mind, and the rest will follow.*

I...well...

Simple for him, maybe. Not for me.

I found the club car. Greece's railways got a lovely influx of cash around the time of the Athens Olympics, and while the patina was wearing off, the nuts and bolts of the train were still sturdy. I plopped myself in a chair covered in cracked polyester, and told the attendant to get me something strong. He came back with a bottle, and I made him wait while I drank it before I asked for three more.

I was most of the way through the second bottle when two paws appeared on the other side of my table. Speedy hoisted himself up, glaring at me the entire time.

"What?" I asked him.

"The hippie wanted me to check in on you," he said.

"Tell him I'm doing much better," I replied, as I rapped my wedding band against the mostly empty beer bottle.

"Tell him yourself. Better do it fast—he's writing an email to his mother."

I thought about that one. "Oh."

"Yeah. He's *that* worried."

"I'm fine," I said, and tried to ignore the guilt that had begun to bore holes in my pleasant buzz.

"Sure," the koala replied, as he flagged down the attendant and ordered water and cereal. The attendant brought these, but made the tragic mistake of serving the water in a shallow bowl, and I had to intervene before Speedy turned him into his toy.

A superintelligent koala's paws work better than my hands. Koalas have extra thumbs for gripping tree branches, and Speedy is smart enough to know how to put them to use in the human world. With the exception of cell phones and other devices that work best with fingers *sans* inch-long claws, Speedy is better than us bipeds at manipulating objects. The attendant watched in horrified amazement as Speedy tucked into his lunch, silverware flashing at a rate never seen outside of knife commercials.

"A *bowl*," he finally said, scorn the only thing dripping from him as he drank his water straight from the bottle, lips be damned. "Like I'm a *dog*."

"He thought he was being polite."

"Fuck a bunch of polite," Speedy grunted. "Carry me back to our room. It's warm there, and I want to go back to sleep."

"Carry yourself," I said, and went to get myself a cup of coffee. I doused this with enough sugar to choke an anthill, but left out my usual serving of milk so as not to alienate the caffeine.

Speedy was still sitting on the table when I got back. We sat and glared at each other for a while.

"I need you to pull your head out of your upper intestine," he finally said. "We're working. You can wallow in misery when we get home, but here? C'mon, Hope, you must have spotted those assholes who got on the train with us at Athens."

I didn't reply, but yes, I had. Hired Goon Squad Version 2.0 was coming with us to Kos, and it was only a matter of time before they made their presence known. They probably wouldn't be so subtle as to jump us in an alley next time, either.

"Here's the thing," he said, his voice dropping to a burry whisper. "It's not like you can stop sleeping. And it's not as if Helen's memories are some sort of *Nightmare on Elm Street* scenario, where you'll get tortured and murdered."

"Just tortured," I replied. "For now. Maybe murdered in the final act. They're her *memories*, Speedy! I feel what she felt, plus I've got an extra layer of yikes because I'm watching it happen in real time and there's nothing I can do to stop it."

"Why would you want to stop it?" he asked, and before I could brain him with an empty bottle, he added, "Everybody who knows anything about this weird world of yours says psychometry and object-reading are bullshit. Which makes sense—how can pieces of glass beads remember their past? They've got no brain, no soul… These memories are coming from somewhere, kitten, and that means there's a ghost involved."

He glanced around the car to make sure no one was listening in before saying, "Helen of Troy? If she's still around, she'd be one supremely powerful ghost. She's a central figure in some of the greatest surviving works of literature in Western civilization. I think you got her attention when you took possession of those beads."

"Fan-fucking-tastic," I growled into my coffee. "So, what? Helen's decided I'm her biographer and she's uploading her life story into my head?"

"No," Speedy said. "I think she's telling you something you need to hear."

I laughed; how could anything in Helen's life be applicable to mine? We were separated by thousands of years, insanely different cultures…

Speedy got that Look on his furry face, the one he puts on right before he starts biting the shit out of you to make sure he's got your undivided attention. Being on the receiving end of that Look is better than dousing your head in a bucket of cold water to sober up.

"All right, say she does want to tell me something," I whispered back. "Why come to me in dreams? *You* can see ghosts—*you* can speak ancient Greek! She can cut out the middleman and tell you what she wants."

"Maybe she can't," he said. "Maybe your hypotheses on ghosts and cultural alignment are right. And even if she could…" He wiggled his freakish fingers at me. "Hello? Genetically-engineered koala here. Try shoving that one down an old dead woman's throat."

"Right, right," I sat back in my seat, and spun my now-empty coffee cup on its saucer. "Think Helen is powerful enough to hop into the future?"

"Definitely. The ancient Greeks were all about fortune-telling. She's probably an expert at it."

"If there's such a thing as an expert at time travel," I murmured to myself.

Speedy heard me and nodded. "You want my best guess?"

"Always."

"Once you took possession of those beads, you pinged on her radar and she decided to check you out. She followed your path into your futures and weighed the outcomes. I doubt she's telling you her life's story because she's bored.

"Her timeline doesn't align with the Mechanism's," Speedy added. "But something that happened in her life will be applicable to yours. She's trying to *help you*, you selfish twunt!

"Now," he finished, as he crawled onto my shoulders and buried his face in my hair. "Go back to our room so we can both go to sleep. I'm tired, and you've got mail."

# CHAPTER 16

On the journey to Aphidna, I had acquitted myself as would any Spartan prisoner, and so they brought me to the king's mother in chains.

The old woman looked at me, and the lines on her face that had grown soft in her son's absence reappeared.

"Another one," she said.

"Mother—"

"Come," she ordered him, and he bound me to a column before he followed her from the room.

I stood until the sun went down, and ignored those who brought me food and drink.

As the stars rose, the old woman returned, a key in one hand and a Spartan dagger in her other.

"Would you like to know how my son has fallen into your father's trap?" she asked me.

When I nodded, she undid my chains, and offered me the dagger.

"Your people are only at home when armed," she said. "Please allow me to welcome you to your new home."

I nodded, and accepted the blade as my own.

She allowed me the use of her toilet and bath, and provided me with clean linens before she asked me to join her in a light meal. We reclined on overstuffed couches as she encouraged me to try new and too-sweet dishes.

"I am Aethra," she said. "A mother who speaks ill of her son speaks ill of herself, but I am deeply sorry that you are here with me tonight."

"They say Theseus is a good king."

Aethra nodded. "He is a good and great king," she said. "He is a terrible man. You are not the first woman he has stolen from her home.

"Though," she added, "I pray you'll always be the youngest."

"Women are his weakness."

Aethra stared at me with sharp eyes. "You are your father's daughter."

I knew she meant Tyndareus, and none of that nonsense about swans. "You've met my father?"

"No," she replied. "But I know his reputation, and I know you've come here because of him. How did they take you?"

I told her of the shrine and the rabbit.

"Clever," she said. "Allowing my son to think he stole you away without notice. Did you know a party from Sparta arrived in Athens this morning?"

My heart leapt; she saw it, and held up her hands to calm me. "No," she said. "You are still a prisoner, and will be for months, perhaps years. It will be politics first, followed by war. Tyndareus has wanted to put Athens in its place, and your abduction is the excuse he needs to do so."

I said nothing for several minutes, as I finally felt hunger and thirst for the first time since my capture. I had allowed myself to eat only what I needed to keep from growing weak; now, I began to eat for pleasure.

"This bothers you?" Aethra asked, mistaking my silence for sadness. "That your father would use you?"

I glanced up from my plate. The surprise on my face must have been plain, as she tried to explain: "He has spread rumors of your beauty far and wide, to pull suitors towards Sparta."

I was stunned. "My...my *beauty?* I am no beauty."

"Truth means little in politics. How better to entice men than by offering them a beautiful princess? Also," she added, "mark how Tyndareus has done nothing to quash this tale of Zeus as your true father. Such a story is a gift to him; your value exceeds that of your sister's."

This made sense: Clytemnestra's face matched my own, but there were fewer offers for her.

"I am not beautiful," I said. "Nor do I want to be."

"Ah," Aethra said. "That's a mistake—every princess should want to be beautiful. Do you expect to be married to a Spartan prince?"

That made me laugh.

"Then you accept that you'll be married to a king outside of Sparta?"

"Of course," I replied. I had known since I was a crawling babe that my marriage would be a weapon in my country's hands. As much as I might wish to stay at home, my leaving Sparta would strengthen it.

"Beauty improves your value. The more valuable you are, the better your father can use you when he decides who you should marry. He is fortunate, your father, that so many men want to wed the child of a god. I would fear doing so, myself."

I remembered the long lists of suitors who had come to pledge for my hand, Theseus and Pirithous among them. Father had not said yes or no to any of them, claiming I was still too young to wed, and the offers of wealth and power had increased as they sought to change his mind.

Clytemnestra thought it hilarious that so many men wished to possess a girl because they thought her to be half a bird.

"Father would never permit my marriage to align Sparta with Athens," I said, as I slowly came to understand how I had been used to bait my father's trap. "He says they are a weak people, and he does not approve of Theseus on the throne."

I saw it now, my father's plan, and I felt pride in him.

Aethra nodded. "Your abduction was a challenge to Sparta's honor, and one that could not go unpunished. Tyndareus will use it as reason to go to war with an old enemy. So now you are here," she said, spreading her hands wide. "I hope that you will join me in making the best of a bad situation. I would dearly regret needing to keep you in chains for the length of your stay."

"I promise you peace," I said to her. "I only wish my father had told me I was a lure for your son—I might not have put out his teeth."

That made Aethra laugh merrily. "A Spartan, come along

quietly? Never. A wolf in a cage must be true to its nature, or all will know they have caught merely a dog."

"Why do you tell me these things?" I asked the old woman. "In a war between Sparta and Athens, I would think you would side with Athens."

"I would, and I will," Aethra said. "But it is only fair to tell you how you have been used— girls who are born to kings are made to suffer for their fathers."

She took a breath to steady herself. "Theseus thinks himself the child of a god," she added. "Not the bastard son of a visiting king who my father sent to my bed when I was barely older than yourself.

"One day, Helen, when a princess is given to you for her own protection, I hope you will remember this, and that you will be kind."

# CHAPTER 17

Kos was...

Well, it's no Athens.

It is, however, a damned pleasant vacation spot.

I was on a Mediterranean beach, wearing a string bikini and one of those ludicrous oversized floppy hats. My koala buddy was neck-deep in warm sand and digging ever lower as he made happy chortling noises, and Mike and I were pretending to ignore Atlas as he played in the nearby surf.

"That is just cruel," I muttered, as I flipped a page of the book I wasn't reading. "What's he doing, anyhow?"

"He's trying to get you to go swimming with him," Mike replied.

"Married woman here, thank-yew-vaary-much."

"I thought you were in medical school," Mike said. "They haven't covered the differences between swimming and sex yet?"

"You go frolic with him, then."

"He's too young," Mike said. "I need a little seasoning on my bones."

I grunted something about minimal age differences and terrible dick jokes, and yanked the brim of my hat down over my face.

I was thinking I'd nap, since sleep had gotten much easier. Napping meant I could expect to show up in my usual dreams of platypuses (platypuseses? platypi?) and roller-skating with my seventh-grade English teacher. Much, much more pleasant than riding shotgun on the life experiences of a long-dead princess.

I didn't exactly miss Helen, but I was wondering why she had stopped checking in. Maybe she had shown me all she needed to, or maybe she didn't like Kos. Or maybe… Hell, what did I know about anything that happened over twenty-five hundred years ago? What I did know was that we'd been here all of two days, and she hadn't shown up once. That was okay, though: kid-Helen appeared to be in good hands when I left her. Evil Dude's Surprisingly Nice Mom was one of those women in her early fifties who had her shit so tightly knit together that she could wear it as a sweater—

Um. Moving on from that analogy.

Let's just say that I was sure that Surprisingly Nice Mom wouldn't allow anything unsavory to happen to Helen on her watch, and that was a huge relief to me.

Strange, how Helen's opinions didn't mesh with my own. I saw Surprisingly Nice Mom as an energetic woman who was still in the prime of her life: Helen thought that Mom was barely a sneeze away from toppling into death.

But maybe that wasn't cultural. Maybe that was just the normal opinion-colored lens of early adolescence. Riding along in Helen's skull was bringing back my own memories of how I used to see the world, and yeah, there were some similarities that couldn't be explained by anything other than pure dumb youth. At least Helen didn't seem to be driven by the usual self-destructive reasoning which passed for teenage logic. Or maybe Spartan discipline trumped hormones…

Heh. Spartan bootcamp. There's an idea for modern miscreant youth. Similar to military school, but with phalanx formations. They could show *300* as their recruitment video. Hell, *I'd* go to that camp!

I snuck another peek at Atlas. Waves were crashing around all him, the spray from the water cast rainbows around his body… It was *ridiculous.*

Speedy hurled sand in my face.

"Jesus!" I said, spitting. He hadn't gotten any in my eyes, but he had nailed my mouth. "Speedy, what the hell?!"

"You were drooling," he said. His ears were back. "Figured you'd want to save what little dignity you might have scraped together before his cousin gets here."

"What?" I was busy licking my arm to get the sand off of my tongue, so I didn't notice that Darling had arrived beside our beach chairs. Her shadow fell on me and I glanced up mid-lick.

The sun was behind her, so her face was lost in a blur of dark features. The lines of her face neck were stark and clean, right until they disappeared under her jacket, and I had the quick impression that she was trying to be ugly.

"Inconvenient time?" she asked, as she sat down in the shade of our umbrella.

I shrugged and reached for a towel so I could scrub out my mouth on the terrycloth. "No. Any news?"

"Yes," the thief said, nodding. "The guard will let us in tonight, and will make sure we are alone."

Let me tell you one of the practically infinite number of problems with trying to track down ancient historical documents: it turns out one does not simply walk into the Library of Alexandria. Or what's left of it.

We've all heard about the Library of Alexandria, and, if you're like me—well, like I used to be before I had to learn all of this crap—you thought it was a big library that held a lot of books and burned down a long, long time ago.

We're not even close.

Keep in mind that the first Library was built in Egypt and had a lot of influence from the Greeks, two ancient civilizations that weren't exactly known for their modest small-scale constructions. Instead of thinking of it as a quaint little building full of books, imagine a library as built by Donald Trump. Words like *ostentatious* and *opulent* didn't even begin to cover it. It was a gigantic shrine to the human experience.

(This Library was part of, and I kid you not, a museum with artifacts from even older civilizations, which contained some pieces left over from the private collections that the Egyptian pharaohs kept before *those* existed. Don't think too hard about this because if you look at it too closely, it becomes one of those illusions when the Thing contains a smaller version of the same

Thing, which in turn contains an even smaller version of the same Thing, and so on until it all tapers off into infinity and/or the first cartoon doodle ever done by a single-celled organism.)

Oh, and the Library didn't burn down just once. It burned down four different times, each time taking part of the collection with it. Those ancient archivists were fast learners, though, and after that first fire, they began creating satellite libraries to store copies of their books. Like most backup systems, not everything got copied over, but enough was preserved to make its mark on antiquity.

Unfortunately for us—unfortunately for the whole of Western civilization, really—the first time the Library burned was *after* Archimedes (and maybe Posidonius) would have studied there. It was possible that most of his original works were torched in that first fire.

However, it is also possible that backups of what survived were made and moved to Kos.

Nothing lasts forever. You have any idea how much paper is lost each year? Fire and water and careless patrons with their indiscriminate application of bookmarks, not to mention those gnarly little bugs which find any organic material to be damned tasty. The paper used in the Library was different than that what we use today, but it still was susceptible to those same destructive forces. Scribes would have made copies of Archimedes' work nearly as soon as it was written, just to ensure there'd be one or two that would beat the odds. These might have gone out to the sister libraries in Alexandria that existed before that first fire, and were sent out to the satellite libraries to help preserve the knowledge after the place started burning down.

One final fact in our favor? Kos was an ancient *science palace*. It's where modern medicine was invented, and where one of the first and best schools of astronomy was established. If ancient archivists were sorting books into piles to send out to various satellite libraries, Kos would have gotten the batch marked "Nerd."

So…

On the one hand, the satellite library at Kos was one of the smallest ones. Most modern scholars tend to ignore it.

On the other hand, we were most likely to find something previously undiscovered at the satellite library at Kos, because its contents were germane to our needs and most modern scholars tend to ignore it. We weren't here because it was *likely* we'd find undiscovered information on the Mechanism—we were here as it was *one of the only places left on earth* where it might be *remotely possible* to find that lost information!

I enjoy grasping at straws. It keeps the reflexes sharp.

But?

Problem: we couldn't get access to the freakin' stuff.

Atlas had tried to work his magic, and they had laughed in his (oh-so-divine) face. Something about approved clearance, and the online digitized archives being just as good as the real thing for his American tourists.

They weren't, though; Speedy needed access to the originals. Originals have liner notes and handwritten personal memos. Little sketches in the margins, maybe. Things that might have been missed.

The solution?

We were going to break in to the Library of Alexandria.

Not rob it, mind! When I say *break in*, what I'm actually saying is *bribe the night watchman and promise to leave all food and drink outside.* I was sketchy about the legality, sure, but everyone assured me this was a time-honored custom among scholars who wanted to search through the archives but couldn't get official access. We wouldn't be caught on camera, and in the unlikely event the cops showed up, a little extra money would send them on their merry way.

Besides, the surviving archives weren't kept in a *museum-* museum. They were kept in a nice climate-controlled basement, and the documents were preserved between pieces of acid-free Plexiglas. When it came right down to it, we weren't committing burglary as much as we were going to sit around and read in a pleasant air-conditioned room.[10]

10  All right, all right. We might have been committing a little bit of data theft.

Darling had gone to arrange it so we could sneak in and out without meeting anyone on the way. Flip open an unlocked back door, plunder the knowledge of the ancient world, and leave with no one the wiser.

Simple as pie.

"When?" I asked her.

"Midnight," she said. "We will have three hours alone."

"That's not nearly enough time," Speedy said, as he jumped up into my lap. I howled and crammed a towel under him. "That's barely long enough to narrow down the search parameters."

"Then we will go back tomorrow night, animal," Darling said. "And then the night after that, until you are satisfied. The three hours after midnight is the window in which we are not likely to be caught."

Atlas came up to stand beside Darling, puffing slightly from his short run up the beach. Darling took an obvious step away from her cousin and hurled a towel at him. This, he looped around his waist, giving him the appearance of wearing absolutely nothing under the towel, and Mike and I were suddenly very busy looking for our respective whatevers in the communal beach bag.

"I'm hungry," Darling said. "I will find you later."

"I'm hungry, too," I said, thinking I might be able to get a decent conversation out of the thief over lunch. But then Speedy said he was hungry, and the five of us ended up at a little spot on the city's main drag.

It was nice. Kos had a large marketplace, and we took a table outside so we could people-watch. Mike sat with his back to the wall, and I sat directly across from him so he could search the crowd behind me without being obvious about it. Every time he saw someone he thought was one of our new goons, he marked it by tearing a piece off of his paper napkin.

Truth be told, I got a little worried when he needed a new napkin.

Somebody had set a hell of a lot of Hired Goons on our tail. <u>Any guesses who that certain somebody was? Hanlon, right?</u>

Semantics. We'd leave all the originals where we found them.

We're all betting on Hanlon? Nobody wants anybody else in the pool?

Okay, then.

I let Atlas order our meals, the compromise being that Darling had to order our appetizers, drinks, and desserts. Both of them tried to one-up the other on finding the most authentic tastes of Kos. Us meat-eaters ended up with fish dishes that tasted almost Italian, and the vegetarians got sweet grains and vegetables baked into flatbreads. All of us devoured what Mike referred to as the Platonic ideal of an appetizer, breads and cheeses in a spicy cream sauce.

Mike and I ordered seconds. And then thirds.

(Yea, though I walk through the valley of the shadow of eensie-weensie cocktail dresses, I will fear no carbohydrate: for I train a minimum of twenty hours a week and after that I go to work...)

We were all feeling decent, I think, but it's hard to have a good conversation when one or more members of a party actively hate each other. So, you know. Play to their strengths.

"Hey, Atlas?" I asked, as I shoveled more of that spicy cream sauce onto a triangle made from hard toast. "Tell me more about Helen. Uh...Helen of Troy."

Mike didn't so much as blink, but Speedy? His ears flattened against his head.[11]

Atlas didn't notice; Darling did, and her eyes went from Speedy to me, *bang-bang*, smooth and quick.

I didn't care. Seriously did not care. Whatever she thought was going on couldn't possibly be anywhere close to the truth, and I was tired of doing Google searches which gave me the same information over and over again.

And, um... Well...

I couldn't remember the names of the other people involved.

What? One old Greek name sounds like any other to me, especially when a language I don't speak is being autotranslated in my subconscious. I was lucky to have remembered Helen's <u>name, and that's</u> because I grew up with a different Helen who

11 Koalas have the best poker faces, but they have terrible poker ears.

kicked me off of a jungle gym when I was five. Wikipedia is plenty helpful about the whole "of Troy" phase of Helen's (the other Helen, not the sociopathic playground one) life, but her Spartan childhood is treated like an afterthought at best.

"What do you want to know?" Atlas asked.

"You said she was a Spartan, right? Start at the beginning and work her timeline."

"As you wish." Atlas tapped a few commands into his phone, and then handed it to me. An old painting was displayed on the screen. A naked woman and a giant swan were standing in an awkward embrace, while two of those naked infant cherubs the Renaissance painters were so fond of played the role of voyeurs.

"Have you heard of Leda and the Swan?" he asked.

"Yeah," I replied. "Part of the Zeus Rape Myth collection, right?"

Atlas closed his eyes just a moment too long, and then said. "Yes. Zeus, highest among the gods, came to Leda as a swan. She was married to Tyndareus, who was one of the kings of Sparta—"

"Spartans had two kings at all times," Darling interrupted. "They felt it stabilized their political system. Tyndareus was the stronger of the two kings of his day."

Atlas waited until his cousin was done before pressing on, trying to sweep me into the cadence of his story. "As the myth goes, Leda had four children, two by Zeus and two by Tyndareus, a boy and a girl each. Helen and Polydeuces emerged from an egg, and Clytemnestra and Castor were birthed as mortals."

"Quadruplets?" Mike asked.

"Possibly, but the myth aligns Castor and Polydeuces as twins, as it also aligns Helen and Clytemnestra. Perhaps Zeus visited Leda more than once."

I grimaced.

"Tyndareus seemed to take pride in the story that two of his royal heirs might have been fathered by a god," Atlas said. "He appeared to favor all four equally, and trained them as he would any Spartan child. Castor and Polydeuces were the heroes of

Sparta, and Helen and Clytemnestra had suitors asking for their hands before they were considered old enough to marry."

"And that would have been…?"

"Age of first menstruation," Darling said, as she drew her knife straight through the center of her fish. "Fourteen or fifteen."

"Nope," I said. "Just nope."

"It was what it was."

"Do you remember what you were like at fourteen?" I asked her. "Nope."

"Yes." Darling glared at Atlas, who was suddenly busy with his phone. "I remember."

"Helen had hundreds of suitors," Atlas continued, as if Darling and I hadn't spoken. "Tyndareus declined them all on her behalf. All of these suitors were powerful men, and many scholars believe that Tyndareus was using Helen's marriage to further Sparta's political reach.

"Some of those suitors did not appreciate being used. Helen was kidnapped by Theseus—"

"Stop," I said, as one of the names I couldn't remember finally clicked in my memory. "*Him*. Who's Theseus?"

Atlas paused. It was not, apparently, one of those questions that made me look especially intelligent. "I think I mentioned him at dinner the other night," he said mildly. "Theseus is one of the best-known figures of the Heroic Age. He is said to be like Helen, the child of both a god and a mortal. He became King of Athens, but he is best known for completing heroic trials."

"He killed the Minotaur," Speedy said.

"Right!" Now I could place the name. "He was the Labyrinth dude."

"David Bowie?" Mike asked, completely deadpan.

"No, his name was Theseus," Atlas said. "He promised to rid Athens of a monster that took a tithe of seven boys and seven girls every seven years. This monster, the Minotaur, was imprisoned in an elaborate maze beneath the city of Crete. Theseus was able to navigate the maze and kill the beast."

"Only because he was helped by Ariadne," Darling cut in. "The King of Crete's daughter. She told him how to best the monster and beat the Labyrinth. After he succeeded, Theseus took her and her younger sister, Phaedra, from Crete, but abandoned Ariadne on an island and married Phaedra instead."

"Man," I said. "Real class act, there."

"It was not the first time he had done such a thing," Darling said. "Theseus had a history of stealing women and then abandoning them. He had many wives, and many more children, but Helen is said to be the last woman he stole."

"Good for Helen," I said. "I bet she gave him hell."

"Perhaps," Atlas said. "Accounts of what befell her while she was his captive are widely different. Some say she was not kidnapped but instead fell in love with him and went willingly, and even bore him children."

I laughed, thinking of a king with blood pouring down his face from where his teeth used to be.

Atlas added, "No matter how Helen came to be with him, the stories agree on what happened to Theseus after she was rescued: he was forced from the throne of Athens. Some sources say he was killed, others say he retired in exile, but they are in agreement on that point."

*Rescued.* There's a relief.

"Did Theseus try to stop Helen from leaving?" I asked.

"The myths put Theseus in the Underworld at the time Helen was rescued," Atlas said. "He had gone to the Underworld to steal Hades' bride, but was imprisoned on a stone."

"In stone?" I asked, imagining Theseus waist-deep in something rock-hard for all eternity. Talk about your perfect ironic punishments.

"No," Atlas said. "The stories say his skin was bound to a stone bench, and he could not remove himself. His cousin, Hercules, finally freed him after many months, but did so by ripping him from the bench. It left Theseus sorely wounded."

"Some versions of that myth claim that Theseus was castrated in the act," Darling added, with maybe a *titch* too much glee.

"In those versions, Hercules tore his cousin from the rock with such force that his legs and buttocks came loose, but his testicles were left behind."

"That is not the most popular version of the Theseus myth, but if myths are grounded in fact, then an injury that resulted in castration would explain why he never took another wife or fathered another child," Atlas said. "Theseus disappeared from public view after Helen was rescued, and the stories that followed his life ceased around the same time."

"What happened to Helen after that?" Mike asked.

"She returned to Sparta with Theseus' mother, Aethra, and all of the women of Aethra's household. Aethra stayed with Helen for most of her adult life as punishment for having played a role in the abduction."

"And then came Helen's marriage to Menelaus," I said. This is where my Wikipedia searches had picked up: I knew that Helen and Menelaus had taken over as King and Queen of Sparta and had ruled for ten years before the whole Trojan War thing got underway. It was nice to know that Evil Dude's Surprisingly Nice Mom—sorry, Aethra—had been wrong and Helen was able to stay in the country she had loved.

"Yes," Atlas said. "As happened with Theseus, no one knows whether Paris kidnapped her or if she went willingly. There are different accounts, and all are said to be true."

Strange, that. Makes you wonder.

# CHAPTER 18

I've committed more than my fair share of crimes in my life, but I've never actually planned any of them. Turns out that when you're killing time before you break into a museum, things slow down to a crawl.

So we went to look for ghosts.

Kos has been settled and resettled over the millennia. Unlike Athens, its Asklepion is a unique site set apart from most other buildings, both old and new. Kos is believed to be the site where modern medicine was first…uh…

Look, I'm in medical school, and I know the majority of medical discoveries tend to come with a body count. Let's just say that Kos was where Hippocrates introduced the idea there might be some questionable ethics involved in cutting patients apart just to see what would happen.

The Asklepion at Kos is *huge*. It's set on the side of a hill, and the view is absolutely killer. Speedy, Mike, and I had ditched the Contentious Cousins back in the city, and it was great to stand alone, quietly, with friends, on top of this marvelous old ruin.

Sorry. *Almost* alone. Believe it or not, a lot of people still travel to the Asklepion to ask the gods for healing. There weren't many of them, but those tourists who had come seeking miracles? You don't travel all the way to an ancient site on an out-of-the-way Greek island for a mild case of eczema. My doctor brain was silently shouting at their loved ones to *get them to a fucking hospital!*

I have a hard time dealing with human misery. There's just so much of it, in so many different forms. All we want to do is live out our lives in peace, and when circumstances mean we can't do that, we crater the peace of those who care about us. When one person suffers, everyone who is connected to them through love suffers, and everyone connected to them suffers, and so on until the love runs out.

Love doesn't run out. That's the best and worst thing about it.

To top it all off? I know for a *fact* that death isn't the end of things. Do you know how refreshing it'd be to tell some of these people that it'll all be okay and soon you'll be able to build your own private Kardashian cave-pool?

But, you know. Then I'm a crazy lady.[12]

"Anything?"

Mike's question brought me back down to earth, and I realized that, yes, I had let my mind wander but, no, I sort of forgot I was supposed to be looking for ghosts and just got pissed off at the futility of the human condition instead.

I settled on saying, "Not so far."

Speedy groaned, the deep heaving sigh of someone who's tired of suffering fools. "Go up and to the left," he said. "Try again at the Avato."

"The whatnow?"

"A meditation center," Mike replied.

"A hallucination station," Speedy snapped. "The Greeks thought the god Asklepios would appear to them in dreams, so they set aside a room at the temple for dream-healing."

"As I said," Mike said, smiling. "A meditation center."

We scaled the old staircase, mostly walking backwards so we could watch Kos drop away below us.

We took the opportunity to wave to those members of Goon Squad 2.0 who had tailed us to the Asklepion.

One of them waved back.

I laughed. "Morons."

"Maybe," Speedy said. "Or maybe they don't care."

I glanced around the Asklepion and spotted a local tour guide an easy distance away. "Shitty place for an ambush. Too

---

12 Sparky asked me once why I wanted to go into medicine when I felt these things so clearly. I said it was because I planned to go down fighting with the corpses of disease and injury in my fists, because those fuckers didn't deserve to keep getting away with their shit.

open. Too many tourists to tell the cops exactly what happened."

Mike nodded. "They'll either wait for us to go somewhere with fewer people, or more of them so nobody's stories will be the same."

"How about we hit the market after this?" I asked them. "Pick up some new souvenirs, lose some unwanted ones?"

Speedy chuckled.

The Avato was a nice place. It probably had a roof on it at some point, but that was long gone. What remained were a bunch of reconstructed columns sticking straight up and supporting nothing but the open air, and the ubiquitous chunks of former buildings lying around. Speedy prodded me until I lay down on one of these, and told me to focus.

"Concentrate." He poked me between the eyes. "You got those beads on you?"

I did: I had strung them on a sturdy hemp lanyard and was wearing them as a necklace. (Yes, I was wearing a priceless artifact. I thought I might need a physical connection with the dead queen. Sorry.) I yanked them from where they had been hiding under my shirt, and let them dangle on their cord.

"Good," he said. "Helen's willing to talk to you, so maybe that'll be your backstage pass to meet the rest of the ancient ghosts."

"She's not talking to me, Speedy. She's shoving her adolescence into my head."

"So? See if you can get Archimedes to start showing up in your dreams. Then we can all go home and you can review the data at leisure."

"There are so many assumptions crammed up the butt of that idea," I sighed.

"Try. I'm getting sick of this country."

"I can't go to sleep on command," I told him.

Mike settled himself beside me on the rock in the lotus position. "Do as I do," he said. "You don't have to sleep, but you should relax."

"Right," I said, and turned myself into an upright pretzel.

We meditated, Mike and I, our eyes closed and our faces tilted up towards the afternoon sun. Speedy kept watch on the edge of the rock, sometimes sitting upright like a chubby gray meerkat.

(All right, I might have peeked a few times. What? We were surrounded by bad 'uns.)

Mike was good to me. He called it after an eternity of ten minutes.

"Nothing," I said.

Speedy sighed and flumped flat on the rock.

Mike knelt on the rock and slowly turned in that aikido shuffle that makes me wonder how he has any knees left. "Question for you," he said, once he had completed his circle. "Would you feel the presence of ghosts if one has already been around you?"

"Don't follow," I said, as I dug into my bag for some water.

"If Helen's here, then—"

"Oh!" Speedy launched to his feet. "Good one. Maybe Helen's already here, and she's got you desensitized to other ghosts."

I blinked at the open stretch of hillside. "If Helen *is* here, and if she's that powerful," I muttered, "why can't I see her? God, this is the culture problem again, I just know it!"

"Call your husband," Speedy said.

"Wouldn't do any good," I said. "That chip in his head doesn't come with an autotranslate program. You're the only one who can communicate with her, and you can't see her, either."

"*He* could see her," Speedy snapped. "And he could pipe in their conversation via your phone, so I could hear it and translate it."

I tried to shoot this one down, but he made a damned good point. "Fine," I said, and hit the button on my ring.

Let me tell you about cyborgs and the out-of-body experience.

Everybody in OACET can take themselves out of their native headspace and put it into a spectral avatar. Mike says it's

basically astral projection, in which the mind can travel outside
of the body, and he says monks and mystics have been doing
this for ages. Cyborgs do this by using electromagnetic fields;
I have no idea how the monks and mystics do it. Sparky and I
use it to keep in touch when we're apart (see: really amazing
cyborg phone sex).

But…

When cyborgs go out-of-body? Their avatars can see ghosts.
All ghosts, not just the super-powerful ones that us psychics can
perceive when our brains are rooted in flesh like normal. We
think it's because their implants help them tune into whatever
frequency the ghosts exist on. Uh…the spectrum in which the
ghosts exist…

Sorry. The metaphysics is (are?) confusing to begin with,
and the language starts tripping it all up. What I'm trying to say
is that the implant removes the barriers between the living and
the dead, and lets one speak with the other.

I **know**, right!? It's a really big fucking deal. In my opinion,
it's an even bigger deal than the implant allowing the cyborgs
to connect to any and all networked machines. Machines are
this *tiiiiiiny* little dot on the timeline of human evolution, but
life and death have walked with us hand-in-hand that whole
freakin' way.

This has given me, Sparky, and the rest of the gang
conniptions. We're trying really, really hard to keep the worlds
of the living and the dead separate. Knowing there's an Afterlife
is the ultimate spoiler, and we're not about to wreck that for
anyone.

(Do *not* get Mike talking about this stuff. Still waters run
deep, and down near the bottom there are hidden rapids: Mike
is fanatical about keeping the Afterlife a secret. He says that life
is about the journey, not the destination. Religion and belief,
despite their balls-out screaming litanies of flaws, have helped
provide a path for everyone from the most devout follower to
the most hardcore atheist, and this path is—arguably—taken
as a matter of choice. Throwing proof of an Afterlife in there

would shatter the ideas that serve as the foundation of those paths. Yeah, they could be rebuilt over time, but who are we to destroy humanity as we know it?[13])

So we try to keep the ghosts a secret. We're not too worried about anyone in OACET accidentally spotting our ghosts—by *our*, I mean those ghosts who are native to the United States and who American psychics can see without too much effort—because our ghosts follow a…dress code of sorts. Unless they're in a place where they feel secure, like my house, our ghosts tend to appear as small blue winged pixies when they're on this side of the mortality line.

Dressing up like creatures of myth is apparently a time-honored tradition among ghosts. They want to keep their existence a secret, too, and the living are much less likely to associate "blue thing" with "dead human" when they can confuse it with "elf" or "chromatically-challenged leprechaun".

Greece has this enormous catalogue of screaming monster-horrors. Also, nymphs. I guess I expected anyone hanging around the Asklepion to look like one of those.

A few moments after I pressed the hidden button on my ring, Sparky arrived in the usual pop of bright green light before he resolved himself into a green facsimile of my husband.

"Hey, Sweetie," he began, and then stopped cold. He straightened, his avatar changing from my casually-dressed husband to a besuited politician in the blink of an eye. "What am I looking at?" he asked.

"You tell us."

"Four ghosts. Three men and one woman. One man in an old-fashioned business suit, two in some sort of armor. The woman is wearing a toga. She's their leader; the way the others are standing means they're deferring to her."

Eh, so much for dress codes.

"Oh, good," I said. "She's the one we want to speak to. We're

13 Seriously. We're a bunch of schmucks and a talking koala, and we know firsthand what happens when you go public with a major conspiracy. Based on humanity's track record, taking an even *bigger* Full Disclosure Bomb to modern civilization will end in blood. War. Probably mass genocide as various factions decide to resolve their old religious disputes. Like hell that's our call to make.

about ninety-nine-point-nine percent sure that's Helen."

"Helen...Helen of *Troy*?"

Do you know how hard it is to get Sparky to crack when he's in politician mode? I grinned like a freakin' lunatic.

"Yeah, she started showing up in my dreams after that hot guy sold me her beads... Never mind, it's a whole long story," I said. "I'm pretty sure we should start calling her Helen of Sparta, though."

"Ah."

And then he bowed. *Bowed.* Like you would to a royal—

Right. I'm not too smart.

I stood and bowed, too. And, since all psychics can see and hear a cyborg's digital avatar, so did Mike.

Speedy, who can also see Sparky's avatar, began to clean himself with loud slurping noises.

"What does she look like?" I whispered to my husband. I had to ask: that gangly girl in my dreams wouldn't be launching ships any time soon. Past-soon. Thing. God*damn* I hate time travel.

"Not what you expect," he whispered back. Then, louder and not to me: "Do you speak English?"

A long pause.

"Speedy?" Sparky said, still staring at what seemed to be absolutely nothing. "Introduce us in Greek, and ask them if we might have their permission to talk via an electronic device. Face the same direction I'm facing, and use the dialect Helen would have spoken, please."

The koala grunted and scampered off of the stone block to where Sparky's avatar was standing, and...

Well.

I *could* do a line-by-line of what happened, but let's just say we lived through a kids' riddle, the kind where it seems like there's an easy answer but it's mostly just confusion in need of a punchline. Even the ghosts didn't speak the same dialect of Greek, so Speedy had to translate not once but multiple times. This is the gist of it:

> Koala chatter in Greek >> Ghosts debating
> amongst themselves >> Ghosts replying to
> Sparky >> Koala translation in English >>
> Debate amongst the living >> Koala chatter in
> Greek >> Ghosts debating amongst themselves
> >> Ghosts replying to Sparky >> Wash, rinse,
> repeat for thirty minutes.

By the time we were finished, the ghosts understood that
we were looking for the Antikythera Mechanism. Sparky had
shown them a green digitized image of the machine, and the
ghosts were extremely excited to learn we were hunting for
information on its creation. It also seemed they were willing
to help; Helen said that she was good friends with Archimedes,
and she knew exactly where to find him.

(Which meant that Archimedes was still around and *eeeie!*)

There are a few other takeaways from this conversation.

I finally saw adult Helen of Sparta's face in my cell phone.
Yes, she's absolutely breathtakingly beautiful, but so's Mount
Everest. If you've been thinking of Helen as the approachable
kind of beauty, the kind you find in a sunlit meadow with flowers
and butterflies? Rethink that *right fucking now*. She's a frozen
murder mountain. I now sincerely believe that face could have
really launched a thousand ships; I also believe those ships were
sailing in the opposite direction to get the hell away from her.

She was impressed that I had managed to acquire what was
left of her necklace. I tried to get her to promise to stop coming
into my dreams, but she arched one eyebrow and I felt my teeth
clench shut. Dreams. Good. Yes. Hello, Queen Helen, please
make yourself at home in my head.

And that one last thing.

This is the part that weirded me the hell out, and I'm going
to retell it without the confusing pauses in translation so you
can share in my panic attack.

Half an hour was all that Sparky would allow himself for out-of-body travel. It's physically taxing: projecting and maintaining an image of yourself halfway around the world is *exhausting*. Not many other cyborgs could spend that much time in their avatars all the way in Greece, and the only reason Sparky can do it is because he's got enough metabolic mass to offset the energy consumption requirements of his chip. Towards the end, his avatar was getting slightly blurry around the edges.

That's when (I'm told) Helen grabbed my face in both hands and looked me straight in the eyes.

"I am tired of this world," she said. "The beast waits below the island. Set us both free."

Now. That's what happened from Sparky's perspective.

From mine? I felt my head seized by invisible hands with incredibly strong fingers, and a cold chill settle into my stomach as a frozen wind roared wordlessly in my ears.

People, I ask you, is it any wonder that normals are terrified by ghosts? I knew what was happening (husband calling my name in an eerily calm voice, koala translating the words of a furious dead queen, Mike holding onto my hands so I didn't slug said queen in her invisible jaw…), and I'm still poking the goosebumps back into place.

Then? She was gone, along with her ghostly entourage, and Sparky left to go back to his own body a moment later.

The three of us living non-cyborgs found ourselves standing on a sunny stretch of the Asklepion, with at least eight Hired Goons surrounding us in a loose circle some distance away, confused expressions slapped all up and down their faces.

"We doing this here?" I asked them. When they didn't answer, Speedy translated my question into Greek.

The one who had waved at me before just smiled.

"Right," I said, and me, Mike, and Speedy set off down the hill to pick a place to have a fight.

# CHAPTER 19

Let me tell you the most annoying thing about politics.

Politics doesn't operate on just one level. Political maneuvering operates within its own nigh-infinite sphere of influence, stretching across time and space and persons and communities, and if you think that an offhand comment you made to a friend in the sixth grade can't come back to bite you when you're running for office forty years later, you're a sucker who deserves what's coming.

What I'm saying is, yes, someone had paid a bunch of dudes to beat us up, but causing us pain and inconvenience wasn't their primary purpose. Creating bad press for OACET was one likely reason. Disrupting our efforts to find more information on the Mechanism was another. Then there was the Occam's Razor explanation, which was that whoever hired these dudes (yes, yes, that would be Hanlon, thanks) is just a dick.

But the most likely reason we were getting hired goons thrown at us was because they were a distraction.

Eight goons is an *insult*. Either Mike or I working alone wouldn't have broken a sweat on eight goons; put us together and the goons stood slightly as much chance as a snowball in a bonfire. If, however, we were forced to focus on an obvious threat, that would leave us vulnerable to a sneak attack from an unseen opponent.

My money was on Atlas.

Oh, he wouldn't sneak in to stab us in the kidneys while we were fighting the goons or anything like that, but if you're concentrating on a big threat *here*, it's easy to ignore a small threat *there*. He could swipe any information we found and funnel it back to Hanlon, and we might never be the wiser because we're focused on the big looming Gooncloud on the horizon.

Why Atlas? Well, as soon as I had learned that he had worked with Hanlon, I had both him and Darling checked out by OACET's team of world-class information specialists. Atlas had been in contact with Hanlon much more recently than he had claimed; the phone calls had begun flying back and forth as soon as Ambassador Goodwin had contacted him and asked him to work with me.

On the other hand, Darling seemed to be a good penny: no connections between her and Hanlon had turned up. That didn't mean she wasn't running a con on us with her cousin, but she honestly hated that guy. I think she'd side with me, Mike, and Speedy out of spite.

The goons followed us down the mountainside. We hadn't hired a car or taken the bus or anything, as the Asklepion was an easy (for us) walking distance from our hotel.

When we hit the road, Mike and I started running, with Speedy sitting pretty on Mike's shoulders.

Poor hired goons.

The Asklepion is set on a lovely old mountain with a nice, gentle slope down towards Kos Town. If you're taking a car, it's a smooth and winding road to the top. If you're on foot and you follow the road, you're probably going to get a little puffy.

If you leave the road and sprint down the side of the mountain, nobody short of a mountain goat will be able to do anything about it.

Mike and I ran the three-plus miles back to town. Four of the goons had tried to follow on foot; the other four had gone to their rental cars and were trying to box us in so they could stop and beat us up, but we were having none of that and those cheap sedans weren't built to go offroad. Mike and I ran over rough terrain until the goons on foot were exhausted, and then we put on some real speed. The four jogging goons waved down their friends and piled into the cars. As soon as they did that, Mike and I jumped a nearby highway divider and ran straight down a steep hill into the center of Kos Town.

Kos Town is an old, old city. There are ruins every which way, and streets better suited for carts than cars. The marketplace stretches out over a few blocks, and while most of it has been polished and paved to a nice modern standard, there's a few spots that are ripe for some good old-fashioned pandemonium.

The Kos Market Hall is a lovely indoor shopping venue. We had walked around there the day before, scouting locations and sampling the local foods.

The three of us thought we might have to wreck a good part of it.

Mike and I breezed through the archways that led to the marketplace, a grand total of zero hired goons behind us: parking in Kos Town can be tricky. If we had lost them? Good! We didn't think that anyone would risk jumping us in the middle of a crowded marketplace. A quiet winding road down a mountain, or an alley off of a busy street where everyone is minding their own business? Yes, definitely, pass the brass knuckles. But we thought we would be safe here.

If we weren't? Well, we had picked this marketplace for a reason.

The three of us pretended to browse, returning to many of the same vendors we had visited yesterday. Speedy had taken a liking to an old woman who was selling salted seaweeds, and we killed time with her, gnawing on samples of something I can only describe as asparagus jerky.

Her booth was positioned in front of an alcove. More of a short hallway, really. As best as we could tell, this hallway led to a bunch of stockrooms that were always kept locked. Maybe the owners had a problem with theft, I dunno, but if the goon squad showed up again?

We might have to put that hallway to good use.

Mike and I put ourselves with our backs against the wall, and munched on pieces of seaweed while Speedy told filthy jokes in Greek. The old lady laughed as she scratched Speedy behind his ears, while her fellow shopkeepers and an assortment of locals and tourists gathered around the koala.

Just when we thought we were in the clear, the hired goons began to pop up in the crowd.

"Twelve, thirteen, fourteen…" Mike said quietly, all the while browsing a pamphlet on local restaurants. "They called in reinforcements."

"Show of force," I replied. "They know they aren't going to jump us here."

"There's enough of them to make a reasonable 'Come along quietly or else' argument."

"Well, then," I said, as I rolled my shoulders as nonchalantly as I could. "Let's get this over with."

I took a few steps away from the crowd, pointed at the Smiling Goon, and followed it up with that *come here* crooked-finger gesture. He did, still grinning.

"English?" I asked.

He nodded.

"There are security guards all around us," I said. "You were hired by a third party. Trust me, the guy signing the checks doesn't care if you go to jail. Walk away."

"No," Smiling Goon said, his gaze crawling over the marketplace. We were a goodly distance away from the nearest doors, and it would be hard for him to get us out without making a scene. He flipped open his jacket in a practiced move to give me a quick glimpse of his gun. "Come with us and no one will be hurt."

"Let's do this the easy way," I said to him, and opened my bag to show him a huge stack of Euros. "You're getting paid to beat us up, but not kill us. Otherwise, you'd have taken a few shots at us when we were running down the mountain. Take the money, go back to your boss, and tell him you did your job. Hell, I'll give myself a black eye and walk with a limp for the rest of the week to make you look good."

"No need to rush into a decision," Mike said. He had found an enormous fruit smoothie somewhere, and was working his way down through the strata of pinks and oranges. "Talk it over with your friends. We'll be waiting for your answer."

They did. The hired goons actually *did*. They huddled up and had a hushed meeting about the most logical course of action, and I thought maybe we'd be able to bribe our way out of this one.

"Nope," Speedy's voice came behind us, his ears perked forward to catch every whisper. Some of the folks who spoke English glanced up, wondering what he was talking about; the security guard standing close enough to listen in on Speedy's jokes wasn't among them. "No go. They'll take the money, leave, and then jump us as soon as they can get us somewhere without cops."

"Aw hell," I grumbled. "I hate it when these guys are smart enough to double up on their profit."

The goons broke apart and started to circle us, trying to keep us boxed in while still acting as if they were preparing to leave. Whee, threats.

Smiling Goon came back. "Yes," he said. "We accept your deal."

I hesitated until he scowled and held out his hands. "Money, please."

"Are you *robbing* me?!" I shouted, and clutched my bag to my chest.

The smile vanished from his face in a heartbeat as our trap snapped shut. The security guard came a few steps closer.

Now, this is the part where I was hoping we'd get lucky.

If we got lucky, Smiling Goon would do the math, count the bystanders and the guards and the cameras, and take his posse and leave until things cooled down. We'd still have to deal with them later, but they wouldn't try again until the next day, and by then we might have left town.

If we weren't lucky, Smiling Goon or one of his coworkers would rush us, and it'd be on.

Smiling Goon was definitely the best banana in this bunch. His eyes moved across the crowd, and he took a few steps backwards, his hands up in the air and that too-familiar *What is this crazy lady talking about?* expression on his face.

Sadly? His buddies were too amped to power down.

No luck for us.

Plenty of fun, though.

The man closest to me grabbed my hand and yanked, and I pretended to fall off-balance with a loud scream that got the attention of anyone not already watching. Another goon took a swing at Mike, who turned his smoothie over and dumped the contents on the floor as he stepped out of the path of the man's fist as easily as if he were dodging a leaf on the breeze. But, instead of returning his punch, Mike seemed to trip and fall straight at the goon, and somehow ended up in the goon's half nelson. The goon was quite surprised at that, but didn't question his good fortune and clamped down on the lock.

Smiling Goon and two others turned and ran. Smart.

Or maybe they had just seen Speedy.

Remember when I said that you need to deal with Speedy straightaway, or Bad Things Happen?

The goons had focused on me and Mike, and had allowed Bad Things to Happen.

A low noise started to reverberate within the marketplace. Koalas don't growl, bark, or yip, but if they're decently pissed-off, they can combine all three of these into a sound somewhere between a frog in a blender and a tornado siren. This noise started to creep into his steady stream of profanity, giving his cursing an otherworldly vibrato that I felt more with my spine than heard with my ears. Speedy seemed to grow in size as his fur stood on end. His claws began tapping on the tile countertop in a sharp staccato, a warning for anyone with the sense to understand it.

Then? He *lunged*.

Speedy didn't get his name from his smarts—he is faster than fast. Our default image of koalas is that they are sleepy, dopey dumps of fur. No. Sleeping and creeping are lifestyle choices. Physiologically, koalas can move like cracked-out squirrels if they feel the urge.

And if a koala wants to move?

*Get out of its way!*

Speedy is a practical soul. He took out the nearest goon by springing straight at his face and going for his eyes. He missed, but only because the goon covered his eyes in time. This, unfortunately, left the tender skin of his ears exposed, and Speedy went to town with his teeth.

The goon slipped in the chunky wet crap of Mike's smoothie and fell, screaming. Speedy launched himself off of the goon's head onto a nearby banner, and scrambled up a dozen feet before he dropped onto a second goon. This time, he reached the goon's eyes, and then was off of the second man's shoulders and airborne towards a third victim.

The third goon covered his eyes and ears the instant he realized the koala had targeted him. Speedy unleashed those inch-long claws and went for his mouth instead.

I should mention that throughout this carnage, Speedy is laughing in that multitoned vibrato like a fucking maniac.

It was…disturbing.

Before the rest of the goons could react to those five seconds of koala-perpetuated horror, Mike reached up to grab the wrists of the man holding him in the headlock. There was a brief flash of panic on the goon's face, and then he was airborne.

The *kotegaeshi* throw was perfect. The goon landed in the hallway and slid down the length of it, with Mike blocking the only exit.

It was time for me to go to work.

I grabbed my own goon by his shirt and flipped him towards Mike. Mike grabbed him out of the air and tossed him down the tunnel, disarming him in the process.

Two in the hole, three had scarpered, and Speedy had put four on the floor.

Six goons left. They closed in on Speedy, trapping him on the weeping wreckage of his fourth victim.

I ran forward, calling for Speedy. "Catch him!" I shouted. "Please catch my little koala! *Fifty thousand Euros to the person who brings him back to me unharmed!*"

Bingo bango bedlam.

The marketplace had gone stone-still the instant that Speedy had erupted into violence. Nobody thinks of self-preservation when a small cuddly animal is involved. It's like watching a kitten run amok with a chainsaw—it's so surreal that it takes you a minute to realize that the red stuff isn't ketchup. The promise of money got the tourists and locals to break out of their torpor; those who understood English leapt into action, and those who spoke Greek followed as soon as the translation reached them. They knocked the goons aside in their rush to get to Speedy, who had managed to run straight up one of the tourists and climb onto another handy overhead banner.

One of the six goons still standing was reaching into his jacket. I doubted he was going for his wallet, so I targeted him next. Left hand on his shirt, right hand on his pants, and I swept his legs out from under him before lobbing him towards Mike in a fast *tomoenage.*

"Gun!" I warned.

"Got it!" Mike called.

*Tomoenage* is a sacrifice throw in judo, so I was on the floor when the next goon rushed me, thinking I was easy kickings. I screamed and made a show of scrambling away, but—clumsy me!—I accidentally slammed a foot against his legs, bending both of his knees sideways. I grabbed his shirt as he started to fall, and ended up on my feet with enough momentum to bring the goon with me in a roll.

I finished the roll. The goon ended up on the end of Mike's receiving throw, and joined his buddies in our makeshift prison.

Four goons left.

Oops, my mistake. Four and a half: one of the goons Speedy had maimed was struggling towards an exit. It wasn't even a trick to spin this guy over my hip and put him back on the ground, and then kick him across the wet floor towards Mike.

Above me, Speedy laughed as he shouted obscenities in a dozen dead languages.

I spun on the wet floor and hooked an ankle under another

goon. This guy was a big 'un, at least twice my size and built like a muscly tree. He toppled over like one, too; I heard his head bounce off the concrete.

I pretended to slip as I was getting up, and toppled over sideways. Another one of Speedy's victims had recovered enough to bring himself to crawl for cover, and I fell into a *dakiwakare* where I grabbed him as I was moving and then threw him towards Mike.

The last three goons were trying to rally and close as a group. None of them were making that inner jacket grab-hand gesture that came along with a gun, but they were mad. Like, *mad*-mad. They rushed me all at once, thinking that superior size and numbers gave them the advantage. Wrong. Not in a crowded marketplace in which everyone around you is hollering and stomping and trying to climb up shopping venues to grab the koala full of money.

I swept the leg.

Literally. One move, six legs. Wet floors are *amazing*.

I punted two of the goons towards Mike, who hooked them neatly into the hallway to join the rest.

"Shufflecock!" Speedy laughed gleefully from above.

"*Shuttle*cock!" I yelled back. "Shufflecock is something else!"

"I know!" He ran across a set of suspended lights, maneuvering to position himself directly above Mike.

I glanced at that last goon. Sure enough, his pants had fallen down around his knees, and between that and the leftover smoothie, he couldn't quite get himself upright.

"Fair enough," I muttered, and gave his shoulders a push with my feet to send him sliding into our holding cell.

Speedy dropped down from the light fixture and landed safely in Mike's outstretched arms.

Then all that was left was, as the man once said, some 'splaining to do.

The market was locked down—no one in, no one out—to process what had happened. That wasn't as bad as it sounds: the goons had guns, the market had security cameras, and we had a ton of witnesses who *almost* remembered what had happened but they were busy chasing a koala and didn't someone say something about fifty thousand Euros? With the exception of being covered in smoothie, Mike and I came out of it clean.

Speedy, not so much. He had maimed four dudes, after all, even if those dudes had been trying to rob his friend-slash-owner, and Kos Town didn't look favorably on dangerous animals running loose...

I sighed and gave the cops a stack of Euros to make sure they wrote off the incident as a random monkey attack,[14] and let them know that I would supply the monkey if necessary.

Mike placed a call to Ambassador Goodwin to prep him for any problematic questions from reporters, and asked him to direct any questions about monkeys to the local zoo.

Once the goon squad was hauled off, the checkbook came out again to pay for damages (again, *sigh*), and the rest of those Euros in my bag went to buying the crowd dinner as thanks for trying to help me retrieve my poor lost koala. We turned the marketplace into our own giant reception hall, with the locals teaching us tourists the old Greek drinking songs. Most of those songs had been around since before there was an America. I think some of them had been around since before there was an *England*.

At some point, I sobered up enough to run the room again. I had been doing this all night, of course, but nobody had struck me as weird or dangerous, and now that the doors to the market were locked, I wasn't too worried about Smiling Goon and his remaining buddies popping up for a repeat of the main event.

My eyes roamed over the crowd. Most of the folks there were seriously drunk. I only spotted her because she was sitting quietly by herself.

Darling was four tables down.

She had lost that fantastic jacket, and was wearing the same jeans and short-sleeved shirts as the other women around

---

14 There are more than fifty recent unsolved monkey attacks in the Washington D.C. area. Sparky and I have a monkey in reserve, just in case. Don't worry about what might happen to the monkey. That monkey knows what it did.

her. She had done something different with her hair, and was actually rather pretty in the low light.

And she had been there the entire time.

# CHAPTER 20

You know all of those movies and television shows and comic books where the hero is keeping watch on a rooftop?

Why don't any of those end with the hero toppling forward and tipping off the ledge because keeping watch on a rooftop is *so damned boring* that you can't possibly help but nod off every ten minutes or so?

The Library of Alexandria—what was left of this particular branch—was kept in a museum basement. I had pulled first shift on the roof to keep watch for cops and goons, so that's as much as I knew about it.

Forty feet below me, a door in the back alley opened, and Mike's red hair popped out. I whistled softly, and he scooted up a nearby drainpipe to join me on the museum's roof.

"This is fun," he said, as I handed him the oversized dark hoodie I had been using for camouflage. "It's too bad security is so tight on the museums back home. I could see us sneaking into the Smithsonian on girls' night."

"Sit up here for an hour and then we'll talk," I said. "You guys find anything?"

"Not yet. Speedy's tackling the contents of the room like a general planning a battle. When he strikes, it'll be over before you know it. I think we'll be able to get out of here tonight."

"Nifty," I said, and gave him a quick kiss on the top of his head before I jumped over the parapet and slid down the drain pipe.

Darling was holding the door open for me. "You two can do this?" she said, looking towards where Mike was safely hidden on the roof. "Climb up and down buildings?"

"It's not hard," I said. "The biggest thing you have to worry about is when the drainpipes aren't properly secured to the wall. *That* gets real tricky, real quick."

"Ah," she said, still looking up. "Could you teach me?"

"Sure," I said, before thinking that through to the point where I realized that yes, a thief would certainly find scaling the sides of buildings to be a handy ability. "If we've got time."

Darling grinned at me; I hadn't fooled her in the slightest. "Of course."

The two of us had had a long chat after the marketplace had gone off of lockdown, with me telling her how I found it really, *really* sketchy that she had played stranger and hidden in plain sight for hours.

She hadn't even blinked. Instead, she asked me if I was okay being interviewed by cops while in the company of a known local criminal.

Point.

So why was she in the market in the first place?

Because she had happened to be getting a bite to eat when she saw her employer running down the side of a mountain in full view of the entire town, and by the time she finally found said employer, there was a major brawl underway.

Aaaaand point.

I swear, I'm too involved in conspiracies these days. Sometimes I can't see the forest for those bright red dots from the sniper rifles.

(Still. I had asked Sparky to run her phone records and email history again, just in case. I might trust you as far as I can throw you—twenty-plus feet on a good day—but I hang out with dead dudes who can tell you the best stories about what a fabulous drinking buddy Benedict Arnold used to be. I live and learn so I can live some more.)

"Tell me about this place," I said, as she and I entered the building.

"This?" she said, with an offhand shrug. "It is just a museum. The best items from Kos were taken to Athens years ago. This is just for the tourists, and for those studying at university."

"Have you ever stolen anything from here?"

Darling didn't reply, but I saw the corners of her eyes crinkle as she kept herself from smiling. She took me down a dark corridor and through another door, and then I was standing in the Library of Alexandria.

It had seen better days.

I guess I had expected it was residing in something space-age, with low white lights illuminating long glass cabinets, their drawers stuffed full of ancient knowledge. Nope. Think: shitty vinyl record collection in a teenager's bedroom. Oh, and the kid has painted the walls black and hung a trash bag across the window to keep the light out.

No idea why the room smelled like feet, but there it was.

Don't get me wrong; the old parchments and whatnot hadn't been shoved into piles and left to rot. Everything was preserved between two airtight sheets of flexible Plexiglas, and cardboard bankers' boxes were stacked to the ceiling. At one time, the room had probably been tidy and organized, but years of scholars doing exactly what we were doing had left it in a state of disarray. There was a thick layer of dust across every surface, and the trash cans were overflowing (ah, there's the source of the foot stink). Maintenance hadn't touched this room in a long time.

"I think I need a shower," I said as I looked around the room. "This is just sad."

"Money." Speedy's voice came from behind a wall of bankers' boxes, where Atlas was helping him navigate their contents. "This stuff isn't a priority."

"It's the Library of Alexandria!"

"It's a bunch of old papers," he replied, his nose nearly pressed flat against a document as he squinted to make out a line of tiny text. "Greece has got a metric fuckton of those. Besides, they digitized the best stuff in these archives ten years ago. Now, shut up."

I grumbled something about backup systems and the value of originals, and went to tour the room.

It looked just as bad from the other side. There were tables in the center to serve as workstations, but no chairs. Darling had moved a few boxes from the top of an old filing cabinet and was sitting on this; Speedy and Atlas had staked out the floor.

"Mike thought this was fun?" I asked myself.

"He was helping us organize," Speedy said. "Either get busy or get back on the roof."

"Yup," I said, and moved towards the tables to see what I could do to speed things along.

I swear I didn't feel any ghosts in the Library—I definitely wasn't expecting one of them to offer their own version of help.

Ten feet behind me, two bankers' boxes toppled forward from a single stack, and the lid popped off of a third. A sheet of acrylic-encased parchment leaped out of that third box and fell on the floor with a plasticy *fhwop!*

Atlas made a little yipping noise; Darling whispered something in Greek and made the sign of the Cross. Speedy twitched an ear, but didn't look up from his papers.

"Oops," I said with a shrug. "Clumsy me. I'll go clean that up."

I went to see what the ghost had pulled from the stacks.

So what if I hadn't felt the presence of ghosts? That didn't mean much, since no ghost had been able to push my psychic buttons since Helen had come along. Hey, as far as I knew, the ghost who knocked the boxes over had been Helen herself.

I shoved the two boxes back on top of the third, and took the parchment over to one of the tables.

"*Katadesmos,*" I read, testing the strange word. "Hey, Speedy—"

The koala held up a clawed finger, as if testing the wind. "Fuck yourself in your primary pig hole," he said.

"Right. Darling? Can you translate something for me?"

"Perhaps," she said, warily circling the tables until she had convinced herself that the boxes toppling over was just a freak accident. "My knowledge of some of the ancient dialects is not very good."

Darling didn't do herself justice; it only took her a few

moments to work through the text. "I recognize this," she said. "It is a copy of a document by Tacitus in which he describes the death of an emperor's adopted son."

"Thrilling," I muttered.

"Well, yes," she said, her finger running across the Plexiglas to keep track of her place. "Germanicus was an exceptional Roman military leader, but he did not die a natural death. Tacitus claims he was affected by an illness of magical origin. A rival, Piso, is believed to have cursed Germanicus using several different methods of witchcraft, including the *katadesmos* you mentioned."

"What's that?" I asked.

"A curse tablet," she said. "They have been found all over ancient Greco-Roman territories. They are a scrap of soft lead inscribed with a curse, and pierced with nails or other sharp objects. The Greeks and Romans believed in magic, very deeply. They felt it was a force that bound them to the world."

I nodded; the OACET dossier on the Antikythera Mechanism contained a large section on astronomy and fortune-telling. The fragment of the Mechanism that Rachel and Santino had found was an inscription to show how the machine could be used to plot an astrologic calendar. Curses and astrology weren't the same sorts of things, but they were close enough to share a shelf at the local book store.

"Superstition was a tremendous motivating force in almost all ancient cultures," Atlas said from across the room. "The Greeks were no different."

"I think they were," Darling said, as she slid the page in its protective plastic towards me. "Most cultures tended to impose curses that lasted long after the victim had died. The Greeks and Romans tended to end their curses at the moment of the victim's death. I feel that was because their version of the afterlife had rewards and punishments that suited the deeds committed by each person in life."

I remembered Mike's discussion with Ambassador Goodwin, where he described the punishments of Sisyphus and Tantalus in the Greek afterlife. I knew those stories well—I pay close attention to any story about an afterlife, an Afterlife, or any limbo in between—and Darling was dead-on (hah). The wicked and evil got stuck in Tartarus, that realm of Hades in which eternal torment was tailor-made. Maybe those who used a curse tablet didn't want to step on any god's toes.

"Neat," I said, and went to return the parchment to its box.

So.

Somebody—Helen?—wanted me to learn about ancient curses.

That wasn't ominous at all.

# CHAPTER 21

While in Aphidna, I kept to the regime that I had followed since I was a child: five hours a day to the strength of the mind; five hours a day to the strength of the body; five hours a day to the strength of the spirit.

Aethra was the perfect hostess. At first, she no doubt indulged me in my habits as she felt I'd outgrow them, the soft living of her city lulling me to apathy. She allowed me to shave my head and dress as the local boys, to run for miles across the countryside, to return with wild deer and boar for her table. When my breasts began to grow and I could no longer hide in public, she filled a courtyard with sand and began to hire mercenaries.

I learned much from them. They came from distant lands, and brought with them strange and unfamiliar ways to fight. They taught me new techniques for using a sword, to fight with fists and feet. The women of Aethra's household would watch as I fell, time and again, and as I would stand again after each time I was knocked to the ground.

"Doesn't it hurt?" one of the serving girls asked, as we poured clean water to wash the blood from the sand.

"Of course it hurts," I replied. "But today, this blood isn't mine."

When I wasn't fighting, Aethra taught me what it meant to be a queen.

At home in Sparta, I had had tutors teach me the rules of royalty. How to sit and stand properly. How to dress. How the fashions of the hair and face must be *just so* in one kingdom, and *just so* in another.

Those lessons had taught me nothing.

Aethra let me walk with her as she ran the business of the

city. Aphidna was small in comparison to Athens or Sparta, but it was a border town and there were travelers aplenty. Most of these travelers respected Aethra, and spoke to her as an equal.

Some did not.

I was confused, at first. Aethra, the daughter of one king, the mother of another, plucked and tuned the myriad strands of the busy city until it played a fine song. She was clearly a queen, and just as clearly the source of power in Aphidna. Hers was the voice that decided matters from large to small, and while the townspeople often questioned her decisions, she would sit with them and persuade them to come around to her way of thinking.

Those travelers who declared that they would not discuss matters of economy or politics with her were rarely brutes. They were quiet and soft-spoken, with intelligent eyes. Aethra kept men of her own to manage such travelers. Her men had wise faces and well-trimmed beards, and when they spoke, their words were the queen's.

Once in a long while, the travelers would realize they were still receiving instructions from Aethra, and then they would demand to see the prince.

Aethra would smile as she granted their request.

Aphidnus disgusted all who saw him, a slovenly lump of flesh on a gilded throne. He had been gifted the city some years before, but his best and greatest fortune was that Theseus' mother resided in Aphidna and she needed something to do with her time. No sane man with a working mind should be satisfied with the prince when they had the option of Aethra, yet those soft-spoken travelers who insisted on meeting with him seemed to prefer his judgment over hers.

Aphidnus knew nothing—nothing!—of how the city was managed, and those who followed his advice tended to end in ruin. And yet, so many of those soft-spoken men allowed themselves to be guided by his words. Once they left the city, we could be certain that we would never see them again…at least, not as wealthy, worldly traders.

I watched this pattern repeat itself again and again, and I could not puzzle it out. It seemed a fool's decision. Why, then, did these men who were *not* fools continue to make it?

"Principle," Aethra told me when I finally decided I could not resolve this question without her help. We were walking through the marketplace, the queen's daily custom to allow her to assess the mood of the town. "They would rather suffer the outcomes of poor advice than consider that wisdom can come from an unfamiliar source. Placing principle above sense is so often the ruin of us."

"Because you are a woman," I decided.

"No." Aethra shook her head. "Because I am not what they expected, or wanted, or felt they deserved. Most of those men think that the prince is wise, because why else would he be the prince? Those men decided the word of the prince trumps the word of all others long before they reached our walls. Wisdom from any other source is of no value to them.

"Here is a lesson for you, Helen," said the queen. "Men who refuse to hear women are easy to recognize. They are also easy to rule. Such men ask for a woman's opinion, but what they want is their own turned into honeyed words to make it sound all the sweeter. Easy, then, to put your own thoughts in such a man's head and make him think they are his own.

"Those who follow principle?" Here, Aethra paused to inspect the walls of her city. They stood strong and tight around us. She placed a hand on my arm, and the two of us resumed our walk. "They are dangerous, because they feel in their hearts they know the right of it. You can change a mind with little effort; changing a heart is near to impossible. Listen to me: when you come up against a man who follows principle above reason, you must decide whether it is worth going to war with him, and if it is not, you step out of his way and let him follow his path to its end."

# CHAPTER 22

I coughed myself awake.

Mike woke when I did, lifting his head from my shoulder like a sleepy wolf's. He took a quick glance at our surroundings, determined we were still on the ferry to Rhodes, and stretched.

"What?" he asked.

"Helen," I replied. "She's back. Don't worry!" I added quickly, as Mike's face had fallen. "It was a good memory. Aethra was showing her how to be a queen."

"I hoped those dreams had stopped," Mike said. "We've met her—twice! There's no reason for her to keep ambushing your dreams."

Mike was right. About how we had met Helen a second time, that was. That very morning, in fact. The five of us were sitting in a café, planning that night's raid on the Library, when the entire restaurant turned into a localized hurricane of flying glass and utensils.

Helen doesn't have a mute button, so Mike, Speedy, and I had a few frantic moments of lying and shoving and kicking the Petrakis cousins until they got the hell out of the café. We ended up in a (very) small supply closet, with my (very) tired husband who had just finished a (very) long day of congressional hearings and needed to grab a quick five hours of sleep before a (very) important meeting with the President of the United States and who was Not In The Mood For Such Shenanigans.

The moment Sparky's avatar popped into our space, I managed to blurt out that someone—a powerful dead ghost, most likely Helen—probably wanted to talk to us because stores don't usually have maelstroms and maybe we should have set up some sort of communication system before we had disbanded at the Kos Asklepion.

Sparky's gaze moved from my face to a space a few inches away. "Yes," he said coldly. "It's Helen."

He held up a hand, as if halting someone mid-speech. "Speedy, please translate: Helen, we are doing our part to keep the worlds of the living and the dead separate. We *cannot* stop our activities to address your needs without notice, and disrupting the mortal world *will* cause undue attention. We thank you in advance for your assistance."

By the time Speedy was done translating, Sparky had linked my phone to his perspective. It allowed me to see Helen's predatory eyes as they moved from his face to mine.

I felt like I was being *weighed*.

I stuck an arm out to lean on the nearest wall, my arm passing through my husband's digital body, and the two of us glared in the same general direction.

She nodded to us before she spoke in Greek.

Speedy chuckled.

"What?" I asked.

"She says that the kings and queens of her time announced themselves at the first meeting, not the second."

"Tell her we had shit to do," I said. "Now, what does she want?"

Turns out that Helen had gotten in touch with Archimedes' ghost, and had arranged a meeting for us on Rhodes. She was vague on the specifics, but the gist of it was that when Archimedes was in our world, he divided his time between Rhodes and an island somewhere out at sea. Archimedes had agreed to meet us on Rhodes to discuss the Mechanism.

(Personally, I thought that a teleporting ghost could come and see us much more easily than we could go to see him, but apparently Archimedes hadn't become any less reclusive or geeky after his death. Still, I'd never been to Rhodes and I wasn't about to look a gift eccentric hermit ghost in the mouth.[15])

After that, it was just a matter of coming up with a story that Atlas and Darling would believe.

They were standing outside the café with the staff and the

---

15  If I could see him. Which I probably couldn't. Whatever. I got to go to Rhodes.

rest of the patrons. Helen had wrecked the place. *Wrecked* it. There was nothing left untouched except the windows and the counters. Mike, Speedy, and I were the only living things that had stayed inside during Helen's page, and passing off what had happened was…uh…difficult.

Not with the locals, mind! With them, we shrugged and gasped and thanked our lucky stars we hadn't been hurt. But Atlas and Darling wanted a good reason to explain why we had spent hours plotting out a strategy for our second search of the Library, and now we were ditching that entire plan to go to Rhodes. Especially when I claimed to have received a hot tip that new information had turned up on Rhodes (true), and we had to get there as quickly as possible or we could lose our source (also true).

Then, Darling pointed at the café and wanted to know how in God's name I had managed to take a phone call when all of *that* had been going on!

The discussion got a little heated. Eventually, I had to apply the *"Because I said so!"* brakes, and sent everybody to their respective hotel rooms to pack.

After they were gone, I went to write a substantial check for damages to the café. Bad economy, rampaging guilt, faulty ghost-paging system… Pick a reason. Ben Franklin made me stupid-rich so I can deal with stuff like this when it comes up.

Which it does.

Usually three times a week or so.

Since I was nineteen.

(I used to drink. A lot. Then I helped expose a conspiracy theory and got famous. Now, I just write checks and take an aspirin.)

The journey to Rhodes was a short hop between the islands. We took the ferry. The cousins disappeared with Speedy to discuss the best way to approach a "hot tip" on Rhodes, and, after a quick preventative sweep of the boat for Smiling Goon and his two remaining buddies, Mike and I crashed on a bench in the sun.

Sunlight, Mediterranean sea air, and a smooth-running ferry is the perfect recipe for a nap.

Hello again, Helen.

"She shouldn't be coming into your head," Mike said, after I had described the dream. "It was understandable before we made contact, but now..." He trailed off, looking across the water. The thin haze of an island was starting to emerge on the horizon.

"I don't know if ancient queens have the same opinions about psychosocial boundaries that we do."

"That's irrelevant," he said. "If she can invade your mind to the extent where she can send dreams to you, she could talk to you directly. She's decided she'd rather impose her thoughts over yours. In my opinion, that's an unforgivable violation."

I grunted and pretended he wasn't completely right.

He paused before he said, "I got a reply from my mother."

"Oh?" I said in a very small voice.

Let me tell you about the Old Families.

I'm a terrible psychic because I shouldn't exist. There's maybe three hundred of us—real psychics, that is, not the carnival *step-right-up!* kind—in the entire world. Those traits that make us psychic are hereditary, so with very few exceptions, psychics tend to be born into the same families.

This is *hugely* advantageous, by the way. You've learned from birth that puberty is going to be Especially Awkward for you, because once your hormones come online, so will your ability to talk to caterpillars or whatever. You've got a built-in support network of people who know you're not crazy, and who teach you why hiding what you can do is smarter than parading it around in public. Your family is usually filthy rich, as they've been around for a hundred generations and they've been able to use their abilities to build themselves a tidy fortune. You tend to marry others who are like yourself, who come from similar families, and the two of you produce children to carry on the cycle.

There're only two Old Families in America, and I try not to

make inbreeding jokes around Mike, because he's from one of them. Me? I'm a sport. I'm one of those exceptions that pop up from time to time, a psychic who doesn't come from an Old Family.

They don't like people like me very much.

For a long time, I thought this was because sports could blow their secret. I was lucky to fall in with Benjamin Franklin as soon as I did. He helped talk me through my new weird life, and helped me to see that some decisions (e.g.: freaking out and making a huge scene) didn't have as many positive outcomes as others (e.g.: talking to a psychiatrist who had to respect patient confidentiality). If it hadn't been for Ben, I would have gone to jail or worse. I have unlimited sympathy for sports who weren't lucky enough to trip over a Founding Father.

But that's not why the Old Families don't like sports. See, we don't fit into their worldview. After all, you've spent years telling each other that your family is special because you've got superpowers. You can make plants grow. You can heal injuries. You can understand animals. You can *pierce the veil between life and death!* Why wouldn't you think that the Old Families are leaps and bounds better than the rest of the human race?

It's a knock to this image when a complete genetic fluke pops up out of nowhere who can do the exact same things.

(And? Frankly? I'm much better with the dead than any of them, and they fucking know it.)

They made excuses when I tried to contact them. Oh, they were plenty pleasant, but no means no.

No, they wouldn't help me learn what psychics can do when properly trained.

No, they wouldn't tell me anything about their history, or what notable feats psychics had accomplished in the past.

No, they wouldn't help me figure out why psychics are able to see OACET's projections.

No, no, no. Thank you for calling. Please lose this number, you should never have gotten it in the first place.

Ben wouldn't interfere on my behalf. He said that the Old

Families are respected among ghosts: sometimes the dead need the living, and vice versa, and there are lasting friendships that crisscross the mortality line.

That's fine. I get it. Besides, Mike walked away from his family when he was just a kid, and that's about all the proof I need that I do not need those people in my life.

He did, you know. Mike got the hell out of there when he was twelve. Decided that his family's traditions were built on a pack of lies and self-delusion, and that being born a psychic was like being born an albino; there was nothing authentically special about it, only how it was perceived and packaged.

Twelve. He decided this when he was *twelve*. Psychic-ness doesn't even turn itself on until puberty, so he walked away from a future of wealth and magical powers. He went from living in mansions and summering in the Hamptons to living on the streets, and that's all I know about that time in his life because he doesn't talk about it.

Oh. I do know he kept up with his aikido training while he was homeless.

Mike is *amazing*.

His family? Not so much.

Mike's late uncle, Richard Smithback, had been instrumental in helping Sparky and me unravel the OACET conspiracy. He passed away a few months ago. Despite what he did for us, I don't miss him—he was a dick when he was alive, and dying didn't change that.

His last request to his sister, Mike's mother, was to let Mike back into the family. Both Mike and his mother were trying.[16]

It wasn't going well.

"My mother says that psychometry is a myth," he said.

I sighed. "Lot of myths going around these days."

"I mentioned that," he said. "I also told her we think a ghost has been sending you her memories."

He didn't need to tell me what his mother had said about

---

16 Smithback really should have asked Mike if this was okay with him first, but what can you do? Last requests are last requests, regardless if you're still able to check in and make sure those requests being followed.

that; it was in his voice.

I shook my head. "What hoops do I have to jump through to prove to her that I'm the real deal? I'm not making this shit up!"

"It's not you," Mike said. "It's her—it's *them*. Nobody in my family has ever been sent a dream by a ghost. Therefore? It can't happen. It's a culture where isolationism and close-mindedness are—"

He suddenly lifted himself off of the bench with a fighter's grace and walked away, too angry to remember to make noise when he moved. I stayed put, and watched the fuzzy edges of the island begin to turn into buildings.

When Mike returned, he was calmer, a can of seltzer in each hand. He set one can on the bench beside me. I didn't recognize the fruit on the label (orange with spikes?), but I popped the top and sipped. Pretty good.

Then I settled in for a long wait.

He surprised me. "It's not that they think you're a fake," he said, almost as soon as I had set the soda down. "That's the problem. You challenge how they think of themselves, and they can't accept that.

"They're going to die out," he said. Then, more quietly, "My family is going to die out. They could survive when the world was smaller. They can't adapt—they've trapped themselves, and they don't even realize it."

He let me cover one of his hands with my own, and the boat rolled on beneath us.

# CHAPTER 23

Rhodes is pretty big.

We were there for maybe an hour before I realized we probably should have asked Helen for more details about exactly where on Rhodes we were supposed to go.

I mean, it's not Texas-big. But I figured we'd show up, go to the largest ruins we could find, and then meet Archimedes.

We showed up, went to the largest ruins we could find, and nope.

The city of Lindos is ancient. *Ancient.* They could sell shirts with the slogan, "Lindos: Eleven centuries older than Jesus."

Darling loved it.

"The Acropolis at Lindos is not just a single city," she said, as she rested gentle fingertips on a column of the Temple of Athena. This building was fairly well-preserved. No roof, of course, but it had two walls and a stunning view of the sea. "Many civilizations built new cities upon the ruins of the old. You cannot walk a meter through the lower levels without turning up something of value."

Atlas sniffed at that.

Darling ignored her cousin. "I come here often. Look," she said, and pointed towards the walls surrounding the acropolis. These had been built from smaller stones than those used in the older ruins at their center. "The island made a natural fortress after the Crusades. The Knights Hospitallers came and established a base of operations, and it took nearly two hundred years of battles before Suleiman's forces succeeded in routing them. Would you like to see the gates to their fortress?"

She didn't wait to hear our answer. Instead, she turned and marched us across the acropolis, ending at a steep staircase that blended the natural rock of the island into its elevation. It was impressive, and Darling chattered on about great battles and body counts.

I'm sure it was interesting, but honestly? I wasn't listening.

My ghost sense had started tingling the moment we had set foot on Rhodes. Not in a *Hey! Look! It's Archimedes!* way, but more of a *Hey! Stop walking through my invisible chess game!* way. There were ghosts here—if Darling was right and this was a layered civilization that had seen a metric shit-ton of different wars, there were probably an astonishing number of ghosts here—but none of them were interested in making contact with us. And, as with the ghosts at the Acropolis at Athens, Mike and I couldn't see them anyhow.

Kinda frustrating.

Oh, we also couldn't call Sparky and have him act as an intermediary, because he and the rest of OACET's administration had just gone into a meeting with the President. I have no doubt Sparky *could* split his mind and manage two important conversations at once, but I sure wasn't about to ask him to do it.

Time to put on my big-girl pants and find Archimedes.

"Darling?" I interrupted her. She put down a chunk of rock, which she claimed had been used as a cannonball during a siege of the fortress. "I might have gotten the meeting place wrong. Is there another old ruin on Rhodes?"

She and Atlas made that gaping-fish face that I'd come to associate with my stupid questions. "Ah—"

"Gotcha," I said. "There are bunches. Let's narrow it down—where would Posidonius have set up shop in Rhodes?"

"No one knows, but it is likely he taught here," Atlas said, pointing at the castle and the ruins behind it. "Many of the other sites around the island were destroyed in a massive earthquake not long before Posidonius would have been born. Lindos remained relatively untouched, and the shrine to Athena became the most prominent on the island. It was believed that Athena had spared this city, and reconstruction was centered around it."

"There is another acropolis near Rhodes Town," Darling said. "But it was damaged in the earthquake and never regained its former glory."

Speedy gave a deep yawn and lifted his head from where he had lain slumped against Mike's chest. "Might be worth checking out," he said. "Posidonius was a teacher, and the Odeion at Rhodes survived the quake."

"The Odeion is…"

"A big stage," he said, as he rested his head on his paws again. "Built so a performer's voice could be heard by anyone in the audience, even in the back rows. Teachers used it for their lectures."

"Good enough," I said, and we headed back towards the donkeys.

Yes, I said donkeys. The touristy way to travel to the Acropolis at Lindos is on a donkey. It was a nifty slice of the city—I would have loved to explore if we had had more time.

On the ride down the hill, Atlas nudged his donkey so it fell into step beside mine. He pointed out fancy nouns as we rode, native birds and plants and whatever, before he finally got to the real reason he was small-talking.

"I could be of better help to you if you let me know why we came to Rhodes," he said. "I feel that I have not earned my pay on this trip."

"I'm intentionally keeping you in the dark," I said. "Since everything I do goes straight back to Senator Hanlon."

Pause. Blink. Token protests.

If we had been walking, I would have stopped and gotten in his face for effect, but no, we were bumping downward on donkeys. The best I could do was not to fall off during the angry handwavey parts.

"Atlas? Do me a favor," I said. "Think about who I am. Think about who my husband is. Then ask yourself if you've been in contact with Hanlon recently, and don't bother to lie.

"Thus far, you've done jack shit for me," I added, intentionally ignoring Helen's beads on their new cord around my neck.

"Your cousin's been a lot more useful. So, start earning your keep—tell me what's special about this other acropolis."

I saw his knuckles turn white as he gripped his donkey's saddle, and then relax as he brought himself down. Good.

"The Acropolis at Rhodes Town is not as well studied as those in other locations," he finally said. "It is a large, sprawling site, and much of what once existed has been reconstructed. Excavations, however, have been limited."

"Why?" I asked, but I thought the chunked-up mess of Lindos was a good enough answer: archaeologists thought the exciting stuff was happening right here.

He proved me wrong. "The site is restrictive," he replied. "It is built on a hill, and the temples situated on terraces. There is no mystery to the land; the people of Rhodes shaped it to their purpose.

"For the last fifty years, it has been the Monte Smith Park," he said. "Not many tourists visit it, but the locals go there for recreation. I do not know what you expect to find there."

Neither did I, and that worried me. If we didn't find Archimedes, we'd have to ask Helen to set up another meeting, and second chances didn't seem to be her bag.

It was another hour to Rhodes Town, and thirty minutes after that we were at the new acropolis. Sorry—the *second* acropolis. Like the one at Lindos, the Acropolis at Rhodes Town was ancient, and situated on top of a hill with a view of the sea.

Really pleasant, though. Lindos was a tourist trap, but this one was all open spaces and trees. We hiked up to the top of the hill, where three tall stone columns held up the barest remnant of a temple.

Atlas started playing tour guide. He got about two sentences into describing the acropolis when my ghost sense twitched.

"Hey, you know? This looks like a nice spot," I said. "Take five, guys. I'm going walkabout."

I took off before Atlas or Darling could stop me. Behind me, I heard Mike tell the cousins to hang back, followed by the unmistakable *plop* of a koala hitting the ground.

I paused so Speedy could climb up onto my shoulders (not a courtesy for him, mind, just that a walking koala doesn't dig in his claws like a running koala), and the two of us headed towards the less prettified areas of the acropolis.

"Where are we?" I asked him.

"Temple of Apollo," he replied. "Head south."

"What's south?"

"Fewer people."

"Fair enough."

We wandered to the southern part of the acropolis, making our way around giant rocks that were suspiciously reminiscent of broken buildings. If I had thought Athens was arid, it was only because we hadn't hit Rhodes first. I thought the island's air would be sweet and tropical. No. It was hot and *dry*. The sounds of unfamiliar insects chittered at us from the trees, pausing as we got too close, then screaming at us as we walked away.

Unlike the acropolis(es?) at Athens and Lindos, the preservation efforts at Rhodes were sort of meh. The further Speedy and I got from the Temple, the more haphazard the reconstruction. Nature had been allowed to get a firmer foothold, and whole groves of trees were scattered in and around the ruins.

We found a nice shady spot under an old myrtle tree. I traced the fading edges of a frieze on a worn slab of rock before lying down. Speedy darted up the tree, and I heard a happy sigh as he curled up on a branch just over my head.

"Better?"

"It's no eucalyptus, but it'll do. Check for ghosts."

"I don't have to," I said, as I let my mind wander. "They're already here."

The feeling was *really* strong. Whoever was nearby wasn't a random soldier, bound to the site where he died. No, this was a ghost with a good amount of fame fueling it.

And I still couldn't see it.

"Start translating," I said, and I began talking to the empty air.

I wasn't about to assume that this ghost was Archimedes, so I told the ghost who we were, and why we were here. What OACET was (As if they didn't know. According to Ben, the entire Afterlife is fascinated by the idea of cyborgs!), and why the Antikythera Mechanism might be a Big Deal.

"We're here to learn if something is wrong," I finished, as the koala chattered overhead. "And if so, we want to try and put it right. But we don't know where to look. If you can help us…"

I paused—I'm never sure about the etiquette of gift-giving for the dead—before I tugged my pack towards me and removed the small travel bottles of ouzo that had been clinking around in the side pocket. Hopefully, whoever was watching us would think I was keeping to custom instead of trying to pay them off.

"…we would be grateful."

I lined the three bottles up on the rock, and waited.

Then, with tiny pops of air, all three bottles disappeared.

And I *still* couldn't see it!

"Oh, come on!" I shouted, and flopped back onto the rock.

# CHAPTER 24

Let me tell you my thoughts about ghosts and culture.

These are *my* thoughts, mind. They aren't informed by anyone else, except for this crazy koala who I sometimes bounce ideas off of. These are just my opinions based on what I've experienced, so take that as you will.

After I graduated from college, I wanted to get my shit together. I had been away from home all of a month before Ben showed up, and I thought it best to see if I could get rid of this persistent four-year LSD hallucination before I jumped into the real world. By that time, Ben and I had started day-trading and I had a comfortable nest egg, so I bid him a teary goodbye[17] and went to India.

I didn't see a single ghost while I was there, and I went to Significant Places. Temples. Battlefields. Old ruins. Places where ghosts tend to congregate in the living world.

I don't think they spend much time in places like those, mind, but they do like to check in and see how the old home is doing. Ghosts are nostalgic, maybe, or maybe they use those sites help to ground them. I think those sites function as touchstones between the dead and the living worlds, much in the same way a church or temple functions as a site that brings you closer to your god. You don't need it, but maybe it helps to put you in the right mindset to cross over.

My point is this: I love to travel. I've bounced all over a whole bunch of countries. And I have never, ever seen a ghost outside of the United States.

Helen is the proof I needed to conclude that the strength of the ghost doesn't affect whether or not I can see them. She's

---

17  Teary on my part, since I had convinced myself I'd finally straighten out my head while I was gone and I'd never see him again. Ben just smiled and said he hoped I'd have some good stories to tell him when I got back. Which I did.

freakin' *Helen of ~~Troy~~ Sparta!* She's like King Arthur or Moses—

nearly everybody in Western civilization has heard of her, and she's riding the energy of two thousand years of legendary fame.

Her personality is also proof that she's actually Helen, and not the *idea* of Helen, if you get me. The Helen of poems and movies and whatever is a meek lovestruck beauty; the Helen I've met was cutting hired mercenaries to pieces at the age of fourteen, and age and death haven't mellowed her out. If Helen were a myth running around in ghost form, it stands to reason she would have manifested as that timid little creature from the stories, not a sword-wielding death maiden.

I know Helen's real, and not a myth come to life. I'm a ridiculously powerful ectomancer in my own right. There's only one reason I shouldn't be able to talk to her directly, and that's if we don't occupy the same realities.

Bear with me. I'm going somewhere with this.

Put the specialized physics lingo on the shelf, and accept it at face value when I tell you that ghosts are beings of energy. They can manifest however they want, whether as a tiny blue pixy or a photorealistic spectral image of their former selves, or anything in between. Regardless of how they appear, when ghosts cross over into our world, they are aligning themselves with a very specific reality.

I don't think they get it a hundred percent right.

I think they're slightly out of synch with the living.

This isn't their fault. Not consciously, at least. I think that when they appear in the living world, they manifest on a specific energy frequency. The more (oh God, I need to use airquotes) "in tune" a psychic is to that specific frequency? The more likely it is that psychic can communicate with the ghost.

Psychics don't hit puberty and bam! Ghosts! No. Not all psychics have the ability to see ghosts, and for those who can, it still takes ages of practice to (\*sigh\*) "tune" a psychic's brain. I was friends with Ben for years before I started seeing other ghosts, weaker ones who didn't put off as strong a signal as Benjamin Franklin. The more I associated with the strong ghosts, the easier it was for me to (again, *sigh*) "tune" myself to the weaker ones.

I'm still working on it. Hence, my continued attempts with the bottles of ouzo.

So.

Here we have a strong ghost, a strong psychic, and a successful attempt at offering a tuning agent.

Still nothing.

What's missing from this equation?

A shared cultural identity.

Culture is a funny thing. It shapes every aspect of our lives. How we experience the world is defined by how we perceive ourselves in relation to it. How we relate to others is shaped by our similarities and our differences.

I'm now damned sure that cultural identity is the biggest tuning fork in existence.

Strong ghost. Strong psychic. Successful application of ouzo. Absolutely nothing else in common.

No connection. We're so far out of synch that we might as well be in different realities. Hell, for all I know, we *are*—we might exist in two different planes, intersecting through bottles and beads.

I know, I know, you're asking how I fell in with Benjamin Franklin, since the guy's been dead for a hell of a long time and his culture was so vastly different than ours, right? Well, when it comes down to notable figures in American history, Ben's at the tippy-top of that list. As an American—an American who's always been a huge history buff!—I've accepted Ben as a part of my own cultural identity since I first learned about him in grade school.

Also, Ben isn't as far removed from modern culture as you might think. He, uh... Hmm. I'd like to say he lives for new discoveries, but that's not quite right. Instead, let's say that he's decided to stay grounded in our world for the novelty of it. He loves experiments, science, change... He's immersed in technology and politics, and is enormously entertained by the ongoing evolution of American society. As far as dead people go, he's quite flexible.

He's never stopped inventing, for one thing.

He's made gizmos and gadgets you wouldn't believe. A man of his genius, with functional immortality and access to information from all over the planet? It's freakin' *paradise!*

Ben says he's got a secret laboratory somewhere in Nevada, where he pokes at various scientific problems.

He claims he's cracked cold fusion.

Fun fact: when he was alive, the majority of Ben's experiments weren't scientific, but social. The man was always pressing buttons to see what would happen, and this hasn't changed. He loves dicking around with politicians and scientists, testing this and that and the other thing. He's about as active today as he was when he was alive, and if you know Ben from the historical record, that's actually pretty scary.

Anyhow. Where was I?

Right.

Culture.

Culture *has* to be the determining factor. It can't be personality—in terms of traits, I have a lot in common with Helen of Sparta. Sure, I've never torn the lifeblood from an animal's throat with my teeth, but I can relate to someone who trains with swords for a zillion hours straight and is then obligated to dress up for fancy dinners. If I couldn't make direct contact with Helen, there's no chance I'd be able to make contact with a socially-shy scientist.

Or whoever this new ghost was.

# CHAPTER 25

"I've got an idea," Speedy said, as he dropped out of the myrtle tree. "You got those beads on you?"

"Of course." I tugged them free of the neckline of my shirt to show him.

"Great," he said, as he headbutted me to get me to stand up. "Take them out and let them hang free."

I looped the cord around my right hand as he chittered away in ancient Greek to the empty air.

"Hope that did it," he said, as he climbed up to my shoulders and perched his forepaws on top of my head. "Start walking."

"What are we—"

"Just hold out your arm and walk," he said. "If this works, you'll know."

I did.

The beads moved to the east.

Note that when I say the "beads moved," I don't mean they swayed when I walked. I mean they *floated freakin' sideways* to point due east.

"I'm on a leash," I muttered to myself, because muttering is always the preferred option when your choices are either that or to run screaming for the nearest ghost-proof bomb shelter, which isn't a real thing anyhow so your options are basically just muttering or running around while screaming. "You've leashed me to a ghost. A ghost who we know nothing about. I see absolutely no way how this could end badly."

"Suck it up," Speedy said, as he thumped his forepaws on my head to get me to start moving again. "If he takes you down, I'm going down with you."

Which was a comforting thought, actually. Speedy's not a coward, but he is a prey animal. Risk-taking doesn't benefit prey animals the same way it does predators, so they're hardwired to avoid risks whenever possible. If he thought we weren't going to be led into a flaming snake pit? Well…

Follow the beads.

We went slowly. The dead person on the other end of the beads was very considerate, and would have let me walk at a turtle's crawl if I had wanted that. I got the feeling that the ghost was treating Speedy and me like breakable objects.

Which, you know, we were. Technically.

It was a short walk. The ghost took us through another grove of trees and across a road. We stopped in an open, dusty field. The ubiquitous chunks of buildings surrounded us, but there was little left standing.

The beads pointed straight down.

"Houston? Problem," I said.

"On it," Speedy said, and began speaking in ancient Greek again.

The tension on the beads vanished, as if the invisible someone on the other end had dropped them. I glanced around to take our bearings: once we had left the cover of the trees, Speedy and I went on stage again, and a few tourists had spotted us.

"C'mon Speedy, we've got about five minutes before this turns into a selfie feeding frenzy."

"I know, I know," he snapped.

The beads moved again, but this time they tugged gently on my arm, pointing at the ground beneath our feet.

"Please remind the nice dead person that we can't move through solid matter," I said.

"Already did. Want to call Pat? He can scan the ground."

I added and subtracted time zones in my head. "No, he's probably still in that meeting with the President. Let's see if we can handle this ourselves."

Stalemate.

Leaving me and a koala standing around in the middle of a field.

"Is this when we learn that old Greek ghosts have lost all

meaning of time and have no sense of urgency?" I asked. "American ghosts are usually impatient dicks."

"So are Americans who aren't dead yet. I think he's working. Give him time."

Across the field, I spotted our biggest problem: the Petrakis cousins, coming towards us at a fast walk, with Mike trailing a few feet behind them.

"We might have to sneak back here tonight," I said, just as the beads began to move again. They pointed left, and Speedy resumed pounding on my head as if I were one of the dumber horses in the stable.

I put my body between the cousins and the magic floating beads, and let them lead us a little further east. They stopped moving at the edge of a square crater cut in the earth.

There were some modern buildings nearby, squat white things that looked like large maintenance sheds. These made a good contrast for this ancient hole that had been carved into the bedrock. There were steps leading to the bottom, but these were blocked off with iron grates. Along the sides of the hole were offshoots that appeared to be manmade tunnels. These were large enough to walk through…or they would have been if they weren't covered with more of those grates.

"What's this place?" I asked.

Speedy shook his head. "No idea. Definitely not a must-see on the tourist list, though."

He was right. The rest of the acropolis was flashy, in that old-timey ruins way. This was just a hole surrounded by a cheap iron guard rail to keep the tourists from toppling to their deaths. Which was fitting—the hole looked more like the entrance to a gigantic tomb than anything else. The grass around it was as high as any I'd seen on Rhodes, and there was zero litter.

*Definitely* not a must-see.

For tourists, that is. The beads were doing a fair bit of tugging. Whatever the ghost wanted to show us was at the bottom of that giant hole.

I heard rustling in the long grass, and managed to slam my

hands down over the floating beads in time.

"Atlas, what is this?" I said, all bright and cheery. The beads had stopped moving, which was great because for a moment there it was oh God squirming magic beads in my hand and I'd much rather still be elbow-deep in that basket of snails at the Athens marketplace ...

"These are the Nymphaia," Atlas said. "There are two more on the other side of the road. Why—"

"Neat!" I said. "I want to check them out. They look cool."

Above me, I heard Speedy groan quietly.

"This is not like the Acropolis at Athens," Atlas said. "Public access is limited to certain areas. The Nymphaeum is fragile... look," he said, gesturing towards the barred grates. "We cannot go down."

"Cousin, you should know better," Darling laughed, as she threw her legs over the guard rail. "What the client wants, the client gets."

I took a step forward, all ready to go into my *No, stop, it's illegal!* tirade, but Speedy yanked my hair, hard.

"We might get one chance at this," he said quietly, his whiskers buzzing against my ear. "Our invisible friend is being very helpful right now, but if he leaves, we're standing around with our thumbs up our butts until we arrange contact through Helen. As far as we know, this is Archimedes! Nobody is watching us; nobody cares about us. Let's get in and out and gone."

"Fine," I snapped, as I swatted at him until he let go of my hair.

The koala hopped down from my shoulders and moved to the side of the pit, then barked at Darling to come help him. This turned into something of a production, with Speedy laughing as Atlas and Darling maneuvered the too-wiggly marsupial into the hole.

Mike and I took a few steps back from the pit, and I used Speedy's distraction to catch him up in a whispered rush. "I have no idea how we're going to do this," I finished. "If we could count on the ghost's help, the three of us could sneak back later, but…"

Mike nodded. "Let's see what happens," he replied. "Maybe the ghost just wants to show us something underground, and then we can leave."

"Sure," I said, as Atlas lowered Speedy into Darling's arms using a contraption made from his belt and her bra. "Because it'll be that easy."

Mike and I hopped down into the hole. Atlas paced around the top, sneaking glances towards the maintenance shed.

"If you're going to keep watch, sit down," I said. "A tall lone man standing in a field sticks out."

"He doesn't know how to get into the Nymphaeum," Darling said from behind me. "He doesn't want to get dirt on his pretty clothes."

Atlas shot her a look of pure hate before he swung his legs over the guard rail. He held on to the lowest rung a little too long, and I was *sure* he'd land badly and break something. I was wrong: he wobbled a bit, but he righted himself and set to work straightening his pants.

Meanwhile, I was trying to follow a set of levitating beads while still hiding them from the normals. I pretended to inspect the walls, shielding the beads from Atlas and Darling, and let the ghost lead me around the perimeter of the hole.

We stopped in front of one of the iron grates. Behind was a dark, cool tunnel. A little breeze came out of it, suggesting that it didn't just dead-end at the wall that was barely visible in the afternoon sun.

The beads floated through the grate and pointed down the tunnel.

"Of course," I sighed, tucking the beads back into the palm of my hand. I gave the grate an exploratory tug to see if it was locked. Yup.

"Allow me," Darling said, as she pulled a thin metal strip from an inner pocket of her jacket. I stepped back and allowed the tomb robber to do what she did best—if we could get in and out before this backfired on OACET, I'd be tipping her out heavily at the end of the day.

"Tell me about this place," I said to Atlas while his cousin worked the lock.

"This is one of the smaller Nymphaia," he said. "Think of them as public water gardens. They were shrines to the nymphs, and were used for recreation."

"Water parks? Amazing," I said, as I ran my fingertips across the cut stone. "Were these caves first, and then they turned it into the Nympharium—"

"Nymphaia," Speedy said.

"—Nymphaia, or did they cut the entire thing out of the bedrock?"

"It was cut," Atlas said, picking his way across the stones. "You will notice a regularity to these caves. Most of the Nymphaia were natural grottos, but the Rhodes Nymphaia appear to have been created for the acropolis by tapping into an underground spring.

"Interesting that they chose to do so," he added. "Nymphaia were common, but not within an acropolis, not unless the site already had grottos. To choose to build one here, so far from the other temples…an unusual decision, to say the least. Maybe we will learn their reasons once more of the acropolis has been excavated."

"Yeah," I said, as Darling swung the gate open. "Maybe."

I exchanged a glance with Mike.

Speedy, sitting on his shoulders, gave me the tiniest nod.

Darling led the way. The thief took out a flashlight, one of those small ones with enough wattage to light up the moon, and took us into the tunnels.

"If I remember correctly," Atlas said, "there are holes cut through the bedrock which allow persons in one room of the Nymphaeum to speak with persons in another."

He began to play the tour guide in earnest, showing us alcoves and niches which would have held small objects, and stones which still held traces of ancient art. I grunted at the right times, but mostly I waited for the beads to move.

We reached the end of the first tunnel. There was nowhere to go but take the only turn and go down, so we did, and we found ourselves in a cool, dark cave with a deep pool in front of us. The pool seemed clean enough if you didn't want to swim; the spring that flowed into it kept the water moving, but the rocks were encrusted with algae. It was a fresh green mess.

"No wonder they don't let the public back here," Mike said.

"When this was first built, the spring would have flowed unobstructed and kept the pool clear," Atlas said. "The earthquake likely changed the course of the water. They did some light renovations on these Nymphaia about twenty years ago to see if they could improve the flow of the water, as they wanted to open this area to the tourists. Sadly, they could not, and they have kept the Nymphaia closed. I believe this is the only one of the four where the water still moves."

"Of course it is," I sighed.

"I'm sorry, what?"

"Atlas, Darling...could you tell me about this rock?" Mike called from the other side of the room. "It looks like someone carved it into a chair."

I shot a quick peek at Mike's rock—Mike's decidedly *not* chair-like rock—and allowed the beads to swing free as the cousins moved to the other side of the grotto.

Gravity didn't have time to take over before the beads snapped straight out, pointing over the water towards the far wall of the grotto.

"And of course they are," I said, as I removed my boots.

Mike and Speedy are good. It took Darling at least a minute to notice the splashing noises, and by then I was already halfway across the pool.

"Just checking on some stuff, guys," I said cheerily, as the cousins started to shout. "Thought I saw something shiny in those rocks."

You know what's disgusting? Algae. You know what contains diseases and microscopic parasites? Algae. You know what I'd rather have been wading through? You guessed it—*anything but algae*. I'd thought that basket of snails was slimy, but that was because I had not yet learned the true power of slime.

I fell. Twice. *Me*.

By the time I reached the other side, I was soaking wet, with green tendrils of algae hanging from me like I was a swamp monster. I was not in the best of moods, and this wasn't helped by the discordant hooting that serves as koala laughter. I was convinced that somewhere nearby, a ghost was losing his shit over the spectacle he had created, and I decided that ectoplasmic heads would roll if this turned out to be a dead man's idea of a practical joke.

I stomped around on the rocks to remove as much algae as I could, and then turned my back to the others: Atlas was flipping out, but Darling…

She was a sharp one. Atlas might think that I was a crazy rich girl playing archaeologist, but Darling knew something was up.

I began to run my hands over the wall, more to hide the motion of the beads than because I had any real reason to do so. The ghost resumed its tugging, directing me to a location somewhere further down the wall.

They stopped moving, and pointed up.

I inspected the wall. It looked the same as the rest of the rock face, the only difference being one of those small alcoves that Atlas claimed had been used for displaying art.

I poked around in this alcove. Carefully. I don't exactly harbor a fear of bugs, but there's a difference between *Oh, look at that centipede*, and *Oh, look at that centipede running over my hand and crawling up the inside of my shirt…*

Nothing.

Whatever the ghost expected me to find wasn't here.

The beads began their tugging motion again, but this time it was frantic, and I was dragged a few feet down the bank before the pulling stopped. I heard Darling gasp: I was *not* looking forward to coming up with the lie that would explain all of this.

From behind me came the loud groan of stones sliding past

each other.

Then, a slab of rock, wider than I was tall and twice as high, came loose from the wall and *fell*.

Forward.

Landing in the water.

Pushing a mighty tidal wave of chunky green liquid towards the four people standing on the far side of the pool.

And then I had four swamp monsters of my very own.

"Oops," I said.

# CHAPTER 26

They forgave me when they saw the library.

That was what the ghost had wanted to show me, by the way—the lost library at Rhodes.

After the rush of green water, I turned to take stock of my surroundings (see: find a place to hide before Speedy got close enough to murder me). The hole where part of the wall used to be was definitely new.

The room behind it…

I couldn't see much; there was almost zero natural light in the Nymphaeum, and what managed to trickle into the library barely lit the edges of what was in the room. My first impression was of an overstocked wine cellar. The walls were layered in shelves, and these were groaning under the weight of old parchment. A nearby table was covered in a mix of parchment and fabric, and I could make out the faint smell of ink over that of the algae.

"Thank God and all His little blue ghosts," I whispered. "Answers."

Behind me came a splash, followed by another; I turned to see Mike and Darling rolling oversized stones into the pool, forming a connecting path to the bridge that the ghost had made when it had pushed out the wall. Atlas was splitting his time between yelling at them for damaging a priceless ancient site, and yelling at them for working too slowly.

"Ms. Blackwell!" he called to me. "You cannot enter the room—you'll contaminate it!"

Atlas was absolutely right. I don't know too much about archaeology and forensics and whatnot, but I do know that swamp water is incompatible with pretty much anything you'd like to keep clean.

Well, damn. How to manage this?

There were footsteps as the four of them pounded across the new bridge, and Darling's flashlight illuminated the library.

We all gasped. Even Speedy.

Ghosts aren't big into physical possessions. They've got no need for them, really. But if they decide to keep something, they preserve it. The room was pristine; I didn't even see any dust.

The scope of the place was smaller than I had guessed at first glance. It was about the size of a very large Starbucks, the rock ceiling of the manmade cave lower than was comfortable. I'd say it was almost cozy except for the floor, which was the most beautiful mosaic mural I had ever seen.

It held the night sky.

The room had been split into hemispheres, and the summer constellations chased those of winter across the floor. The master artisan who created it had depicted Leo in stunning golds, the Twins in whites and bloody reds... I lost track of the rest, as my mind would need hours to study how the images of scales and fish and crabs and water were both entwined and separate.

Around this was a border made of math.

I don't know how else to describe it. Numbers and symbols surrounded the art. The two aspects of the mural were separated by a border of blues and golds, and yet all of it was part of the same design.

I glanced at Speedy. From his usual perch on Mike's shoulders, he could see the entire mural. The art didn't catch his interest at all; he was craning his neck to see the mathematics on the far side of the table.

"Formulae," he said. "It looks like an early version of Apollonius of Perga's description of epicycles."

"Which are..."

"How the planets move," Speedy said with a sigh.

"Hah!" I shouted aloud. "There's got to be something here about the Mechanism!"

"Mister, ah...Speedy?" Atlas said. "Can you make out what's

on the table?"

"Yeah," Speedy replied. "I'll have to look at it, but I'm pretty sure it's a copy of Archimedes' lost *Catoptrica*."

My heart jumped at the mention of Archimedes, and Mike and I exchanged wild grins.

"The *Catoptrica*..." Atlas whispered, then began waving and pushing us back away from the doorway. "We cannot go into that room. This is priceless—this is a once-in-a-lifetime discovery! We need a team—"

"Yeah," I said. "You should definitely go call someone and let them know what you've found."

He paused. "I didn't find—"

"Sure you did!" I said. "You and your cousin can take the credit."

"Ms. Blackwell, I couldn't—"

"Yes, you can," I said, and this time I slapped my open palm against his chest for good measure. Hopefully that would shut him up long enough for me to get it through his brain that I didn't want any responsibility for this stuff. "This is a hell of an opportunity for you—for *both* of you. Like, maybe a career-defining opportunity?"

Darling froze as she realized what I was offering. Legitimacy. A way to get out of the black market and compete in the same international marketplaces as her cousin. Maybe even *with* her cousin, if she was willing to take that chance.

Atlas wasn't quite so quick. "I did none of the legwork, Ms. Blackwell. This discovery is yours—"

"We. Don't. Want. It," I said, banging on his (smooth hard broad *yum!*) chest with each word. "You can have it. Why don't you and your cousin go topside where the reception is better, and make a phone call to whoever you know at whatever museums are on Rhodes, okay?"

"Come," Mike said. Speedy scurried down from his shoulders, as Mike took Atlas' arm to guide him back over the bridge. "The faster we make that call, the faster we can come back down here."

The two of them disappeared down the tunnel, Atlas busy fussing with his phone to check if the water had ruined it.

Which left Darling, her bright brown eyes moving between Speedy and me.

"Strip," she said, as she began removing her clothing.

"Say again?" I asked.

Darling peeled that astonishing jacket over her head, followed by a remarkably dry blouse, and... *Wow*. There were some outstanding genes in the Petrakis family. Darling was in much better shape than her cousin. I could have grated aged Parmesan cheese on her six-pack.

"Animal," she said to Speedy. "Come here."

To my absolute shock, Speedy walked over to Darling and allowed her to wrap him in her blouse. He flicked his ears, one at a time, so she could dry them off with a sleeve.

"You heard the woman," Speedy told me, as Darling picked him up like a stray cat caught in a towel. "Strip."

Oh. Right. We were a mess. Anyone would be able to tell we'd have entered the room by the trail of pond water. Getting rid of our clothing took care of most of that; shaking out our hair and tying it into rough ponytails took care of the rest.

Nymphaia are fairly chilly, by the way. Or at least this particular one was; I haven't run around in my underwear in enough of them to make an informed judgment about the rest.

As I stepped out of my pants, the beads around my wrist swung loose, reminding me that we weren't alone.

With us living humans wearing nothing but our skivvies.

Yup.

I reached out to take Speedy, but Darling stepped away.

"The animal will stay with me," she said. "You know what you are here to find, no?"

"No," I said. "I need his help."

"So do I," Darling said, then pointed at the beads. "And I need it more than you do, I think."

"It's okay," Speedy assured me. A slip of white teeth showed through his fur. "Move fast. We've got about ninety seconds before you bipeds need to get dressed again."

"All right," I muttered.

We entered the room together.

I was worried we'd somehow damage it—I had this mental image of all of this ancient stuff going *poof!* and crumbling into dust from the stress caused by our presence alone—but nothing changed. Our footprints didn't even show up on the floor.

Darling and Speedy began to circle the room, lightning quick, touching nothing as they inspected shelves and alcoves for small, portable treasures. As they spoke in low tones about profit margins, I took a moment to myself to just...*be*.

The smell of ink hit me again, stronger this time. I noticed papers spread out across the desk, covered in a thin, light hand. It was easy to imagine torchlight, a man humming to himself as he paged through old documents, a warm drink beside him...

The room was cozy. There wasn't any other word for it. Someone—possible many someones—had loved this place very much, both in their lifetimes and after.

Guilt began to scratch at my conscience as I realized I had violated a sanctuary.

"Last step of the journey, I hope," I whispered, as I held my arm out and let the beads hang loose. "I know you can't understand me, but thank you for your help."

This time, the beads moved slowly, as if the ghost moving them wasn't quite sure where he had put that...thing...where is it...*just* had it...where on *earth* did it go...

Then the beads jumped with an inaudible *There!*

I followed them across the room, ending at a low shelf beneath a writing desk. Darling was watching me, the expression on her face stuck between fright and bemusement. The beads ran over a line of rolled parchments, like a finger tracing the spines of much-loved books, before stopping on one.

I placed a finger on the very edge of the scroll—carefully—and waited to see if it would dissolve into nothing. When it didn't, I began to tug—again, *so* carefully!

It took me maybe a minute to remove this old scroll from its resting place. The slow tugging was almost meditative; I heard Speedy and Darling talking in normal tones, then Speedy shout aloud in a language I didn't recognize.

Tug, tug, tug.

No sign of Mike or Atlas.

Tug, tug, tug.

The scroll finally came loose, and I sat back on the mosaic floor, cradling it in my hands.

It looked no different from the other scrolls lining the shelves in the room. There was writing along an outside edge, probably for an archival system or such. Other than that, it was merely a rolled-up hunk of heavy not-quite-paper.

Something bumped against my shoulder. Darling, her arms devoid of koalas, held out another oversized flashlight.

"It's for smuggling," she said. "There is a hidden compartment around the battery case, to hold documents."

"Thanks," I said. "Where's Speedy?"

"It ran up the tunnel to keep watch," Darling replied. "I don't think it likes me."

"Well, you keep calling him an *it,*" I said. "But that's your own funeral."

Darling helped me package up the scroll, unwinding and rewinding it around the circumference of the battery case to keep it safe. The whole time, she shook her head at the state of the parchment. "This should not be possible," she said. "The items in this room? Too perfect, too well-preserved."

I shrugged. "We got lucky, I guess."

"No," she said, with a meaningful stare towards the beads hanging from my wrist. "No, we did not. What are those?"

"Junk. Bought them from your cousin," I said, as I screwed the flashlight back together. "He says they're old."

"They look old," Darling said, as she stood and offered me a hand up. "I would say they are authentic, but I saw them move on their own. What are they? A trick of your husband's? A small machine, maybe?"

I grinned at learning that any sufficiently advanced weirdness is indistinguishable from technology. Good to know. "Maybe. Did you get what you wanted?"

"Maybe." She smiled, too. "Your animal helped me find some lovely pieces. Many private collectors will be very happy with me, I think."

We moved to the doorway and Darling clicked off her light. Both of us paused in the dim light of the Nymphaeum before we had to cross back into the modern world.

"An amazing discovery," she said quietly. "I am glad to have been part of it."

"This could be yours, you know," I said. "I was serious when I said that I don't want the credit. I could spin the story to claim that the cyborgs were involved, but that'll just create more questions for OACET. It'll look better for us if a team of noted antiquities brokers were giving me a tour and then...oops! Hey, look what we found."

"I am happy with myself," Darling said. "And I want nothing to do with my cousin. He can have his name in the journals without mine beside it."

"What about your mom?" I asked.

Her face went tight. "What about her?"

"Um...she's sick, right?" I said, backtracking through my mindfiles to remember how I had learned—Right. The café in Athens. Speedy. Koala superhearing and eavesdropping on their conversation. "I think Atlas mentioned it."

"Ah," she said, as she bowed her head. "Fame is overrated. Money is not."

# CHAPTER 27

As such things go, the aftermath of discovering an ancient library is just slightly better than unraveling a massive government conspiracy. They're kinda similar, though: at first, nobody really believes what's happened, and when you give them enough proof to choke a horse, they think you're trying to trick them. Then, after the experts weigh in and say you've actually done what you've claimed, the world goes ever so slightly berserk.

Since Atlas wasn't willing to take the sole credit for the discovery, we blamed the whole mess on the koala.

In the press conferences, Speedy sat on the podium or the table or the armrest of the interviewer's chair, and lied his butt off. He said that in his work with the Smithsonian, he had come across a scrap of a rumor that the library at Rhodes had been located underground, and that a second entrance was in the Nymphaia. Photographs of the recent renovation of the Nymphaia suggested this entrance might still exist.

What? No, he wasn't going to tell them where he found this information, or how he could tell there was a hidden entrance concealed behind solid rock from a few photographs. You think he's going to do their jobs for them? Fuck 'em.

Speedy is an asshole, true, but assholes are incredibly useful and having one improves the overall quality of your life.

We ended up with the story that we were blissfully touring the acropolis when Speedy slipped out of our hands and sprinted into the Nymphaeum. Someone had left the gate unlocked so we ran after him to pull him out of the fragile archeological site, but by the time we got to the pool, he had already opened the hidden door.

OACET's hands were clean, and Speedy didn't give one

single shit that his (paws) weren't.

Atlas looked great on camera, by the way. He was finally earning his keep: we would have been up Shit Creek if one of the country's most reputable antiquities brokers hadn't been with us. Atlas' first phone call had been to his contact at the Archaeological Museum of Rhodes, and they had a team on-site within thirty minutes.

Since Darling didn't want in on the action, I gave her a giant chunk of money as a retainer, and sent her away until the press got bored with us. The thief sent me daily updates from a hotel on the other end of the island, along with her ever-growing list of expenses.

Whatever. If a paid week of spa days at a five-star resort bought her silence, it was worth it.

As for me and Mike?

When we weren't doing interviews, we spent our time talking about the ghost of the library.

I wanted to apologize. I hadn't realized that locating the library would be the end of it for him. He had stayed there for maybe thousands of years, and he had helped us. Now? His sanctuary was public knowledge.

By the way, that ghost who had helped us?

*Archimedes himself!*

We had managed to speak with Helen again. The queen said that Archimedes had retreated to a quiet island until the living humans left his home alone. Remember how I said that Speedy had started shouting in another language when we were exploring the tomb? That was when he told Archimedes to clear out his stash and get anything he wanted to preserve to safety. All of the work he had done over the centuries? Well, from what the experts at the Museum told us, the materials in the library all dated to before the great earthquake, so at least Archimedes had managed to save his best stuff.

Still. In my mind, we had driven a very old man from his home.

Mike offered old zen kōans instead of advice, all of which

sounded lovely until you realized that they had multiple meanings, and that if you dug around in those then it was obvious he thought we had driven an old man out of his home, too.

I was beating myself up over the whole thing but good.

In the meantime, we studied the scroll.

There was a ton of information on that scroll. Short version? It was a firsthand account of how Archimedes was able to create a device like the Antikythera Mechanism without any messing around with weird supernatural sources.

*Yes!!!*

Mission accomplished, folks! We didn't have to worry about any wibbly-wobbly timey-wimey aftershocks such as, oh, being wiped out of existence.

Long version?

Well, it's an incredibly cute story, so here's the full translation.[18]

*I am reluctant to put down these words, as they will show how my greatest discovery may have been made while I was relieving myself in the woods. Honesty, however, is the mark of the furious cocksnack and holy balls, woman, I could be watching* Dancing with the Stars *reruns,[19] so I shall endeavor to preserve this event as it happened.*

*Poliadas, a good friend and a generous one, declared I had been spending too much time alone, and took me from my workshop to the nearby forest for a day's rest. After a pleasant meal of fish and wine, I felt that telltale pressing upon my bladder, and walked a good distance from my friend so as not to show him the fate which was about to befall his generous repast.*

*I began to water a pile of fallen leaves. By chance, the weight of a portion of my urine fell within the bowl of a leaf. I watched as* the leaf tipped forward. *I thought the leaf would tumble from the*

18 It's straight from the koala's mouth and I didn't pay him to do it, so it's likely Speedy has taken some liberties with the word choice and phrasing.
19 Like so.

pile, but when the liquid emptied out, the leaf righted itself. This happened many times, until I found myself to be out of urine.

Finding this to be an unusual behavior for a leaf, I bent and examined the mechanism that allowed a cup to be filled, then emptied and righted. Beneath the leaf I found two slim sticks, laying in a cross. One of these sticks was long and fixed; the other, short and flexible.

I rushed back to Poliadas' table. My friend was not around, having walked in the opposite direction to find his own private spot in the woods, so I seized a jug of wine and ran back to the leaf and the twigs. I repeated the process of pouring liquid into the leaf, and watching it empty and return to position.

Over and over, I poured wine into the leaf. I found the shorter stick to be the source of the action, where it was forced to submit to the changing weight of the leaf. Once freed from this burden it sprung up, renewed! But! The shorter stick could only climb so far and no further, its upward movement fixed by the length of the longer stick.

Most interesting was that I learned the rate at which I poured wine into the leaf did not affect the response, merely how long it took to occur. I found a handful of soil, and poured this into the leaf—as with the liquids, the leaf shook loose its load when it had taken just enough and no more.

I continued to observe this process until the old leaf could no longer ignore the pressures I put upon it, and its structure crumbled away. When I looked up, I found Poliadas staring at me, before his eyes moved to the now-empty jug of wine.

"Archimedes," he said, saddened at the loss of the wine. "Why are you playing in the dirt like a boy?"

"Look," I said, and duplicated the weight of the leaf with my finger. The shorter stick obliged, and bent beneath it. "This is amazing!"

"Archimedes," my friend laughed. "What could be of interest to you in such a thing?"

"Here we have a connection between two objects, and this connection is controlled by weight," I replied. "This force is *generated by the one, and limited by the other."*

*"Ah."*

*"Have you heard of the water clocks of Ctesibius?" I asked him.
It was a fool's question: such clocks were famous works of art,
controlled by gears and powered by water. "They have a similar
operation, but rely on the force of water to function. Imagine,
Poliadas, a clock that does not need water to drive it!"*

*"Impossible," my friend said, and his was a brilliant mind so
he knew I'd listen to his words. "The action of the clock cannot
occur without water. The clock's movements require a source of
power."*

*He was right, and I pondered the problem for the next seven
weeks.*

*I built many clocks during this period, all the while trying to
find a means of driving them without the need for water. I came
across many solutions, but all of these were temporary. I had no
way to store the power needed to maintain an accurate clock.*

*Out of frustration, I built the simplest device that I could—
three gears turned by a hand crank. I operated this device for
hours, writing notations on each gear, observing its functions with
the hope that I might become inspired with a strategy through
which such a simple device could be powered.*

*No solution to that problem presented itself. Yet, as I stared into
the gears and watched the small black inks of my notations move
in a predictable pattern, I could not help but observe how the
gears provided a regularity of cycles. I found myself constructing
equations from these notations, and realized that while I had not
been able to solve the problem of the clock, I might be able to
create a new type of machine.*

*I began to experiment again, but this time I ignored the matter
of earthly time and instead applied my studies of heavenly cycles.
I was able to construct an orrery of bronze, and could use this to
predict the movements of the Sun, the Moon, and the five planets.*

And then, after that first orrery worked, Archimedes got more
creative and made the same thing, only bigger and more complex.
A few kings thought that this was awesome and hired him to build

*other, bigger shit, and Archimedes wrote all of this down before*
*he built the Mechanism anyhow so the rest of this manuscript is*
*irrelevant. I'm fucking done here; let's go get falafels.*

Mike and I thought that this story was the best thing since unsliced bread. There was no way we could deprive the world of it—or Archimedes, as it was such a catchy tale that it would help fuel his reputation—so we decided to put it back.

No reason for us to hold on to it, right? Thanks to this scroll, our work in Greece was done.

I slipped the scroll into Darling's flashlight thief-case, and Mike and I went to revisit Archimedes' library.

It took us maybe eight seconds to learn that getting an item into an ancient library was much more difficult than sneaking it out.

If this had happened when we were back home, I would have called on Ben or another friendly powerful ghost to pop the scroll into its resting place. But? Just like how I've never seen a ghost outside of the United States, I've also never seen an American ghost in another country. Maybe it's a territorial thing, I don't know, but Mike and I were on our own. I sure as hell wasn't about to call Helen and ask her to play errand girl.

We waited until lunch before heading to the acropolis, as we figured that was the most likely time to have a low ratio of guards to scientists. Nighttime was ridiculous: the threat of modern-day tomb robbers had motivated all of Rhodes to play sentry. None of the locals were going to allow their treasures to be taken from them, and since nearly twenty percent of the population was unemployed, there were a *lot* of volunteers patrolling the acropolis.

(Hopefully, they'd never learn that one of the first living humans to explore their newfound library had already made off with everything that could be crammed down her very ample cleavage. Um...let me clarify. That wasn't me; I'm talking about Darling. My cleavage is anything but ample and I had just snagged that one scroll.)

The site was crawling with people. Mike and I were spotted the second we arrived on the hill, and there was plenty of waving and cheering. Another unintended consequence of finding an ancient site? The arrival of all of the reporters who needed to cover the story. These reporters needed to eat and sleep, so they visited the hotels and restaurants, and after hours they visited the clubs... If nothing else came of this, we had given Rhodes some good publicity and a temporary economic shot in the arm. That made me happy; that seemed to make *everybody* happy.

We smiled and waved back, and began walking through the gauntlet of guards. We made it as far as the inner corridor of the Nymphaeum before we bumped into resistance.

The Nymphaeum had been drained, and the algae had been scraped off and hauled away. Portable dehumidifiers chugged all around the manmade grotto, making sure moisture didn't penetrate the layers of plastic sheeting that had been hung over the entrance to the library.

I think I had paid for those dehumidifiers and the generator running them...I couldn't remember. I had written a lot of checks recently.

Anyhow.

They didn't want us to go into the room. The woman running the operation insisted we stay outside; we could look through the layers of clear plastic, but we couldn't go inside, oh no.

She was a hard nut to crack. I'm sure we would have been turned away if Atlas hadn't already been in the library.

He came out to see what the commotion was, and he inadvertently gave us one of those movie moments that rarely happens in real life, you know the ones, where the character slowly emerges through a veil, gradually coming into focus, and then? *Bam!* Luscious eye candy. Yeah, usually that character is a woman and usually the veil is gauzy silk instead of industrial-grade plastic, but the principle was the same. Me, Mike, and the female archivist had to stop to remember where we had put our brains.

"Is there a problem?" Atlas asked the archivist.

"No, Mr. Petrakis," the archivist replied, her face going bright red. She was about my age, maybe a year or two older, and definitely on board the Atlas Train. "They wanted to see what we've been working on, but—"

She never got the chance to finish. Atlas grinned at me as he looped his arm through mine and escorted me through the plastic, the archivist gasping behind us as she prevented Mike from following.

"Stay close," Atlas said. He released my arm, but his hand traveled down to that not-quite-butt region of my lower back. I let it stay there; no need to come out swinging. "We are trying to preserve as much as we can, and it is safer if you do not touch anything."

"Sure," I said, as I looked around the library. The two of us were the only ones in the room. The library was well-lit with LED lamps positioned on stands, but the lamps had been kept on their dimmest settings and covered in thin white silk to protect the materials in the room. The effect was like moving through the haze of a million soft candles. The gorgeous mosaic floor had been covered in a heavy white cotton cloth to protect it from foot traffic, and the edges of this cloth were piled around the base of the walls in voluminous clouds of folds. There was a portable radio in the corner. Classical music was playing. I don't have an ear for that stuff, but it sounded Mozart-y.

No wonder the archivist hadn't wanted us around—I'd seen hardcore porn with more understated set design.

"We are doing the catalog from the top to the bottom," he said, pointing towards the highest shelves. These were now empty. "It has all been photographed to preserve its order. What you found, Ms. Blackwell, is a unique example of daily life from the Hellenistic era. Simple details, such as which groups of parchment were placed upon the same shelves, may provide insight to a world many generations removed from ours."

I nodded and muttered a comment that had nothing at all to

do with the fact that a ghost had been moving those parchments around during that entire time, and unless that ghost had been extremely thorough when he moved out, there might be an inexplicable paper coffee cup or candy bar wrapper lying in a corner.

I often wonder about the accuracy of the entire historical record, but, you know. Most of life is just made of varying degrees of bullshit anyhow.

"What have you found?" I asked.

"So much!" Atlas stepped away from me and moved to the open space in the center of the room. The desk and the items on it hadn't been touched. "This appears to be a lost treatise by Archimedes himself. Many of our discoveries seem to be related to mathematical formulae in some fashion. And there is the art, of course," he said, as he bent down to lay a gentle hand upon the heavy cloth and the floor beneath it.

He was as giddy as a kid in the modern equivalent of a candy store. I realized I was smiling.

"Ms. Blackwell..." Atlas met my eyes and stood. "I want you to listen to me. I want to tell you something, and you must believe me."

I dropped my shields. I don't know why I did it—I guess it was because he was so earnest—but I let his emotions hit me. Sincerity and joy were the two that I could recognize. The rest? I don't know. I'm nowhere near good enough at reading emotions to get through the complex layers that make up a mind.

All I knew was that Atlas Petrakis wanted to cut through the lies.

"I have told Senator Hanlon to never call me again," he said. "I am no longer going to feed him information."

"*Former* Senator," I said absently as I brought my shields back up. I really don't like reading people; I was beginning to think that maybe some of those underlying levels of emotion were lust, because a casual hand on my lower back wasn't enough to get my panties steaming and *holy shit* I suddenly wanted to see exactly how well that table had stood the test of time. "Why not? According to Hollywood, playing both sides is a long-standing tradition with art brokers."

"Because…" He paused. I got the impression that his brain was moving faster than his English. He lowered his voice and took a few steps towards me. "Because you found this place. I saw you do it, and I cannot explain it.

"I do not know what to do with you," he said, leaning in close, and I smelled spices I couldn't recognize. "You are a businesswoman, aggressive, calm…then you are a child stomping through a pool of water.

"And then you find *this*," he said, pointing to the room. "You claim you are here to bring fame to your husband's organization, but you won't take credit for what you have found. I don't know why you are really here, or what other discoveries you want to pursue, but if this is what you bring with you, then I *must* be part of it! Hanlon cannot offer me what you can."

"That's…very honest," I admitted. "But I'm sure what I've been searching for is already here in this room.[20] As soon as you find it, Mike, Speedy, and I are going home."

He reached out and laid his hands on my shoulders. I was wearing a sleeveless shirt, and his skin was *so* hot against mine. "You cannot leave," he said earnestly. "This room, this is a miracle!"

I peered around Atlas to check on Mike. He was still outside, the archivist steadfast in her efforts to keep anyone else out of the room. If I didn't get a distraction soon, I'd have to leave with the scroll and beg Helen to teleport it back to its original location.

"Shoulda brought Speedy," I said.

"What?" he asked, his dark eyes searching my face. His hands began to move down my shoulders…

"Oh, just that he would enjoy what you've done here," I said. There was a worrisome lack of oxygen in the room, and I took a quick step away from him to see if it was easier to breathe when

20 And if I stepped outside of the room, then it would be outside, and if I went back inside, than it would be inside, and if I went back outside…

there was some distance between us. Nope. "It's...neat."

His eyes were unbelievably dark as he took my hands in his own. "Ms. Blackwell—Hope—"

He pulled me towards him again; I *let* him pull me towards him again...

God and libido only know what that was going to turn into, as Mike finally managed to convince the archivist to let him into the library.

"Hey Mike!" I shouted, as he came through the plastic, the archivist behind him. "Atlas was about to tell me about the floors! They're really...neat..."

The archivist's face went bright red as she saw Atlas standing with his hands on my shoulders.

Ah. Jealousy. *Perfect.*

"Or..." I said, as I leaned against Atlas and slipped my hand into the back pocket of his jeans. "You can show me that thing you were talking about?"

"Thing?" Atlas asked. "What do you—"

"That *thing!*" I said, and this time I goosed his butt. Hard.

"Yes," he said, eyes wide. "Yes. That thing. Of course."

I began to drag Atlas out of the room, but I also managed to snag the archivist by her waist on the way. "You weren't lying," I said to Atlas, before the archivist could break away. "She *is* really pretty!"

After that, neither of them were paying any attention to Mike.

With one hand on a (firm juicy) butt and another curled around a strange woman's hips, it was awfully hard to drop the flashlight, but I managed. The heavy cloth layered over the floor caught it and muffled the sound.

Mike found me a few minutes later. I had broken free of both Atlas and the archivist, and was taking selfies with the locals gathered at the metal fence around the Nymphaeum.

"We good?" I asked.

"We're good," he replied. "Atlas and Rebecca?"

"Rebecca? Oh, the archivist. I think they're over there," I

said, and dipped my head towards one of the nearby supply buildings. "I told them to start without me while I did some fast public relations."

"You're a horrible tease," Mike said.

"Me? Never! It's a well-known fact that I have the attention span of a goldfish," I told him. "Who's down in the Nymphaeum now?"

"Nobody."

"Well, hell," I said, as I duckfaced with a giddy tweenager. "Guess we're the ones standing guard over the place until they're done romping in the hay. Boning on the lawnmower. Whatever."

And that's what we did.

# CHAPTER 28

When Theseus came to Aphidna to visit his mother, I hid in plain sight, and her household worked with us to keep me away from her son.

By the age of sixteen, I had already had my menses for two years. The first time I spotted the bedding, Aethra made me reopen a wound on my leg and told the maids that I had sparred too roughly the day before. The maids were not fooled, but they understood; Theseus was brutal to them. I found clean rags when I needed them, and the soiled ones vanished as if by magic.

To be fair, there was no need to go to such lengths in our deception. Theseus rarely came to the city without an escort, and with him came his women. Beautiful, all of them, many beginning to swell with his bastard children. Three days before he arrived, Aethra would hire the largest mercenaries she could find, and I would make that morning's lesson a study in pain. By the time Theseus reached Aphidna, my face would be all bruises, and the king's mother would brandish a leather strap and tell him that, in spite of her best efforts, I was still an unmannered beast. She made sure I kept my hair and clothing plain, my breasts bound tight… He rarely looked at me during these meetings, showing favor instead to his beautiful whores.

Until the day he arrived unannounced, and caught me in his mother's garden.

He was traveling to a neighboring city, a last attempt to win allies for his impending war against Sparta. It was a trip that gave him reason to pass within a league of Aphidna, and he came to his mother's house to rest. Aethra and I were taking a late lunch when a maid rushed in, the king several short steps behind her.

There was no time to hide.

He failed to recognize me, and the beginnings of a lusty grin had begun to form on his gaptoothed face. Then, he spotted the Spartan dagger at my waist, and knew.

"Oh, mother," he said, not moving his eyes from my body. "You play a wicked game."

"One you have lost," Aethra said, as she moved to shelter me from her son. "Her brothers are mere days from Athens' door. Let her return to her family in peace, and you can save your honor."

"The war will end once I wed her," he said, and came at me.

"Don't be a fool, my son!" Aethra shouted, trying to push him away with her words, but he took his own mother by her shoulders and hurled her to the damp earth.

She fell hard, and my blood rose.

*No more.*

I put myself between the king and Aethra. I pressed a hand to his chest, and felt his skin burn. "Enough," I said to him. "Your mother has treated me like her own daughter—I will not allow this."

He covered my hand with one of his own, and used the other to pull me against his waist. He was erect; the household gossip of the maids had prepared me for the feat, but not the fear. "My wife," he snarled. "Helen of Sparta...*mine!*"

I answered him the best I way I knew how; I took the dagger his mother had given to me, cut him across the meat of both thighs, and then copied these wounds in the heavy muscles of his arms.

They were not killing wounds; I would not murder Aethra's son, no matter how I might wish it. They were, however, hard wounds. The last, the one I made in his left arm, was the worst of them, as he realized at that fourth quick stroke that I was crippling him and tried to pull away. That cut ended in an odd upward curl, a bloody fishhook marked upon his flesh.

He tried to come at me again, and I stepped away before he toppled to the ground.

"Put him in a bed," I told the maids, as the ruined king moved towards me. I stepped backwards, keeping time with his stuttering crawl. He would never touch me again. "Not mine and not his mother's, and call for the seamstress to stitch him back together."

He had enough fight left within him to beat his fists against the face of the first woman who tried to help him. I kicked him across the jaw and made a fifth cut while he moaned into the earth.

That fifth cut was quite wicked of me; all the maids of the household smiled.

# CHAPTER 29

I woke screaming.

Hey, *you* try riding along in a dead princess's body as she castrates a man, and see what *you* do, all right?

Speedy twitched in his sleep. I nearly woke him up to talk over Helen's most recent dream-memory, but thought better of it. He was done with Greece. I needed to get him to his home territory before he started getting dangerously irritable. Emphasis on *dangerous*.

I tied my hair back, threw on some clothes, and went downstairs.

Mike found me in the bar an hour later. I had a large glass of whiskey in one hand, and those three little beads on their new lanyard in the other. The beads had stopped chirping at me days ago. I wasn't sure if I was happy or sad about that. I guess I was hoping the liquor would tell me.

Mike sat down beside me, and held up two fingers to the bartender. He waited until his own whiskey arrived before he nudged me with his elbow.

"You okay?"

I nodded. I was three shots into a decent buzz, and feeling much better than I had when I had woken up with somebody else's memory of slicing a scrotum off with a dagger.

I told Mike about the dream.

To say that he flinched would belittle the subtle art of flinching. Instead, I'll say he placed his drink on the bar, ordered another double, and drank all three glasses—both of his and mine—without tasting any of them.

"Yep," I said. "That."

"Dear Lord," he said. "We've got to get her to stop sending you these dreams."

"I don't think she's going to stop until I do something for her," I began, as the bartender swept away our glasses and replaced them with new ones. "It's like what Speedy told me—she's sending them for a reason. She's not going to let me go until she's done."

"Okay," he said, shaking his head as the whiskey hit him. "Let's figure out what she wants, and go do it."

"I wish it were that simple. She's not good at communicating," I said. "Or maybe I'm not good at understanding the message. So far, these dreams have been about her kidnapping and imprisonment. Why aren't they about that big thing that made her famous? Why aren't they about what happened in Troy?"

"Good question," Mike said.

"Or…maybe they *are*," I realized, and my stomach sank to my feet. "Maybe this is just the preamble, and then I get to watch another twenty years of politics and war. Which…well, I'd love to know what really happened in the Trojan War, but I don't have the time to watch it now, and I definitely don't have the time to tell the rest of the world—

"Oh *God*," I groaned. "What if she wants me to be her public image consultant? What if she's tired of being portrayed as this meek blonde waif in a dress, and she wants me to fix it?

"I don't know how to do that, Mike!" I grabbed his arm, and he signaled the bartender for another couple of drinks. "How do I make all of Western culture change their image of Helen of Troy to Helen of Sparta? *I'm not that good!*"

"Easy," Mike said, as he pushed the whiskey into my hands. "You're just guessing. Let's talk this through. What has Helen actually said she wants you to do?"

I thought back to what Helen had told me at the Kos Asklepion. "*I am tired of this world*," I quoted. "*The beast waits below the island. Set us both free.*"

"Good," he said. "So we've got an island, a beast, and a command. She wants you to set them free."

"Speedy thinks she's helping me," I said. "That she's popped into the future and seen where I'm headed, and wants to prep me on what's coming."

"Speedy's almost always right," Mike said. "So, she's helping you, but she also wants you to help her? Why would Helen ask you to set her free? She's a powerful ghost—she's not limited by physical constraints."

I huffed out a long breath. "What do we know about the Afterlife?" I asked. "Beside the part where you get to build your own dream house."

"Damned little. It's more limbo than reality. You wait there while you decide whether you want to move on from this life to the next."

"Yeah," I said. "So why does she think she's trapped? She could pick up and move on to the next life whenever she wants."

Mike mulled this over. "I'm a Buddhist," he finally said.

"You've mentioned."

"Buddhism is big on the problem of getting trapped within cycles of your own making. Much of what holds us back are barriers we impose upon ourselves. These are mental barriers, not physical—they'd apply to dead humans as much as living ones."

"I'm with you," I said.

"Now, who's most likely to stay behind as a ghost?"

"Soldiers, politicians, and creative types who want to continue their experiments or projects or whatever," I said. It was a good rule of thumb that if someone felt invested in the welfare of the world of the living, they'd stick around. I didn't like battlefields; *way* too many dead people still fighting over causes long since resolved. "Fame alone doesn't tie a ghost down—if it did, we'd be swimming in James Deans and Marilyn Monroes."

"Exactly," he said. "Ghosts stick around because they feel they have to. Maybe some of them don't accept that they already have the ability to move on to the next life...maybe some of them don't think they have the *right* to move on."

"That would explain the battlefields," I sighed.

Mike nodded. "If we accept that ghosts think they still have obligations," he said. "That feeling of responsibility means they feel compelled to follow patterns they already have the power to break."

"Sounds good," I said. "So, if we follow this logic, what? We've decided Helen's sticking around because she feels responsible for something…maybe…?"

"Yes, but how does an island fit into this?" he asked. "And which island? There are hundreds of them around Greece."

"Not to mention the beast," I said. "Which is a very vague term, and could mean anything from Theseus' ghost to a llama with a bad combover."

We slumped over our drinks.

"We need more data," I said, as I poked at a salt shaker.

"Yeah, we do," he said. "We're just grasping at straws here."

"Think we could just call Helen and ask?"

He didn't reply.

"Thought not," I said. I threw a bunch of money on the bar, and went back upstairs to bed.

# CHAPTER 30

My brothers were waiting at the gate.

They had grown in our four years apart, but I would know them anywhere: Castor and Polydeuces, the pride of Sparta. Leaders of the Dioscuri. Hard and wicked men.

They did not recognize me.

I let them into Aethra's household, and their eyes moved past me before they jerked back to my face.

"Soft living," said Polydeuces, the first words I had heard from my family's own lips since I was taken captive. "They have turned you into an Athenian whore."

I hit him hard enough to split his cheek open, and laid him flat with a kick I had learned from one of Aethra's hired mercenaries. When he finally caught his breath, he began laughing, and gathered me into his arms.

"Sister," he said. "It's time to come home."

"Long past time," I said. "What kept you?"

"Father," Castor replied. "He wanted to be sure that Theseus would never control Athens again."

I laughed, perhaps a little too well. "Never," I promised them, as I led them to Aethra's reception hall. The queen sat, waiting, the women of her household gathered around her. Their fear was thick enough to taste; the Dioscuri were proud of their reputation as killers of the wicked and unjust, and these women had helped imprison their sister.

"Where is the king?" Polydeuces asked, as he circled the room like a hunting wolf. "He is supposed to be in this house."

I looked to Aethra, who closed her eyes and waited to see if I would finally slit her son's throat.

"He is on his way to the Underworld," I said. "If he has not already arrived."

"Your doing?"

I nodded. "He was a coward, a thief of women. If he lives, he will never repeat his crimes—I have made sure of that."

"Where?" asked Castor, and I nodded towards the bedroom where Theseus lay wrapped in his pain. My brother held out his arm, and I slipped mine through his.

He felt like home. I rested my head against his shoulder for a brief moment, and then took him to see the king.

Six days had passed from when Theseus had come upon me in his mother's garden. The healers kept changing the poultices, but the smell of ripe infection assaulted my brother as he pulled aside the bed curtains. The king twisted within his fever dreams, moaning of curses, of monsters...

"Well done, sister," my brother told me, pride in his voice. "Well done, indeed."

"He might yet live," I admitted. "He's quite strong. But if he does..."

I threw back the sheets to show Castor that last wound.

Even the Dioscuri can feel revulsion. My brother recoiled from what I had done to the king.

"Helen..." he began, but could not finish.

We heard screams from the great room, and we hurried to see Polydeuces take his sword to the first maid.

"Stop," I said, my command ringing through the hall.

My brother pulled his sword from the woman's chest. He wiped it on her robe before he held it out to me. "Apologies, sister," he said. "The right is yours."

"Aethra has been like a mother to me," I said. "And these women helped protect me from her son. They will not be harmed—*never*. Not while I live."

Polydeuces saw what he had done, and was ashamed. He bowed before Aethra.

I will never know what he planned to say, as the maids began to scream for another reason.

The sounds of their terror and anguish had woken something in the ruined king. Theseus stood in the doorway, black blood seeping from his wounds and yellow tears pouring down his face. He wore nothing, and my brothers froze at the sight.

I did not. I took up Polydeuces' sword and pressed it to the king's neck.

"Do it," he hissed.

"No," I said. I took a step back and let the sword fall to my side.

"Do it, or I will kill all who you love," he said, and his mad eyes turned towards Aethra. "I will start with *her*."

I turned my back to him and walked away.

"They come with us," I told my brothers, as I pointed to Aethra and her maids, and ignored how the ruined king howled behind me.

# CHAPTER 31

The archivists working in the library found the scroll two days after Mike and I left it there. Atlas tried to get me to come down to the library to look at it: I declined, and sent Mike in my place. Mike said the scroll had been placed in a clear Plexiglas tube for protection, and Atlas had donned lint-free cotton gloves to remove it and show him the elaborate sketches of Archimedes' orreries.

Mike says he *oohed!* and *aahed!* in the proper places, and that Atlas still didn't realize that the abnormal discoloration in the corner was actually a three-day-old coffee stain.

I made reservations for a flight out of Athens the following day.

But...

*"The beast waits below the island. Set us both free."*

Now, as Speedy put it, we had two options. One? We get on the plane, head back to America, and the queen could go fuck herself...so to speak. If the cultural barriers between the living and the dead worked the way I thought they did, we'd never see or hear from Helen again. I probably shouldn't go back to Greece, but, you know, I could easily avoid an entire country if properly motivated.

The second option was to tell her we were planning to leave unless she could give us better instructions.

Speedy wasn't for that *at all*. He kept harping on the tornado in the coffee shop, and said that if things got that bad when the queen was trying to get our attention, she'd probably do a damned fine job of killing us if that's how she wanted the meeting to play out.

I figured it wouldn't hurt to be polite.

Probably.

Speedy, Mike, and I rented a car, and drove back to Lindos to visit the Temple of Athena. We had researched the hell out of possible locations on Rhodes that were associated with Helen, and there's a story in the *Lindos Chronicles* that Helen had dedicated two bracelets to Athena at that particular temple. Helen plus bracelets equaled the closest we could come to forming a physical connection to the queen on Rhodes.[21]

We hoped it would be enough to get her attention.

Mike and I did without the donkeys, and we arrived at the top of the hill just before the last tours of the day left the acropolis. I bribed the guards to be busy somewhere else for an hour, and the four of us—me, Mike, Speedy, and the bright green avatar of my husband—arranged ourselves along the plinth of the Temple of Athena at twilight.

I cupped the three beads in my hands and joined Mike in meditating our butts off on the image of the dead queen.

It was almost full dark before Sparky nodded at the open air beside us and said, "She's here."

"Speedy?"

"On it," the koala said, and started spewing Greek.

The queen's face on my phone's screen grew dark, and a whole bunch of gigantic loose stones that were lying around the plinth detached themselves from the earth and began floating towards us. *Fast.*

I rose, took a few steps towards the space where Helen stood, and shouted: "Stop!"

The stones dropped and clattered against the plinth. Some of them were huge, bigger than me and Mike put together; I really didn't want to have to explain how those got up there to a guard. Or an archaeologist. Or a mortician.

"Tell us what you want," I said. "No riddles. No shortcuts. We don't speak the same language, so dumb it down for us!"

---

21 Maybe. While we were researching locations, we found a lesser-known myth called "Helen Dendritis," or "Helen of the Tree." In this myth, Helen came to Rhodes after the Trojan War, was betrayed by a friend, and was hanged from a tree until dead. So, yes, there is a dedicated shrine to Helen of Troy on Rhodes, but we decided against using that one because of the part where it celebrates her murder and thank you, but we were actively trying to *not* piss her off, so no. Just no.

The queen's eyes moved from me to the koala on my shoulders. Speedy translated; Helen replied.

"She says she wants us to go to the island," Speedy said. "Kill the beast, set them both free. No new information. She's getting really angry," he added, as if I couldn't see the rocks beginning to twitch and levitate again.

"No shit," I said. "Tell her we would, if we knew which island. This is Greece—there are hundreds of them!"

Speedy spat out the words as quickly as he could.

"Holy crap," Sparky said in a low voice.

"What?" Mike and I asked, but the queen's laughter through our phones was our answer.

"What's happening?" I whispered to my husband.

The koala shushed us; Helen was speaking.

"Huh," Speedy said.

*"What?!"*

"She apologized," he said. "She says she's forgotten what it's like to be limited by time and space."

Okay.

Bear with me while I explain this part, because I've never seen anything like it before, and I doubt I ever will again.

The floating stones began to swing around us in a tight circle.

Now, when I say *stones*, what I'm really saying is *pieces of ancient buildings the size of cars*. This made for a very... unpleasant experience.

The stones twirled and danced, and I got the impression Helen was taking her time about aligning them in a specific order.

Then, the stones stopped. They hung there in midair, one of Archimedes' orreries without the need for the limits of gears.

The stones plummeted to the ground and cracked apart. The shards—the unnecessary pieces—were swept aside as if a large invisible broom had passed across the plinth. What was left behind were carefully cut sculptures, with brand-new bumps and ridges all over them, positioned across the temple floor in a too-regular order.

As a finishing touch? The shards that had been swept aside came flying back in a dusty whirlwind, grinding themselves down into fragments the size of sand. This sand was laid across the plinth in waves. Literally, waves. As in: this sand was moving in ripples like the surface of the ocean. I could see eddies and sounds around each of the large stone sculptures.

The creepiest part of this whole creepy process? The waves floated at my thigh. I pushed my hands through them, and there was an inch of pulverized stone which felt smooth and silky, like warm, dry water...and there was just open air beneath this.

Okay.

I hang out with Benjamin Franklin on a daily basis. As far as powerful American ghosts go, only George Washington has more juice than Ben. I've seen those guys do amazing, magical things for nothing more than the sake of personal convenience.

Both of them working together couldn't have put on a telekinetic display of this magnitude.

The four of us wandered around the plinth, waves made of dust crashing around our knees and our jaws hanging somewhere around our navels.

None of us wanted to admit that what Helen had just done—the precision and the size of it—had no place in a sane reality.

Sparky recovered first. "I think..." he began, and then launched his avatar into the air. He flew fifteen feet straight up for a better view. "I think it's a map of an archipelago."

"Which one?" I asked.

"A Greek one."

"Thank you, Mike. I mean, which Greek archipelago? And which island?" I asked. "Do you think we have to search them all?"

Maybe Helen understood more English than she let on, I don't know, or maybe comedic timing transcends language barriers. Whatever the case, that was the exact moment a bolt of bright white lightning shot down from the heavens and *set one of those giant stones on fire!*

"Ah," I said, as I watched the rock melt into a pool of red-hot slag. "That one."

# CHAPTER 32

The ruined king came to Sparta seven years after I thought he was dead.

I was pregnant with my fourth child; had I realized the old man was the man who had kidnapped me, I would have had him slain before he could enter my home and pollute the air my unborn babe and I breathed.

I sat, stiff and heavy on my throne, as I attended to the needs of my country. My husband was away, engaged in the trade of war, and I was alone on the dais. It had been a hard winter, and the fire in the center of the room burned as hot as my men could make it.

Petitioners came and went, their concerns defining their lives and mine for the time it took me to address them. I consulted with Aethra often; she was always by my side of late, as we waited for my child's time to come.

The last petitioner was announced. An old man shuffled towards me, his face hidden by a heavy cloak. When he reached the dais, he pushed his hood back and sneered.

He had meant it to be a shocking revelation, I am sure, but even his own mother could not recognize what Theseus had become. He had aged fifty years in seven, his limbs thin, his face a skull within skin.

I recognized him by the scar on his left arm, the long white line that ended in a fishhook that spun up towards his heart.

So did Aethra; I heard her gasp at what her son had become.

I nodded to the nearest guard. "Kill him."

"Hold!" There was still enough command in the old king's voice to freeze even a Spartan warrior. "I will speak with your queen before I die."

I held up a hand to the soldier. "He knows he will never leave this room," I said. "Let him speak."

What a fool I was.

"Helen, Queen of Sparta," Theseus spat. "You've brought me to ruin."

I said nothing. There was no need for me to point out what was obvious.

Aethra had the mother's prerogative of chastising her son, and so she did. "The fault is yours, Theseus," she said, moving ever closer to my throne. I placed my hand over hers, and felt her quaking; she had so nearly escaped seeing her son die in front of her. "Had you left this girl alone, you would still be a king."

"And whole," I added. The members of my court chuckled, but I knew my words were petty as I said them. The Dioscuri had told all of Greece how I had brought down the king of Athens, and every man in the room knew what Theseus lacked beneath those beggar's robes.

His face grew wild with rage.

"Dog's bitch," he swore. "Whore of a queen. Mark me—I bring your doom."

I kept my own face calm as I studied him for traces of disease. I saw none, but that did not mean he had not brought sickness to my court.

"Oh?" I asked, pillowing my chin on my hand.

He removed a dagger from his robes. Its black blade was short and straight; its handle too heavy for throwing. Still, I nodded to my guards and they closed around him, spears at the ready.

"I have been across the sea," he said. "I found an Egyptian who taught me their magic."

The old king bowed his head and began to whisper in a language I did not know, and the guards looked to me for guidance.

Before I could tell them to run him through, Theseus snapped to his full height. "Helen of Sparta!" he shouted. "Hear me! You are cursed! I curse you, your children, your entire line! Your kingdom, cursed! The Age of Heroes ends with you, Helen!"

His voice dropped to cold fury. "I pledge my shade to this," he said. "You will never know another moment's peace. Not in your lifetime, and not after death. This I vow."

Theseus drew the black dagger across his own belly.

The old king's guts poured from him as he toppled forward, into the fire, and he burned while he screamed my name.

# CHAPTER 33

Sparky and I were sitting on the roof of my hotel. We had a great view of the ocean. We were both pretending to watch it.

Yeah, I could have woken Speedy or Mike, but when you've watched a man eviscerate himself before burning alive? Well, you don't want to be with anybody but the one you love more than anyone else.

We were getting close to the half-hour mark. Neither of us wanted to be the first to say that he should go back to his body.

"I'm tired of ghosts," I said quietly.

"Me, too."

"Everybody's hurting. Pain should stop once you die, not…" I didn't know what to say, but Sparky knew what I meant.

"Not continue, not become worse, and definitely not spill over on to anybody else," he said.

"Yeah."

He held up his left hand; it still had all of the fine details that were always stamped into Sparky's avatar, but these were starting to run into each other at the edges. The image of his wedding band started out as crisp, the Celtic knots twinning into each other; as I watched, the lines began to run like water.

"You've got to go," I said.

"One last time," he said. "While it's fresh."

I sighed, and repeated everything I could remember about the most recent dream. I included all of the details. Even the smells.

"The thing is," I finished, "I'm damned sure Helen doesn't believe in curses. She didn't believe the bullshit that Daddy Dearest was a god, so why should she believe in magic?"

"Well," Sparky said, his eyes going distant as he read something online, "Sparta had a string of bad luck right around that time. There was a plague, then Helen was kidnapped by Paris, and then the Trojan War began."

Damn. Pile enough bad luck on one set of shoulders, and even the most cynical person might bend under the weight. "That may be," I insisted. "Still. She wasn't superstitious."

"But she was religious, right? Even though she didn't believe Zeus was her father? You said she worshipped Artemis?"

"Yup," I said. Many of the dreams from when Helen lived in Aphidna were of her traveling to worship at various shrines. "Not quite sure how much of that was devotion and how much of it was an excuse to get out of Aethra's house for an afternoon, though."

"Maybe she didn't believe that Zeus was her father, but that didn't mean she wasn't religious. Or even superstitious. In any case, watching a man die in front of you after he placed a curse on your entire country would probably shake anybody's resolve."

"Why didn't any of this make it into the mythology?" I asked. "You'd think a death curse by a disgraced king would make some mark on history!"

"If I were Helen, I'd make sure nobody would repeat that story. Ever." He wasn't speaking just as my husband at that moment; there was a healthy helping of the Cyborg King in there. "It'd be eliminated from the public record, to keep the rumors from causing more damage."

I winced. I knew Aethra survived through the Trojan War, but there were no guarantees for the soldiers and the other members of court who had witnessed Theseus' dying declaration.

(Also? It's never comfortable to be reminded that while your husband had never made anyone—airquotes again—"*vanish*," politics is a filthy shithole of a business, and there's always tomorrow.)

"Well, whatever else comes of this, we know why Helen wanted me to learn about ancient curses," I said. "Mike and Speedy both think Theseus is still out there."

"The beast beneath the island."

"Yeah. The ancient Greeks believed in the concept of a soul, sort of. They called it a shade. It was part ghost, part spirit, and it lived on after the body died. I'm definitely not looking forward to meeting one of *those*," I said.

He turned towards the ocean again. I wrapped my arms around where his body should be; I felt his energy run through me, tense and ready for whatever was coming.

"I want to ask you to get on that plane home," he said quietly.

"You know I can't."

"I know," he said. "But you saw what Helen did with those stones at the Temple. Theseus is an even older ghost than she is, and probably as powerful. How do you fight something like that?"

"I'll figure it out. I've got Mike and Speedy with me. "

He didn't reply.

"Go," I said, pretending to bump my forehead against the green expanse of his back. "You're probably burning up. Get in the shower, and bring down your core temp before you cook yourself."

"Yes, doctor."

He turned; we kissed. Fuck you if you say he wasn't really there.

I grinned up at him, then pushed against the illusion of his chest until he vanished.

My phone rang a moment later.

"You good?" I asked.

"Yeah." Sparky's voice sounded very far away. "I'm okay. Listen, Sweetie—"

"I'm sure," I said.

"Call me if you need me."

"Always," I said, and hung up on him before I started to cry.

I didn't see any reason to go downstairs, other than that's where the liquor was. So I made another phone call.

Twenty minutes later, Darling arrived with a bottle of vodka in one hand and a large paper bag in the other.

"That was quick," I said to her. "I thought you were staying at a hotel down the island."

"I've been shopping in Lindos today," she said.

"Shopping, as in…"

She laughed as she settled herself beside me. "So quick to judge, yet you did not mind at all when your animal helped me to loot the library."

"What did you get out of that, anyhow?" I asked, as I inspected the vodka. I hadn't heard of the brand, but there was a blue fairy on the label. I took that as an omen.

"Ah. Well, I found it curious," she said, "that the items the animal recommended I take did not align to the library."

"Come again?" I took a pull straight from the bottle. The vodka was ice cold and perfect. A good omen, then.

"I had them examined by a man I trust. It seems those pieces were written at least four hundred years after the library would have been lost. Strange, no?"

I groaned. "Speedy, you *shithead.*"

Darling smiled. "Will you tell me the whole story now?"

"Sorry. Can't."

"That is what I thought you would say," she replied. "I would very much like to hear why documents I personally removed from a sealed room cannot exist."

I took another long drink.

"I see. Well, I also would like you to know I have enjoyed our partnership," she said, as she passed me the brown paper bag. "I have made quite a lot of money from it, and I thank you for that."

"I honestly didn't know Speedy would con you," I said, then added: "I probably should have guessed, though. That's my fault."

"Oh, you shouldn't worry. I was still able to sell them—I just could not claim they came from the newly discovered library. That decreased their value, but not by too much. There was quite a bidding war among collectors."

"That's good, I guess," I said. I opened the bag to find a jacket identical to Darling's own amazing camouflage parka. "Oh!"

"I noticed you were admiring mine," she said, almost shyly. "It is custom; I hope I guessed your size correctly. A friend of mine in Athens makes them. It is waterproof, resists fire, and the fabric cannot be torn.

"Here," she said, as she helped me slip the jacket over my head.

I stood and made a few quick turns and bends. The jacket fit perfectly. There were hard items on either sleeve. I examined the one on the left; the face of a digital watch stared back at me.

"My friend believes there is no need for clutter," she said, as she showed me the cuffs on her own jacket. "In the field, one item must do the work of twenty. There is a watch in one sleeve, and a GPS in the other."

"Heh," I chuckled. "I can't remember the last time I carried an actual watch."

"I know you will probably never need them, but better safe than sorry, yes?" she said, and patted the rooftop beside her. "The GPS has to be recharged every two weeks, but the battery in the watch should be good for many years. They are both shockproof and waterproof. You'll have no cause to treat them gently."

"Thank you," I said to the thief, as I sat down beside her. "I would have liked to have gotten to know you better."

"Then tonight, we talk," she said, handing me the bottle of vodka. "And when you return to Greece, you will return as a friend, and not an employer.

"Perhaps," she added with a wink, "if I get you drunk enough, you will finally tell me how you found that library."

# CHAPTER 34

Helen's mysterious island was inhabited.

I didn't expect that. I thought it'd be a tiny speck in the middle of the sea, but no, it was an island of about eight square miles, with a small fishing village on the east shore. Plus sheep and WiFi.

Speedy and I hung back at our rented speedboat while Mike went to check in with the locals. He took all of the utility tools we had brought, plus a couple thousand Euros. He came back with nothing except a very strong ouzo buzz and the weird bit of trivia that nobody in the bar had ever hiked up the lone mountain on the island.

Which was all we needed, really.

We waited until full dark before we pulled the speedboat around to the other side of the island, and then we started walking.

Let me tell you about hauntings.

Real psychics laugh our collective asses off at the frauds. If you're ever invited to a haunted house or a cemetery for a séance, and a woman in purple and eighty clunky necklaces rolls her eyes back into her skull while crooning, "I sense a strong presence," you have our permission to get up and leave. Don't worry about breaking a circle, or upsetting the spirits. If there are any ghosts around, they aren't strong enough to do shit to you if they cared about a circle getting broken. Which they don't. Because that's dumb.

I'm not saying that haunted houses don't exist, mind. They do. Human beings—alive or dead—are territorial buggers. You'd think we'd get over this once our physical selves stop taking up space, but our minds have more control over how we occupy the world than our bodies. Once you get rid of paltry details such as eating and sleeping, we're free to obsess over everything else, and the dead tend to obsess over the living.

The living have invaded their space. Worse, the living are *changing* it! This is offensive to the dead on a deep emotional level. It's rather like buying a house and the previous owners get pissed because you've torn down their wallpaper. From their point of view, the house was fine when they left it: they spent days poring over samples to find the perfect combination of paisley, weeks getting the seams to line up correctly, and went loopy trying to find a paint color for the trim that didn't clash. Then you went and tore their hard work down because you didn't want to feel like you were living inside of a necktie.

Reasonable, rational ghosts will usually recognize that they no longer own that house. They'll stand aside and bitch amongst themselves as the wallpaper gets chucked in the dumpster, but they accept their time is over.

Insane ghosts are a different story.

If you walk into a so-called haunted house and you feel that something is wrong, that's not due to the presence of a ghost. There's a part of our lizard brain that can tell when something is wrong with a place, and this has nothing to do with an invisible dead dude waving his arms and shouting, *"BOO!"* Ben says that feeling of wrongness is a shift in the local energy, an atmospheric effect like a pocket rainstorm. Maybe it was caused by a traumatic event; maybe it blew in from somewhere else like a cloud. If left alone, it'll dissipate over time.

But? If people who expect the place to be haunted—the evil kind of haunted—keep visiting it? Their preconceived notions of how a haunted house *should* feel will help to fuel the negative emotions associated with that place. It's a never-ending cycle of bad feelings, resulting in a creepy-crawly ambiance that'll give you nightmares.

It's probably not because of a ghost, though. Powerful ghosts almost never haunt a place. Places are boring.

Note how I said *probably* and *almost*.

Some ghosts—a very small number, so small they don't

much affect the overall math—are just *fucking nuts.*

Not mentally ill, mind. Mentally ill people don't tend to cross back over into the living world once they've gone over. Personally, I think they stay in limbo until they decide to move on, as they've finally found peace. So when I say *fucking nuts,* I'm talking about ghosts that are just fucking nuts.

Psychopaths, mostly.

Fortunately, most psychopathic ghosts don't have the juice behind them to do any serious damage.[22] If they did, there'd be unexplained massacres every other day instead of just once a decade or so.

Now, I'm sure you're asking what happens when a powerful *sane* ghost decides they want to set up territory in the living world. It happens, obviously (says the woman who found Archimedes' private library). When it does? The living will never even notice it's happened. When a ghost decides to set up shop, that location vanishes from the living mind.

It's the places that you don't even notice that are haunted by the powerful ghosts.

There's that road you know by heart. You know the one, you've driven down it maybe a thousand times, and wham! There's a building you've never noticed before. And then, you forget about it for maybe a year, until there it is again! This happens over and over and over, a building blinking in and out of the holes in your mind. *That's* where you could find a ghost with some real juice behind it. If you could remember it long enough to search for it. Which you can't.

Someone had made an entire mountain disappear from the collective memories of those who lived a stone's throw away.

I was hoping that someone was Helen. The alternative was…

---

22 I've always been a little worried about the cult status of serial killers. Once, Ben and I ~~got drunk~~ sat down and had a long talk about what might happen if a psychopathic ghost built up some serious fame. We decided the odds were against it, but also that I should stay the fuck out of London's Whitechapel district, just in case Jack the Ripper was waiting for a lady psychic to come along.

Also? History is full of murdering assholes, and I've never heard of most of them. It'd really, really suck to be wandering alone down a country road in Southeast Nowheresville and find out the hard way that it was haunted by the ghost of Somebody-Something the Mangler. Sticking fame into people is dangerous for *so* many reasons.

Boy howdy golly-gosh, was I ever looking forward to confronting Theseus. Really.

The mountain was shallow, not steep; it was an easy climb, and we made it to the top with plenty of time before dawn.

Mike and I like the night. We like it a *lot*. If society wasn't so hell-bent on running on daylight, I think we'd sleep until the sun went down.

We've both got more energy at night, too, which is why I was shouting on a mountainside at midnight.

"Theseus!" My voice bounced down the mountain and rolled across the valley below. "Helen sent us! We want to talk!"

Nothing.

I shouted until I started to go hoarse. I waved Helen's beads around. I had Speedy translate, in case the two psychics and the talking koala on his mountain weren't enough to wake Theseus' ghost.

Nothing.

"*Beneath* the island," Speedy finally said. "*Beneath.*"

"Yeah, yeah," I muttered, and went into my backpack. I came out with three tactical flashlights, and passed one of these to Mike, and another up to Speedy where he was settled on Mike's shoulders.

Tactical flashlights are awesome, by the way. I had Sparky send me a dozen of them via express mail when we realized we had to go explore an island. They're modular flashlights with dual heads, and can be used as a standard flashlight or a lantern, or even a glowstick at a rave, depending. We were carrying all twelve of them, in case we found ourselves in a bad situation.

No weapons, though. Just the Puukko knife at my belt, and that would be less than useful against a ghost.

We started searching for the cave.

There had to be a cave, right? If we wanted to go beneath the island, there had to be a cave that would let us go inside. Either that, or we were waiting for Helen to open the door for us via straight plagiarism from Ali Baba or Gandalf...

Nothing.

"We're getting pranked," I said, as I stomped a path through a virgin thicket. I was wearing camp shorts with tall hiking boots, but some of the upper branches made it past the thick leather and my knees were getting cut to pieces. "There's an Afterworld betting parlor, and this is some ghost version of *Rat Race* where Helen's got fifty bucks riding on how far she can push us before we tell her to go fuck herself—"

"Found it!" Mike called.

"Oh, thank God," I said, and turned to join the boys.

My psychic sense twitched.

I dropped to the ground without thinking. I landed flat in the thorns, true, but tiny scratches and punctures are a small sacrifice when bullets are involved. I heard Mike and Speedy shouting through the gunfire, and yelled at them to take cover.

Whoever was working the gun stopped firing. "Ms. Blackwell?" called a vaguely familiar voice.

"Oh for fuck's sake," I whispered. "Smiling Goon."

Bullets. He was using actual bullets. Hanlon's marching orders had changed: it was now A-OK to turn Mulcahy's wife into a leaky corpse if he could get away with it. Or maybe Smiling Goon was just fed up with me—he wouldn't be the first, and I'd make damned sure he wouldn't be the last.

"I will assume you are not dead," came Smiling Goon's voice from the other side of the thicket. "And there is nowhere for you to run, yes? Not through these thorns, not without making noise enough to find you. Come out, come out, and then we will talk."

"Fuck you, fuck you," I muttered to myself. "And then I would *die*."

I grabbed some nylon cord out of my pack, left my flashlight lying on the ground behind me, and started to crawl towards Smiling Goon's voice.

It wasn't hard. Smiling Goon really should have asked Hanlon what my husband and I do for fun on weekends. My best friends are soldiers and spies, and their version of entertainment comes just short of murder. Sparky and I compete in this one paintball league that should be tried in The Hague for war crimes. I know from (painful) experience that it's actually easier to crawl through a thicket than walk through one, because down low is where the rabbits live. Slithering through a bunch of bunny poop is nasty, true, but if you're a smallish woman who's resigned to a little bit of filth, it ain't even a trick. Especially not when the local warrens have been undisturbed since Helen was alive; the trails were as big around as beach balls.

I moved through the thicket. It was easy going, and I was wearing the jacket Darling gave me so I was camouflaged with the earth. Even with that in my favor, I needed to keep slow to stay quiet, and the Puukko knife had to come out for the tight spots. Speedy and Mike covered the sounds of my progress by shouting at Smiling Goon from the cover of the cave; Speedy hurled a few insults so ripe and choice that a second goon broke cover to take a few potshots at the cave's entrance.

So. Smiling Goon wasn't alone. Good to know. I changed directions and shuffled left, and after five minutes of stealthy crawling, I was peering through the archway of the bunny trail at a pair of boots. I bided my time until he was busy laughing at something Speedy said, and yanked.

I wasn't trying to pull him into the thicket with me; I'm too small to drag a full-grown man anywhere. Momentum, however, is my best friend, and I had him out cold and tied up before he realized he was no longer standing. Then, I dove back into the thicket to wait.

Sure enough, a third goon came over to check on his suddenly too-quiet friend. I watched as he prodded his friend with the toe of his boot, and then I grabbed his stationary leg. This goon let out a cry as he fell, but Speedy and Mike managed to cover that up with their running commentary.

A kick to the head to knock him out, a few loops of cord around his wrists and ankles to keep him on the ground, and I snapped his thumbs for good measure. Done.

Two down.

I slid back into the thicket. My gut told me that Smiling

Goon had all the brains in this operation, and he wasn't going to let me catch him as he was checking out the bodies. I began to circle around the thicket again, keeping the clearing where the goons had been standing on my left.

After another fifty yards of creeping through the thicket, I finally spotted him. The moon was down, and Smiling Goon was a dark shape against the sky.

I kept crawling. From behind me came Mike's voice, asking Smiling Goon if he had given any thought to the consequences of his actions...

I rather hoped he hadn't. That way his ass-kicking would be a surprise.

I was almost within grabbing distance when his face lit up in a sudden bright green halo; for a brain fart of a moment, I thought he was OACET, but then I realized he was checking a digital device.

There was a flash of white teeth, and Smiling Goon brought his gun up to point directly at me.

"Hello, Ms. Blackwell," he began. "Did you think—"

And then he wasn't saying anything, because Darling Petrakis was crushing his skull with a rock.

# CHAPTER 35

"What are you doing here?" I hissed, as I grabbed Darling and pulled her into the thicket. "Get down! There might be more of them!"

"I don't think so," she said, as she slithered down the rabbit trail behind me. "We came up behind them, and I saw no more men."

"We?"

"Atlas is here," she said. "I made him go back down the mountain until I found you."

"Do I want to know?" I asked. "Actually, yeah. I do. Why are you *here?*"

"Because you let her tag you like an endangered manatee," Speedy said as he came into view. He was bigger than the average rabbit, but he could walk comfortably in the tunnel. "Did you get all three of them?"

"Yeah. How do you know there aren't more?"

"Mike's been keeping them busy while I scouted for you," he said. "I hear two unconscious men, and the one who was conscious isn't making any sounds at all."

"Right," I said, and stood up. The thicket ripped at my hair, but that fantastic jacket kept my skin intact. Speedy started to climb up my legs, but I swung down to grab him before he reached my thorn-torn thighs. He settled on my shoulders, chuffing slightly from the excitement.

Darling stood and turned towards the base of the mountain. It was enough of an opportunity for me to swing her into a chokehold and press my knife against her throat.

"Tell me what he meant," I said. The edge of the knife wasn't quite cutting her, but it was a near thing. "Tell me what he meant when he said you tagged me."

"You idiot—"

"Shut up, Speedy," I snapped. "I want to hear it from her."

"Your jacket," she gasped. "The GPS…"

I glanced at the GPS embedded in the jacket's sleeve. "I didn't program it."

"You *id-eee-ot*," Speedy said again, this time drawing out the word. "*She* programmed it before she gave you the jacket. She could use it to track you anywhere."

I craned my neck to look at him. "You knew about this?"

"Yeah."

"Why didn't you say something?"

He did that rolling motion that passed for a koala's shrug. "Figured we'd need her."

"You knew she'd show up in time to save my life?"

"Sure," he said. "Why not."

I released Darling and shoved her away from me, hard. She tripped and went sprawling into the thorn bushes.

"Get Atlas up here," I snapped. "We're gonna have a talk about boundaries before I send you back home."

I yanked Speedy off of my shoulders and carried him like a football until we were a safe distance away. "You knew she tagged me, and you let them follow us here?" I whispered.

"We'll need them," he whispered back. "Don't get rid of them."

Behind us, Darling put her fingers to her lips to give a short blast of a whistle.

Speedy directed me to the cave, where Mike gathered me into a bear hug.

"I'm covered in bunny shit," I gasped.

"Don't care. What's going on?"

I gave him the rundown of my last fifteen minutes, ending with Darling's arrival and Smiling Goon's murder. "I don't think I saw him die, but he's definitely dead by now. Skulls can't do what his did."

"What about the other two?"

"Out cold and tied up. I broke their thumbs so they can't

untie themselves."

"Good," he said, then peered out of the cave's entrance to watch the Petrakis cousins carve their way through the brambles. "Speedy?"

"We *need* them," Speedy insisted. "We probably won't get out of this alive without them."

Mike raised an eyebrow. "Explain."

Speedy squirmed until I let him go, and then sprinted a few feet away. "Lemme go get them," he said. "Then I'll tell you."

The koala darted into the thicket and was gone.

"Not good," Mike said.

"Nope."

"What's that joke about escaping the hungry lion? You only have to be faster than the other guy?"

"Yup," I said. "Darling's pretty quick, though."

"Her cousin isn't."

"Nope," I sighed. "Want to beat 'em up and leave 'em here?"

"Tempting, but that's a shitload of bad karma. They're adults—let them make their own choices."

"Right," I said, and went down into the brambles to get my gear. My flashlight was blinking away, a little beacon sitting next to my pack, and I had retrieved them and returned to the cave before Speedy managed to bring Atlas and Darling up the path.

Darling looked no worse for wear. Her cousin, however, had lost his polished edges on the hike up the mountain. His hair was tousled, his shirt untucked... I swear, he was all the more sexy for it. Some women love diamonds; I love stones.

"Go home," I said to them. "Whatever the koala's told you is a lie. He wants to use you as cannon fodder if we get in a tight spot."

Speedy slapped one forepaw against his face and grumbled under his breath.

"Ms. Blackwell," Atlas said, his jaw set in a hard line I hadn't seen on him before. "I do not think you can order me around any longer. You made it clear I am no longer your employee."

I winced. I had avoided all contact with Atlas since our

encounter in Archimedes' lost library; it still hurt to think about that moment when my self-control had nearly snapped and blown my underwear into ribbons. After he had found (a-hah-hah) the scroll, I had sent a courier with a glowing letter of recommendation to Atlas' hotel room, along with a bank deposit slip for the fairly obscene sum of money I owed him. He had tried calling, and then sent a note, and then sent flowers with a note, and had then come upstairs to bang on my door. Mike had gone out to tell him thanks, but no thanks.

What? I hadn't expected to see him again. Definitely not in a cave on the side of a missing mountain.

(Which begged the question—how had they found us? The GPS, obviously, but did that mean that you could track a person to the mountain because you knew that the person existed? Or did Helen just not have a firm enough understanding of modern technology to know that she needed to blank out the GPS's signal? Too many questions, too fast.)

"I also am no longer your employee," Darling said, as she settled herself on the floor of the cave. She was carrying her own gear now, a small and badly-beaten backpack with all manner of doohickeys hanging from various straps and clamps. She began to tug on these to test them with the absentminded precision of an experienced explorer. "As we are here now? Tell us how we can help."

"You can leave," I replied.

"You have no authority over us," Atlas said. "We have settled all debts, and now we are free to tour the country. I told you I wanted to be part of your next discovery, and I *will* be. Put me to work."

Darling gave me a wry shrug. "We are not going to leave," she said. "You might as well tell us why you have come here, to this out-of-the-way place, and how we can help."

I opened my mouth. I had *no* idea what was going to come out—hell, I might have even started talking about ghosts!—but Mike saved me.

"Satellites," he said. "OACET has access to satellites with

ground-penetrating technology. They located the hidden library under the Acropolis at Rhodes Town this way. They've got a line on a second hidden room, but reaching it is…dangerous."

"It's *lethal!*" I jumped in. "There was an earthquake, and cave-ins, and…and booby traps…and…"

"They're lying," Speedy said. "They just want the treasure for themselves."

I glared at the koala; he glared back.

"They're coming," he said.

"You're going to get them *killed*," I snarled.

"Better them than us," he said.

"Excuse me!"

"Oh, shut up," I snapped at Atlas. "There's no treasure. There's just a manipulative furry prick."

"If it helps," Speedy said to Atlas, "you'll probably be the one who lives."

I threw my hands in the air. "Fuck it! Fuck it *all!*" I pointed at the cousins. "You promise to stay between us? To turn and run if things get rough?"

They nodded.

"Fuck it all," I growled again, and hoisted my pack.

Then I led us down into the beast's lair.

# CHAPTER 36

The cave wasn't a cave.

Oh, it had started out as one, I'm sure, but we hadn't gone more than twenty feet into the dark before it turned into something utterly different. The walls lost those caveish nooks and crannies and became smooth. The floor had a gentle slope downwards, and at times there were a couple of stairs to ease the descent.

I had expected to feel the press of the mountain around us, but there were no tight places. None. Walking was easy, with breezes coming from hidden holes carrying the night air to us. We kicked up a bit of dust as we went, but all of us marveled at how clean the place seemed to be. No bats. No rodents. No snarling beasts (ghostly or otherwise).

I stayed at the front of our small party; Mike and Speedy brought up the rear. The two of us kept our flashlights moving as we searched for hidden whatevers. Up, down, ceiling, floor... Nothing stood out as a trap. This cave was nothing more than a long rectangle carved into rock.

There were twists and turns, of course. More than once, our flashlights showed that the tunnel seemed to dead-end in a flat wall, only to continue after a sharp turn.

We didn't talk much, but it wasn't too long before Speedy started saying, "Right" or "Left" whenever we reached an intersection. I'd use a black Sharpie to mark the direction we turned on the walls and the floor, just in case, and ignored Atlas as he kibitzed about ruining priceless archaeological sites.

After about fifteen minutes of this, I finally realized where we were. "Holy crap," I said. "It's a maze!"

"Labyrinth," Speedy corrected me.

"Who built this place?"

"I do not know," Atlas said. "It is larger than any underground dwelling made by the ancient Greeks or Romans."

"Are we below sea level now?" I asked, as I laid a hand on one of the smooth walls.

"Almost," Speedy said. "Another hour, then yes."

"That's unsettling," I said, as I scrubbed my hands together to get rid of the chill from the rock. "Definitely unsettling."

Mike and I switched positions every so often; the one riding point needs to stay fresh. During one of these swaps, we all stopped for a break, and Mike took me aside.

"I had thought we'd have met Theseus by now," he whispered.

"I know," I replied, and took a quick sip from my water bottle. "What do you think he's waiting for?"

Mike shook his head. "Can you feel anything?"

I closed my eyes and leaned against the wall, trusting Mike to keep watch. The mountain felt…hollow. "No," I whispered back. "It feels like…nothing."

"Is that good or bad?"

"Hell if I know," I said, as I hoisted my pack and took the lead again.

It was two hours after we entered the Labyrinth that I started balking at Speedy's orders. Well, not me—Helen. I wasn't consciously aware I was doing anything until we reached yet another intersection, and Speedy told us to take a left.

I turned right.

"Hey, dumbass," Speedy snapped. "Your other left."

"Um…" I began, as I shone my flashlight down the right-hand tunnel. It looked like every other featureless section of the Labyrinth. "I think we have to go this way."

"You realize I've already got this place worked out?"

"Yup," I said. The psychic section of my brain was starting to twitch. "But—"

"Let her lead for a while," Mike said to Speedy.

The Petrakis cousins weren't too happy about that. They exchanged a nervous glance.

"Ah, Ms. Blackwell—" Atlas began.

"Hope's gonna lead for a while," Speedy said.

"Got my back, Mike?" I asked.

There were muffled grunting noises as Mike transferred Speedy from his shoulders over to Atlas'. "Always."

I shut my eyes and began to walk.

(Not tight, mind you. I'm not a complete idiot. I kept them at about half-mast and watched my feet so I wouldn't accidentally slam into a wall or shuffle off a ledge into empty space. There's letting instinct guide you, and then there's being a higher-level organism who doesn't rely on instinct alone, because sometimes instinct can be a myopic dick.)

I moved through the corridors, my entire world condensed to nothing but my feet and the ground around them. I turned right...right...left...

We kept descending.

I gradually became aware of a light pressure on my shoulders. I could barely feel it; it blended into the straps on my backpack. I shuffled out of my pack and dropped it, nearly oblivious to the discussion over who should carry it for me.

With the pack gone, I realized that the barely-there pressure felt like a woman's hands. She kept moving me forward; at intersections, she pushed and pulled me into position.

Not instinct, then.

After a time, I couldn't feel Helen's hands anymore.

Step, step, step, one foot in front of another.

"Oh my God!" I heard Atlas say.

The concern in his voice snapped me out of my trance. I clung to a nearby wall, shaking my head to clear it. "What?" I asked.

"Look," Darling said, as she shone her flashlight forward.

The beam dropped away into the black.

"Holy *shit*," I said, as I peered over the edge. "This is straight out of the Mines of Moria."

The chasm was massive; it seemed to split the mountain in two. The remnants of a stone bridge jutted out where the tunnel stopped.

End of the road.

"We can't cross this," Mike said. "It's not humanly possible, not without better equipment."

I didn't reply. I thought it might be humanly possible, if the human in question was Helen with her telekinetic rock-smashing abilities, and wondered how on earth we could explain something like *that* to the Petrakis cousins.

The pressure on my shoulders returned. I found my feet moving towards the sheer drop.

"Hope? Hope, perhaps you should stop. *Now.*" The concern in Atlas' voice grew the closer I came to the edge of the chasm.

"There's a path," I said, as I spotted the shadowed edge of a very shallow niche cut along the chasm wall.

There were stairs down to the path, if you knew where to look for them, and somehow I did. I heard Darling's gasp as it seemed as though I was stepping into thin air, right before my foot landing safely on the first rock riser.

"Hold on," Mike said, as he set Speedy on the ground before fishing through his pack for a spare flashlight. He hung this from a rocky outcropping by its lanyard, a signpost to guide us back to the top of the stairs.

This makeshift lantern swayed on its cord, and we all stared as the shadows below us moved slowly back and forth.

"That," Atlas said, "is a long way to fall."

Then it was just a matter of clinging to the rock face as we made our way down into the dark.

It took *forever*.

Atlas had the worst of it. Speedy, Darling, and I had much less overall mass, and we were able to tuck ourselves tight against the wall. Mike is Mike: the man might have had an extra fifty pounds of muscle on Atlas, but he's as sure-footed as a mountain goat. I think Atlas held his breath every step of the way; just I was starting to worry that he'd pass out and fall into space, the ledge spilled open into a wide, comfortable path.

"This looks promising," Darling said, inspecting the walls. Unlike the Labyrinth's smooth walls, the region around the chasm was rough and natural. Darling's light showed that the rough edges of the cave became smooth again further down the path. "I think this is part of another manmade section."

"What tipped you off?" Speedy said, as he climbed up to his usual spot on Mike's shoulders. "The fucking stairs?"

Atlas collapsed on the Labyrinth's floor, and stared down into the chasm. "We should be able to see the bottom by now," he said.

"Why?" I asked, and pointed up.

Atlas followed my gesture, and saw that Mike's lantern was hanging barely twenty feet above us. The angle of the cliff meant that the path we now stood on was hidden; the lantern was close, but all we could see of it was its light.

"That climb felt longer," Atlas muttered.

Mike clapped Atlas on the back. "Fear is the mind killer," he said. "You must face your fear—"

"C'mon, Muad'Dib," I said, as I yanked Mike away from the still-trembling Atlas. "Let's see where this new road takes us."

"Wait." Speedy clapped Mike across the top of his head. "Take a few steps to our right."

Mike obliged, closing the distance between them and the rock face. From this angle, the lantern was directly over their heads. Speedy stood on his hind legs, placed his forepaws on the wall, and scampered upwards, his claws finding easy purchase in the seemingly sheer cliff.

Darling watched him, bemused. "You could have climbed up or down walls at any time, animal?"

"Shut up and give me some more light," Speedy said. I shone my flashlight towards him, and the koala began chuckling. "Here," he said, drawing a claw across the rock in a vertical line. "Do you see this?"

"Yes," Atlas said, his voice slow and full of caution. "The scraping against the rock? As if something has been dragged up."

"Or lowered down," Darling said excitedly.

"There's a lot of these marks," Speedy said, as he began to

descend towards Atlas' open arms. "Lots of trips. Enough to cut into a rock face."

"We're getting close," I said. "Not exactly sure what we're getting close *to*, but we're definitely getting close."

I moved my flashlight down the broad path. The black chasm yawned beside us, but ahead was…more light?

"What is that?" Atlas asked, as he noticed the glow from a few hundred feet down the path.

Darling joined her flashlight's beam to mine, and began to laugh.

Okay.

Have you ever been minding your own business, walking down a city street, and then you turn a corner and suddenly you're in a park? Not just any park, but one that's *so* idyllic, *so* perfect, that you expect Dick Van Dyke to show up and start dancing with some animated penguins?

Now apply that scenario to miles and miles of dusty, dark tunnels. You're wandering through this gross mushroom kingdom, trying your everlovin' best to ignore the tons of rock sitting above your head and how if you need to backtrack it'll take you at least an hour of steady jogging to reach the cave's entrance, and then your flashlight hits something yellow.

No, not just yellow—*gold.*

Gold.

*Gold.*

An entire cave *full of gold.*

Not the raw, still-to-be-mined kind of gold. No, this gold had already been removed and smelted and hewn and whatever the ancient Greeks did to turn ore into gorgeous refined gold.

I don't remember the walk down the path. I remember Mike's hand around my upper arm, keeping me from breaking into a run. The reflection of our flashlights against all of that gold was hypnotic: I've never seen anything like it before or since. There was this *richness* to the light that I can't describe. It was almost sensual. I thought I could feel the weight of all of that gold on my skin. That light *promised* things.

The five of us stood in the entrance to that treasure room, staring.

There were shelves cut into the rock walls, and these held stacks of gold bars organized into gleaming pyramids. Along the middle of the room were metal chests, their lids open to show the wealth of coins within. A little closer, and there were pottery urns, overflowing with gemstones, and old wooden tables covered in ancient jewelry, with rich rugs and fabrics spread out beneath them...

And there, against the far wall, were the weapons.

I realized Mike had both of my arms in a vise grip. "Don't," he said.

I blinked a few times. Somehow, I had managed to take another few steps towards the room. He had stopped me a hair short of the threshold. I stared wistfully at the rack of pikes a short hundred feet away. "Thanks," I said.

"*'There is no wealth but life,'*" he replied. I didn't recognize the quote, but he followed it up by pointing into the room. "It's...wrong. I don't know how, but it's wrong."

"It's clean," Speedy said. He had his forepaws on Atlas' head, and was peering at the mountain of treasure.

I started to move into the room, and Mike grabbed my arm again. "Not *safe*-clean," he said.

"Oh?" I asked, and then I stopped to think about it. "Oh."

The room was spotless. Not in the well-loved way of Archimedes' library, but wholly and completely devoid of any sense of human habitation.

"This is like the lost library," Atlas said, as if to convince himself. "A room, perfectly preserved..."

Speedy scoffed against his hair. "Keep telling yourself that," the koala said. "I can see the little hairs on your neck standing up."

All of us knew that treasure room wasn't like Archimedes' library. Part of it was the dust; the rest of the Labyrinth was dirty. Not from the presence of animals and insects, but from the settling of the earth alone. The treasure room didn't even have a skim coating of dust. It was all bright and shiny and new.

I glared at one of the wooden tables. I don't know what I expected—maybe that it would crumble and turn into a pile of rotting fungus before my eyes?—but it had suddenly become a very sinister table. The rug it was sitting on was all golds and silvers and blues, woven together in patterns I had never imagined, and as clean as it had been vacuumed that morning.

"Yup," I said with a little shiver. "We've all seen this movie."

Atlas was standing a couple of feet behind Mike, staring over his shoulder at the wealth of a nation.

Darling was watching me.

I stared wistfully at the weapons. "Tell me there's no chance any of that is Damascus steel," I said to Speedy.

"Are you kidding?" he said, as he scurried down Altas' body. "If this room is dated to Archimedes or later, every single weapon here might be authentic Damascus!"

I groaned.

Damascus steel.

Screw the mountains of gold. Forget the king's ransom in jewelry. Give me an authentic Damascus saber in mint condition, and you can keep the treasure.

"I didn't think it existed," Atlas said. "The stories… I thought such troves were myths."

"Guess not," I said. "Too bad it's not meant for us." And I turned to put the room behind me.

To find Atlas pointing a gun at Mike's head.

"Yes," Atlas said. "It is."

"Oh come *on!*" I shouted. "*Now* you've got to be a dick? We don't care about the treasure! Haven't you figured that out?"

I was enraged. Seriously furious. He had given me permission to read him, and I had, and he had seemed honest and open and delicious and—

Okay, maybe I was just mad at me.

I looked over at Darling, and she was smiling. Not at me. At her cousin.

"Oh *fuck* me," I said, as I began rubbing my temples. "Smiling

Goon was using a GPS to track us to the mountain, too. He got the coordinates from you two."

"Took you long enough," Speedy muttered.

"Shut *up!*"

Speedy rolled his eyes. "You know," he said, "if you weren't such a *shit* psychic, maybe you could prevent stuff like this from happening."

"Psychic?" Darling asked, as she took the gun from her cousin's unsteady hand. The way she held it made the gun change from a toy to an actual threat. "What is this, this psychic?"

"Her and Mike," Speedy said, as he climbed up Mike's legs. Wise choice: Mike had already taken a gun from Darling once, and she was keeping her distance from him, so if anybody needed to be unencumbered by a koala to fight her for the gun, it had to be me.

Plus, if Speedy had tried to use me as his personal mobile tree unit at that particular moment, I probably would have punted him into the chasm.

"They're psychics," Speedy continued. "They can see ghosts. Everything that's happened, every weird thing that you can't explain? It's because we've been working with ancient Greek heroes."

"Ixnay on the ychicpsay," I muttered.

"Why? Hanlon's already told them that strange shit is afoot," Speedy said. "Isn't that right?"

Darling nodded, very slowly.

"How can you be working with Hanlon?" I snapped at her. "I had you checked out!"

"I did not know of Hanlon," she said. "Not until after the library at Rhodes was found. One of his men approached me— the one I killed on the mountain—and said that my cousin had called Hanlon and told him he would no longer work with him. It was my job to fill my cousin's role, and to convince Atlas that he had been wrong to walk away."

"Hanlon threatened you," I guessed.

She nodded again. "I was not given a choice," she said. "It was easy to convince Atlas that he had made a poor decision after you sent him that letter. He was already considering paying you one last visit before you left Greece."

Darling stared directly at her cousin. "He does not take it well when a woman tells him no."

And with that, she shot Atlas in the head.

# CHAPTER 37

Even Speedy gasped.

We watched as Atlas' hands started to come up, but the message got lost somewhere between them and what was left of his brain. Gravity took over, and his body fell to the ground.

"I have been waiting to do that for twelve years," Darling said, as she savagely kicked his corpse until it toppled into the chasm.

"Oh my sweet Lord," Mike whispered.

I realized I was clinging to his arms, and him to mine; neither of us had ever seen something so...so *cold*.

Darling glanced over at us. "Stop," she said. "Don't worry. I won't hurt you. All I want is the treasure."

Speedy snapped out of it first. "She's lying," he said. "Hanlon wants information. He wants to know how you found the library. That's why she's here—that's why she saved you from the same goon squad she told how to find you. She needs you to trust her so you'll tell her your methods."

"Then why'd she kill Atlas?" I gasped. Some part of my subconscious noticed that Darling hadn't put down the gun.

"Because she wanted to, and this was as good a time as any. After we're dead, who's gonna know?"

Mike and I took a few steps away from Darling. I realized just in time that we were about to cross the threshold of the treasure room, and I shoved both of us to the side.

That put a rock wall at our backs, which was okay. Very okay. Rock was good. Rock was solid. Rock didn't explode into chunky red mist and oh God we were breathing *pieces of Atlas*...

I started to gag.

"Calm down, please," Darling said. "I'm no threat to you— the animal lies."

"Sometimes, yeah," I said. "But he's not very good at it, and he's almost always *right*."

The thief let the barrel of the gun dip as she searched our faces. Whatever she wanted to find there didn't exist. She sighed, and the gun came up again.

"Hanlon is a very powerful enemy," she said. "I like you, Hope, I do, but he would kill me when you would not. Tell me how you found this Labyrinth, and the library."

"Ghosts," I gasped. "Helen of Sparta's ghost, specifically. And, Archimedes' ghost, I guess, but I've never actually seen him."

"Helen of Sparta?"

"Helen of Troy, whatever. I thought she was Helen of Troy at first, too, but it turns out she kills deer with her teeth." I knew I was babbling. I couldn't help it; there were *pieces of Atlas on my face*.

"She's telling the truth," Mike said. We were still clinging to each other, and while his voice was steady, I could feel him shaking.

What? Mike and I are truly awesome at beating people up. We draw the line way, *way* before killing, which is weird if you think about it—who knows better than psychics that death isn't final? But death is a serious change and can be a terrible tragedy, and apparently, watching it happen hits us really hard.

Fuck you if you think this is a weakness of character. I'd rather feel than not.

"It would be easier if you told me what is really happening," Darling said.

"It's true!" I insisted. "She's here right now. The tunnel? How I knew the route to this room? And…and Archimedes showed us his library! He's probably here, too. I think he has another workshop here, but really we're all just waiting for Theseus to try to kill us. Well, not the ghosts, though, since they're already—"

Speedy reached over Mike's head and slapped me. He didn't pull his claws, and put three shallow scratches across my cheek.

It worked. I came back to my senses, one hand pressed to my

cheek to push down the pain.

"Better?"

"Fucker," I said to him. Then, to Darling: "Fucker."

"Tell me what's going on," she said.

"Fine," I snapped. "Ben Franklin thought there might have been a temporal oddity with the Antikythera Mechanism. He sent us here to Greece to learn its history. Along the way, I picked up Helen of Sparta, and she's put us on a quest to undo Theseus' curse. Helen's an absolute badass, by the way, and she's probably really pissed at you right now, so don't be surprised if you get crushed between two giant rocks.

"Oh," I added. "In case you're wondering, we learned that Archimedes made the Mechanism without looking into the future, so our reality probably isn't going to unmake itself. Not because of this, at least. You're welcome."

I can't describe the expression on Darling's face. It was...

Well. I can't describe it.

When her expression didn't change for five whole seconds, Speedy began to translate what I had said into Greek.

"No. *No!*" Darling shouted. "Quiet!"

She took a breath. "Hope? Tell me what has happened—tell me how you discovered the library, and this place. This does not have to be the end," she added, with a nod towards the treasure room. "There is enough wealth here to keep Hanlon from us."

"Liar," Speedy said. "You're planning to kill us, report back to Hanlon with some bullshit story, collect your money, and then sell off the items in this room one at a time until you die of old age. What a total money-grubbing cu—"

"Shut up, animal!" Darling shouted, and took a menacing step towards Speedy. She caught herself just in time; she had nearly put herself within Mike's reach. "Oh," she said to the koala. "So clever. I think you should die first."

"*Now* we're back on script!" Speedy chortled. "You had me worried when you shot your cousin—I did *not* see that coming."

"Enough," she said, and gestured at the treasure with her gun. "Into the room."

"Um—" I began.

"Yes," she said. "If there are traps, I expect you to spring them for me. One at a time, please, and walk quickly."

She broke into a horrible smile. "Make the animal go first."

I shifted to the side, preparing to jump her, but Speedy made a quick *hsst!* noise and shook his head at me. He then scurried over Mike's shoulders and down the front of his body.

Mike and I exchanged worried looks, but, you know. Superintelligent koala.

Speedy walked straight towards the treasure room. As he was about to cross the threshold, he paused.

"I liked your cousin," he said to Darling. "I'm gonna *love* watching what's about to happen to you."

"And what is that, exactly?"

Speedy cast a glance at the shining mountains of treasure before him. "Something nasty."

He broke into the theme from *Ghostbusters* as he strutted into the treasure room, his gait way too confident for a koala on his way to his doom.

Speedy almost never sings, which is a pity because it's really pleasant to hear. "He's got a good voice," I said to Mike.

"*I ain't afraid o' no*—thank you!"

Darling stared into the treasure room, watching the walls, the ceiling, the floor, searching for the first of the traps.

She didn't look over her shoulder, which was a shame.

For her.

Speedy, Mike, and I, on the other hand, had a very good view of the open air behind her, and we saw that this was quickly turning a very distinctive shade of blue.

"Guys?" Speedy shouted from fifteen feet inside the treasure room. "Get in here. *Quickly.*"

Mike and I did what the superintelligent koala ordered. Darling stayed put.

Again, a shame.

Behind her, the blue turned from a hazy mist into vapor trails, twining together as they relearned the physics of mass.

I bent down and scooped up Speedy, and he leapt from my arms to Mike's shoulders. "Get ready to run," he whispered, as he hunkered down and wrapped his legs around Mike, and we humans strapped our flashlights into their holders.

"Hey, Darling?" I called. (What? I had to try.) "If you drop the gun and promise to play nice, we'll protect you. No hard feelings, okay?"

She laughed. "Thank you, Hope. I do like you, very much, but..."

"Yeah," I said, as the blue mist finished solidifying. "Business first."

Darling's head came off of her body like butter meeting the edge of a red-hot knife.

I didn't scream this time, not even when her blood splashed over my chest. I was too preoccupied with what had killed her.

One of the most powerful monsters in the ancient world was staring down at me.

Minotaur.

*Min-o-taur.*

A bull's head on a man's body, and everything was scaled to fit the bull, not the man. It loomed over us, ten feet tall, with muscles on top of muscles and a set of sharp, shiny horns.

The weapon that had separated Darling from her head was covered in blood, and I couldn't see what it was until the Minotaur obliged me by bringing his right arm into combat position. A labrys, that wicked double axe of legend, rose up above our heads.

"It's blue," I think I said. I don't actually remember speaking, but the voice sounded like mine. "It's completely blue. Shouldn't a Minotaur be...not blue? Brown, maybe?"

A voice that sounded like Mike's said, "It's a ghost."

"Oh," said the voice that sounded like mine. "Good. Ghosts are good. Maybe...he was...protecting us from Darling?"

The Minotaur snorted.

I've *never* spent any time around livestock. *Ever.* So when that snort bypassed my ears and hit my amygdala, it was speaking directly to the part of my genetic heritage that still remembered how good life could be high up in the trees where there were snakes and leopards and venomous creepy-crawlies, but an almost zero percent chance of getting *gored*.

Minotaur.

Versus the two worst psychics in the world and their tiny companion of sentient fluff.

Although, if you flip that script…

Two of the best living martial artists and the most intelligent being on the planet, versus a bunch of glowing electrons.

Poor Minotaur.

# CHAPTER 38

Let me tell you what you need to know if you want to survive a fight with a ghost.

Mike and I fight with ghosts all of the damned time. We love it. *Love. It.* Ghosts are the ultimate sparring partners when you want to test lethal techniques you absolutely cannot use on anything with a pulse.[23]

However, most of the ghosts I know aren't good fighters. The Founding Fathers, bless their undead hearts, are strong believers in punching as hard as they can. That's the beginning and the end of their combat skill set. Dodging? Nope. Kicking? Please. They learned this particular thonk-bonk style of fighting when they were alive, and if they're solid enough to participate in a physical fight, then that's how their physical bodies will fight. None of that misting back-and-forth between solid and vapor like you see in the movies, because who the hell has that much concentration?

This is important: ghosts are only solid when they want to be, but when they're solid, they remember what it's like to *be* solid. Sensations. Pleasure. *Pain.*

Hence, if Bully McGillicutty was real enough to swing an axe, he was real enough to get the shit kicked out of him.

Not that that was our Plan A, because the only way to truly win a fight with a ghost is to avoid that fight altogether.

Ghosts might feel pain, but if we lopped the Minotaur's head off *à la* Darling's corpse, that wouldn't kill it. At best (for us), the Minotaur would experience a major earth-shaking revelation of shock and awe that would require quite a bit of recovery time.

At worst (same)? One spectacularly sore and pissed-off Minotaur that never forgets how *it's already dead.*

---

23 More than once.

So, if you want to survive a fight to the death with a ghost? You *run*.

Mike and I scattered. He dove to the side while I charged the Minotaur with a battle cry.

It roared and swung its axe.

The Minotaur missed me by a mile, mainly because I had turned my charge into a diving roll and had zipped through its legs before running as fast as I could in the opposite direction.

For the record, I will have you note that I did *not* hit the Minotaur in his jimmies. It would have been easy—they were *right there* in all of their barely-covered-by-a-loincloth dangly blueness. But there was a chance that we could still reason with him, and once you punch someone in the junk, Minotaur or not, that chance goes away.

I actually yelled this at the Minotaur as I scampered down the tunnel. I don't know if he understood English—"Hey, I coulda nut-punted you but I didn't, okay? Bye!"—but I figured that maybe the thought counted.

There was a bellow behind me, and the ground started to shake with the *Thump!Thump!Thump!* of pounding feet. I turned a sharp corner and started running straight-out, the light from my flashlight illuminating a tunnel with none of the usual chunky pointy bits one would expect in a natural cave, with another well-defined intersection up ahead.

Oh goodie. The Labyrinth had *levels*.

I ran straight at the wall in front of me. The plan was to do one of those Parkour-style flips over the Minotaur, and then run back the way I came. Fortunately, I remembered at what might have been my very last second that Minotaurs are taller than most of the dudes I practice freerunning with, plus a bonus set of pointy horns, and changed that flip from overhead (*clonk*squish*gore*) to sideways (*whee!*woosh*zoom*).

The Minotaur bellowed again as I dodged around him, and it swung that wicked labrys at me. I grabbed the labrys' shaft and used it to whip my body forward.

On my way up and over, I had a clear view of the Minotaur's

left arm. It had a scar running from its shoulder to its elbow, ending in a nasty curve that reminded me of a fishhook.

I suddenly regretted not having paid more attention to the Minotaur's dangly bits while I was down there.

The momentum from the labrys put another few long lengths between me and the Minotaur. I shot up the same tunnel I had just run down, and when I reached the end, I tossed my flashlight over the edge of the chasm. I screamed, too, and tried to taper my voice like I was falling. Then, for good measure, I chucked a few decent-sized rocks after my flashlight.

Then I tucked myself into a tiny ball behind another large rock, pulled Darling's handy camouflage cloak around me, and waited.

The *Thump!Thump!Thump!* slowed, then stopped. From beneath the edge of the hood, I saw a pair of blue bare feet walk up and down the edge of the chasm, right at the spot where I had pretended to fall to my death.

After a moment, the feet vanished.

I don't mean the Minotaur walked on—I mean that it *vanished.*

I waited a few more long moments for a labrys to split my head open, and when that didn't happen, I started creeping towards the treasure room.

Keep in mind I had no idea if this would work. The Minotaur and the Labyrinth? Pretty much synonymous. I figured that the Minotaur had some sense of where trespassers were located when they were in its domain: that's why it had appeared when Speedy had cleared the threshold of the treasure room. But was this an all-encompassing sense? Did it know exactly where I was, right this moment?

I was betting no.

Ghosts are only human, after all.

And this particular dead human most likely had experience with a particular kind of living human, which is to say that its only social contact for however long it had been lurking in this hole tended to be brief and bloody.

Unless, of course, the Minotaur was just an ordinary bored dead dude who enjoyed moonlighting as a monster. If this was the case, I was screwed. But I could *see* this ghost—out of all of the ghosts in Greece, this one was strong enough to cross whatever socio-cultural boundaries that had prevented me from seeing the others. As I slunk down the tunnel in the dark, finding my way back to the treasure room by feel alone, I knew that any ghost strong enough to manifest as the Minotaur would not stay in this dusty horror hole unless it thought it absolutely had to.

After an eternity of groping around in the dark, the reflected glow from the gold in the treasure room began to light the tunnel. I kept low and quiet, and made my way to the room as quickly as I dared.

As I reached the opening to the treasure room, I heard Speedy's voice: "Come on in."

"You sure?" I whispered back.

"Just get in here."

I scooted inside, pausing at the invisible threshold which functioned as a doorbell for a legendary monster. "You better be right about this," I muttered as I crossed it.

Speedy, sitting amongst a pile of gems the size of his nose, said nothing for about five seconds. Then: "Okay, good. Wasn't sure that would work."

"You bastard."

"Hey," Speedy said, as he lifted his forepaws so I could pick him up. "We're learning as we go."

I let him climb up to my shoulders as I gazed around the room. "You guys have been in here the entire time?"

"Yeah. Thanks for leading it away. What is it?"

"I'm not sure," I said. It was getting hard to think: there was so much I wanted to see and touch and explore…

"Focus," Speedy said, whipping a paw across my head. "That thing could show up at any moment. Tell me what happened, and what you think it is. Your gut instincts are usually spot on when it comes to ghosts."

So I told him about the brief chase down the tunnels, and how I had tricked the Minotaur into thinking I had fallen off of the ledge. He was especially interested in the scar—"Are you *sure* it was the same one you saw in your dreams?"—and kept looking around the room as if taking inventory.

I couldn't blame him. It was hard to concentrate while standing in a dragon's hoard.

Sorry. Minotaur's hoard.

It wasn't the gold and gems that had grabbed me; it was all of the *things*. They were all ancient, and so many of them chimed at me with the same pushing, pulling sensation that I was learning to associate with objects with deep histories. As I walked around the room, vertigo rose up, and my knees began to give way...

I touched the three beads around my neck, and the feeling of falling into the abyss disappeared.

"Fuck yeah," I whispered to myself. "I'm already Helen's bitch, y'all."

"What?"

"Nothing," I told Speedy, as we paused by an overly ornate shield the size of a smallish car. It was covered in raised reliefs that were too detailed and complex to make out without dropping everything for serious study, but I managed to spot the sun and the moon at its center, with the constellations spaced out around them.

"Think Sparky could lift that?" I asked the koala.

"Easily."

I grinned. "Nice."

"Hope," Mike whispered from across the room. "Come and see this."

He had a naked sword in his hands. It was a claymore, that enormous metal weapon of William Wallace/Mel Gibson fame.

It fit him.

"Damn," I said. "That looks good on you."

Speedy whopped me across the head again. "Do the math."

I had no idea what he meant until I did, and then I needed

to sit down on the floor for a moment to recover.

Claymore.

Scottish claymore.

Scottish claymore from the 16th century.

"Oh hell," I said. "We're not the first to discover the Labyrinth."

"Probably the first to have lived this long, though," Mike said, as he carefully repositioned the claymore on one of the weapons racks. "There's a pocket watch on a table by the east wall. That's the most modern item I've found."

I shuddered at the idea of cell phones lost within this golden mess. It's all well and good to think that a Minotaur's been murdering explorers for millennia, but it gets a little more real when those explorers are part of *your* millennium. I wondered if the more modern items had belonged to psychics who had gotten past Helen's defenses, or if the queen had the occasional off day.

Or maybe we weren't the first she had sent down into the Labyrinth...

I was suddenly very doubtful of Speedy's version of events, how Helen had seen my future and was trying to help me. Speedy is usually right, but when he's wrong, he's dead wrong.

"All right," I said. "What's the game plan? Try and sneak back up to the surface, or keep going down?"

"What's further down?" Mike asked, as he tested the balance of a gladius.

"The Labyrinth keeps going," I replied. "That claymore was more your style."

"The blade's too long for fighting in close quarters," he said with a sigh. "Did you see any of the layout?"

"No," I said. "I was in and gone as fast as I could. The lower tunnels look identical to the upper tunnels, though."

I heard a rushing clatter of coins as Speedy shoved the contents of a nearby table onto the floor.

"Speedy!" I whispered, horrified.

"Time's more important than trying to be sneaky," the koala

said. He had taken another Sharpie from Mike's pack, and was sketching out a grid in broad black lines on the two-thousand-year-old table. "You were right: the Minotaur's sense of this place isn't absolute. If it were, it wouldn't be searching for your body. I'm guessing it has a limited awareness of certain locations. This room is one of those; it knows that someone never left it. That's why it didn't pop in when you crossed the threshold; since Mike and I stayed put, that awareness was already active. It'll swing back and check on us when it can't find you."

"Hope, come and pick your poison," Mike said in his normal tone.

I left Speedy to turn a priceless artifact into so much graffiti, and joined Mike by the weapon racks.

It was...

Okay.

Take a moment and pretend you've trained in the martial arts from when you were a little kid. It might not be your entire life, but it's a huge part of it—you've spent the better part of your existence accumulating factoids about fighters and fighting.

Then, without any warning, you're deep in a hole with the weapons of generations of warriors. You recognize *all of them*, fresh and shiny in their ghost-preserved stasis.

Which one do you choose?

Most of them were Greek. Obviously. Mike and I would have both gravitated right to the Japanese weapons, if there had been any. We had both trained on those, and when you're going into battle against a ginormous predeceased monster, familiarity is a big plus. But no, it seemed as if no one from Japan had ever stumbled into the Labyrinth, or, if they had, they hadn't been packing.

I walked past a king's ransom in weapons, trailing my fingertips across them as if waiting for one to speak to me.

Some of them did.

My hand closed on a xiphos, the short sword that defined one-on-one combat for the Spartans.

I tested its weight. It felt good and right and—

I shook myself as I replaced it on the rack.

"No," I said. "*My* fight. Not yours."

"You okay?" Mike asked me.

"Nope," I said, as I moved down the row. "I think Helen wants to ride me into battle."

"Ah."

"Yeah."

Mike went to gather up the sheath to his gladius. "Why would she do that?"

"Because the Minotaur is Theseus," Speedy said from atop his gigantic sketch pad. "Or what's left of him. Get over here."

I grabbed something off of the rack at random, more to have the weight of a weapon in my hands than any rational selection. Then, I joined the boys at Speedy's table.

He had been drawing the Labyrinth.

Speedy's an excellent draftsman; he had used solid and dotted lines to break up the sketch, and I could tell at a glance that the solid lines showed the path we had taken to reach the treasure room.

He was reading my face, and nodded. "I guessed at the rest," he said, tapping a claw on a dotted line. "Patterns repeat."

"You think it's this big?" Mike asked. The map spread across the entire table. If Speedy had drawn it to scale, the treasure room was a shoe closet dangling on the edge of a mansion.

"Yup," the koala said. "I need to take a few turns through the lower section before I can get a feel for the layout, but if the same architect designed it, I'll be able to take us straight to the center."

"The center?" I asked. "What's there?"

"Something more important than this," Speedy said, waving at the mountains of gold around us. "Something so important that its creators set this room out as bait."

"Okay, okay, I gotcha," I said. "Anyone looking for treasure would have come straight into this room if they made it this far—you can't miss it—and bam! Minotaur murder spree."

"Exactly."

"What did you mean about Theseus and the Minotaur?" Mike asked.

"It's a ghost, right? Has to be a person in there somewhere," Speedy said, and then netted the claws on his front paws together. "Name another person in the mythology as closely linked to the Minotaur as Theseus."

"But Theseus killed the Minotaur," I said.

Ever received a look of pure scorn from a marsupial? It withers the soul.

"Or," I amended, "Theseus *didn't*, because there's no such thing as a real Minotaur."

"Bingo," Speedy said, as he added a few flourishes to the map. "But say you're an ancient Greek king, and you've done some really shitty things during your life. Say you're part of a culture which believes that your Afterlife will include punishments and eternal torment befitting the crimes you committed in life. To top it off, you don't die in battle, which might have redeemed you. Instead, you walk into the throne room of the queen you blamed for your misfortune, and you lay a death curse on her and her kingdom."

"Oh, *shit*," I said. "Maybe... Maybe since you're the ghost of a king who's still celebrated in Western culture, you've got the power to stick around for millennia. But you're popular not because you made treaties or peace or whatever, but because your name is synonymous with a monster's. So you... What? Theseus got his mental wires crossed along the way and *became* that monster?"

"Just a guess," Speedy said, as he finished his sketch. "But that scar means it's a good one."

"Remind me to never go looking for the ghost of Saint George," Mike said.

I cringed at the idea of a firebreathing saint.

"Why would a ghost keep a scar?" Mike asked.

I knew the answer to that one. "It's part of his identity," I replied. "Helen *hurt* him—she changed how Theseus thought of himself."

"And if your dreams are her memories," Speedy said, "then we know he's sticking around to hurt *her*, and she's sticking around to keep him in checkmate. If he can't find the mental wherewithal to get rid of that scar, he can't shake the idea that he's cursed."

Mike leaned against the cave wall, and I felt a wave of sadness flow from him. "That poor soul."

"You mean that rapist fuckhead who kidnapped little girls?" I asked.

"I mean the human soul that's trapped itself down here for thousands of years," he replied. "Whatever his crimes were in life, he's paid for them."

Mike couldn't hear the women's screams still running around in my memory, so I didn't say anything.

"So," Speedy said. He pointed at his map, towards the space at its center that was defined in broken lines. "Do we go up or down?"

Mike and I came over to lean against the table. "What happens if we go up?" I asked.

"The Minotaur feels all of us cross the threshold, and it appears."

"And if we go down?"

"Same damned thing."

"And if we stay here," I said, looking around the room. "It appears."

"Eventually," Speedy said. "It's a ghost, so time's practically meaningless to it."

"Except whoever's inside that monster is really messed up," I said. "It thinks it's got a job to do. Can we even leave the mountain without fighting it?"

"Maybe if we hadn't gone inside the treasure room. After this, I doubt it."

"Well, then," Mike said, as he moved to unbuckle his new sword from his waist. "We don't fight him—we help him."

Which might have been a stunning idea, except the Minotaur chose that moment to appear behind him.

# CHAPTER 39

I hadn't even gotten my mouth open to shout Mike's name when the labrys slashed through the air.

It was cool, though; Mike had read my body language and was already halfway across the room, snatching Speedy off the table as he ran.

"First right, second left, first right!" Speedy yelled as the two of them sped from the room.

"Gotcha!" The Minotaur lunged at me; I swung my sword, and felt it cut through muscle and bone. The monster bellowed in pain as one of its legs came apart at the knee. Another whipping motion, and I took off the hand holding the labrys.

Then I was out of the treasure room and racing down the tunnel.

And learning—quickly—that I didn't have a flashlight.

"God *damn* it!" I muttered, and skidded to a halt before I accidentally launched myself into the chasm.

I took a deep breath, turned, and walked back into the treasure room.

Mike's pack lay beside the table that Speedy had used as his sketch pad. The Minotaur was a dozen feet away, flat on the ground and moaning in pain. The golden glow of the room had changed; now that the Minotaur was the only source of light, the treasure reflected an eerie blue-green hue.

Very, very unpleasant.

I kept a wary eye on the monster as I circled the room. Mike had kept a few spare flashlights clipped to the outside of his pack. I grabbed two of these and strapped one to my thigh and the other to my belt as quickly as I could.

The Minotaur watched every move I made, venom in its eyes.

"Well," I said, as I picked up my sword again. The Minotaur flinched, and I lowered the blade so I didn't look like a threat. "I'm betting this is the first time you've experienced pain in…I dunno. Ages.

"I'm supposed to set you free," I added. "Any advice?"

The Minotaur bared its teeth at me, and then it and all of its associated parts dematerialized into a blue mist.

"Didn't think so," I said. I hoisted the sword and sprinted out of the room.

I followed Speedy's directions through the Labyrinth. At the third turn, I heard Mike call my name in a low whisper.

I followed the sound: they had found a hidey-hole on an upper ledge overlooking two intersections. I climbed up the wall and told them what had happened in the treasure room.

"Great," Speedy said with an eye roll. "You reminded the monster that it's really nothing but a ghost. Thanks."

"Would have happened anyway," Mike said.

"And now it knows we can hurt it," I said.

"Which just motivates it to bring its A-game," Speedy said. "Theseus was a warrior. Somewhere in those motes of blue light are his memories. Do you really want to test yourself against a legendary Greek hero?"

"Actually, yeah, that sounds pretty amaz—"

"Oh *God*, just shut up," Speedy said.

"I think that's a fantastic idea," Mike said.

"See?" I told Speedy.

"No, I mean, we should remind it that it's a human being. We can't reason with a monster."

"Um." I raised a finger. "I should mention that from what I saw of Theseus in my dreams, the Minotaur might be an improvement. I don't know if we can reason with it, even if it does remember it's really a man."

"Well," Mike said, "it's worth considering. We can't fight him. Not over the long term."

"What are we missing?" I asked, as I peered over the ledge. I saw nothing except darkness. The Minotaur either didn't know where we were, or was still licking its imaginary wounds. "Helen wouldn't have sent us here if it were a lost cause. We've got to be able to do something that she can't."

"We know she's here," Mike said. "She's been steering you."

"Call your husband."

"No," I told the koala. I didn't—*couldn't*—want to see Sparky until this was all over. I was having a hard enough time keeping it together without bringing him into this mess. "We're missing...something."

"What's at its center?" Mike asked.

"Hmm?" Speedy flicked an ear at Mike.

"It's a Labyrinth, right? That sketch you drew. What's at its—"

"Yes! Of course!" Speedy nearly shouted. Then, in a whisper: "Come on."

He scurried down the wall and danced on all fours until Mike and I reached the ground. I scooped him up, and we started another slow descent.

Talk about nerve-wracking. Those two-plus hours in the second level of the Labyrinth were among the worst of my life. At every moment, we expected the Minotaur to lunge out and skewer us on its horns. Also? It was a ghost, which meant the floors and walls couldn't be trusted.

(I was kind of hoping the Minotaur would try to manifest through a wall, which would mean it would have to solidify as it did, which would mean there was a high possibility that it half of its body would get trapped in the wall until it could sort out its molecules, and God only knows how long that would take but at least we'd know where it was until that happened. The anticipation was murder.)

Mike led the way. Speedy rode on my shoulders, keeping watch behind us. We traveled slow and steady, our swords at the ready. Mike kept his sword low to the floor, ready to come up and gut the Minotaur at a moment's notice; the saber I had grabbed on a whim was much lighter, so I rested it on the shoulder unoccupied by a koala, ready for an overhand swing.

My saber was Damascus steel; that had made me smile.

"How do you imprison a ghost?" I asked, sometime late into the second hour. I hadn't felt Helen nearby; I assumed that meant Speedy was leading us in the right direction.

"It lets you," Mike said.

"Or you get an equally strong ghost to keep it in check," Speedy said.

"That's still just a trick of the mind," Mike said. "On a subconscious level, a ghost has to consent to being trapped."

"Maybe," I said. "But we know that different ghosts are stronger and weaker than each other. That's a fact, not a trick of the mind. There're natural laws at work here; we just don't know what those are."

It took Mike a while to reply.

"I'm not saying you're wrong, but I don't like that idea," he finally said. "One human imposing their will upon another... That shouldn't be allowed to happen in life, let alone after death."

"Law of the jungle, baby," Speedy said. "The strong will always dominate the weak."

"Well, the jungle can go suck eggs," Mike said.

We were all quiet for a few more moments. Then: "Suck eggs?" I asked.

Mike sighed with the deep resignation of a man who is still many lifetimes away from enlightenment.

"How old are you? Ninety zillion?"

"Here's another question," Mike said. "Who built this Labyrinth?"

"Atlas didn't know," I said.

"That might be worth learning," he said, as he ran his fingertips along the nearest wall.

We tripped over Atlas' body sometime during that second hour. Pretty much literally: Speedy was riding on my shoulders and keeping watch low, while I was leading the group and keeping watch high, when Mike grabbed the back of my jacket.

"What?" I whispered, my sword ready, and then saw the... uh...squishiness in front of me, wearing a familiar shirt and pair of jeans.

"Oops," Speedy said with a toothy grin.

I took a deep breath and reminded myself there were many good reasons why I shouldn't murder a koala in cold blood. They were an endangered species. They were cute. They were... There were probably other reasons, but screw me sideways if I could think of any at that moment.

"Just as I thought," Speedy said, pointing up. The walls were rough, cave-like, and they kept going up. We could still see the light of our lantern, hundreds of feet overhead. "The chasm was in the natural part of the cave."

He leapt off of my shoulders and ran up the wall a few yards, his claws tracing more of those scratches in the rock face that suggested heavy items had been lowered down to the bottom.

"What are you thinking, Speedy?" Mike asked.

"Ask me again when we get to the center," the koala said, as he returned to my shoulders. "We're nearly there."

And then, five minutes later, we reached the center of the Labyrinth.

It had been lying in wait for us. Speedy's predictions of the layout had been completely accurate, except he thought there should have been one last hard left turn before we reached the center. Whoever built the place had decided, no, we don't need that last turn because we're just going to mess with anyone who makes it this far instead.

Mike and I were tired and our reactions were getting slower, but we still stopped short well before the threshold. The central chamber was dark, with a faint ghostly blue light coming from somewhere within. I tried to peer inside to see if the Minotaur was the source of the light, but felt the invisible hands push me away.

"Uh, guys?" I said, as my hiking boots began to slide across the Labyrinth's floor. "Helen doesn't want us going inside."

I slid backwards until Helen decided I had reached a safe distance, and released me. Then, something grabbed my chin and tilted my head towards the ceiling.

"Hope?" Mike asked, concerned.

"She's getting handsy again," I said. I brought up a flashlight and scanned the area in front of my eyes. "Do you see anything up there?"

"Maybe," Speedy said. He jumped from Mike's shoulders like a giant housecat, and began to scale the walls again. "Yeah. Toss me a light."

I lobbed one of my flashlights at him. He caught it in his teeth, then shone the beam up and down the walls around him. The light vanished in one spot; Speedy had found a well-camouflaged hole.

"It's a hidden passageway," the koala said. He ran a few steps across the wall, then disappeared into same spot that had eaten the light. Mike and I exchanged an uneasy glance when he vanished, but Speedy's head popped out from a second hole on the other side of the doorway. "It looks natural, not manmade. It's an alternate route into the central chamber. We can avoid the threshold altogether. Can you get up here?"

Mike gave me a boost so I could join Speedy in his hidden niche, and then I helped Mike to scale the wall. On the far side of the passageway, we paused to examine the room below us.

It was big, about the size of a decent-sized home goods store. Unlike most of the Labyrinth, this room looked like a natural cave instead of a manmade structure, with rough walls and a floor peppered with miniature hills and valleys. It held two objects: the first was a large white marble stature of a warrior woman, her Spartan xiphos extended and pointing downwards. Her breasts were bare; her body nothing but hard muscles; her face the most deadly kind of beautiful.

"Helen," I whispered.

The stone sword of the long-dead queen was aimed at the second object in the room. A fire pit waited below her blade, where ghostly blue flame flickered around a black dagger with a straight edge and a heavy handle.

"There," I said, nudging Mike with the side of my fist. "That's the dagger Theseus used to kill himself."

"And that's what Archimedes has been working on for the

last two thousand years," Speedy said.

Mike and I looked at the koala, and then followed his gaze up to the cavernous ceiling high above.

"Oh *wow*," I whispered.

Archimedes had had a long time to perfect the art of his orreries. A solar system turned above us, slow and glittering in glass and precious metals. There were comets and planets and moons, all rotating in a celestial dance around three large objects. I tried to find recognizable features—the continents of Earth, or the rings of Saturn—but nothing seemed familiar.

Behind this spectacle, written in gold letters across the roof, were formulae. Countless (sorry) numbers in gilded paint had been painstakingly applied in luminous equations. The blue light from the fire below made it glow like a star-filled sky.

Speedy's eyes lit up as he read it, and he chuckled.

"Nine, ten, eleven… Doesn't our solar system have eight planets?" Mike asked.

"Yup," Speedy said. "But this isn't our solar system."

Mike and I let that sink in.

"Oh," I said in a tiny voice.

"Oh, indeed," the koala said. He seemed unable to look away from the grand orrery above us. "We're taking photographs of this before we leave," he said. "This is more lifetimes of labor than I can calculate."

"The planets?"

"No," he said, shaking his head as he broke away. "That's window dressing. The money is in the math."

"All right," I said. "Photographs later. Mystery now. What's going on here?"

"Looks like we were right; Helen is here to balance Theseus," Mike said.

"I'll bet she's entombed in that sarcophagus," Speedy said.

I blinked and reassessed the room below us. What I had taken for a marble statue on its pedestal was actually a statue balanced on top of a large box.

We had found Helen's tomb.

"If I had to make an educated guess," Speedy said, "When Sparta began to go into decline, Helen had Theseus' dagger thrown into a deep cave. When that didn't fix things, she ordered her people to use the same cave as her own tomb after she died. They stuck her down here, along with her share of the spoils from the Trojan War as her grave goods."

"This isn't a cave," I said.

"It was once," Speedy said. "No ancient civilization could build a Labyrinth like this. Two levels under a mountain? Miles and miles of smooth walls? And how did they move this statue down here, when it's larger than some of the tunnels? I call bullshit on that feat of engineering. You saw what she did with rock and stone at the shrine—I think Theseus has been building this place for two thousand years."

"Theseus? Not Helen?"

"She's been busy making the normals ignore this mountain. But he's deluded himself into thinking he's a Minotaur, right? What else is he gonna do during that time than shape his own cage? Maybe just at the rate of a couple of feet a day, but time plus energy equals Labyrinth."

"This is hell," Mike whispered. His voice was rough. "This is hell for both of them. We've got to end this."

"How?" I asked. "If it's something simple, like snuffing out that fire, why hasn't Helen done it herself?"

"Because this is Theseus's kingdom," Speedy said. He poked one paw out over the edge of the ledge, as if testing the air inside the central cavern. When nothing happened, he began to climb down the wall, one cautious step at a time. "The only thing she's been able to affect down here is you, Hope. You're *hers*—she's been pushing you around, but that's it. She didn't intervene with Atlas or Darling, and she hasn't sheltered us from the Minotaur. She can't. All she can do is keep Theseus imprisoned in this mountain."

The koala reached the base of the wall. He paused. "Got me covered?" he asked.

Mike and I replied by drawing our swords.

"Thanks," Speedy said, and planted his forepaws on the floor of the central chamber. He counted to ten before he turned and ran back up the wall to join us.

"Maybe it only works with humans," I said, before I remembered that Speedy had been the one to trip the threshold to the treasure room. "Never mind," I muttered, and jumped down from our hidden niche.

I walked a slow circuit of the central chamber, my Damascus saber at the ready, with Mike and Speedy keeping watch over me. When I completed the circuit with nary a sign of Minotaur, they joined me on the floor.

I knelt beside the fire pit. The black dagger was suspended in midair, the blue flames coating its blade.

"What does your gut say?" Speedy asked.

"It's been fifteen hours since we last ate anything substantial, and I'm a moron for not grabbing a bottle of water when I went back for the flashlights."

"Don't make me bite you."

"Right." I sighed. "I think it's a seriously bad idea to touch that knife."

"Okay then," Speedy said, and the two of us backed away from the fire.

"Hey, guys?" Mike called to us. "Come and take a look at this."

We crossed the room to where he stood by the base of Helen's tomb. The far side had been set up as a shrine, with personal objects strewn about the surface of the marble sarcophagus.

Most of these looked as if they had belonged to a woman. I saw a hairbrush, some jewelry, trinkets and small statutes...

"Theseus moved all of the gold to the treasure room," I guessed, "but he didn't touch anything that was Helen's."

My eyes snapped back to the jewelry. Lying on top of a polished bronze mirror in an olivewood frame was a long string of glass beads.

"No way," I muttered, as I removed the lanyard from my neck. I cupped Helen's three beads in my hand before I placed them next to those resting on the mirror.

The ones I had been wearing were beaten all to shit, and the ones on the mirror appeared new and still shone with their gold casings. Other than that, they were identical.

The mirror flared bright blue.

"Guys?" I said, as I put some distance between me and the mirror. "Do you see that?"

"No," Mike said.

"Maybe." Speedy paused, then added, "Whatever it is, it's hazy."

"It's Helen," I said quietly, as the dead queen appeared in her mirror.

She was still a ghost; the mirror showed her in blues, just like when I viewed her through a cyborg-filtered cell phone.[24] She tapped the other side of the metal where the three missing beads had joined her own.

"Yeah, I brought them back," I offered lamely. "Nice to finally... Hi."

The woman in the mirror pointed at something behind me.

"Aw, hell," I muttered, as the blue flames in the fire pit rose to engulf the black dagger. "I bet this'll be good."

---

24 I *know*, right?!

# CHAPTER 40

Helen had given us ample warning. The Minotaur was knitting itself together from the flames, growing taller and more solid by the moment. It was extremely dramatic, but slow as molasses. Mike and I had plenty of time to position ourselves on either side of the fire.

When the monster finally took form, it stared at me, fury burning in its eyes. It huffed and puffed a couple of times, and then let out a savage bellow that shook the grand orrery above us.

"Eeek," I said, and stabbed the Minotaur in his thigh with my sword.

Mike hit the monster at the same time. He got the Minotaur's left side; I got its right. We maimed the monster using Helen's system, with long slashes through the meat.

Mike even mimicked the little fishhook at the end of the scar on the beast's left arm.

The Minotaur collapsed into the fire, yelping like a hurt puppy before it vanished.

"I know I'm tempting Fate here," I said to Mike, "but I expected more from a mythical monster."

"He *is* a couple thousand years out of practice," Mike replied, almost apologetically.

"East corner!" Speedy shouted from the top of Helen's statue.

We turned towards where the koala was pointing. This time, the Minotaur appeared at the far end of the room in a single mighty puff of smoke, reforming into flesh almost instantly. It lowered its head and charged.

"Now *that's* what I'm talking about!" I said, as I brought my sword up to guard.

There was no doubt that the Minotaur was rusty. It made

plenty of rookie mistakes as it relearned what it meant to have mass. Its feet would get crossed as it turned. The weight of its horns kept twisting it off-balance. Sometimes it remembered it was carrying a labrys, and sometimes it didn't.

But...

As we fought, the Minotaur slowed its attacks. It would wait for me or Mike to close, watching our technique before responding. This made the Minotaur a much better fighter.

Still not a great fighter but, you know. It tried.

Let me give you an example.

Mike's taller and has more upper-body strength than I do: he's got the reach and the heft. Me, I'm light and quick. When we first started fighting, Mike would go in high to do damage, while I went in low to cripple its legs. Each time, the Minotaur would roar and swing at Mike, who made a larger target, and I'd take it down. This strategy worked pretty well for about fifteen minutes, with Mike *whamwham**slash!*** on the Minotaur's arms and torso, while I'd *ziiiiii**phamstrings!***

On the fifth exchange, Mike and I made the nearly fatal mistake of assuming that the Minotaur would swing at him instead of me. I came in close and low, and was nearly cut in two as the Minotaur changed its overhand attack to a very effective underhand swing.

"Whoa!" I shouted, as the labrys came at me like the world's biggest, sharpest golf club. I rolled to the side, and felt the edge of the labrys pass through the back of my jacket.

"Too close!" Mike yelled.

"Yup!" I yelled back, as I kicked the Minotaur hard enough to shatter its nearest ankle. The monster went down but didn't cry out; Mike followed this up with a clean swing which decapitated it. The head and body stayed put for all of five heartbeats before they disappeared, and then reformed, whole, in the fire pit. "It's learning!"

As Mike and I kept picking it to pieces, the Minotaur began to show some intelligence. Its attacks became less about rage and more about precision, with the beast using its size and mass as secondary weapons. Mike would go in to hit it low, and the Minotaur would start to swing its labrys to retaliate, then turn that into a feint and come in with its horns. I'd bring up my sword, and it would aim a kick at where it thought my chest would be. And so on, and so on, and continued for what seemed like *forever*.

It was like sparring with a very gifted child.

A very large, heavily-armed gifted child who would never get tired, and who was gradually learning that pain was nothing but a state of mind.

Mike and I began to work the Minotaur in shifts. It was a delaying tactic, nothing more; the person fighting the monster had to expend twice as much energy, so it's not like the one who was resting got that much more value out of it than when we worked together. During these breaks, the one who was resting went over our game plan with Speedy, which could be summed up as: *Any new ideas on how we can get out of this situation?* and *Fuck no, just try not to get killed.*

During one of these shifts when I was fighting the monster, I came in close and...

Slipped.

I don't know on what, okay? I guess someone left a banana peel lying around the Labyrinth.

I face-planted. Right in front of the Minotaur.

Mike was there to cover me almost as soon as I hit the ground, but it wasn't necessary—the Minotaur wasn't attacking. Instead, it was making a little huffing noise.

It took me a moment to realize the Minotaur was laughing.

"Hope?" Mike said, his eyes fixed on the monster. "Move about twenty feet away, then come at me."

I was still trying to catch my breath. "What?"

"Fight me. Bow and attack."

I pushed myself away from the Minotaur, slowly. Mike did too, backing up, gladius at the ready but no longer directed at the monster.

The Minotaur watched us with its blue-black eyes, but didn't move.

When we were a safe distance away from the beast, Mike and I bowed to each other, just as if we were in his dojo back in Maryland. Then we went at it, hammer and tongs.

Or, saber and gladius. Whatever.

We came in hard, metal on metal, and pushed off as if that first contact hadn't shaken both of us more than the entire last hour of skirmishes with the Minotaur. Mike used the gladius like a katana, two-handed with long, serious swings. My saber was light and flowed like water, and I was in and out, in and out, faster than thinking.

He swung; I shot in close. I turned; he was right there, his blade bearing down on me, his size and reach making up for my speed. He'd step; I'd follow. Up, down, up, down, the sound of ancient steel ringing in the room as we struck and parried.

Neither of us were trying to get past each other's defense; it was a tournament to see which one of us would make the first mistake.

It was me.

I'm not Mike's equal—nobody is. I overextended, just a fraction of a fraction, but it was enough for Mike to slide in past my blade and tag me with the flat side of the gladius.

He stepped away, his sword at middle position.

We bowed.

Speedy, perched atop the bare breasts of marble Helen, hooted and cheered.

I turned to the Minotaur and bowed.

I'll be damned if the monster didn't return it.

And then I took the Minotaur to school.

Our first few formal exchanges were pathetic. The Minotaur had been fighting me and Mike for over an hour, and it seemed determined to use the same hack-and-slash techniques that had allowed us to pick it apart. On most of our exchanges, I had to hold back from seriously hurting it: the Minotaur kept extending its labrys too far, or it failed to guard its neck, or any one of the many hundreds of careless combat errors that it couldn't seem to avoid.

"Dude," I finally said. "Stop. Just *stop!*"

The monster froze in place.

I showed the Minotaur a mistake it had been making with its feet by mimicking its pose, then shuffling into a stronger fighting stance. "It's all about the core," I explained, as I tapped my sternum with my thumb. "You have to get your central body aligned before you can concentrate on anything else."

Speedy, standing on top of Helen's boobs, translated this into ancient Greek.

The Minotaur whipped its head towards Speedy, Mike and I forgotten. The monster stared at the koala as a sad crooning noise escaped from its throat.

"Oh my God," I whispered to Mike. "This is the saddest thing I've ever seen."

The Minotaur glanced at me and Mike, then back up at Speedy, whimpering.

Over the last hour of combat, I thought that maybe we were getting through to Theseus, that maybe there was something of that man left within the monster. But that whimpering... Oh God, that *whimpering!* There was nothing sane in that noise—it was the sound of pure agony. Whatever kind of man Theseus had been? He didn't exist. Not anymore. Countless centuries spent in what amounted to solitary confinement had stripped him of his mind and personality.

Worse? There was still something human within the monster. Something that had a sense of humor, that was trying to socialize, that was reaching out to connect with the language it recognized...

I suddenly knew why Archimedes had chosen to come here when he had the alternative of his cozy library sanctuary, and why he had built a window to the stars a mile underground.

"Speedy?" Mike said. "Talk to him. Tell him we're travelers who've heard stories of a great warrior living in a mountain. Say that after fighting him, we're convinced those stories are about him, and we'd like to learn more about how he came to be here."

"And if you want to get out of this alive, don't be a wiseass," I added.

"Really?" Speedy snapped. "I thought I'd just cut to the chase and tell it that its immortal enemy sent us here to destroy it. You don't think that'd go well for us?"

The koala resumed speaking in ancient Greek.

The Minotaur panted in shallow gasps, grasping the air around the statue as if Speedy's words could be felt as well as heard.

"It's not answering," Speedy said.

"Keep talking," Mike said. "It's the familiarity more than the conversation."

Mike approached the Minotaur, very, very slowly. Then, as he was standing beside the monster at the base of Helen's statue, he laid a hand on the Minotaur's arm.

The Minotaur's blue-black eyes moved from Speedy to Mike, and its bull's nose flared.

"Would you like to sit down and talk?" Mike asked, before gesturing to a spot on the ground near the fire pit.

I sat, smiling like an idiot with the saber across my lap, just in case the Minotaur didn't quite get the gist of Speedy's translation.

The monster's eyes shot between me and Mike, unable to process what was happening. Mike cupped a gentle hand under its elbow, and guided the Minotaur to where I was sitting by the fire. The beast stared at my legs, then the ground under its own bare feet, as if the concept of sitting was too alien to imitate. It had to watch Mike stand and sit a couple of times before it bent at the waist and pressed its hands against the ground, then crabwalked on all fours until it got the hang of a flat surface under its limbs.

Those horns must have been heavy. It fell over twice. Both times, Mike helped it back to a sitting position.

Neither Speedy nor I laughed.

Then, Mike began to talk.

He spoke of peace, mostly, and those traps we create for

ourselves. He didn't lunge right into it, of course—he started with a story called the Lost Son. Long story short? A man was convinced his son was dead, and when the son turned up alive, the man decided the boy couldn't be his son. The moral of the story is that our assumptions of what is true and what is not true can deprive us of happiness.

That's what Mike talked about. For hours. *Hours.* He talked until his voice was all but gone, and even Speedy with his superhearing had to come down from the statue to make sure he caught all of the details.

Speedy translated every single word.

I sat and watched the Minotaur.

(Along the way, the Minotaur's head began to droop. When Mike was busy with hand gestures and something about an Eightfold Path, I elbowed the creature in its side. Those horns came up, and I pointed at Mike. "Listen to him," I said, as sternly as I could without interrupting the story. "You *will* hear what he has to say." The monster gave a pained sigh, and fixed its full attention on Mike.)

Mike spoke of love, and loss, and the human experience. He spoke of ideals that we all hold on to as children, concepts such as being better—larger—than ourselves.

Of grief. Of grieving. Of fighting when we shouldn't.

And knowing when to let go.

And then, as easy as sugar dissolving in the spring rain, the Minotaur slipped out of our existence.

The three of us stared at the space where the Minotaur had sat. There was nothing left of it. No labrys, no semisolid mist. Nothing.

"Um..." I began, as I gazed around the room for any trace of ghostly blue. "Did it...go to bed?"

Beside us, the fire in the pit snuffed itself out.

It took our eyes a moment to adjust to the change in the lighting. The flashlight that Speedy had left as a lantern on the hidden ledge was still on, but it was a tiny beam of light in a very large room. We flipped on a few more flashlights, and shone these around to see if we could spot the Minotaur.

"Whoa," I said, as my light hit Theseus' black dagger. It was crumbling into pieces. "I'm going to take that as a positive sign."

"Yeah," Mike said, as he stood and stretched. "That was our good deed for the decade. Let's get out of here before we learn if that was a load-bearing monster."

"One sec," I said. My legs were so deeply asleep they might as well have been made of wobbly bees. I staggered over to the base of Helen's statue.

Helen wasn't in her mirror.

"Well, goodbye to you, too," I said, as I wrapped the three beads around the handle of my Puukko knife. I placed it and the beads on the mirror, and tried to ignore how I felt a little emptier than I should. "Happy hunting in…wherever. I hope you've finally made it to your own personal version of the Elysian Fields. Try not to murder anyone who doesn't deserve it."

I turned to rejoin the boys, and knelt so Speedy could climb to my shoulders. He buried his face against my neck.

"Tired?"

He whuffled softly before saying, "Like I just ended a week-long bender at the zoo. Can you imagine the power it took to keep something like Theseus' ghost imprisoned? *Damn*."

"Yeah, Helen was something special, that's for sure," I said as I fell in beside Mike, both of us dragging our swords along the ground. "Let's go home."

We paused to collect Atlas' body, because recently famous handsome men and last known associates and oh *God* we were so tired and we still had to lug a corpse up a hollow mountain. I used my sword to chop off his head and its hard-to-explain bullet hole, just to make it that much easier for us. I guess I put a little more strength than I needed to into the swing, and that's all I'll say about that particular experience, other than I absolutely do not need to repeat it. Ever.

Damascus steel, man. Incredible edge on that stuff.

We left Darling in the Labyrinth.[25] Along with the treasure. *All* of it. Swords included; we stuck those back in the racks where we had found them. On our way out of the treasure room, we recovered Mike's and Darling's packs, and the three of us fell on the water and energy bars like ravenous wolves.

I really don't remember how we got Atlas' body up those narrow stairs to the first level of the maze. Rope was involved, and more than a little swearing.

When we finally reached the first level, we knew we were on the home stretch, and we retraced our path in exhausted, blissful silence. It wasn't until we were nearing the entrance to the Labyrinth when I realized that Mike was humming softly.

"What's up?" I asked quietly, so as not to wake the sleeping koala clinging to my chest.

"I feel good," he said. "I helped to right a very old wrong. That's a rare opportunity."

"Yeah," I replied. "I don't even want to think about what might have happened if you weren't here."

"Good lesson to learn, though," he said, elbowing me playfully. "Compassion over cruelty."

Behind us, Atlas' body gave a particularly hard lurch to the side as we hit a steep part of the slope, and we fell quiet as we put our backs into it. Speedy muttered a few obscenities in his sleep.

"I think Helen had a different solution in mind," I said, as the light of day appeared at the end of the tunnel. "But yours was better."

I left it there. I didn't know the ending that Helen had envisioned, but I knew she wouldn't approve of how Mike had handled the Minotaur. Too nice. Too polite. Not enough suffering.

As for Mike, I would never dream of telling him he had probably managed to bore a ghost to death.

---

25 It's not like we left her body where she had died. We buried her as best we could, and each of us said a few words over her grave. Funeral services performed by psychics and super-geniuses are fairly unique; our eulogies were all different versions of *Sorry, but I told you so.*

# CHAPTER 41

In the end, we decided to keep the mountain and its trove a secret. There were a few good reasons for this: first and foremost, if Speedy, Mike, and I discovered two major archaeological sites within the space of a single week, everybody would know there was something hinky happening behind the scenes.

Second, there were some dead bodies that couldn't be properly explained, and Mike and I were too tired to get rid of them. Not just Atlas' and Darling's, mind—there was also Smiling Goon's, and when we went to untie the two other goons, we found their heads had been crushed as if by a gigantic telekinetic fist.[26] So we get to feel guilty about *that* for the rest of our lives and beyond. Thanks, Helen.

And?

Last but not least, the Labyrinth didn't belong to us. It was a sanctuary for the ghost of Archimedes, and there might have been others who dropped in from time to time to visit a lonely Minotaur. Who were we to come along and throw them out? We decided to leave it up to them as to whether they'd allow the cave to be rediscovered now that Helen's protection had been removed. Archimedes had the juice to keep it hidden, if that's what he wanted.

Speedy was too quick to agree that we had to leave the mountain to its ghosts. I think he was hoping to return someday. I had snapped a few photographs of the grand orrery with my phone, but he had thrown a fit over the resolution and nearly refused to leave. It was only after I reminded him that we knew a legion of cyborgs with digital avatars who could walk through walls that he consented to being carried home. But he kept looking at the photos until my battery died, and I got

26 We buried them, too, and their eulogies were mostly apologies about poor life choices and how it sucked to be on the receiving end of Not Thinking Things Through.

the feeling he wanted to explore the Labyrinth until he found the notes Archimedes had used to make that amazing celestial calendar from the other side of our galaxy.

(Ben's assurances to the contrary aside, I also think that if Time doesn't like to be made into anybody's bitch, Space is probably just as strict. Speedy will never get any real information out of that cave. It'll be like Ben said—lost, until we've thoroughly explored and gotten bored with Alpha Centauri, and then the grand orrery will be discovered and scholars will come up with all kinds of explanations to justify how something that can't exist, does.)

We slept in a heap at the base of the mountain until the wee hours of the morning, and then we dragged the headless body down to where we had left the speedboat. We loaded what was left of Atlas onto the boat, and drove around until we found a likely spot for a shipwreck. Then, I left Mike and Speedy on a good-sized rock, turned the boat around so it pointed towards a second good-sized rock some distance away, and changed into my skimpiest bikini.

It took a few horrible minutes to wrestle Atlas' body into the driver's seat, and another few heart-stopping moments to get the boat up to its maximum speed while I worked the controls around it. I was *beyond* happy when I finally jumped ship.

Mike says the crash was quite excellent; the explosion, not so much. That was fine; by that point, the body was definitely more battered than burnt.

Once everything was wrecked to hell and I was safe on the island with the boys, I pressed the button on my fancy future ring.

Sparky stayed with me until the Hellenic Coast Guard picked us up.

None of us needed to fake how close we were to collapse. I babbled something about Atlas and the crash and *oh God just find him!* and when they did, they quietly told me that his death had probably been quick.

Very true.

Ambassador Goodwin met us in Athens. We stuck around for an extra day to answer questions[27], and he told me how very sorry he was that our stay in Greece had been so...eventful. He seemed really glad to see us get on the plane to go home.

Sparky and Ben were waiting for us at the airport.

Speedy and I fell into Sparky's arms; Ben was nowhere to be seen, but I felt him nearby. Mike and I staggered downstairs to the baggage claim while Sparky navigated Customs for us: sometimes it's good to be the Cyborg Queen.

We watched the endless parade of suitcases and trunks and duffle bags, all spinning around on the International carousel, and we leaned against each other to stay on our feet.

My hand went to my neck, as if searching for three beads on a lanyard.

"You miss her?" Mike asked.

"Yeah," I said, nodding. "I watched her grow up, you know? It's not as if we were friends, but..."

He dipped his head so it rested against mine. "I'm sorry, Hope."

"Eh." I shrugged. "I'll reread *The Iliad*. I haven't read it since junior high, and now that we know what Helen was really like, I'm sure it'll be good for a laugh."

"You want to know what I can't figure out?" Mike asked.

"Oh God, no." I sighed. "No, I don't."

"Why Ben sent us to Greece in the first place," he said. "It's not like discovering one more fragment of the Mechanism would change its history."

"He wanted to know its origins," I said. "To learn if it disappeared as an accident, or as the result of someone tampering with time."

"Yeah, I get that," he said. "What I don't understand is why this was important enough to send us to Greece *now*."

"Because...time...thing..." I muttered.

He kissed me on the cheek as our bags popped out

---

27 I also used that time to track down Darling's mother, because more guilt. Turns out she'd already been dead for a couple of months, so take that to mean whatever you want about the state of the Petrakis family, or Darling, or my shitty judgment.

from behind the plastic flaps. "Thanks for the wonderful Mediterranean vacation, Hope," he said. "Call me when you want to do this again. I'm going to need to spend about a month hiding under my bed to prepare."

I stood by the carousel for another few minutes as I watched my bag go around and around on the track.

Speedy had figured it out—the instant I had told him Ben was sending me to Greece, he had figured it out.

I grabbed my bag, and turned in Ben's direction. I could imagine my best friend shrunk down to the size of a dime, smiling at me in his flying blue pixy form from a concealed hidey-hole.

I think I had figured it out, too, but that was one of those things I didn't want to hear spoken aloud. If I was right...

Well.

That was a problem for another day.

# CHAPTER 42

That would have been the end of the story, except Helen wasn't quite done with me. My dreams had been my own since we defeated the Minotaur, and I had assumed that meant she was satisfied with the way things had turned out and had moved on.

I still missed her.

"Hey, Hope?"

I was tired. I mean, I was *tired.* I was catching up on two weeks' worth of missed classes. I didn't need to open my eyes and see the black bulb of a koala's nose pressed up against mine.

But Speedy was whispering, and since he's got no problems waking Sparky and me up whenever he damned well feels like it…

I slipped out of Sparky's arms, tucked my new copy of *The Iliad* onto the nightstand, and followed Speedy down the hall.

During our three-week trip to Greece, the contractors had gotten plenty of work done on the greenhouse. The glass was in, the irrigation was down, and some of the landscaping was beginning to take shape. Sparky and Speedy had this master plan to put a free-flowing stream down the center of the room, ending in an enclosed rocky pool.

A grotto, if you would.

Dawn was just starting to come through the windows. The light hit them just right, the two objects lying on the flat rock in the center of the pool.

A Finnish Puukko knife and a piece of polished bronze in an olivewood frame.

I felt my heart catch.

"How—"

"Dunno," Speedy replied, as he hopped from rock to rock.

He landed beside the mirror. "But she's here."

I took a moment to run my hands through my bedheaded hair. Not because of vanity (...mostly...), but because I needed time to think. Why did she track us down? And why bring these two items? It must have required a massive amount of energy to move them halfway across the planet and into alien territory. Why not bring gold or gems or...

She hadn't brought the Damascus sword I had used to fight the Minotaur. I was okay with that: once you butcher someone with a weapon, that's pretty much all it is to you. I didn't need a constant reminder of how easy it had been to cut off Atlas'—

Right. No sword. Good thing.

The Puukko knife belonged to me. Maybe Helen had decided to return it. Ghosts had no use for mortal weapons, after all, and the beads that I had left wrapped around its hilt were gone.

Fair enough; those beads had been hers anyhow.

The mirror, though...

"She wants to talk to us?" I asked Speedy.

"Kitten," he replied, "how the fuck would I know?"

"Right," I said, and I yanked my pajama pants up to my knees so I could stand in the water and talk to Helen of Sparta through her magic mirror.[28]

I paused before picking it up, because...

Well. Some things are easier than others.

When I did, a woman's face stared back at me.

It had more soft edges than I remembered, or maybe Helen had changed her appearance. In either case, she looked happier than the last time I had seen her. She nodded when she saw me, and brought her index finger to her side of the mirror.

I thought maybe I was supposed to touch it, like an E.T. thing, but no; her finger brushed against the surface of the mirror and left a burning blue trail in its wake.

Helen was writing something.

"Can you see this?" I asked Speedy.

"All I see is a blue haze," he said.

"Okay," I said, and dipped my own fingers in the water. I

28 I KNOW, RIGHT?!

began to write on the rock, mimicking the shapes of Helen's letters.

"*Charita katatithesthai tini*," Speedy said, before translating this to: "*Lay up a store of gratitude*. She's thanking you for a mighty favor done on her behalf."

"Damn," I whispered. "I thought she had left without saying goodbye. Tell her she's very welcome."

Speedy did. His voice was low and—I *swear!*—respectful.

Helen nodded, and wrote another word.

"Goodbye," Speedy said, and Helen began to pull herself away from the mirror.

"Wait!"

Helen stopped moving.

"Speedy, translate for me. Please."

I began talking. I really didn't want to flub all over myself in front of freakin' Helen of Sparta, but she seemed like one of those people with things to do and my words came out in a chattering flood.

"I'm sorry the only thing we remember about you is that you were beautiful," I said. "I don't know if you plan to stick around after this, or if getting rid of Theseus is what you needed before you felt you could leave this world and move on, but I'd love to know what the real deal was with the Trojan War.

"I think…" I paused. "I think it'd be a great shame if nobody ever learned your side of the story."

In the mirror, the woman moved her dark eyes from mine to Speedy's; even though he couldn't see them, he still shivered.

When he had finished speaking, Helen looked back at me. A finger tapped on the reverse of the mirror, an unconscious gesture, as if the ghost were thinking.

She nodded.

# NOTES

As always, this book wouldn't have been possible without my husband, Brown.

My thanks goes to the beta readers who were so very generous with their time. Gary, Tiff, Joris, Kevin, and Jean, your help is deeply appreciated. Also, thanks goes to those who helped Hope find her voice in the earliest drafts. I was struggling with how to best write a character with Attention-Deficit Disorder, and your feedback put me on the right path.

Danny, thank you for the copy edits, even though one day we will come to blows over your insistence on italics.

Some lunatic calling herself T. Kingfisher wandered into my garden one day, said something cryptic about moths, and handed me the cover art before vanishing in a cloud of vivid orange agastache. I bet she's been up to remarkable things—you should probably go check out her books out as soon as you've finished mine.

My heartfelt thanks goes to everyone who's supported me over this past year. It's my first year of being a full-time writer and artist, and I couldn't have done it without you.

Finally, the story of Helen of Troy has been retold here in very broad strokes. I've stayed within the landmarks of her early life—her childhood in Sparta, her kidnapping by Theseus, and the years she spent in Aethra's house—but have otherwise taken full liberties with her history and personality. In this, I have kept to the storytellers' long tradition of using Helen as the plot demands. I hope, in my version, she has at least found some peace. As for the spelling of Greek names, Joris recommended the Loeb Classical Library, and I found this resource to be invaluable. Any error is mine.

K.B. Spangler lives in North Carolina with her husband, and as many dogs she can sneak into the house without him noticing. She is the author and artist of <u>A Girl and Her Fed</u>, where Speedy, Hope Blackwell, Patrick Mulcahy, and the Agents of OACET are alive and well. The ghosts are well, too, thanks for asking. Additional information about these and other projects can be found at <u>kbspangler.com</u>.